The Tales of the Scorned— Dark Romance

A Femme Rage Charity Anthology

The Tales of the Scorned
Book 3

Ava Jay   CJ Riggs   DK   E.L. Emkey   Kamila Garaz
KM ROGNESS   Lamia Lovett   Nicole Banks
S. Manship   Sasha Onyx

Copyright © 2025 by Tilly Ridge

All rights reserved.

No part of this publication may be reproduced, distributed, or transmitted in any form or by any means, including photocopying, recording, or other electronic or mechanical methods, without the publisher's prior written permission, except as permitted by U.S. copyright law. For permission requests, contact tillyridgeauthor@gmail.com.

No portion of this book was created or facilitated by artificial intelligence. No part of this book may be entered into artificial intelligence technologies or systems for training said systems.

The story, all names, characters, and incidents portrayed in this production are fictitious. No identification with actual persons (living or deceased), places, buildings, and products is intended or should be inferred.

Designations used by companies to distinguish their products are often claimed as trademarks. All brand names and product names used in this book and on its cover are trade names, service marks, trademarks, and registered trademarks of their respective owners. The publishers and the book are not associated with any product or vendor mentioned in this book. None of the companies referenced within the book have endorsed the book.

E-book Covers and Interior Formatting Images by The Bloodied Soul Creative

Volume One and Two Paperback Covers by Suzi at Suzi Antoinette Designs

Volume Three and Four Paperback Covers by Tasha at Occult Goddess Designs

Formatting by Tilly Ridge

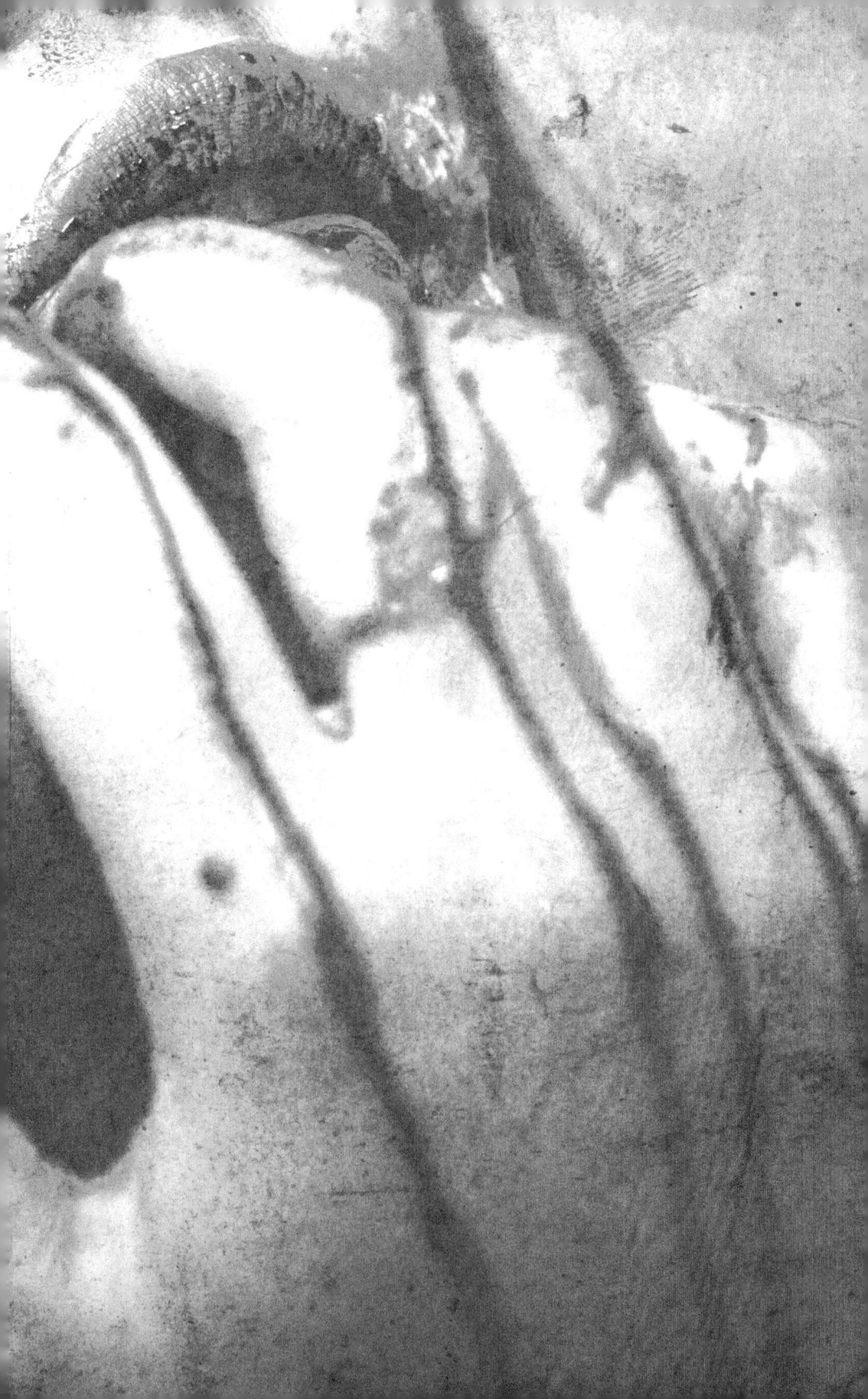

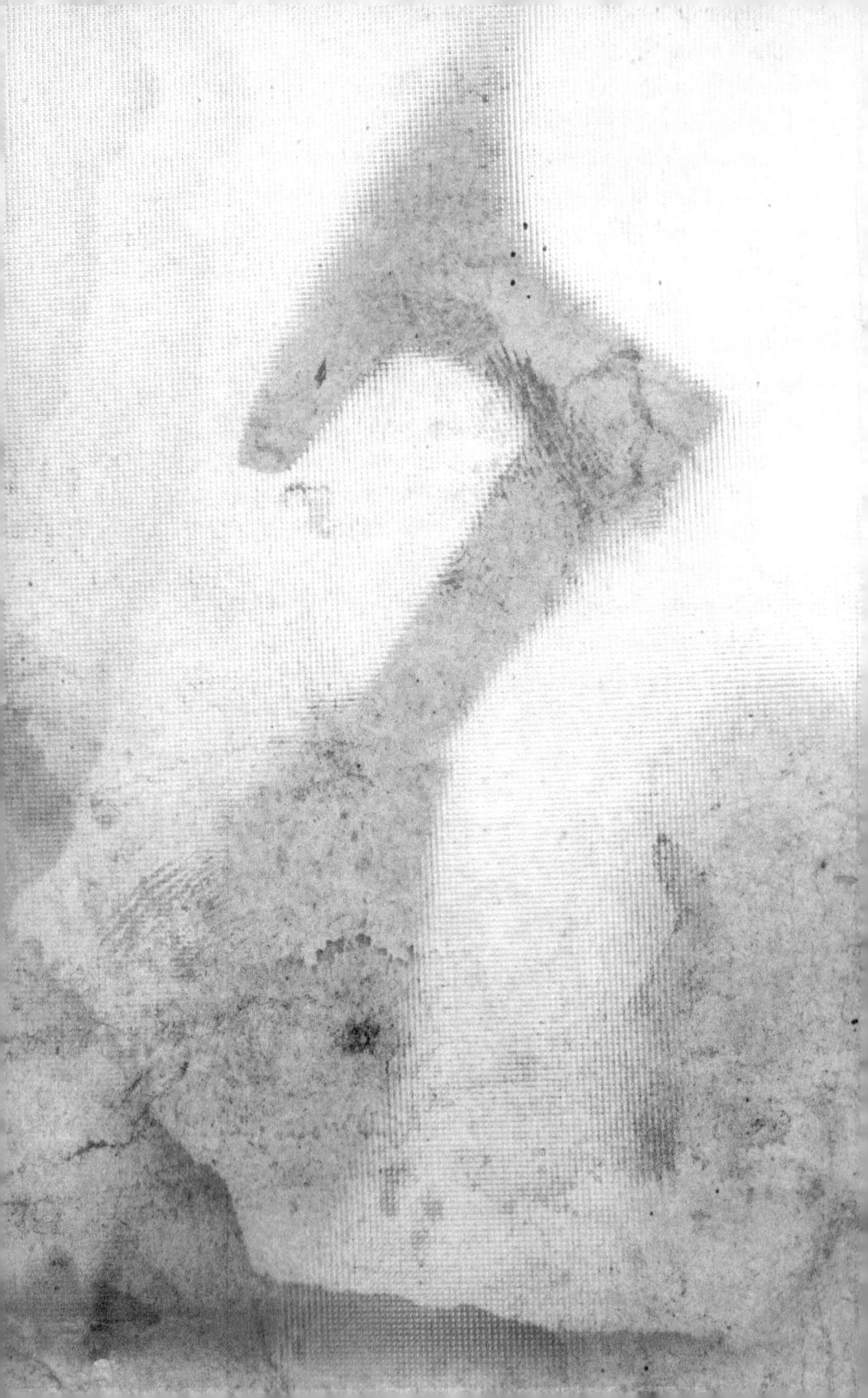

Resources

All funds made from the sales of these works are being sent to the three charities and foundations listed below.

Lilith fund:
    https://www.lilithfund.org/

The Brigid Alliance:
    https://brigidalliance.org/

Planned Parenthood:
    https://www.plannedparenthood.org/

Find your local abortion fund to donate locally:
    https://abortionfunds.org/find-a-fund/

If you would like to donate, the websites are linked, but check with your local clinics as well. And if you don't have spare funds, your time and attention can be even more impactful. Most have social media to share posts from, peaceful protests you can attend, donate time to the clinic itself, and so much more.

Mostly, I want to provide a space to talk about the basic human rights and healthcare of uterus owners and the obsession certain governments have over controlling our bodies.

Speak of it.

Learn about it.

Know the facts.

And the most important thing is to know how to protect yourself and your fellow uterus carrying community. They can't take our knowledge away from us. Talk to the next generations about it, too. They want us to think these topics are too taboo to talk about. I'm here to tell you they're not taboo at all.

We are NOT going back.

Resources:

Abortion. Our Bodies, Their Lies, and the Truths We Use to Win by Jessica Valenti:

> https://www.jessicavalenti.com/abortion-book
> Jessica's substack for information:
> http://abortioneveryday.com/
> Reproductive Health Access Project:
> https://www.reproductiveaccess.org/
> https://www.reproductiveaccess.org/resources/
> Midwest Access Project:
> https://midwestaccessproject.org/

*No participating authors, organizers, or service providers are affiliated or endorsed by any of the chosen organizations. We are a community of individuals bound together by a single wish, to protect the right to reproductive healthcare in all forms.

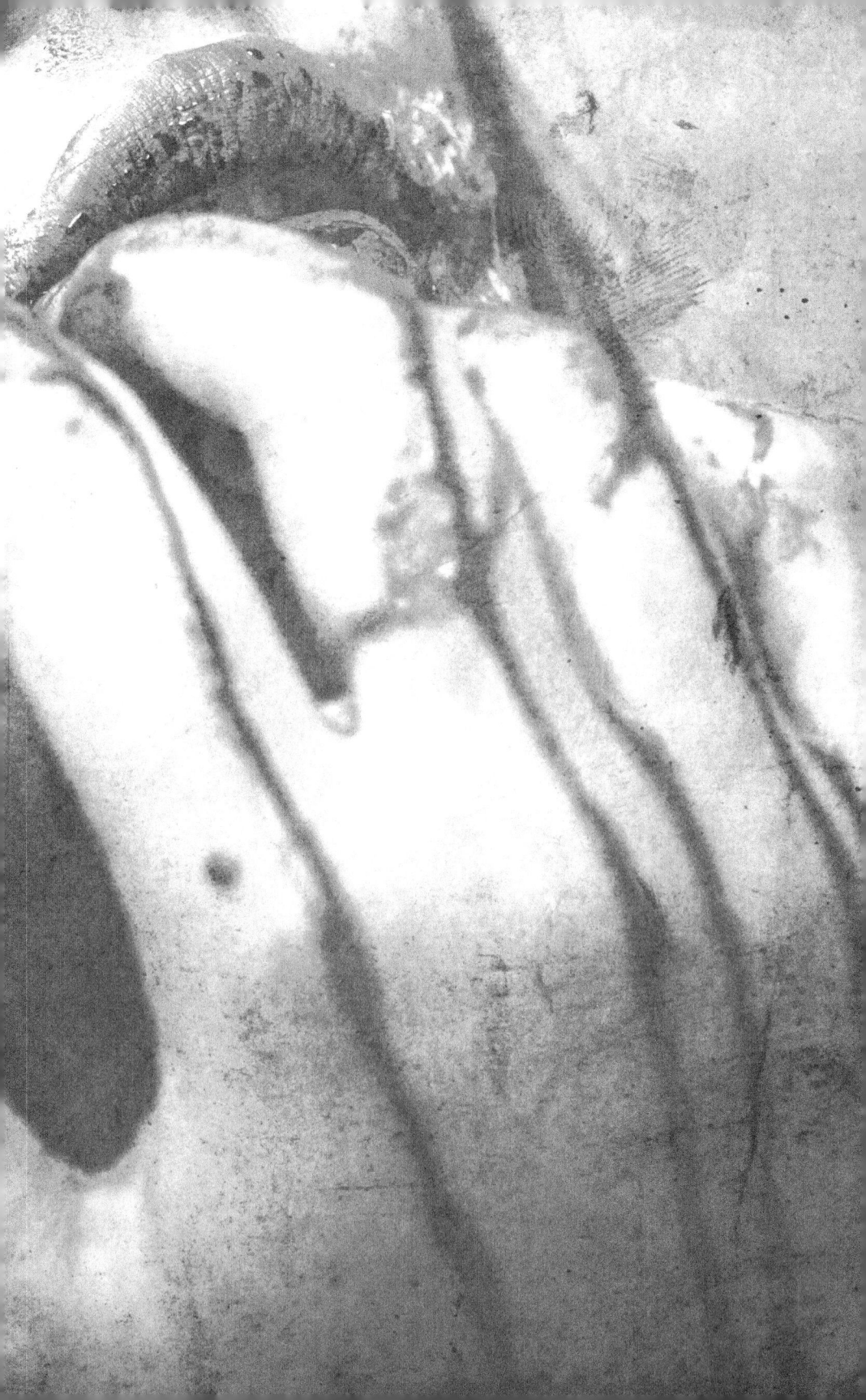

Thank You!

Thank you to these people for making this anthology possible!

The Bloodied Soul Creative, this anthology would not have left the ground if it weren't for Anna. From organization to graphics, emailing, and endless admin work, thank you so so much for donating your time and skills, Anna. This is as much your project as it is mine! She is also the designer behind the E-Book cover!

https://thebloodiedsoulcreative.carrd.co/

Tyla and Kaycie have been so so helpful with admin work as well! Tyla took care of our service providers, and Kaycie helped out with the influencers.

Tyla- https://www.daturadaze.com/

Kaycie- https://www.instagram.com/contentbykaycie/

Alexa, thank you so much for drafting up the contract for the anthology and donating that time and service!

https://www.instagram.com/abookybrunette/

To the cover designers who donated their time and services for the cause, thank you so much! You both crushed these covers!

Volume 1 & 2: Suzi Antoinette Designs

https://www.suziantoinettedesigns.com/

Volume 3 & 4: Occult Goddess

https://theoccultgoddess.com/

Lemmy at Luna Literary Management was gracious enough to donate ARC management for the anthology. Thank you, Lemmy, for everything you have done!

https://lunaliterary.com/

To all the editors who offered discounts for your services, thank you!

To all the influencers who signed up and shared about this project, thank you! I know it may seem small, or that you aren't doing enough, but it truly helps the cause so much!

And to the readers, thank you from all of us! Thank you for showing interest and reading these stories! Each page read is money directly helping these causes that we all care so deeply about!

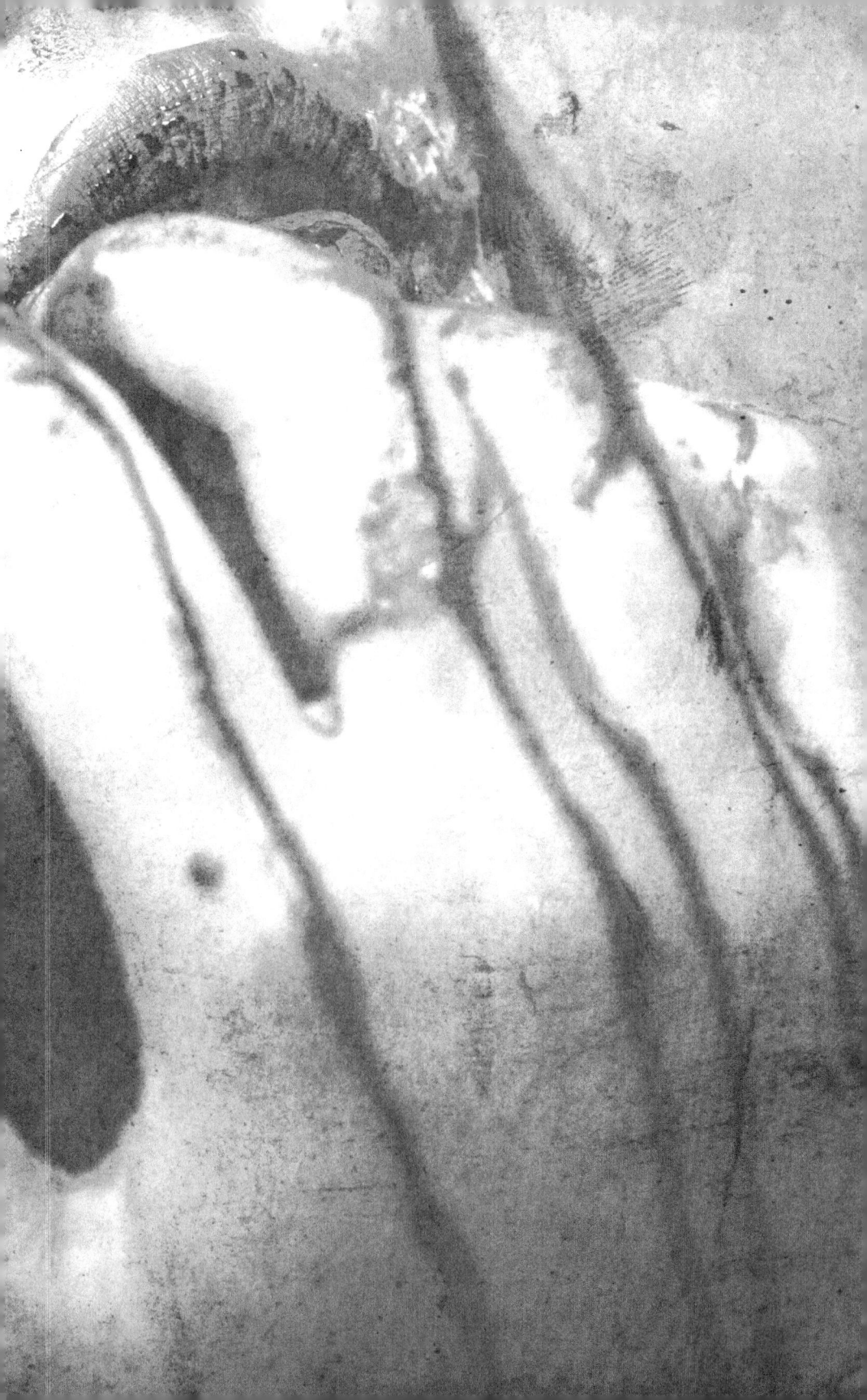

Content Warnings

With how things have been getting censored around women's health, the last thing I wanted to do was get this book banned because of the content warnings. We have placed them at the very back of the book to try and prevent the bots from picking them up and banning them solely because of the content warnings.

These books contain very dark and heavy content. Please do not hesitate to check the content warnings before diving into each story. Warnings are listed under the author's name in the back.

These stories range from morally grey romances all the way to erotic horror. The only rules were they needed to be based on feminine rage.

Your mental health matters more to all of us than anything; protect it.

Playlist

This playlist was a combined effort from the anthology's participating authors. Be warned: It is full of femme rage.

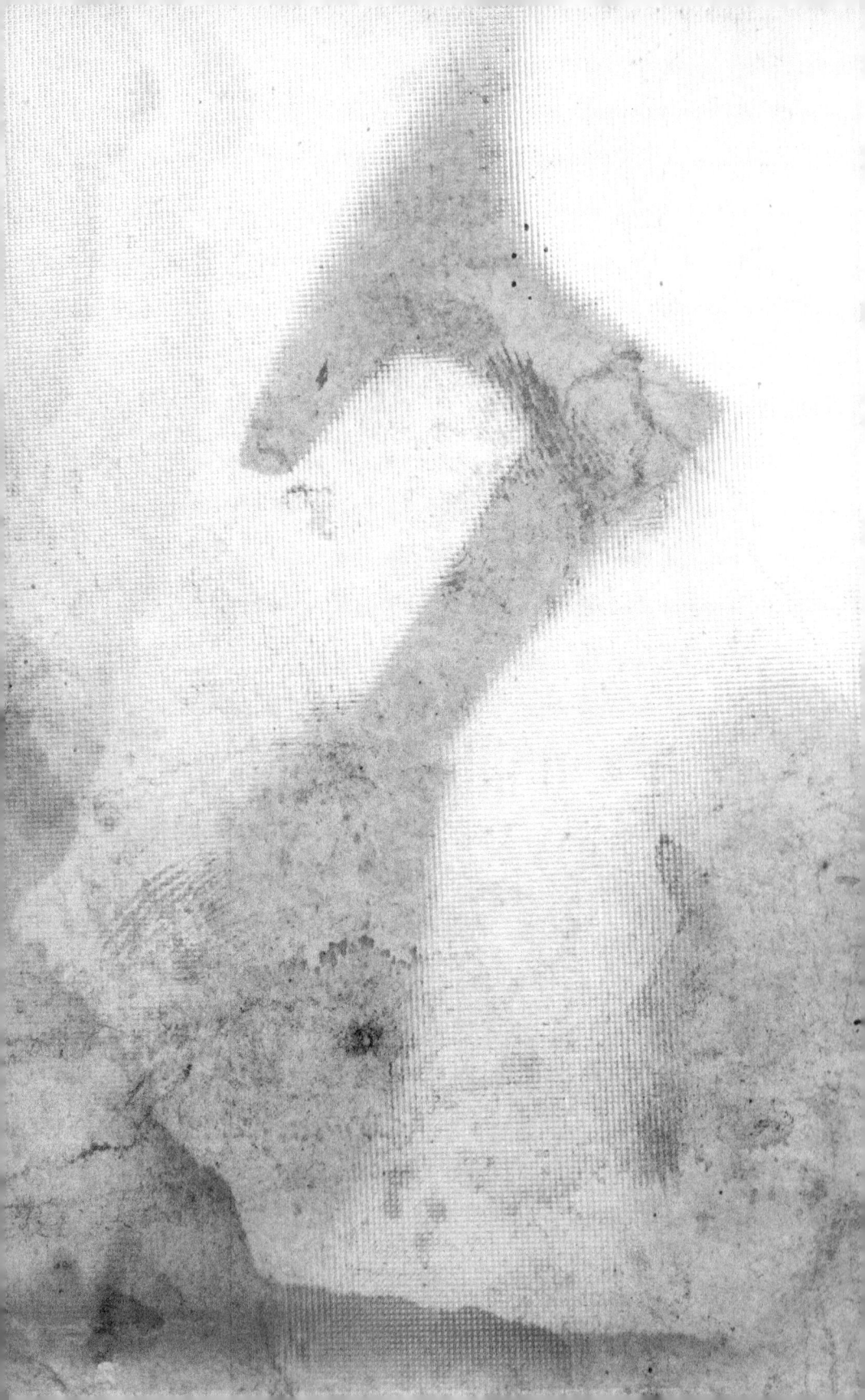

Contents

BURNT, BITTER, BETTER	1
A Preying on the Predator Extended Prologue	
Ava Jay	
OUR BODIES, OUR CHOICE.	59
CJ Riggs	
WHEN SILENCE SCREAMS	111
DK	
STONE	157
E. L. Emkey	
SILHOUETTES OF SIN	223
Kamila Garaz	
YOUR WORST F*CKING NIGHTMARE	283
KM ROGNESS	
SOROR MORTEM	325
Lamia Lovett	
FURY	361
Nicole Banks	
MANEATER	409
S. Manship	
NAUGHT BEFORE ONE	461
Sasha Onyx	
Content Warnings	545

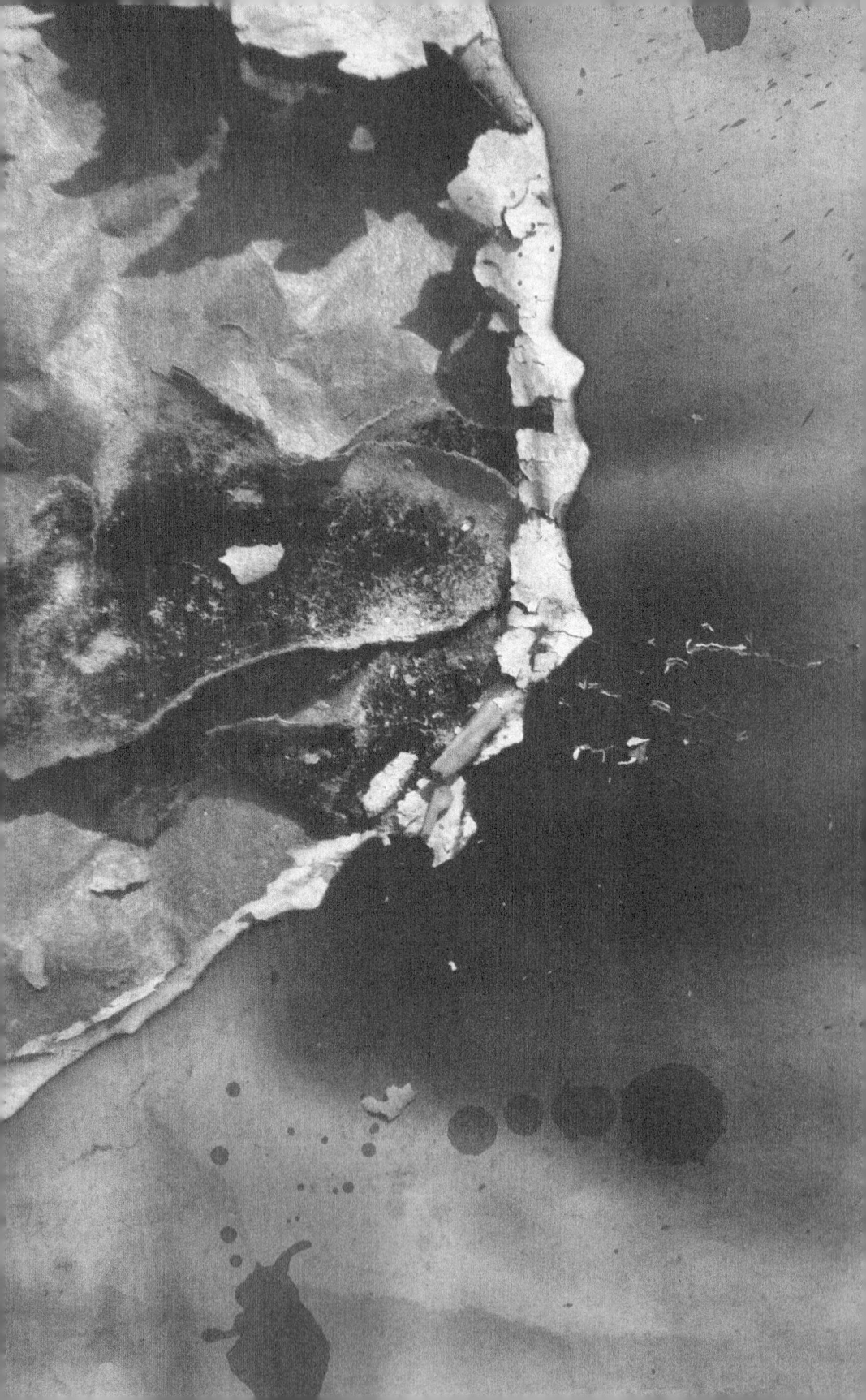

Burnt, Bitter, Better

A Preying on the Predator Extended Prologue

Ava Jay

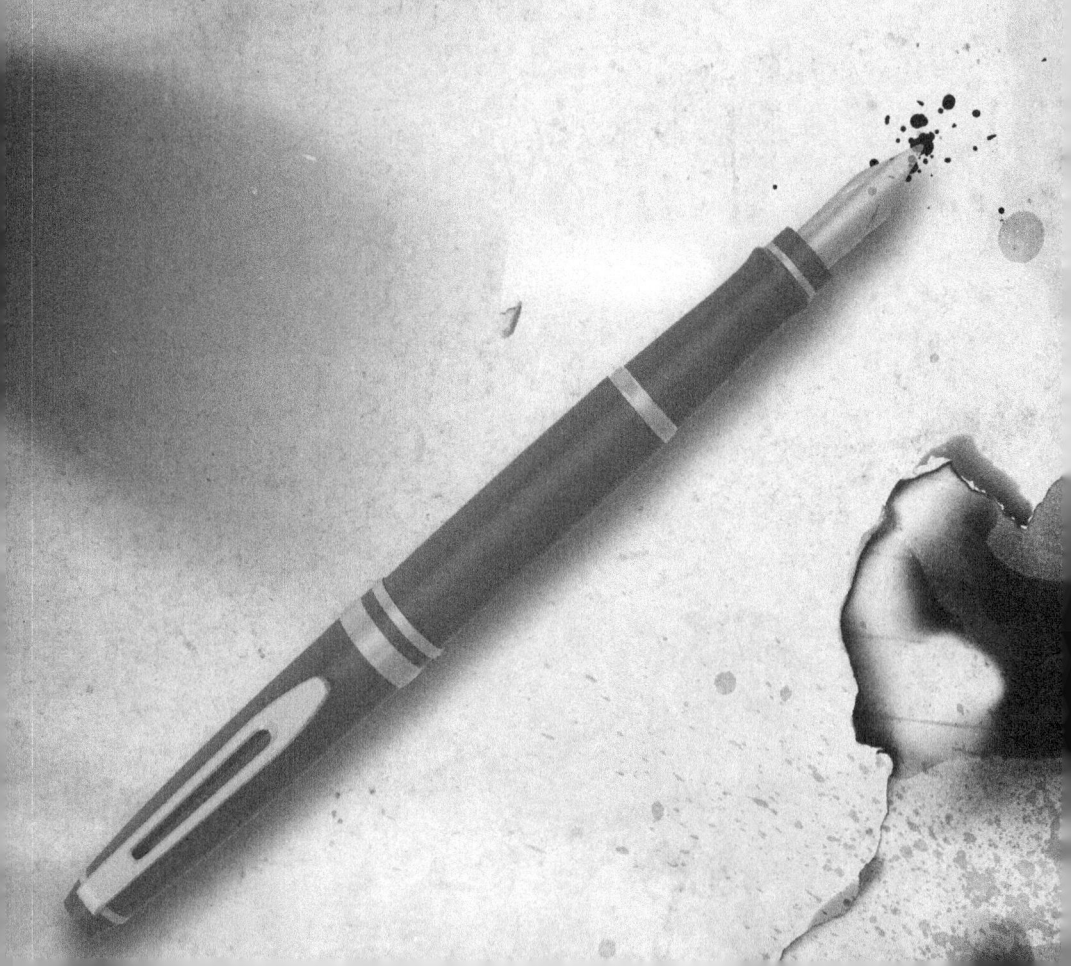

Chapter 1
Brielle

Two Years Ago

Tears stream down my face as I pull my best friend from the bed she lies in with her boyfriend. I yank her by the arm into the attached bathroom, flipping on the light switch and wincing at the harsh yellow lighting as my knees shake trying to get to the toilet.

"What is going on, B?" She rubs her eyes in an attempt to adjust to the light, closing the door behind her when she realizes I'm already dropping my pants.

"I need your help to get it out." I sniffle the snot threatening my upper lip back into my nose.

She finally looks at me, and my eyes meet hers in return.

"Oh my god, B, what the fuck is going on?" she shrieks at me. Her hands begin shaking, but I can't focus on her right now. I need to get it out.

"Felicity, I know this looks gross, and I know you just woke up, but my tampon. I need to get it out." The angle my hands are reaching into my vagina is all wrong. I can't even feel the string. My panic heightens, and I can't breathe.

"Felicity, I need you to help me get it out. Now," I plead with her. We've been through so much together, and as I pull my blood-soaked hands away from the core of my body, I know this is our friendship reaching a new place. There is no one else I would ever trust to help me like this. She drops to her knees in front of where I sit on the toilet, legs spread as far as I can force them. My hips and thigh muscles burn at the spread, but I know she needs to be able to see in this shitty fucking lighting.

"Okay, I can do this," she says, more to herself than to me. I'm covered in blood. The toilet seat is smeared, and I slide around on it involuntarily from the combination of sweat and blood.

Her small hand shakes as she reaches toward my center, and I lock my teeth together and hold my breath. I can feel the moment her two fingers enter me, and I'm praying to the god I don't believe in that she finds it quicker than I could. I feel every movement of her fingers against the raw flesh inside of me. Each tear becomes more noticeable as she digs inside my vaginal canal. As much as I can be, I'm thankful for the amount of alcohol coursing through my bloodstream, otherwise I'm sure this would hurt a whole hell of a lot worse.

I wince as I feel what I assume are her fingers spreading apart, trying to grab at the tampon lodged so far into my cervix that it's hardly reachable. Her hand pushes so hard against the outside of my vagina that new tears begin to run down my cheeks. Each tear drop is a hot contrast to the cold concrete flooring of this garage turned apartment. The light flickers on cue with my body jerking. I look down at her between my legs, her face turned away from my body as if to give me what little privacy she can.

The smell of the room is that of piss and cigarettes. Speaking of which, I need to find my pack. A fucking smoke would help tremendously.

"I think I feel it!" she says, and I look back down at her. I feel it before I see it. Her knuckles scraping against the aching skin inside of me. Then she's pulling the soaked tampon out of my vaginal opening. I have about a one second head start before the vomit is coming out of my mouth. I barely turn my head when the acid and chunks spew onto the gray floor, splattering harshly against the wall and sink cabinet.

She drops the tampon into the toilet between my legs. It's swollen with blood and whatever else, and it looks fucking disgusting, even to me. The sound of it splashing into the water below will haunt my dreams, undoubtedly. She stands to her full height and rushes to the sink, twisting the old knob with her hand that lacks blood stains.

"Fuck, B, do you want to shower off? I can get you a towel." She moves to grab a towel from under the sink when I speak.

"No." It's the only word I dare to push out of my mouth right now. When I stand, I feel the pressure in my pelvis, and the tear in the waistband of my favorite biker shorts makes my lip quiver. I pull them up anyways, wincing when the seam rubs against my raw labia. Everything inside of me is beginning to break loose with the weight of the situation.

"I need a cigarette," I whisper as I move to wash my hands too. I watch as the watered-down blood snakes down the drain. Crimson ribbons swirl as I replace the copper scent with the dollar store vanilla soap. After rinsing my hands and drying them with the towel that has probably laid on this counter for six months, I grab the bottle. It's not even antibacterial soap. Fucking disgusting.

"Let's go outside for a smoke," Felicity instructs. My feet carry me through the threshold of the bedroom, back into the living area where I pass the pull-out mattress. Out of the corner of my eye, I see a glimpse of what was once my bright-red blood, settled into the wrinkles of the rustled sheets.

Walking into the cool night air, I take a deep breath and feel my back slide against the metal siding of the garage exterior. A cigarette appears next to my face, and I part my lips. Felicity tucks the cigarette into my mouth and lights the end while I take a hard pull. She asks questions, talks at me, asks more questions, and finally, she leaves me out in the cool night air alone, returning to her boyfriend's bedside. I don't know how long I sit there, staring into the tree line and listening to the cars pass by on the highway.

I must fill my lungs with smoke for hours without a single line of conscious thought while the sun slowly rises. When Felicity comes back out, I briefly hear her asking me if I'm ready to head home. I nod, stand on stiff legs, and get into the car.

Chapter 2

Brielle

Present

Another six months goes by with another therapist to unload the bulk of my trauma onto. Somedays it feels like a never-ending carousel of strangers with too many years of education under their belts, holding a notepad and dissecting me like a lab rat. Maybe I'll print my story on a trifold pamphlet for the next doctor.

At least this one is nice to look at.

"You're clinically depressed, Brielle. You have to take the meds to know if they work," Jonathan says, keeping his voice soft and disarming, a practiced coo. I've heard this line so many times over the last eighteen months.

What. The. Fuck. Ever.

I'm not clinically depressed. I'm empty. It's been almost two years since my "give-a-fuck" was ripped away from me. It's been almost two years since my "best friend" abandoned me. Two whole years of white-hot rage simmering the blood that courses through my veins. Two years of trauma that has been simmered down to a tiny little check box asking me if I've "lost interest in daily activities."

Obviously.

"What emotion are you feeling right now, Brielle?" Jonathon's voice snaps me back into the sad beige reality of the moment. His tone oozes the kind of patience that is meant to coax me out of my shell, make me feel safe and what not. I ponder his question for a moment, searching for the feeling in my chest, the one that burns there beneath the surface.

"It's like anger, but more," I say. I have this rule of thumb with therapists. I don't expand my answers beyond the basics of the question unless asked. I preserve my energy instead.

Jonathon, who insists I call him Jonathon as if I'm a child who feels cool getting to call the teacher by their first name, sits calmly across from me. Everything about this office is designed to make me feel more comfortable. It doesn't. He knows it, I know it, but he still tries. Even his posture is perfectly poised to feel more like we're having a chat amongst two casual friends. He sits in his black leather chair, legs spread with his elbows on his knees, leaning forward with both hands locked together, sure to make eye contact with me. I haven't felt anything for a man since that night, but if I did feel some sort of attraction, Jonathan would be the perfect specimen.

He's a gorgeous man. Objectively, that is. His crisp white, long sleeve button-down shirt hugs his biceps, letting you know he cares about his physique. His tie is tight around the collar of his throat, and I briefly imagine pulling him by it, like a dog on a leash. I think a leash may suit him, he wants to be led through my mind anyways, he might as well wear one.

"Care to elaborate?" he questions me, waiting for more.

"No," I answer simply.

"Brielle, we've been over this several times. I am not trying to lecture you, but therapy is worth nothing if you don't truly let someone in your head. You can recount your story a million times, to a million people, but we will never find resolve unless we explore the emotions you're harboring for the situation." His tangent is long and quite unnecessary. If he would just ask the right fucking questions, I'd tell him anything he wants to know. Something inside me snaps for a brief moment.

"You ask shit questions and then wonder why I give you shit answers. I come in here with a clear objective, and you argue with me about what I do or don't need." I wish I could say that my bitter honesty shocked this man, but his facial expressions remain even and collected. "If you want to know something specific, then just fucking ask it. I'm not fragile, I just don't give a fuck anymore. All I want is my life back." The sentence starts with heated anger, but by the end of it, the exhaustion settles in, and so does the fear of having another session end with no real progress.

My words hang in the air, thick and heavy, but his face remains calm as he mulls over my words.

"Have you tried exposure therapy, Brielle?" He shifts back in his seat deliberately, leaning casually with his fingers interlocked over his stomach.

"What do you mean?" I ask, one eyebrow raising as I lean to my side to rest my head on my knuckles.

"Have you tried exposing yourself to things that make you uncomfortable, is what I mean. We've discussed your celibacy and your struggle for intimacy within romantic relationships due to the understandable fear of sexual contact, so I am asking if you've tried exposing yourself to these types of situations alone, on your own terms." He grabs his notebook and writes something down. Truth be told, him not taking many notes during our sessions is something that makes me feel less analyzed. So many therapists before him have made me feel like a lab rat, constantly writing down god-knows-what, and some not even bothering to look at me while I speak. I wouldn't doubt if they had been doodling, or maybe writing down how many breaths I had taken per hour.

He's not mincing his words, I'll give him that. Jonathan has piqued my interest, but only slightly.

"I suppose not. Self-exploration has never been a hobby of mine," I answer him truthfully.

"You don't masturbate?" he quizzes me, and a moment of uncertainty passes over his eyes. When I told him to cut the shit, I didn't think he would ask me if I flick the bean.

"No, I don't get the urge the same way I used to. Sure, sometimes I get a flitter in my stomach, but these days the thought of trying to do something about it makes me panic," I reply, my thoughts running rampant with what is to come next.

When I think about what sex used to be for me, I no longer feel the urge. I don't feel that horny ache or the emptiness in my core like I once did. I don't watch porn and get turned on by the moaning and grinding. Sometimes the romance movies are even too much. The love and passion, it makes my heart ache. My chest aches remembering what it was like to be touched so easily then.

Jonathon nods his head as if I've confirmed something for him. He moves to unbutton his sleeves, slowly rolling them up his forearms, seemingly lost in thought. My eyes immediately draw to the tattoos lining both of his arms. Intricate dark ink has made a home on his skin. I let my eyes linger, tracing the lack of pattern. How interesting. I suppose I've never seen him in anything other than a long-sleeve button down. It looks like the good doctor has depth after all.

"I'm going to give you…homework, of sorts." He stands and rounds his desk, pulling out a different notepad. His tall frame leans over the small desk as he scribbles words across the page, before tearing the sheet of paper from the binding, folding it once, and extending it out in my direction. I can't help but think that if I was normal, I would be drooling over this man.

"When you get home tonight, I want you to do some research on the phrases and concepts I've written here for you. Start at the top of the list, do not jump ahead, and do this slowly. Don't pressure yourself if things feel too much. Light some candles, wear clothing that makes you feel comfortable, have a glass of wine, those sorts of things. My personal cell phone number is at the bottom of the paper. If at any point, things become too much, give me a call. I'll answer." I nod my way through his little speech and push the folded paper into the tiny pocket of my jeans.

Who the fuck is designing the pockets on women's jeans? I think toddler pants have the same size pockets as mine.

"Do research, try to get horny, got it." I roll my eyes up to check the clock on the wall. One minute left of our appointment, perfect. I feel like a rebellious child trying to get out of the principal's office, but really, I'm just over it. I want to go home, crawl in bed with my dog, and be left the fuck alone after another hour of my life down the drain.

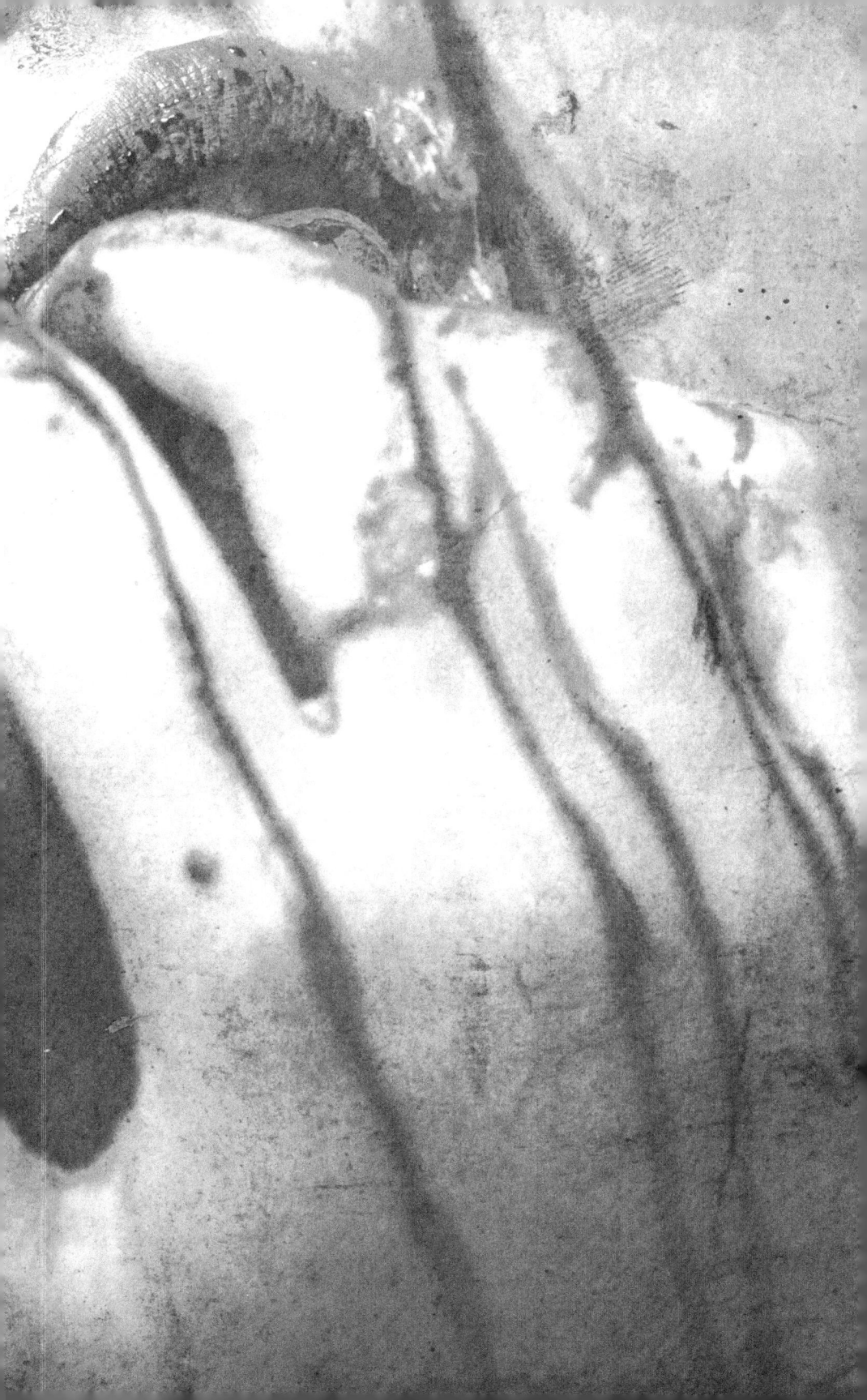

Chapter 3

Brielle

Present

Living alone has its perks, really. I get to eat this big-ass bowl of ramen noodles in my bed, in peace. The only slight annoyance is when my dog begs, which is rare.

After burning my hands on the microwave-hot bowl, I leave it to cool on my nightstand, pulling my laptop onto my lap for the "research" portion of my homework from Jonathan. The list isn't long, and they're not terms I've *never heard* of. I start my internet search with *Femme Domme*.

Immediately the search engine offers me a site explaining how to become one. What is the meaning of femme domme? What is it like to date a dom femme? There's even a femme domme boot camp? Okay, so, this is boring so far, and far more reading than I want to do. I search for the definition of femme domme instead.

"A woman who is the dominant partner in a sadomasochistic relationship, either physically or psychologically."

Great. Now I have to google sadomasochistic too. Fucking annoying.

This search leads me on an entirely different path, one that I'm not sure I can truly stomach. Before I realize it, my hands are shaking, my noodles have gone cold, and there is a feeling in my stomach that I can't dismantle. Slamming my laptop shut, my breaths come slower, more shallow. I feel sick. I feel the black hole inside my chest spreading even wider, sucking my breath, and heart, and brain into it. Suddenly, it's registering just how unhealed I am. It registers just how far away I am from having a normal relationship with another human being. I can't even read about sexual terms or watch porn for educational purposes. It's been so long since I've felt this way. The bones in my chest are being sucked into the black hole, and I just can't breathe.

I try to stand, but my legs don't get the memo, and my knees hit the floor with a crack on the hardwood. Tears blur my vision as the memories begin flooding in, I barely note the salty drops hitting the cold floor beneath me, dripping off my face as I hyperventilate. I'm slowly being sucked back in time, and my vision starts to fade. I crawl toward the bathroom, so close now. A few more feet, and I'll be in the doorway.

Move your fucking body, Brielle.

My hand reaches for the counter and slaps around for the stupid orange bottle that I shoved into the back of the cabinet months ago. The memories are catching up to me, my brain is skipping moments as each one embeds itself into the forefront of my mind. Before I realize what is happening, my body is on autopilot. I briefly register the pills on the floor and a dry circle in my mouth. Haphazardly pulling myself over the ledge of the tub, I turn the water on, and it freezes my skin.

There I sit, scooping water into my hands, pushing it into my mouth. My clothes are getting heavier on my body as if to weigh me into this moment, but it's too late. My vision fades, and the smell of black spiced rum taunts my tastebuds. I'm forced to relive the nightmare another time.

Brielle – Two Years Ago

Felicity passes a shot across the table to me, and I realize I haven't peed since I started drinking. Fuck, I don't want to break the seal. Everyone knows that once you go pee the first time during drinking, you'll be screwed going pee every fifteen minutes after that. Damn it, I need to change my tampon anyways.

Scooting my chair away from the table, I give Felicity a look, and she just gets it. That's how best friends are. She completes me, and I couldn't imagine life without her. I bite my tongue to prevent the mush that is ready to pour out over my love for her. Fuck, I'm drunk.

"I can't believe you're breaking the seal this early!" she taunts me with a wink

hanging onto the end of her words. The wink sends butterflies straight to my stomach. God, I love her. To be near her, is to love her. Felicity has this care-free, effortless vibe about her. If I had a dollar for every person in this room that, at the very least, wants to fuck Felicity, well I'd probably buy a greasy cheeseburger to hang out with all the rum in my stomach.

I giggle to myself over my own inner commentary as I enter the bathroom. I pull my phone out of the waistband of my shorts before pulling them down so I can sit on the toilet. Four missed calls, ten unread texts. Shit. Henry is pissed, and I don't have the energy to deal with that. I fire off a text to let him know that I have shit service and hope it sends. I don't know why I bother anymore. The sex is good, but he's unbearably controlling, and we've only been seeing each other for three months.

I set my phone down on the bathroom counter and pull the tampon out of my bra to replace the current one. My period has been so heavy this cycle, I'm worried I should've brought an extra. I'm not the purse carrying type, so usually whatever fits in my bra is what gets to come with me on each adventure. Removing my current tampon, it's clear that I definitely should've brought an extra. We're going to have to leave so early in the morning because of this. As I'm inserting the new tampon, a loud succession of bangs on the door startles me, causing me to angle the tampon in my vaginal canal wrong. I try to push my finger around inside of myself to readjust the cotton mass, and the weird pressure seems to ease up a small amount.

I hurry and pull my shorts back up to wash my hands thoroughly. Turning back, I push the flush handle down with the toe of my shoe while I dry my hands on my shirt, before grabbing the door to bitch at whichever guy is so rudely pounding on the door.

Swinging the door open, Adam's icy-blue eyes look down at me as he leans into the door frame.

Adam has been on my tail all night, flirtatious comments, grazing his hand over my waist or lower back to nonchalantly squeeze past me in the kitchen, and now here he is. Staring down at me like he wants to eat me for a midnight snack.

I can't deny my attraction for Adam. Part of me is curious. His full lips are plump, and for a second I stare at them and wonder what they would feel like sucking on my clit.

Whoa. Okay, period hormones have entered the chat.

"Can I help you with something?" I raise one eyebrow in defiance, knowing very well that he obviously needs in the restroom. I cross my arms under my breasts and pop my hip to lean on the opposite side of the door frame.

"You definitely can, but that's a conversation for later." He smirks, continuing to chew the minty gum while his charm drags me in closer.

"Oh, whatever you flirt." I smile and push against his chest, moving out of his way to the bathroom. He catches my wrist as I leave the doorway.

"Wait up for me? Let's have a smoke together." His smile is still there, and his grip on my wrist is surprisingly hot. The devil couldn't get to me, so he sent horny little hormones that sneak into my answer.

"Sure, I have a shot waiting for me in the kitchen though, so, I'll meet you outside?"

"I'll see you there." His voice is warm as his fingertips drop from my wrist. I make my way back into the kitchen to find—

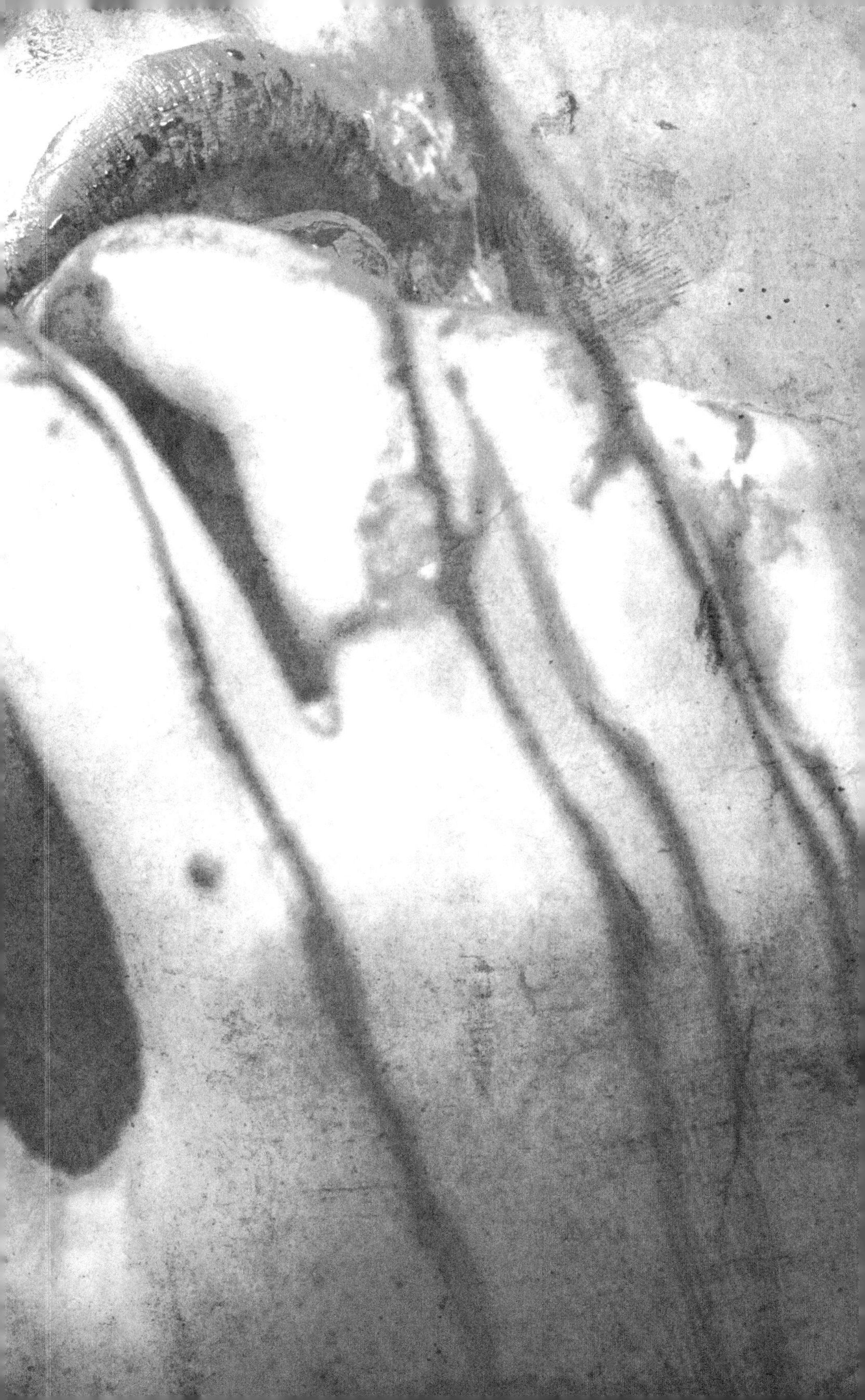

Chapter 4
Brielle

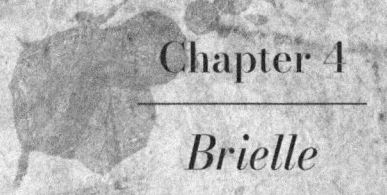

Present

I wake coughing up water. At some point in my panic-induced blackout, I must have slipped under the water. My body shivers, slowly registering the situation I'm in. Ice-cold water surrounds me, and chunky orange vomit floats too close. I look over the side of the tub and realize I've been in here for a while. Water has overflown the tub and the entire floor is a puddle. My little dog stands at the opening of the bathroom barking at the water. He hates water.

My body is so cold and rigid, even leaning forward to turn off the faucet feels like the most work my body has ever known. Twisting the knob with pale, stiff fingers, I pull myself back over the edge of the tub. My shoulder ache with the strain of using the toilet for leverage as I force myself into a standing position. Grabbing my phone, I stare at the paper in hand and slowly dial the numbers printed on the bottom of the small white paper.

Chapter 5
Brielle

Present

Our phone call moves quickly.

"I need help, please. I d-didn't know who else to call." My trembling voice trails off, and the fear begins to creep in that I am asking a man to help me in such a vulnerable state. I don't have anyone else to call, though. My mom would've been my lifeline, and I would call her if she was still alive, but outside of her, I have no one. I lay here curled into a fetal position, shivering, and completely alone. I feel the tears before registering that I'm crying. My body is in a state of shock. I'm lost in my thoughts when I hear a knock at the door, but my body is frozen with the fear of letting anyone in.

When no one is there to answer it, the sound of the door breaking open reverberates through my entire apartment, and my body rocks with unsteady nerves. Every heartbeat ricochets through my skull. I can't do this. I've changed my mind, I think. He can't be here. The smell of him is in the room before my eyes take note of his presence. Cashmere and dark musk. My eyes pinch shut hard and pinpricks invade my vision. If I open them and see him now, I will well and truly lose my shit.

I try to speak but my voice breaks into chopped fragments.

"P-p-please, I changed my mind, y-you can't be her-re," I stammer, kicking and pushing myself into the corner of my bedroom. Something falls off my nightstand but I don't open my eyes to see what it is. The floorboards creak ever so slightly, and I know it's him moving closer with careful steps.

"I can be here, I am here. Why are you sopping wet, Brielle?" Words pour out of his mouth in a calming, honey-like tone. The way he would probably speak to a skittish animal rather than a broken twenty-something-year-old woman.

I curse myself internally for calling this man. What could he possibly do for me? I am best on my own, and that is why I am always alone. Dealing with these episodes by myself is all I've known. This situation is *unknown*, and it terrifies me. The muscles in my eyebrows begin to tense and cramp from clenching.

"B-black out-t. In-n the bathtub-b." My body shakes against my will, and my teeth chatter through each syllable.

"How can I help you right now? What would work best for you? And don't tell me to leave, because only a crazy person would leave you in this condition." The concern and determination in his voice tempts me to open my eyes. As if a curtain is being pulled. I consider which option is safer: opening my eyes and having the ability to see an attack coming, or keeping them closed and retreating into my mind if an attack comes on.

I decide to open them, slowly.

My vision is blurred from the pressure, but I make out his shape in the warm light from my bedside lamp. He squats before me wearing the same outfit he had on earlier today, the only difference being the way the top button of his shirt is now undone, and his silky-black hair is tousled. The muted light softens the sharpness of his features but does nothing for the intensity of his presence. As he comes into focus, long black eyelashes bat at me, and I realize he is still expecting an answer.

"C-cold," I manage to whisper. "Can y-you get me clothes?"

He appears pleased with my response. He rises and crosses the room to my closet without a word. The hangers scrape against the metal rod they hang on like nails on a chalkboard. A few moments later he returns with a black worn-in thermal shirt and a determined look in his blue eyes.

"Where do you keep your comfortable pants?" His eyes dart around the room, narrowing in on my dresser.

"Third-d drawer down."

He opens the drawer as told, pulling out a gray pair of sweatpants that I never reach for. Mostly because they're at least two sizes too big. Before I can instruct him any further, he opens the top drawer of my dresser and must immediately realize the error because he closes it just as quickly. He recovers in a split second and moves on, opening the second drawer. He grabs a pair of fuzzy socks and places everything on the end of my bed.

"Do you need help getting dressed?" His words are careful, as if he's asking more than his words imply.

I shake my head quickly, not able to look him in the eyes.

"Okay, I'll wait in the living room." He takes a step back. "Don't take too long or I will come to check on you."

The command causes a shiver to wrack my body, but I can't tell if it's from the cold or the tone of his voice. I don't have time to ponder the thought much longer before he's out of my bedroom, and the door is closing behind him.

The soft light from my lamp continues to cast a warm glow in my room, and I'm thankful that I chose the amber lighting rather than harsh white.

I still have to grab my own underwear out of my drawer, but I don't mind the fact that he left that job to me. I pull on the soft seamless panties followed by the baggy sweatpants. My shirt collar snags on my wet hair, and when I release the soaked clumps, water continues to dampen my back.

Once my socks are on, a deep breath fills my lungs before my hand wraps around the door handle, and I'm exiting the room.

Jonathan sits on the edge of my couch with his elbows braced on his knees and hands laced tightly together. His eyes are glued to the ground beneath him.

"I'm decent," I whisper the words, picking my nails absentmindedly waiting for him to look at me. "I'm going to sit on the other side of the couch. Please stay on your side, try not to make any fast movements. Please."

"I understand. Sit, please. Let's talk." Jonathon sinks into the couch a little further, turning slightly so he has a better view of me once I sit down.

Chapter 6
Brielle

Present

"I think it was just all of the sexuality. You have to understand that being sexual, seeing sexual things, none of it has a place in my day-to-day life. It's not something I've had a need for in a long time." Exasperation laces my words, and I glance at the clock on the wall.

"You don't have to stay, it's very late, and I'm sure you have someone to get home to." My voice is carefully neutral, though part of me half-hopes he will leave, and the other half hopes he stays. It's nice to have company for once. It's always me and my little furball curled up together in painful silence. I crave human connection though, painfully so, even just someone to talk to casually.

The realization sobers me quickly, this man is my therapist. Someone who usually gets paid to listen to my bullshit. I don't have the nerve to ask if I'll be paying for the time he's spending with me now, the damage is already done anyways.

"You can't live the rest of your life avoiding intimacy all together," he says this matter-of-factly. As if there aren't people who live without sex.

"Are you saying that asexuality isn't possible?" I retort, narrowing my eyes in his direction.

"No, I'm saying asexuality isn't possible for you." He quirks an eyebrow at me. He seems to be quite comfortable on my couch, and I almost feel like two friends bantering.

"And what could possibly make you think that?" I'm genuinely searching for his reasoning.

"Because you want to be loved. You desire to feel 'normal.' Our sessions may be short, but there is a reason I'm deemed good at my job. My patients have a high chance of growing from the things that plague them, and it's because I take the time to learn them. The time to study them. The assignment I gave you tonight wasn't for nothing. It was a small test, which we will move on from. The fact that you tried to look into the list I made for you tells me you want to work on the ability to be intimate again, otherwise you wouldn't have bothered." He takes a sip from his water bottle before continuing.

"You're scared and that's understandable. Even if you don't realize you're scared, you are. No matter what, we will keep working on getting you closer to the life you want, we just may have to force you into it." I gawk at him.

Force me into it? That's how I got this fucking trauma in the first place. My brain moves a million miles per hour with the utter fucking confusion of how that could possibly work. Pushing me outside of my comfort zone is risky enough as is, but forcing me into anything will only make me shut down.

"Being forced to be sexual is what got me into this situation in the first place." I roll my eyes, and he chuckles. The man actually has the audacity to laugh at what I'm saying. "I don't want to be forced into anything."

"Okay, maybe forced wasn't the right terminology, I—"

I cut him off before he can finish his sentence. "You're damn right it wasn't the right terminology. I was raped, and your idea to fix it is forcing me into a sexual experience?" My voice echoes off the walls, and I realize my nails are cutting into my palms. I look away from him while I try to collect my thoughts. Relaxing my posture, I can feel him watching me while I pull several deep breaths into my lungs.

"What I meant," he starts softly, "is that maybe you need to have the control. Maybe you need to be the aggressor, of sorts." He leans forward intertwining his fingers with his elbows on his knees the same way he does in his office. I admire his physique. Now that I have a closer look, his day clothes do little to hide it.

"Me be the aggressor? I don't want to hurt anyone..." I'm more confused now than I was at his force comment.

"No, you'd only hurt people who want to be hurt, Brielle." His voice drops and his words hang there for a moment.

My mind spins with the confusion of the moment. "Who would want to be hurt?" I let out a sigh of annoyance.

Are we playing twenty-one fucking questions?

This man is making me feel like an idiot child. Like I know nothing, because I keep having to ask for more details.

"Lots of people would want to be hurt by a pretty girl like you, Brielle." His words are coated in maddening confidence, like this statement is the surest thing he has said all evening.

Something stirs inside of me, I feel the strangest flutter in my stomach, and I can't truly place the feeling.

"Oh?" I don't mean for the syllable to come out so unsure. The image that took over my mind in his office today resurfaces. Jonathan in his form fitting suit, while I pull him by his tie like a dog on a leash. The image resonates with me in an unexpected way, and I go further. The image grows to him on his knees in front of me, his gaze pointed up at me, pleading.

"Are you imagining hurting me?" His deep-blue eyes lock with mine, unflinching.

"Yes. In a way." The honesty is sweet and raw on my tongue. My therapist is in my home at an indecent hour, what is the point in being anything but honest? "I was imagining leading you around my apartment by your tie, you on your knees in front of me, begging for something that I couldn't—no, wouldn't—grant you."

"And what is that?" His voice is low and steady as he asks.

"Forgiveness." The word cuts through the air like a blade. Silence takes up residence between us, waiting, until he speaks again.

"Would you like to conduct an experiment with me, Brielle?" His words are spoken with a slow building smile. It's almost boyish, the way his lips barely twitch upward with curiosity gleaming in his eyes.

"It depends, are you going to force me into something?" The question is more of a demand for an answer.

"No, the opposite actually." Jonathan's smile deepens, his gaze flicking down to his folded hands for a moment. It's like he enjoys every bit of my animosity.

"I'm not opposed to it, no." I try to remain nonchalant though my curiosity is piqued.

"If you're free, I'd like to come back over tomorrow evening after work. All I ask is that you let me in and have an open state of mind."

I hesitate to answer as I try to calm the rapid beating of my heart. "I can try."

"I'll see you tomorrow then, around 6 p.m., here."

"Okay." I can only muster one word as he collects his coat, nods his head to me, and walks out of my front door.

This day couldn't possibly drag by any fucking slower. I'm not quite excited for what's to come this evening, more anxious to get on with it. Probably because for once it feels like someone is paying attention to me again—actually me and not just my brain—since the assault. He's trying, really trying. It's the most dedicated a therapist has ever been to me. The most present anyone has been to me in such a long damn time.

The way Jonathan looked at me last night, the way he asked me what I wanted to hear while having someone on their knees…moved me? No. It didn't move me. It shook me to my core. It rattled something that has been frozen in place for years. I felt something that wasn't anxiety and emptiness for once.

Fuck.

It's rare, so rare, to feel anything else. Feeling something other than the numbness has invited more anxiety. I don't know if I am yearning for more of this frenzied unsureness, or less.

Pulling my phone from my pocket, I check the time once again. Barely past three o'clock.

Sighing, I give up pacing the house and tidying spaces no one would notice but me. I surrender to the plush pillow top couch and the uneven rhythm of my rickety ceiling fan humming.

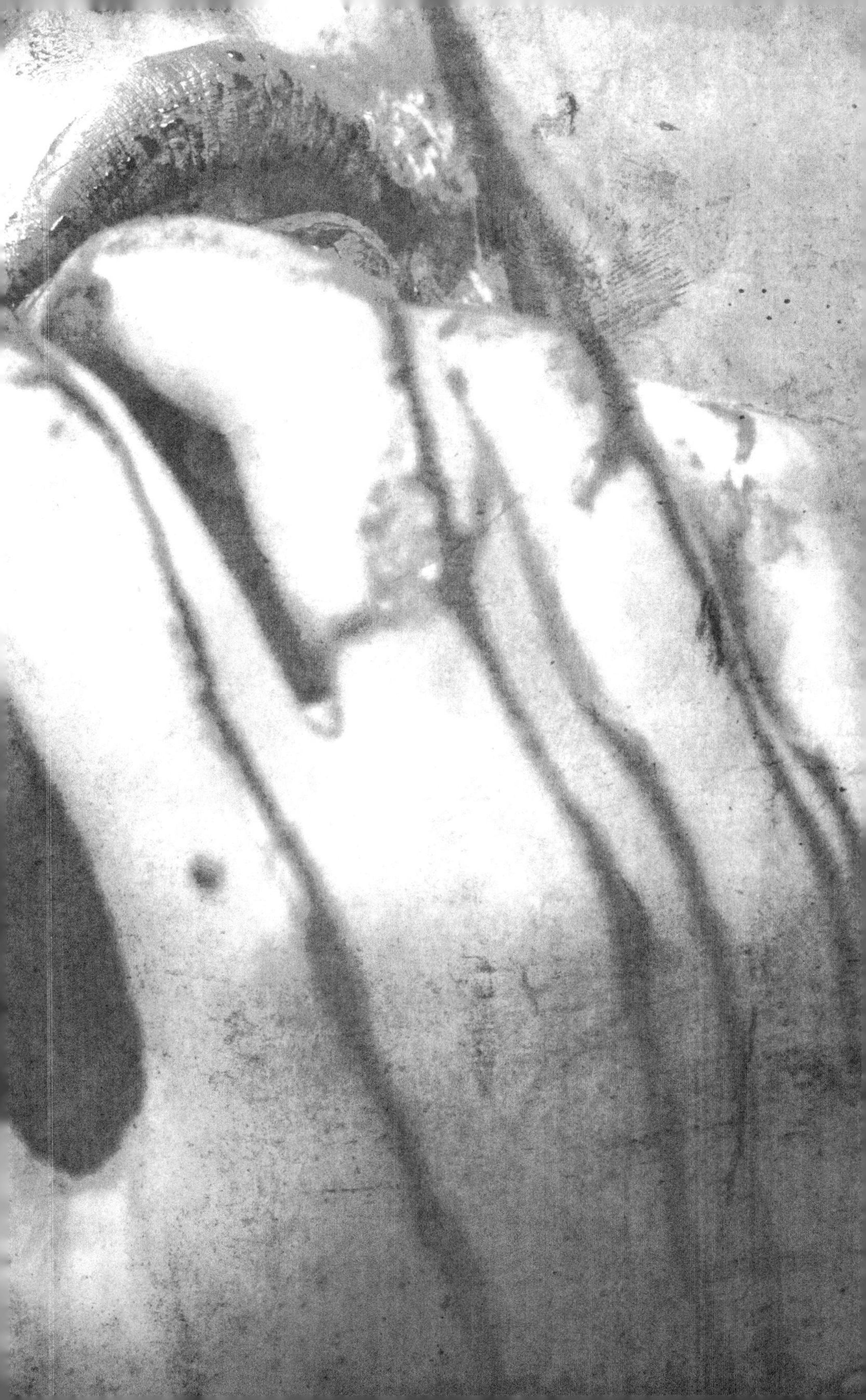

Chapter 7

Brielle

Present

The alarm on my phone jolts me from my sleep. It's a pity because I was enjoying the rare dreamless daze. Two and half hours of blissful, uneventful sleep did wonders for my body. I can feel it within a few moments of being awake. I have renewed energy.

With only thirty minutes until Jonathan said he'd arrive, I move with purpose straight toward the shower. My steps are quick and deliberate, each one shedding a scrap of the clinging lethargy, and dressing in something less slouchy.

I don't know what outfit the occasion calls for. My closet is nothing but a collection of clothing specifically curated to help me hide away from prying eyes. Oversized, baggy sweatshirts, jeans, leggings. All things to help me blend in with my surroundings.

After a good scrubbing with my pink shower loofah and citrus vanilla body wash, I catch a glimpse of myself in the mirror. Damp, jet-black pin-straight hair clings to my face, and there's a slight flush to my cheeks from the warmth of the water. I find myself reaching for the makeup bag that I haven't touched in months. Everything in it is most likely expired, but I feel the old urge to get dolled up again.

I tap the screen of my phone where it lays on the bathroom counter and realize I only have twenty minutes until Jonathan said he would arrive. My stomach tightens as I dump the remnants of a beauty routine I once had onto the bathroom counter, grabbing mascara and eyeliner deciding they'll have to do.

It's funny how we don't seem to lose the muscle memory of things we have done a thousand times. With quick and practiced strokes, I sweep a small wing onto the corners of my eyes and apply coats of nearly dried mascara to my lashes. I look in the mirror and see a crumb of the person I once was. My hair is still wet, but I don't have much more time. I rake a brush through the wet mess and call it good enough. I give myself one more glance before pinching the apples of my cheeks for a faint blush before leaving the bathroom.

Rounding the corner of the kitchen island, a sturdy knock on the door nearly causes me to jump out of my skin, and I mentally curse myself for being so jumpy. I knew he was coming. My habit to overanalyze every move that I make causes an onslaught of reasoning with myself about why I'm acting the way that I am, and unfortunately, I can only deduce that it's due to nerves.

I care about what this man thinks. I want this man in my home. I want him to find me alluring. How fucking annoying.

Leaving him to wait a moment, I strike a match and light the candle on my kitchen island. The soft glow flickers against the setting sun outside, and the creamy dessert scent begins tangling with the air. I don't know what he has in store with this little experiment, but a little mood lighting and a sweet scent filling the room couldn't hurt my nerves.

When I open the door, the sight before me steals the air from my lungs.

Jonathan looks criminally handsome, his presence filling the doorway as though the space was made just for him. He's dressed so sharply, a pang of regret hits my chest because of how lazily I've dressed myself.

"Hello, Brielle." His words are silky smooth, and they slide into my ears, planting themselves with frustrating ease.

He's wearing the same outfit he did yesterday, when he suggested I do my "research." That tie…that fucking tie is still knotted ever so neatly at his throat.

"Hi," I manage, my voice catching in my throat. "Come inside, please."

"You look lovely," he says, his tone sincere. His words hang there for a moment. Lovely? I don't know what to make of it. There are so many emotions dancing in my chest.

He steps inside, hanging the jacket he previously had draping over his arm onto the coat rack next to the door before giving my elbow a reassuring squeeze. When he slips past me, the smell of him is rich and intoxicating. He smells of amber, and oak, with a hint of sweetness.

I inhale the rich masculine notes and allow them to shove the nerves back down my throat.

"H-how are you?" I ask, my voice embarrassingly shy.

He glances up at me from the space he's settled into on the couch, offering a kind smile that disarms me.

"I'm well, and you?"

I fixate my gaze on his teeth. His smile feels so warm and inviting.

"I'm also, well. Well, I'm nervous." The confession tastes sour on my tongue. I don't want to be nervous. I want to feel normal.

"Why don't you come sit with me? We can talk—"

I cut him off. "Okay."

Slow steps lead me the short distance to the couch, and I can't help the hyperawareness of my surroundings. The way his legs are casually spread apart, you can see the relaxation and confidence dripping from his aura.

"I-I, I don't think I want to talk. I want to try whatever we're doing and get on with it," I whisper.

"Okay. Move closer to me." Jonathon pats the middle of the couch. Swallowing hard, I follow the order. "I want to talk about some triggers for you, and some things that you would be against no matter the situation tonight. I don't want to cross any of your boundaries while making such big steps."

"Don't touch my stomach. At no point should you touch my stomach." My voice comes out firmer than intended, but I think that's a good thing. Still, my mind begins backpedaling, racing toward memories I keep running away from, but Jonathan's voice brings me back into the moment.

"Noted, no stomach. Can you show me how far the border extends? Past your ribs, just under your ribs, how low onto your hips?" His question sinks in while I stare at his hand between us on the couch. It's calculated positioning. After seeing Jonathan for months, I realize that every word, every movement, every slight inflection in his voice is planned and calculated. He is always a step ahead of me, warming me up to the idea of being close to him without ever really crossing a line.

"Just, don't touch me anywhere unless I ask for it, please." My voice falters, and I look away not wanting to meet his gaze. Embarrassment rises in me, wondering if he has to have these conversations with other women, too.

"I won't do anything unless you tell me to. You're in complete control," he replies, his voice smooth.

"I'm in complete control?" My brows furrow slightly.

"Within reason, yes." Jonathan nods, confirming with a steady expression.

"What are your boundaries or triggers, Jonathan?" The words come rushing out before I have a chance to stop them. If he knows mine, I should know his.

"Very good question," he says, his voice laced with amusement. "Though, I don't have any."

I blink, confused, staring at him.

"You have no triggers or boundaries? So, if I wanted to put something in your ass, you would be good with it?" His smile doesn't falter as he lets out a breathy laugh.

"I suppose with the proper communication and preparation, I would be okay with it." Astonishment must consume my features judging by the unsure look on Jonathan's.

"We don't have to do anal by any means. You asked, so I answered—"

"No, I know." My words effectively cut him off. "Can I touch you then?" I rush the sentence out, trying to override my anxiety. There are so many emotions flowing through me, but every part of me says that this is an opportunity to get part of my life back in a controlled environment.

You can do this. You can do this.

"Yes. How would you like to?" His question is light and seemingly reassuring.

You can fucking do this.

"I'd like to start with holding your hand." Instead of a response, he raises his hand in offering. I study it for a moment, before reaching mine out to take it.

There is an instant jolt of panic and excitement. His hands are warm, and they lack the rough calloused edges that I vividly remember of Adam's. Not like his at all—and that sentiment allows me to fill my lungs with air.

I continue my exploration of his arm, my fingers trail slowly, studying it as I slowly work my hands up the sleeved forearm and bicep. His skin is warm beneath the fabric, firm yet inviting. I glance to meet his eyes, ensuring that my touches are okay. His features remain calm, his breathing still even, and his body is open to my touch. I continue. One of my hands holds onto his muscular forearm, as the other begins a careful path over his chest, smooth against the material of his shirt.

Unfortunately, or maybe fortunately for me, this seems to be working. A part of me still sits with unease, a quiet voice in the back of my mind reminding me of the past, but it feels distant in this moment. I feel safe touching this man.

I let my fingers move higher, venturing onto the small patch of exposed skin on his chest, where I dip my fingers into the collar of his shirt to feel his warmth under my fingers, nothing stopping me from feeling the smoothness of his skin.

That's when I hear it, the shift of his breathing. It deepens and slows.

It's hunger, but not for food nor comfort.

It's something raw, something vaguely familiar, yet a new feeling I can't remember having felt before.

"Can I climb into your lap? I'd like a better vantage point," I say, my words suddenly much more sure.

"Yes." He sighs. "Please."

Chapter 8

Brielle

Present

I quickly move to straddle his lap. Having a man's broad thighs between my legs is creating a deliciously addicting adrenaline high. I want every molecule of the control that he is giving me.

"Will you touch me, slowly?" I ask, my breaths uneven. "Start low, with my calves or something." My hands are in the silky strands of his hair now as I study his changing expressions. They change with each of my movements. When I give his hair a light tug, a crease begins forming between his eyebrows followed by a haze over his eyes.

That look. That look is familiar to me.

Lust.

He wants me, craves me even, but he has truly given me the power to call the shots. When his fingertips trace a line of agonizing lightning across the bare flesh of my thigh, I can't help the way my hips rock ever so slightly.

"Can I kiss you?" I hate the way my words are desperate with need. Even if I don't really know what it is that I need yet. Just more. More of him.

When my lips touch his, it's a light kiss at first. It's unsure for both Jonathan and myself, neither of us knowing where this kiss may lead. I know we are both feeling the gravity of this moment, and the second his lips part, I think my brain splinters open. My body fills with yearning, and the uncontrolled rocking of my hips deepens.

There is an ache between my thighs, and I'm desperate for friction as his strong and steady hands grip onto my thighs, tugging me to rock into him harder.

Our mouths move in a synchronized tango, dancing together and exploring each others taste. My fingers move on their own accord, unbuttoning his shirt to find more of his bare chest to touch. I feel the loss of his hands on my body when I realize he's helping me release each button. When his lips pull away from mine, I let out a small whimper at the loss of warm contact.

"Straddle my thigh," he says, breathless yet assuring me of the light command.

"Why?" I ask, my own breathless tone matching his.

"You've trusted me this far, trust me now," he breathes, nodding again, continuing to assure me that I'm safe. I do as he says, because I do, trust him.

When the pulsing between my legs meets his thigh, I feel like a ravenous dog. Jonathan lightly grabs my ass and pulls me forward, rubbing my clothed center against his thigh again.

"I don't want to push you, and this is all on your terms," he breathes. "But I want you to rub yourself against my thigh, until you come for me." He punctuates his words by pulling me toward him again, and the electricity sparks even through my lounge shorts and panties.

It feels so fucking good, but I don't even know if coming is possible for me.

"I-I—" I hesitate. "I don't know if I can...come," I admit shyly.

"You can, you can take an orgasm from me, can't you, Brielle?" From the moment those words leave his lips, I know they'll stick with me forever. I can take anything that I want from this man. He's here for me, and as I take control, rubbing my clothed pussy over his dress slacks again and again, I confirm it.

"Yes," I moan. "Yes, I can."

"Talk to me, pretty girl. Are you going to come on my dress pants? Make a mess for me?"

"Yes," I repeat, moving my hips quicker now and making a small effort to rub my own thigh against the growing bulge in his pants.

"Fuck," he groans. His grip is tight on my thighs again as he helps me work myself against him. There's an undeniable heat forming between us, and I want to touch him, see him, feel him. I let one hand wrap around the back of his neck while the other's nails scratch down his chest.

"Kiss me," I plead, and he does more than that. His lips spread mine open as his tongue dives between my lips and tangles with my own. The intrusiveness of it both shocks me and sends a wave of pleasure to my core. The adrenaline pulsing through my veins is unlike anything I've felt. My mind juggles the thought of how wrong our affair is and how exciting it feels.

His tongue continues to explore and dance with mine while my orgasm builds undeniably, and suddenly, I'm pulling away to pant and beg. I barely know what I'm begging for, but my body is aching for more.

"Please," I beg verbally, finally. "I need, I don't know. More, I think."

"Do you want my fingers inside your tight little pussy? Or would you like my tongue, lapping up your sweet juices?" His voice mixed with words that I have only dreamed of being spoken to me nearly push me to the edge of the climax cliff alone. But my core still aches, possibly to be filled.

"Fingers," I pant as I look down at him and meet his eyes. His blue eyes are like a cool glacier staring up at me, filled with burning lust that melts away the insecurities and unsureness that vie for my attention.

Jonathan's eyes never leave mine as his hand snakes between us, pushing the fabric between my legs to the side. I feel his fingertips brush against the tender skin there. His mouth drops open ever so slightly as his first finger dips between my folds, swirling my undeniable wetness and inserting just the tip of his finger into me. My pussy clenches, fighting to keep him there before he inevitably draws the tip back out and brings it up to my clit before circling the swollen nub dutifully. I struggle to keep my eyes open when he applies slightly more pressure. The feeling of his broad fingertip circling my small clit has my eyes rolling into the back of my head before I can stop it.

Suddenly I feel his hand and fingers retract, and my eyes snap open. I watch him while his gaze is fixed on my center where he holds my clothing to the side, giving him an open view of my pussy. I begin to shy away before his movement catches my eyes. He brings the same middle finger that was just soaking in my folds to his mouth, before sucking the finger into the knuckle.

His eyes close as he grunts, his hips bucking once before the finger pops back out with an audible sound.

"You taste so fucking sweet, Brielle," he groans when his eyes open again and land on mine. A shiver wracks my body, my need at an all time high.

His hand dives back between my legs, and he wastes no time pushing his middle finger inside of me. The moan that escapes me is unholy because the way he feels pushing his thick finger into me is sinful at best, and damning at its worst.

"Oh, fucking, fuck—" My words are cut off by his movements as he begins thrusting his finger into me. The pressure returns on my clit, as he rubs in painfully slow circles while pushing his finger in and out of me.

My wetness is audible in the room, making the whole scene more erotic.

My body rolls again as ache deep within me heightens.

"Can you take another finger, baby?" he asks, his voice dripping with adoration. I feel another finger testing my entrance, and I look down to watch his expert touch rub through my pink folds.

"Uh-huh," I murmur to him while I watch. The second finger pushes into me, and stars explode over my vision. Instinctually, I try to force his fingers deeper by settling my hips, and my efforts are successful. Once seated on both fingers, I feel the position of his hand change as he continues rubbing my pulsing clit, the sudden movement causing my core to weep.

When I look down again, a gush of warm liquid cascades from my pussy in waves as I moan and grind into him again. I can't care, everything feels so fucking good that my body feels like it's on fire.

"God fucking damn, Brielle. I didn't know you'd be a squirter. Fuck, you've made such a mess, baby." The noises my pussy makes becomes so much louder with the added liquid. I'm fully riding his hand now, taking everything my body needs from him.

"Keep talking, gonna come," I say around a moan.

"Your tight pussy is sucking my fingers in, baby. I want you to squirt all over my face next, can you do that for me?" He buries his face in my shirt, nuzzling his face between my breasts while I continue to fuck myself with his hand.

"Are you going to come for me now? I feel your pussy tightening and throbbing around my fingers. Let go, come all fucking over me, baby." He pants as he stares up at me again.

"Yes, yes…Oh, yes!" Everything fades as I pinch my eyes shut, pleasure rolling over my body in waves. The liquid soaks us both once more, and it feels like it doesn't stop. It feels as if I come over and over again, with years of missed opportunity. Before I even come out of my orgasm fog, Jonathan picks me up and plants me on the couch, pushing my legs open wide while his fingers keep pumping in and out of me. The sight of him is so fucking sexy that my pussy continues to spasm around his fingers.

"Squirt on my face, let me drink you in," he commands me, and then his tongue is flat against my clit. He licks repeatedly, arching his fingers inside me until I feel the build again all while his eyes burn holes into me. One hand reaches up to caress my breast through the thin fabric, easily finding my nipple before tugging it gently.

With a few more crooks of his finger, I'm coming again, and he continues his punishing thrusts with his mouth open wide, collecting every bit of juice that my pussy squirts before I watch his Adams apple bob while he swallows.

Jesus christ. I've never seen something more unexplainably sexy than this. His clean shaven face sparkles in the dim light with my arousal, and if my body wasn't so spent I'd try riding his face again. Jonathan's slow licks finally come to a halt as he smiles up at me, pure satisfaction glinting in his glacier eyes.

"That was…wow," I hesitantly comment. What is the protocol after sex? Good job? No, I'm not telling him that. Does he still want to…go all the way? Fuck, I didn't plan for that. I didn't plan for any of this. When Jonathan stands to walk away, it feels as if a rush of cold water washes over me. This moment is very sobering, as everything that has just happened sinks in.

A man touched me, fucked me with his fingers, and I let him. Not only did I let him, I enjoyed it. I orgasmed. My mind begins to drop further into the spiral as he walks away from me. Before I know it, I've sunken back into the bad place. The place where only my darkest memories hide, where the scariest part of my psyche roam free.

Chapter 9

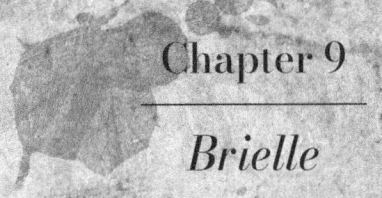

Brielle

Two Years Ago

The nurse's words play on repeat in my mind while tears blur my vision. "Congratulations! You're pregnant, dear," she says with pure glee. I don't fault her. The old woman with stories hiding within her smile lines probably just likes the smell of baby feet or whatever.

"I—" My mind spins. How can this even be possible? "I don't understand how that's possible. The last time I—" My pause hangs heavy in the air while she watches me expectantly. "The last time I had sex, I was on my period."

"Well, it's rare but the human body is capable of miracles!" she exclaims.

Her joy is so thick you could cut it with a butter knife. But it doesn't matter.

The knot in my stomach, nor the fertilized egg stuck in my uterus, budge. My heart races nearly as fast as my tires on the pavement. Hands gripping ten and two, my mind shuts off.

"I don't want it. I don't want this pregnancy," I whisper, only loud enough for the nurse to hear.

"Oh dear." She pauses. "I fear it's too late for the morning after pill. Abortion isn't in our state…" Her worried eyes pull at my heart, and I imagine this woman would give the best hugs. I wonder briefly if my own grandma gave good hugs. I wonder what she would say to me right now.

The blood drains from my knuckles as I grip the steering wheel tighter. The tears begin to dry as Felicity's words cut through the last straw.

"You were drunk. Lot's of people fuck when they're drunk. That doesn't mean he raped you." My fist smashes into the solid plastic of the steering wheel with every word that I recall from her. When my tires jerk loosely on the pavement sending me over the yellow line briefly, everything clicks.

No heartbeat. No pregnancy.

Suddenly my tears dry as the speedometer reaches eighty miles per hour. It's a split second decision. One minute I'm speeding down the cold and foggy country highway, and the next minute happens in slow motion.

My hands rip the steering wheel to the right, and for the first time in weeks, my mind shuts off. I watch as the car hits the metal railing, and I see the world around me spin. When I hear the crunch, I lose my sight, the world goes black, and my body feels warm. The second crunch seems far into the distance. Like I'm only hearing it through a speaker.

I don't know how long I sit in that dark space with myself when the crunching stops. I must drift in space for a while because I begin to grow cold.

The next thing I know, everything is bright. My eyes are sore, and it hurts to open my eyes. Unfortunately my ears begin to catch up with my eyes, and I hear a faint beeping. I realize quickly that I'm connected to several different wires and IV lines, and most likely other things that I haven't registered yet.

When my eyes are finally able to open fully, I register the bright hospital room and something ungodly hanging out of my mouth. My throat aches and it becomes hard to breathe properly. The beeping speeds up as a nurse comes rushing into the room while I frantically pull at the tube in my throat. She removes it with ease, causing me to cough.

The nurse gives me the rundown of my injuries, and tears well in my eyes when I look down at my leg wrapped in a beige cast. Her next words turn my blood to ice.

"I'm sorry to say, but your baby didn't make it."

All I can do is nod. I feel another hot, wet tear slide down my cheek.

I've been in a medically induced coma for just over a week to let my body heal from my injuries. She tells me about the surgery to remove the shards of glass and tree branches from my stomach, and how lucky I am to be alive.

Lucky. What an odd thing to say.

A tree branch stood between my life and my death. A tree branch ended the unwanted pregnancy. I don't say that. Not that I can do much talking with a throat as sore as mine anyways.

"We couldn't find your next of kin…Would you like us to call someone for you?" she asks me, pity etched into every word.

I shake my head, looking away from her to look out the window of my second, *maybe third floor room. I continue crying, even once the words are distorted in my ear. Eventually I fall back to sleep, I think. I don't dream, though.*

Present

I wake up in my bed with broad arms around my midsection. It startles me, and I slowly peel the top arm off of me so I can sit up and check my phone. I wipe the little bits of sleep sand from my eyes as I tap my phone that is surprisingly plugged into the charger. It's three in the morning and there are no notifications on my phone screen. Notifications be damned, I plan to create my own on someone else's phone.

I open the social media app to type in the name I'm searching for, and the profile pops up immediately. Once I've sent my message, I lock the screen and set my phone in my lap. Looking over my shoulder, I see Jonathan is still asleep. God damn this man looks like a dark angel. I'm lost in thought, realizing that not only did the fine specimen in my bed dress me and put me to bed during a breakdown, but he was also able to give me a mind shattering orgasm beforehand. And he's still here.

The last week has been unreal. I don't know what to make of it. I would ask my therapist, but he's lying in my bed gently snoring. Fucking weird.

My phone chiming breaks me free of my thoughts. I read the message while absent-mindedly biting my fingers as I mull over my choices, finally deciding to do my makeup once more in a twelve hour time frame.

I make quick work of the application process before I'm quickly grabbing my keys off the hook while pulling on my cardigan. Making my way out into the cool temps of the night, I only start my car once I'm in it. If my car starting wakes Jonathan, I'd rather it be too late for him to ask questions. The drive is short. I guess that's what happens when you live in a small town, everyone you know or may need to see is only a few minutes away.

The orange street lights shine into my car, and the drive is strangely relaxing. My mind, my body, feel at peace. Even thinking of the scars littering my stomach as I drive a breezy forty-five miles per hour, I feel okay. And I think I'll feel better soon.

Pulling into the driveway that my tires haven't graced in two years, I see the same cracked orange flower pot on the concrete slab in front of the garage that's regularly emptied for cigarette butts. The door to the main living area opens just as I shut my headlights off.

There he stands. The same shaggy blond hair, the same overly blue eyes. The same dirty white T-shirt. Adam, in the fucking flesh.

The dumb idiot shoves one hand in his pocket and waves at me with the other. A boyish smile crosses his face as he motions me into his home. I take a deep breath before opening my door, keys in one hand and my phone in the other as each step I take crunches the gravel beneath my shoes. Walking up to greet him, he pulls a pack of cigarettes from his pocket.

"You want a smoke?" I nod. I haven't smoked in about a year, but I take the cigarette and let him light it for me. Taking a long drag off the cheap cigarette, I let the smoke fill my lungs, finally speaking on my exhale.

"You still live here, huh?" I gesture around to the run down garage-turned-home.

"Yeah, finally bought it from my folks. Remodeled some inside, you wanna come in?" He raises his eyebrows and gestures toward the door. I wave my cigarette at him in response.

"You can smoke inside." He opens the door and walks inside, leaving the door open for me.

I walk in behind him, looking around at the supposed remodels. I guess, to someone, this shit-hole could be considered remodeled.

"You still drink?" Jesus christ. When you don't talk to men, they will just keep questioning you until you do, I guess.

"Sure." I pull out a chair at his kitchen table, plopping my ass down on the scratchy fabric chair from the 1990s.

"Sure?" He holds out a shot glass toward me. Black spiced rum. My stomach churns, but I take the shot and chase it with another drag off of my cigarette. "That doesn't sound very convincing, but the way you slammed that shot does. Damn, girl."

"I wrangled black spiced rum once, I can do it again." I smile in his direction, a smile that doesn't quite meet my eyes while I tap the table. "Plus, you should be taking two to my one. You're like double my size." My laugh is effortless, like I don't have a care in the world.

"Oh, you want to drink like that?" He winks at me as he takes his shot and immediately pours himself another. "I guess I'll agree. You've lost weight, not that you really had any to lose, but you have."

"You know what they say, twenty when you hit your twenties." I roll my eyes and let him pour me another shot.

We sit here talking for an hour or so. I let him absentmindedly talk, continuously drinking, beer after beer, shot after shot. When his words begin to slow, I've only actually had three shots. This rum is strong, but my hunger is stronger. I want to replace the memory of waking up to him between my legs with a new one, a better one.

I stand up and round the table, and when I'm a step or two from him he swivels his chair around to face me. Walking myself into his vicinity rewards me with his hands reaching out to rub up my thighs. I let him, thinking of Jonathan's in the same place only a few hours ago. I close my eyes and imagine it's him for a moment, leaning my head back and letting my own hands fall onto his shoulder. The mental imagery is ruined by the sound of Adam's voice.

"Do you remember the last time you were here?" Is he fucking kidding me?

"I doooo," I sing-song the words, trying to keep my cool.

"I could make you feel good again." I think I'm going to fucking throw up.

"Is that so?" I look down at him and slowly wrap my hand around his throat, forcing him to look up at me. "I think I could make *you* feel good."

"I'm down for whatever you're down for." He smiles up at me with drunken lust-filled eyes. My hand travels up the column of his throat, where I hold his jaw, brushing my thumb across his lip.

"Yeah? I like things rough now. Rougher than you liked it back then," I tease, but there's a lot of truth in my words.

"I think I can handle it." He squeezes my ass to punctuate his statement. I lean down, my breath skating across his skin, tempting him closer as his eyelids flutter.

"How about, I meet you in your bedroom? I need to grab something out of my car, but I wont leave you waiting long." Reaching over to pour him one last shot, I hand it to him. "You're going to need this." Bringing the shot glass to his lips, he tilts his head and swallows the amber liquid.

I stand to give him space to walk to his bedroom and watch as he stumbles, his footing not lining up with his body. He turns around, pure drunkenness seeping from his every movement. I shake my hands at him, shooing him away.

Chapter 10

Brielle

Present

Once he's in his room, the walk to my car moves quickly. Hitting the unlock button on the fob and opening the door swiftly, I reach into the center console and fumble in the dark until my hand lands on the small metal. I stuff it into my bra and jog back inside. Once inside, I notice Adam's pack of cigarettes lying on the table and grab one for each of us before heading toward his bedroom door. He's already half-naked, laying in his bed like a shit-faced starfish in nothing but his boxers. My mind reels at whatever kind of shit stains are probably residing there.

"See, told you I wouldn't take long." My tone is cheerful knowing what's to come.

"Any time is too long, I don't like waiting." I know. I know he doesn't.

"Play nice, I brought you a cigarette."

"Fuck yes," he says as he stuffs the pillow under his head so he can look at me.

Climbing the bed and tucking my own cigarette between my lips, I straddle him and slip his between his lips as well, leaning forward to light our cigarettes at the same time with the lighter. The lighter flicks off and I toss it on his nightstand for now. Slowly, so slowly, I begin rocking my hips over his groin, though, he's already hard with just my being on top of him. I continue taking drags off my cigarette as he watches me grinding against him, and I let my hand fall to my stomach to slowly lift my shirt. Slipping my hand into the waist band of my pants, I begin rubbing slow circles over my clit while drunk eyes watch me.

Adam's cigarette lies limply—far too much ash on the end—between his fingers while he focuses on my body and tries to use his other hand to rock me against him, but he's out of rhythm. Reaching out to rest my cigarette in the ash tray, I climb off of him to remove my pants, and he starts to try to pull his boxers down.

"No." I stop his hand. "Get me ready first," I say as I climb back onto him, naked from the waist down.

I crawl up his body, pulling his arms under my knees where I hover over his face. His eyes are barely open now as he gazes up at me licking his lips.

"You're so we-et for me," he slurs and licks his lips.

I am absolutely not fucking wet for him. But hey, who am I to correct an idiot in his position?

"Mmhm," I hum, swaying my hips slightly to taunt him. "Lick me, now."

He doesn't hesitate against my command. He sits up and eagerly begins to lick. Too bad the pressure is all wrong. His tongue pokes and prods at my soft flesh, and thank god his eyes are closed because he doesn't see me roll mine. I sink all of my weight onto his face and arms, determined to give myself something from this experience. Continuing to rub myself against his face, I bring my pussy over his nose before sliding back to his mouth where his tongue desperately tries to keep up, but I refuse. I drag myself over his nose once more and watch as my pussy lips cover it completely.

He doesn't know he should worry, so in that time frame I'm able to reach into my bra and bring out my secret toy. Grabbing a fistful of hair, his eyes finally open when I don't move my pussy off his nose. Poor thing has his tongue in my entrance and my clit on his nose.

I hold him there for a moment, searching his eyes for something that tells me I'm not making the right choice. Sadly, his eyes are drunk. They seem like they're telling me yes, especially if I use the logic he used the same night he raped me and left me with an unwanted child that I almost took my fucking life for.

"Remember when you said you could handle me?" I moan, even though it's fake.

He begins tapping my leg, and his eyes become panicky.

"I just don't think you like to play as rough as I do after all, Adam." My switchblade flicks open, and just as swiftly as the blade, I plunge it into his eye.

Bright-red blood instantly pours off of his face and begins soaking into the stained pillow case beneath him. An anguished sound comes from between my legs, but I tighten my grip on his hair before dislodging the knife from his eye and thrusting it into the other. A spray of the warm crimson splatters against my bright-blue top.

I press my core into his face a bit harder, knowing that he'll pass out soon from not only the pain, but also the lack of oxygen. Releasing his hair and stripping off my shirt, I pull myself off of him and begin pushing my shirt into his gaping mouth to prevent any screams he has left from being heard. My bare feet tap back toward the living room area, before padding back to the bedroom where Adam lays, barely twitching. I pour what's left of the rum over the shirt in his mouth and watch my pretty blue garment drink in the liquid.

Grabbing my leftover cigarette from the ash tray and the lighter off the nightstand, I first light the cigarette, then the edge of the shirt, watching it catch flame before stuffing the lighter into my bra. As the flames grow, I notice a glint in his eye and realize I almost forgot my switchblade. I pull it free before tucking it back in my bra as I collect my panties and pants.

Since I don't particularly care for sweating, I pad out of the bedroom because it's getting fucking hot. With the cigarette between my teeth, I'm able to quickly maneuver my clothes back on and slip back into my shoes. I take one more peek into the bedroom, and like I'd hoped, the bed has caught fire, and Adam still hasn't moved.

I know I said I'd make him feel good, and I truly did mean it. He feels good to me now. Dead that is.

Before I leave, I grab my phone, and his. Just in case the whole place doesn't burn, I'd like to pretend I'm trying to cover my tracks. I just have to hope he's not logged into any social media accounts anywhere else for now.

Before I leave, I steal the pack of smokes from the table. A parting gift to myself, I guess.

The drive back home is even more relaxing. The orange lights still gleam in the early morning light, and in the few moments I have, I watch the sun begin to rise. The pink hue is other worldly. My chest feels lighter, everything feels…*good*.

My driveway comes into view quickly, and I waste no time jumping out of my car and tiptoeing inside. My little dog's collar clicks against his tags as he waddles his butt toward me. I scratch his chin but hurry to check my bedroom for Jonathan. By some miracle, he still sleeps in nearly the same position I left him in. My eyes close in relief, and I allow a deep breath to fill my lungs. My feet carry me weightlessly to the shower where I tuck my bra, panties, and pants into the bottom of the clothes hamper after stripping down. The mirror stares back, exposing the droplets of blood against my pale skin. I don't flinch when the shower knob squeaks in protest. I don't flinch against the feeling of the warm water running over my body. And I don't flinch when the bathroom door opens while I'm rinsing my shampoo.

"Hey, I'm sorry to barge in, is everything okay?" Jonathan's voice is groggy and soft, caring.

I pull the shower curtain to the side, exposing my full body to the cool air, giving him an unobstructed view, scars and all. He's already pitching morning wood, but I don't miss the way the bulge in his pants twitches when his gaze lowers across my breasts and down to the V of my thighs.

"Shit, good morning," he says as his eyes rake back up to meet mine.

"Would you like to join me?" I ask, keeping my voice soft to match his.

"Are you sure that's okay? That's a big step, Brielle. I don't want to pressure you, or make you feel—"

"You're not, I don't…You don't have to feel pressured either," I whisper.

"I don't," he says as he pulls his shirt over his head before pushing his boxers and pants down at the same time.

His large body takes up so much space in my tiny shower, and it forces one part or another of my body against his. There are butterflies freaking the fuck out in my stomach when I raise my hands to touch his chest, raking my fingers over the tattoos as water droplets cascade over each vein and muscle.

"I want you to fuck me. Show me what it's supposed to feel like again. Don't ask me if I'm sure, don't be gentle, just…just take me."

"Okay." He invades my space and pushes his body against mine, his growing erection hard against my stomach while he pushes his hand into my hair to cup my neck. His kiss is searing, molten fucking lava as his mouth commands mine.

Our lips are dancers, moving together to the mixed beat of our hearts thudding within our chests. His hands find the backsides of my thighs where he hoists me up, using his body to pin me against the shower wall.

"If at any point it gets too rough, tap me anywhere three times, I'll stop, no questions asked," he says into my open and panting mouth.

"Okay, yeah." My voice comes out as a whimper, my core undulating and searching for friction.

He looks down between us and guides his thick cock to my entrance, and I watch as the tip nudges at my opening.

"Fuck." Jonathan pants, leaning his forehead against mine as he slowly pushes further into me. I moan. Fuck, I'm moaning so loud the sound reverberates off the tiled walls.

I don't have time to process because his cock pushes through the barrier of muscle inside me as he sinks to the hilt.

"Oh, my, fucking god!" I plead, and he starts moving.

He fucks into me with punishing strokes, and my body goes entirely limp. Jonathan supports my entire weight, fucking into me over and over and over.

I'm boneless in his arms, and all I hear is his muddled curses, my moaning, and the sound of my lower back repeatedly slapping against the tiles. I feel free. I know I will be sore, but for once it's a soreness that I welcome. Being ravaged this way feels too fucking good.

So good even, that it feels like I'm getting away with murder.

The end...for now.

FIND BRIELLE'S LOVE STORY WITHIN PREYING ON THE PREDATOR. YOU can preorder here now!

Acknowledgments

I want to give a special nod to the organizer of this spectacular anthology.

Tilly Ridge, the woman you are, you are an amazing human being. I spent several years writing and deleting before you came along and basically told me to nut the fuck up. Thank you for giving me a space to finally tell Brielle's story and in a way that goes to amazing charity organizations.

I adore you a scary amount. I wouldn't be here without you.

Thank you.

Red, my partner in crime. I love you.

Thank you for being you and never ceasing to believe in me.

I do believe we're owed a bottle of wine after this one, yeah?

I'd also like to thank chocolate milk. The true star of the show, my fuel writing this story. Never change, Choccy.

About Ava Jay

Ava Jay is a Midwest based author in her mid-twenties. Ava spends her time juggling mom life, being a spouse, taking care of too many animals to count, and daydreaming of more plots than she can write.

Ava's primary focus is romance, no matter the trials her characters must face to earn their happily ever after.

Website: https://avajay.carrd.co/

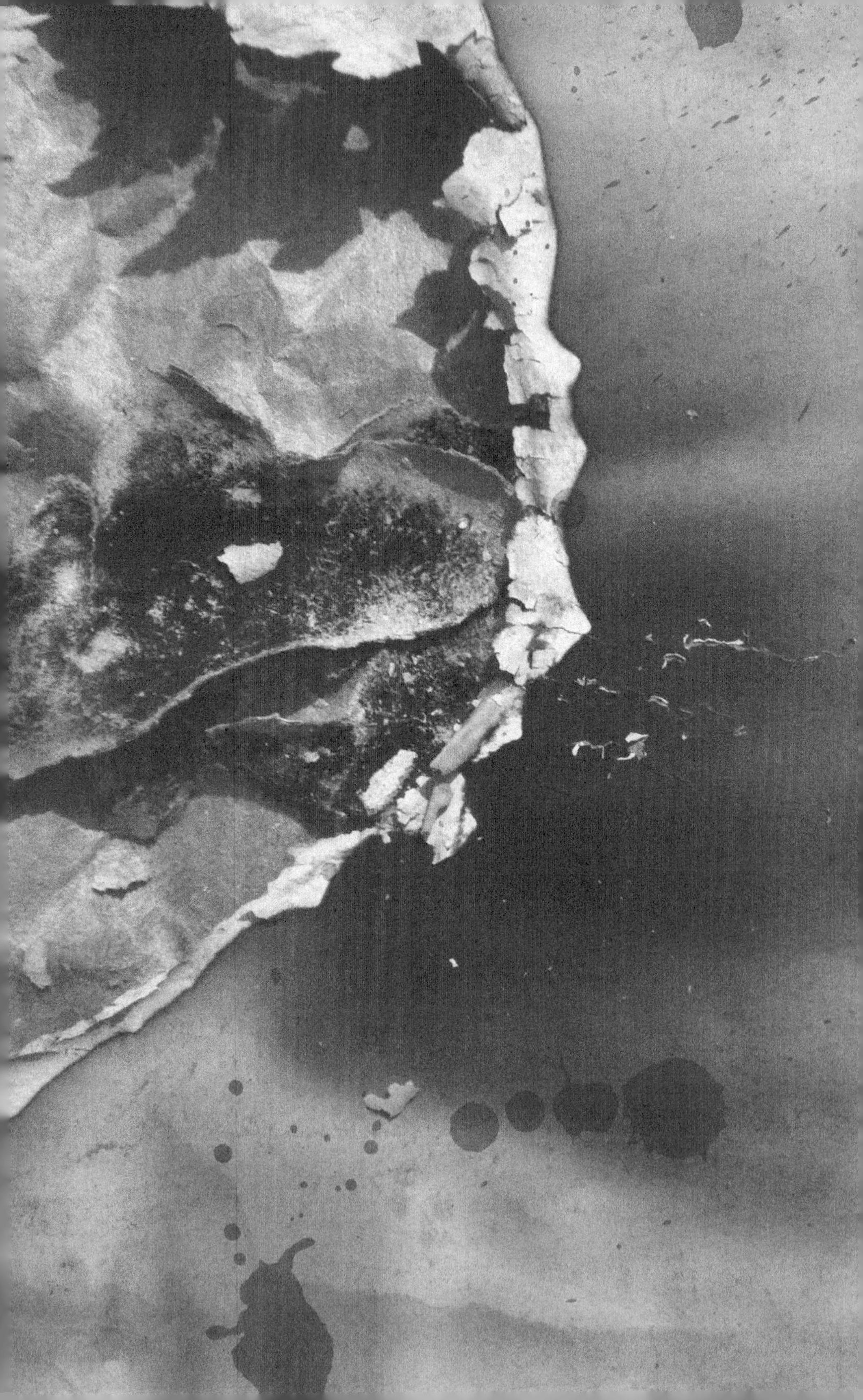

Our Bodies, Our Choice.

CJ Riggs

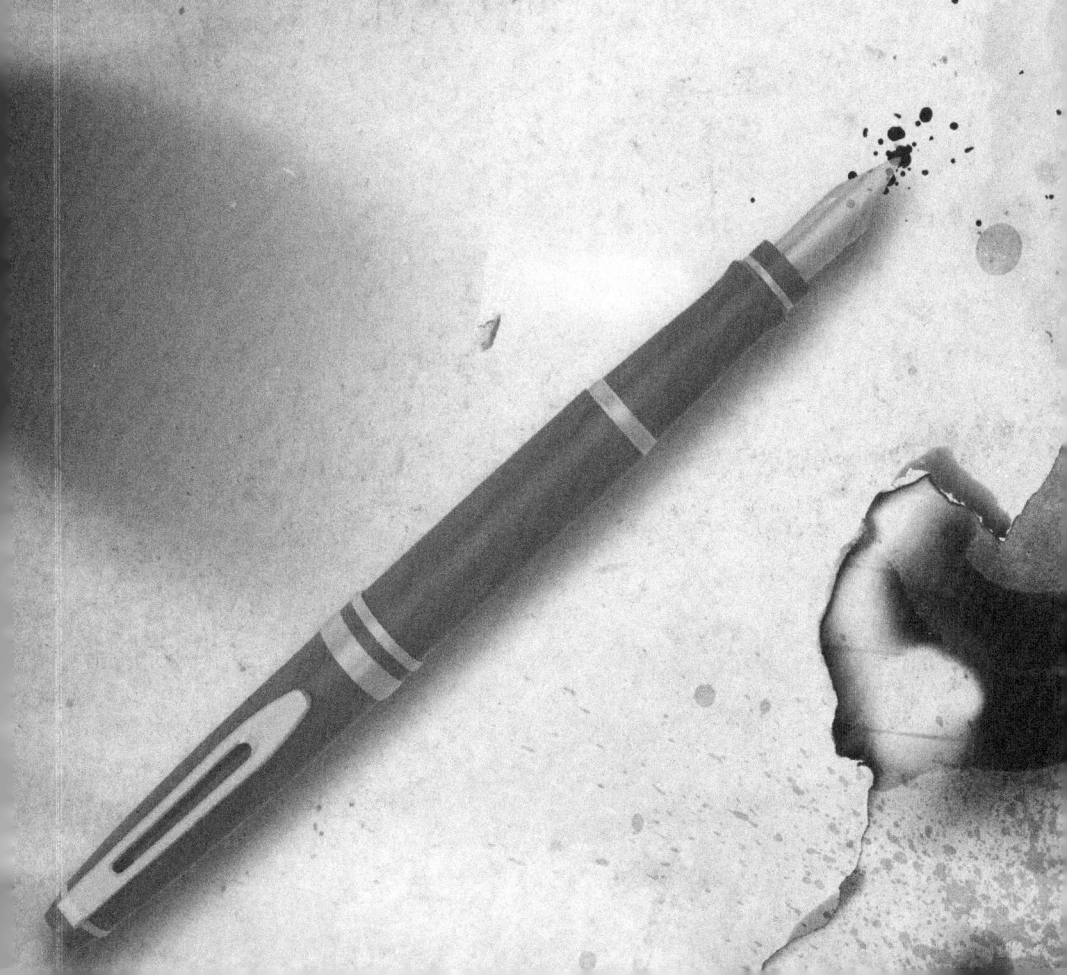

Chapter 1

Elise

Missouri.

I haven't taken my eyes off the computer screen since this ingrate started spewing his shit at four p.m. Listening to hate speech from the oversized fuck-hole that is his mouth, is driving me crazy. There clearly wasn't enough chlorine in his family gene pool because how in the fuck… did anyone create such a snivelling little cunt like him.

The man in question; Robert Evans.

Apparently, women and '*the gays*' as he so disgustingly puts it, have become unreasonable, uncontrollable, and we all need to be stopped before we ruin the country and take over… or some bullshit like that. And according to this motherfucker, I hit the top three on his shit list.

"It's fucking laughable how fucking stupid you women are." Robert laughs, snatching the microphone from the table he sits behind, and bringing it closer to his mouth.

"*Pendejo,*" I mumble, screwing my face up slightly because even though I'm sick to fucking death of hearing this little *chingada madre* talk so much crap, I'm surprised he isn't shitting out of his mouth.

"After all that time protesting, chanting, and walking the streets together, crying about how we all need to take a stand… well, we did, and *we* fucking won, while you…. failed."

His laughter at the screen fills me with fucking rage. But I remain stoic. I just continue eating my dry roasted peanuts, watching this man continue to dig his own grave.

"Men are the better sex. We are far more superior, stronger, more intellectual, and just all around *better* than you!!!"

"How long have you been listening to this shit?" My sister Bekah says as she stops beside me, crossing her arms in front of her chest.

Popping another peanut in my mouth, I shrug. "Too long."

"Well, turn it off. The Coursing is starting in a few hours, and we need to get out of the state and into the safe zone as quickly as—"

"You'll never have any rights, whores. Because what I know—and every other fucking man in this country knows—is that it might be *your* body, but it will always be *our* fucking choice." He begins laughing hysterically. What little expression I had on my face, drops. Both me and my sister standing there in silence. "We own you. We control you. We are the superior species overall."

There are red hearts from people liking his live feed, bouncing all over the screen; comments flying through the chat, shares, follower count… everything is getting higher.

"How long do we have?" I ask, turning to face Bekah.

"Five hours until we need to be on the bus, but—"

"Good. Call Daisie, tell her I need a favour, and I need it quickly."

"Elise, we can do this another time, but right now—"

"Now, Bekah!" I snap. "The full works, make sure she knows *nothing* is to be missed.

"Okay."

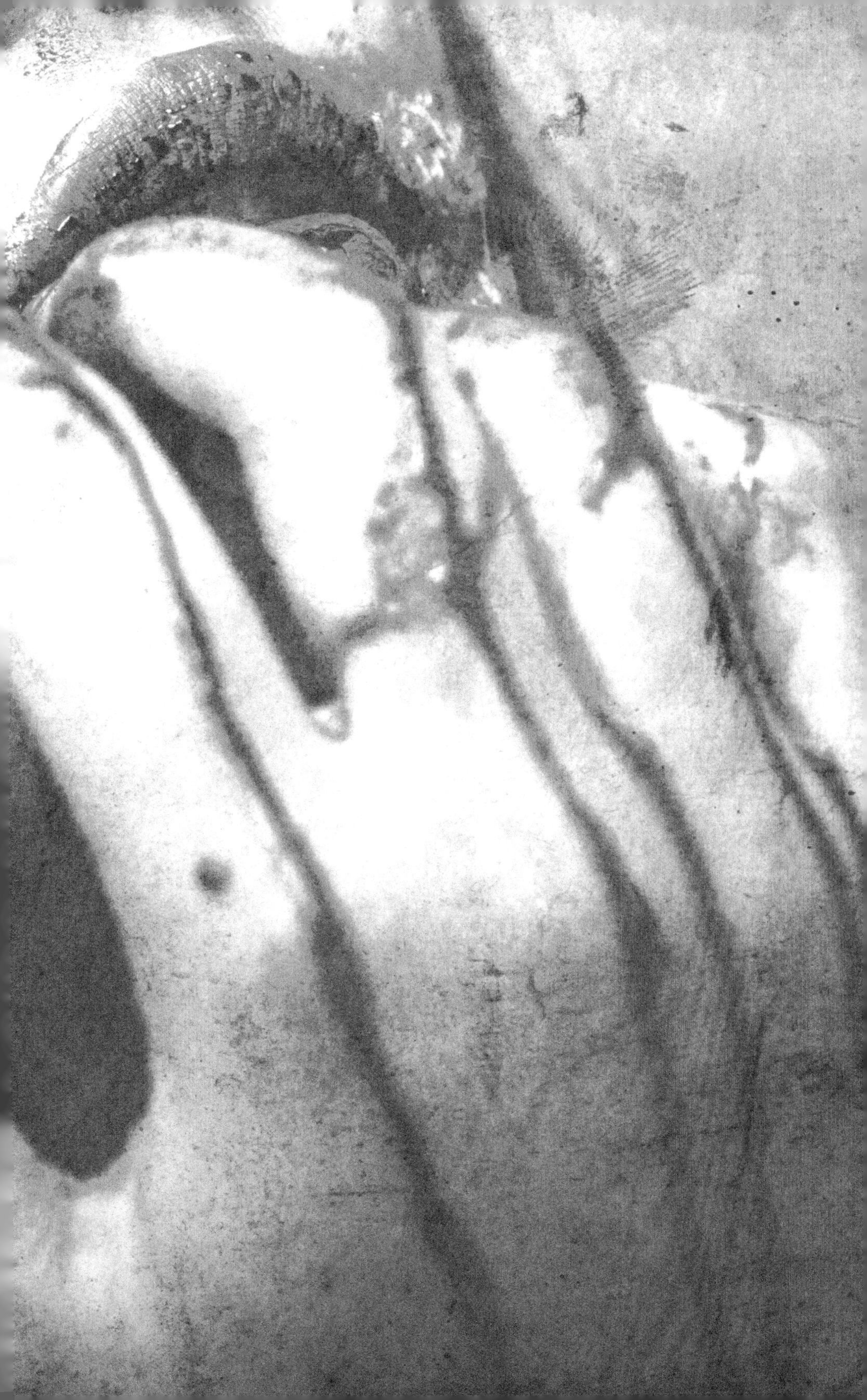

Chapter 2

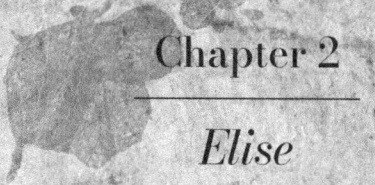

Elise

1 year Later

C**oursing**.
Noun
The sport of hunting game animals such as **hares** with **greyhounds**, using sight rather than **scent**. "Hare coursing."

That's what the original definition is anyway.

Except now, instead of actual animals… it's humans.

Once every six months, it begins with an alarm and a twelve-hour window where all of us are in danger. American's fought for this. Marched for it. Stormed the Presidential Palace and eventually, the President himself endorsed it.

The news tells us he endorsed it through fear of an uprising from the American people, but those of us who are smart, know it's what he wanted all along. Handing out fearmongering tactics within every speech, buying news channels and funding them to show the bullshit propaganda he thought up. Taking our concentration away from the real issues at hand.

The removal of any free thinker.

"What do you have for me?" I ask Daisie the moment I walk into her private office. Her house is situated on the outskirts of The Coursing border, which enables us to be safe. After all, this isn't country wide yet. It's being tested within Missouri for the first year, and then eventually—just like healthcare rights—each state will decide on whether they want to engage in it or not.

"Everything..." Her sultry voice filters through the air the closer I get. "And anything you need."

Daisie is the most beautiful woman I've ever laid eyes on. Her long baby pink hair, that's always tied up into space buns, sits beautifully against her alabaster skin. She's got bright blue eyes that stare deep within your soul, and a voice so soft she would be the perfect phone sex operator. We've been best friends for ten years, and I've been in love with her for each of them.

The moment I saw her walking across the school yard at seventeen —her hair was coloured teal back then—I just knew that she was going to be someone I would only ever love from afar.

Why? Because she's straight.

It doesn't stop me fantasising about her, though.

My mind is filled constantly with thoughts of Daisie, and even though I've tried as hard as I can to stop the sexual urges, I can't. Perfect curves on a short stature, with beautiful elven features that make her look almost ethereal. Most of the time, when I'm alone, I imagine all the things I shouldn't. Like how her touch would feel across my deep, golden hued skin, or how she would react beneath mine. Would she crave me as much as I do her? Do her moans of ecstasy sound like heaven?

I come up behind her as she sits in the black, high back swivel chair at her computer. The red and black, checkered mini skirt and tight fitted black vest she's wearing are doing nothing to help my composure.

Resting one hand on the back of the chair, I press my other to the tabletop and lean over her shoulder, just to get a look at what she's doing. Really, it's to get a whiff of how she smells. Honeydew with a hint of white oleander. The perfume she's always worn, and that same bottle sits in my bedside table at home.

Don't judge me. I'm in love with the girl, alright.

"I finally managed to get into everything, Elise. Bank statements, his real address, where he works. *Fuck*, I even have his social security number and where he really went to school. The same goes for all of his friends."

"Good job. You've done amazing with this." I praise her. A light blush creeps up the side of her neck before it covets the highest points of her cheeks. I lean in a little closer to her, reaching my hand forward and pressing the tip of my finger against the computer screen.

"What's this? I thought we checked there for him already."

Clearing her throat, she readjusts her position before answering. "This is where he stays when everything begins. Usually it's empty, but he makes sure that it looks that way so nobody suspects him being there."

I turn my head to her, our faces a lot closer than before. The heavy swallow I take is more audible than usual before I continue to speak. "Does CCTV footage prove that?" I ask before looking back at the monitor.

"Yes. He doesn't hide it very well either, mainly because he's so cocky now he doesn't think anyone would dare to come for him. I managed to track his cell phone location, and at least three or four times a month he comes here, either early morning or late at night."

Daisie leans back in the chair, the back of her shoulder resting against my thumb, and I can't help myself—I need to learn to assert some form of control on my actions. Lifting my thumb from between the chair and her, I gently dance the pad of it over her exposed skin.

"This is great." I offer her a smile as I look at her. "You've done brilliant as usual."

Fuck, those eyes of hers.

Chapter 3

Daisie

My heart flutters every time she looks at me that way. The small touches, how gentle her voice is when she speaks to me. All the times I've caught her staring my way and never said anything. Because she's my friend. My *best* friend. And there would be nothing worse in this world than losing her if she didn't feel the way I do.

Elise. Is. Stunning.

God, she's more than that. She's everything. Hazel eyes and beautifully plump lips. Smooth looking, tawny skin covering every inch of her. Elise is tall, lean from years working out to get herself in perfect shape, her hair styled into a short pixie cut that helps accentuate all her perfectly angled facial features. I've tried everything I can to fight the feelings I have for her, but since everything has gone to shit in Missouri and she's protected me every single time, they've only grown stronger.

I've always seen myself as a straight woman, only ever dated men.

What a mistake that was.

I swallow hard before clearing my throat again. "So I think this is the best place for the four of us to hit tonight, because—"

"You're staying here," Elise counters, cutting the end of my sentence off before standing up and righting herself.

I swivel my chair around to face her. "I'm sorry?" I frown.

Rubbing her hands over her face, she sighs deeply. "I need you to stay here so you're—"

"Safe?"

"Exactly. Look, D—"

"No. Why?" I cut her off, standing from the chair and stepping towards her.

"Just drop it." Turning away from me she makes her way towards the door. "Stay here, where you're safe, where I can protect you. And when everything's done, I'll—"

I move faster than her, placing myself in front of the steel door and locking it. "I'm not staying here."

"Yes… you are," she counters, resting her hands on my shoulders. As she tries to move me out of the way, I stand rigid. Refusing to do what she wants. "Daisie."

"Elise." I cross my arms in front of my chest. There's no way I'm staying here while she goes out to that building with her sister.

Groaning, Elise drops her head back with her hands resting on her hips. "Please, D, don't fight me on this. I've thought long and hard about everything, and I don't think that—"

Reaching up, I grab her by the chin, tugging her gaze back to me. "You can at least look at me when you're about to lie."

"Lie?"

Okay, not the best choice of words I could've used.

"Yes, lie." I know she's about to get pissed off. The vein in her forehead is already throbbing. "You want me to stay here because you don't think I can do it. Not because you want to protect me." I step forward, closing the space between us. "It's because you think I'm weak, isn't it."

"What? No, that's not it at all. It's because I—"

"Oh, don't bullshit me, Elise. Just fucking say it. You don't think I have the capacity to murder someone. That's it, isn't it."

"Daisie—"

"Just fucking say it!" I shout. "Tell me to my face. Then at least I'll know how you really feel about me!" I egg her on. "That you think I'm weak, that I can't do what you guys are about to, that—"

"Is that what you think!?" she barks.

"Yes!"

"That's bullshit, D, and you know it. I've never once called you fucking weak."

"If that's not it" –I raise my arms to the sides and drop them, my palms slapping against my bare thighs— "then what is it, because I sure as hell don't have any fucking idea why you want to keep me locked away like Rapunzel while you go off and—"

"Daisie, stop," she begs.

"And I also don't understand why you're doing this to me!" I'm speaking faster than the words are forming in my brain. "Is it because you don't want me around you anymore?"

"Daisie…"

"Is it because all you think I'm good for is hacking?"

"I never said that." She screws her face up.

"Is it because you think I'll fuck something up and get us all killed?"

"What? No! Fuck… no it's not that, it's—"

"Then what!?" I shout. "What is so fucking private that you can't tell me—"

"Because I love you!"

My lips part, as though I'm going to speak, but no words can form right now after this admission. I must have it wrong. A friend, she loves me as a friend.

"Fuck!" she shouts, causing me to jump. But not in fear. More so because she has never once raised her voice at me in the decade we have been friends. "Don't you *ever* think that *I* think… you're weak. Jesus Christ, Daisie, I don't want you there because I fucking love you!" Elise slaps the back of her hand into her other palm frustratingly.

Turning from me, she leaves me standing there with my mouth agape, moving to sit on the edge of my computer desk. Elise's fingers curve around the edge of the wooden desk so tightly that her knuckles turn white.

"If something happened to you, if you got hurt, if one of those fuckers touched you… I don't think I could ever forgive myself. Let alone live with it." Looking at me she continues, "It fucking eats at me, D. I drive myself fucking insane. Wishing I didn't feel the way I did, that I could just fucking stop thinking about you every second of every fucking day but… I can't. So forgive me if I want to keep the woman I love safe from the grimy hands of rapists and fucking sexists!"

Taking a deep breath, she continues speaking, as though she's finally able to release all the pent-up emotions inside her after however long.

"If you truly believe all those things you said, then you really don't know me at all."

Dropping her head in defeat, the silence between us is palpable. The connection of my clumpy boots play out as the only sound in the room, as I slowly close the space between us. Stopping between her legs, I take both my hands and raise them to either side of her face. I lift it to look at me and the moment I do, I see all the pain in her eyes.

"I'm sorry," I breathe. "I don't believe you think that of me for even a single second. I shouldn't have said it. Forgive me." Leaning in, I angle my face towards her and gently press my lips against her plump ones.

Moving her head to the side she sighs. "Don't do that. I don't want you to feel like you have to."

Bringing her attention back to me I raise an eyebrow. "When have I *ever* done anything because I have to?"

Silence.

"Exactly," I murmur. "So, please just… kiss me before I lose my confidence and go bury myself somewhere from embarrassment and—"

I'm cut off.

No words are able to be formed because the woman I've been in love with for as long as I can remember, is kissing me. With her soft mouth pressed against mine, I can't halt the low whimper that descends from my throat. Running the tip of her tongue against the seam of my mouth, as though begging for entry, I happily oblige.

And the moment I do, she eases it inside. Tenderly sliding her tongue against mine in a deep meaningful kiss. My skin ignites with gooseflesh, running from the bottom of my spine, all the way up into my hairline. Feeling as though this is the first kiss I've ever experienced, a kiss so perfect that none previous can compare. I underestimated my imagination greatly, because this is unlike anything I expected from her.

Elise's hands grip my waist, fingers squeezing tightly at the skin And in reaction, I wrap my arms tightly around her neck, bringing myself flush with her body, silently demanding more from her.

"Please," I beg her.

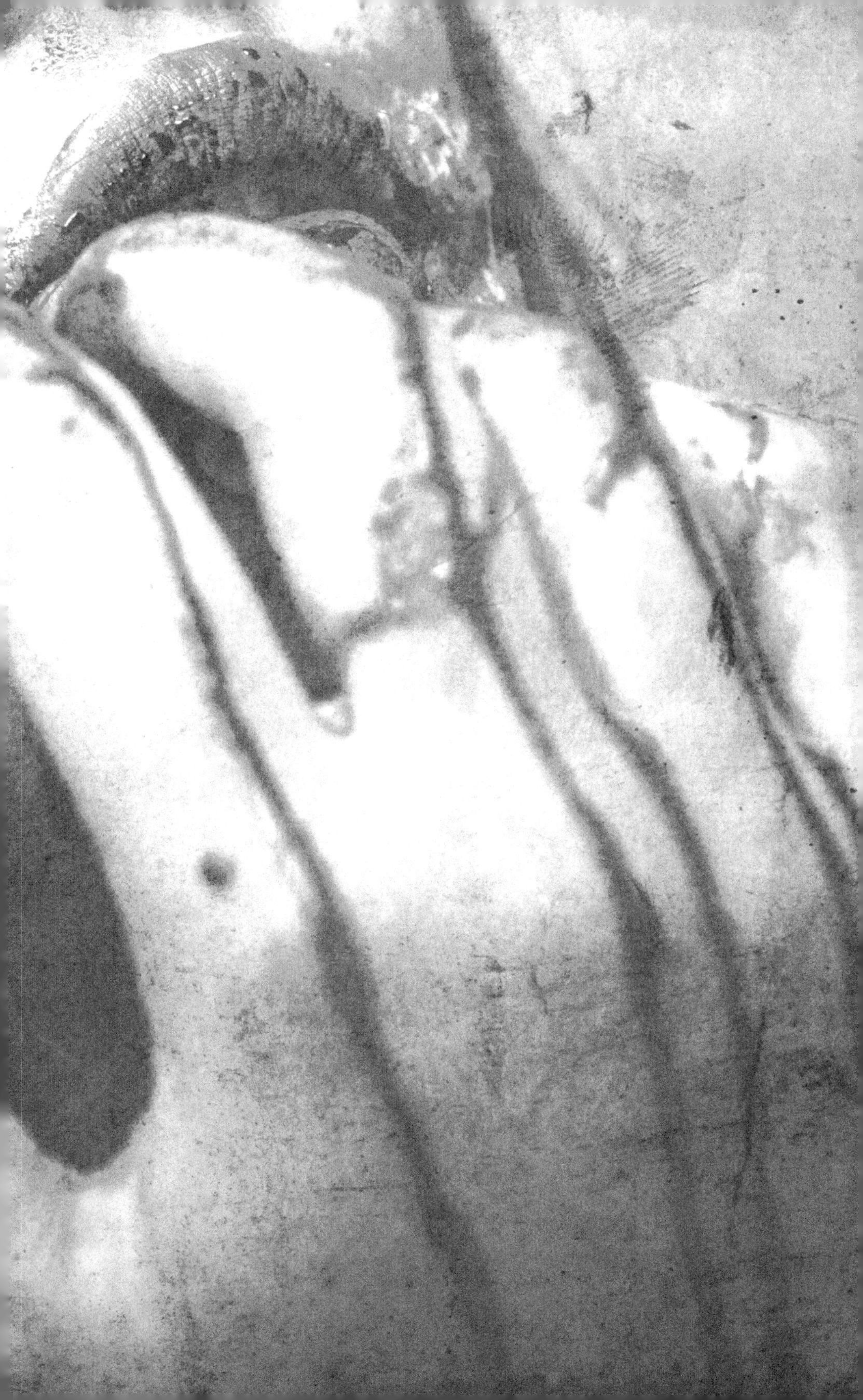

Chapter 4

Elise

Her plea of need makes every single hair on my arms stand on end. It's soft, and so fucking sweet that my body reacts to it almost instantly. Craves more of it.

I lower my hand over her full ass, gripping each cheek in my hand, before I lift her up from just under the thighs. With her knees resting on the edge of her computer desk, I bring her closer to me. Holding her in place with one hand on her lower back—the space between her legs pressed flush against my groin. Devouring her mouth all while I touch her.

I've wanted this with her, and never in my wildest dreams did I think I'd get my wish. Her body reacts to mine so perfectly. The delicate whimpers she keeps releasing with every roll of my tongue over hers are nothing like I had in my mind, they're a million times better.

"Fuck, Daisie," I breathe against her mouth. And the moment those words leave my lips, I feel the lower half of her body grind against mine. But before I get a chance to feel it again, she freezes, and in that moment, I pull my lips back. "What's wrong?" I ask, brushing the strands of bubble-gum coloured hair from her face.

"I... just realised I don't really know what I'm doing here."

Releasing a light chuckle, I brush my lips over her jawline, peppering subtle kisses as I go. "You don't have to be an expert at this,

D," I mumble against her creamy skin. "Just do what feels good for you."

"But what about you?" she questions while I continue to kiss her, moving my lips along to the shell of her ear and down the delicate column of her neck. "I... I want—"

"What do you want, baby?"

She hums in enjoyment. "Mmm, that feels good."

"Whatever you want, if it feels good for you, then it will for me. Trust me on that."

"Okay." The word comes out breathy as I continue to roam my lips down to her collarbone.

Pressing my hand a little more firmly to the space just below her ass, I stand up and turn myself before sitting down in the computer chair. With Daisie still straddling me, her legs either side of my hips, I pull her head closer to me before whispering lightly in her ear. "Ride me. Roll these perfect hips of yours and make yourself come," I tell her.

I'm desperate to feel her fall apart in my lap and watch the expressions her face makes when she comes. Her eyes meet mine as she leans back to look at me, flicking left and right, checking to see if I'm being serious.

Placing my hands on either side of her hips, I hold them firmly in my grasp before pulling her closer to my groin. And with just the right amount of pressure —when she finally moves—her clit will rub perfectly against the seam of my jeans. The part that covers the zip. I'm aching to touch her, my own pussy already throbbing with the need to not only do that... but the need to taste her too.

"Will you touch me," she asks just before she begins to very slowly, but surely, dry hump me.

Fuck.

"Yes," I reply, keeping my eyes trained on her because I don't want to look away for even a second. "But... only when you ask me to."

Daisie closes her eyes, resting her hands on my shoulders and dropping her head back slightly. Her pace picking up a little more, all before she releases the sexiest little moan I think I've ever heard.

Jesus. Fucking. Christ.

Flicking my eyes down, I watch the lower half of her body grind back and forth against me. Her mini skirt has ridden higher, revealing her thick thighs and the rose tattoos that sit right at the top. The silky black thong she's wearing is drenched. Her peaked nipples are visually alluring pressed against the thin cotton fabric of her vest.

She's fucking glorious to look at.

A sight I never want to forget.

I keep my hands on her hips, desperate to touch her in ways I've only dreamt of, but refusing to give myself what I want until she asks for it. Until I know she wants me as much as I do her. This might be something in the heat of the moment, sure, but with the way she's giving herself to me, I believe it's more than that.

"Oh," she moans again. My pussy further becoming slick with need for her. "Elise."

Fffuck... you're killing me, D.

She's not the only one that's breathless now. Whose lungs are constricting tightly because fuck *me* if having her grind her pussy against mine isn't the best feeling in the world.

"What do you want, Daisie, tell me."

Please fucking ask me to touch you already.

"I want to come... please." Her begging is euphoric.

"Then come for me, baby."

"Not like this." Her moaning escalates an octave higher.

I'm about to fucking lose it. My restraint is killing me more than she is.

"Please... oh, fuck."

"Say it, baby. Beg me for what you want." I push her further. Praying for the words to leave her mouth.

My heart is beating a dozen times a minute and the goosebumps over her skin tell me she's close. Quicker than I expected, too. I didn't think it would even go this far before she got up and walked away from me.

"Please touch me, I want to come but... on your fingers." Her words even more breathless than before.

Yep, someone could kill me now and I'd die a happy fucking woman.

"Say it again," I demand. "I want to hear you say it again."

She leans forward, her hands cupping my cheeks, and she kisses me deeply. It's rough and desperate. "Fuck me, please."

Without wasting another moment, I grab the fabric of her black vest, dragging it down her chest to reveal that—as always—she's not wearing a bra. My other hand crests the space between her pussy and mine, and I curve two fingers around the silk material of her thong before tugging it to the side. Running the pads of my middle and index finger along her wet slit, I groan in response.

"Fuck, Daisie, you're drenched."

"Put your fingers inside me, please."

"So polite."

The moment I do as she asks, she throws her head back, showcasing her perfect breasts to me. Bending my head towards the right one, I wrap my lips around her pert nipple and suck it into my mouth, while simultaneously thrusting my fingers in and out of her all the way to the second knuckle.

"Right there… Oh, my fucking God!" she cries out, and Jesus, if this is what she really sounds like when she's being fucked, I'll never stop. "You feel so good, don't stop."

Her husky pleas do everything to spur me on—and if her trembling body is anything to go by, I know she's hungry for more. Popping my lips from her nipple, I hoist her back up into my arms and lay her back onto the counter. Splaying her gorgeous body over the wood.

Her skirt is ruched to her waist now, and the material of her thong is still pushed to the side. Wrapping my fingers around it, I yank it clean from her body, tossing it somewhere in the room. Her pink pussy is on display for me and all I can think about is what she's going to taste like. Covering her body with mine, I kiss her hastily.

"Tell me I can taste you. I need to hear you say it." This is her first time with me, with a woman, and I won't ruin that for her by only thinking of myself and taking what I want.

Whimpering into my mouth, Daisie kisses me with just as much ferocity as I do her. In this moment, it feels as though we have always been this way. That this was how it was supposed to be between us from the very beginning, and I want every second with me right now to be perfect for her.

She deserves that much.

She deserves everything.

Whining, my girl gives me exactly what I asked for. "Elise, eat my pussy. I'll go fucking crazy if you don't," she mewls between kisses.

Fuck, finally.

I kiss my way down her body, from her neck to the curvature of her collarbone. Over the swells of her tits that are still perched over the fabric of her top, and down her stomach to her bellybutton. Everything about this woman drives me crazy. I'm hungry for her in every way possible. I'm full of pent up, inconsolable need for every part of Daisie, and finally I'm going to get to taste her.

Hoisting both of her legs over my shoulders, I hover my mouth over her smooth mound and descend upon it, covering her clit with my mouth and sucking. All while simultaneously using both my thumbs to spread her pussy lips wide open. giving me full access to her dripping cunt that I've fantasized about for as long as I can remember.

That very first swipe of my tongue over the full extent of her core is extraordinary—a flavour I will never get enough of. Her pussy smells just like that mint shower gel she frequently uses, and the taste… honey with a slight salty tang, and *fuck* if it isn't heaven.

Her body begins to tremble and shake while I devour every inch of her. Flattening my tongue, I lick her from her tight little hole before flicking the tip of the muscle up and over her needly little clit. The moment I do, Daisie releases a sweet little moan that sends shivers down my spine.

"Holy shit!" she purrs fervently. "Right… there."

Her back curves up from the wooden tabletop and her fingers find my hair, threading through my soft curls, tugging tightly.

"Fuck, you taste so good, baby," I growl from the deepest part of my throat, allowing the vibrations to ripple over her sensitive core.

Her thighs begin to tremble and shake, strangled moans of ecstasy grow louder as the moments pass. Matching my moans of lust and unrestrained need for her so perfectly they both merge into one, perfect symphony.

"That's it, baby. Let yourself go for me," I croon.

As her thighs begin to constrict around my neck, so do her fingers in the tight tendrils of my black hair. She's crying out in pleasure and I'm fucking ecstatic that I'm the one to give it to her. That I'm the one she trusts enough to have her first experience with a woman.

"Elise, *fffuck*…" Gritting her teeth and releasing a guttural moan from her throat.

Gripping her knees, I widen her legs. Moving her right, boot clad foot to the edge of the table, I remove my mouth from her pussy and stand, crowding her body. Her whimpers of woe make me smile—my girl is so needy, and I can't wait to watch her fall apart. I brace my left forearm beside her head on the table and curve my hand under the back of her skull.

Without wasting any more precious time, I slide two fingers inside her pussy, feeling the narrowness of her core contract around my digits. Curving them up, I begin to stroke that perfect spot at the exact angle to have her screaming my name.

"Holy FUCK!"

"So tight," I whisper against the curve of her neck, groaning at the sound of her voice becoming more high pitched with every stroke I give her. Tilting my head slightly, I look at the tortured expression on her face. Her features telling me she's eager to last as long as she can, but she's desperate to come.

"Open those beautiful eyes, baby. Look at me," I beg her, pressing my thumb to her clit, rubbing it in circles and fingering her in unison. Her lids pop open, displaying those ocean blue eyes that I've come to adore so much.

"Can I touch you?" Her pleading words crack me instantly. Offering her a simple nod, she lifts her hands to the waist of my jeans, popping the button through the loop and jerking the zip down as quick as possible.

Wrenching both my jeans and boxer shorts down with her thumbs, I widen my legs some and pull her into a more seated position while still giving myself enough room to keep touching her.

I watch as she licks three of her fingers and I smile. "I'm wet enough for you, there's no need for that." I wink.

A gentle blush creeps up her cheeks as she grins widely in response. "I want you" —her fingers press against my pussy, instantly finding my clit, and I moan at the contact— "to come with me."

Rotating her fingers to match my speed, I'm breathing heavier than I ever have before. Nobody touches me. I'm what they call a 'no touch top'. But for her, *shit*, for her, I'll give her anything she wants. I've never heard myself moan unless it was from giving pleasure to others, so when the sound of my breathing changes to a raspy groan, I can't help but let the words roam free.

"*Fffuuck*, Daisie. That's... Jesus Christ, there. You're doing so good, baby."

Hooking her fingers around the back of my neck, she pulls me flush to her, crashing her lips to mine. Absorbing my every moan, swallowing them down instantly the same way I do with hers. Our kiss is rough, aggressive, and in this moment, it's absolutely carnal.

"Look how wet you are for me, Elise," she mewls, curving her fingers to my hole, and before I know it, she's gliding them inside me, thrusting into me from below with a swiftness that matches my own.

"Christ, you fuck me so good. Don't stop," I beg, my voice jumping an octave. "Make me come, fuck me, Daisie, make me yours."

"You're already mine."

My eyes pop open, staring straight into hers.

"You always have been. Because I love you too."

In that moment, everything comes to a standstill, and I'm lost for any words that could explain the validity of what she just said to me. So I let her have her moment of rendering me speechless. My orgasm begins to build higher; her face contorts as she vigorously holds onto her own.

"I'm so close," I tell her. "Wait for me." Squeezing her eyes shut, she grits her teeth and the moment she curves her fingers to the perfect fucking angle, I lose it. "Now!" I cry out. "Come with me now!"

Porn star screams release from the both of us as we jump over the cliff and into a euphoric orgasm of our own creation. Her cunt gushes over my hand, her cum squirting, coating my skin and the walls of her pussy contracting beautifully.

Daisie grips onto me, pulling me down onto the desk with her as we patiently wait to come down from our high.

"How long do we have until Bekah gets here?"

Checking my watch, I smirk at her. "Forty minutes, why?"

"Wanna go again?" she asks, and I can't contain my laughter.

Chapter 5

Elise

Crickets chirp outside the blacked-out van while we watch Robert and his three friends venture towards the so-called abandoned warehouse that's in his name. The time on the dashboard reads 8:48 p.m., which means there's only twelve minutes left until the alarm finally sounds, and everything turns into chaos.

It's the day people everywhere—for different reasons—have been waiting for. Where the building is situated, most people wouldn't venture out this far. It's too dangerous and being out in the open like this is a sure-fire way to get yourself attacked, or better yet, killed. Bekah and Daisie are going through the black duffel bags, making sure we have everything needed for the rest of the night.

But my attention is strictly dedicated to keeping watch. I've checked my handgun six times before we left the compound, repacked my duffle five, leaving me with one thing… making sure nobody enters the building other than those three men.

"Daisie, pass me the plastic sheeting, I have space in my bag," my sister, Bekah, says from behind me, bringing me back to reality. The rustling of plastic assaults my ears, but still, my eyes never leave. Not until I watch them enter the building, and the soft golden glow of their torches dances behind the newspaper covered windows.

Enjoy your last moments of freedom, assholes.

"Hey," Daisie says, resting a forearm on each seat up front. I turn to face her, the corner of my mouth turning up. "You good?"

I raise my hand, softly cupping her chin. "Always, D." Leaning forward, I press a kiss against her soft lips. "Are you okay?"

"Uhh." I hear my sister interrupt. Both me and Daisie turn to face her, a smirk brightly covering my face. "When did this happen?" Bekah points between both me and Daisie.

"Yesterday, while you were on your way over." I wink.

"Finally," Bekah groans.

"What do you mean finally?" Daisie frowns.

"Oh, come on. With the way you've been looking at my sister… it was obvious to everyone, but Elise, how infatuated you were with her," Bekah jokes, tucking her Glock inside the holster attached to her hip. "At least I don't have to listen to my sister's incessant yearning over you anymore."

Daisie turns to face me. "Yearning, huh?" She fights the smile on her face, teasing me with those beautiful blue eyes of hers.

"We'll talk about it later." Rolling my eyes, I press my lips to the space between her brows and breathe her in.

"Remember what I said." I pull away from Daisie and focus on both her and my sister. "No fucking around. We go in and we get the job done."

Bekah claps her hands together furiously with excitement. "I don't think I've been this excited since I slept with Danny Masters behind the Science building."

"The Quarterback at our school?" Daisie questions.

Bekah nods. "Uh huh." Holding both her hands inches apart she mouths the words, *'This big.'*

"Bullshit," Daisie chimes in. "There's no way."

"Trust me, it was so big I thought it was going travel up my stomach and out of my oesophagus."

"Jesus Christ." I chuckle silently.

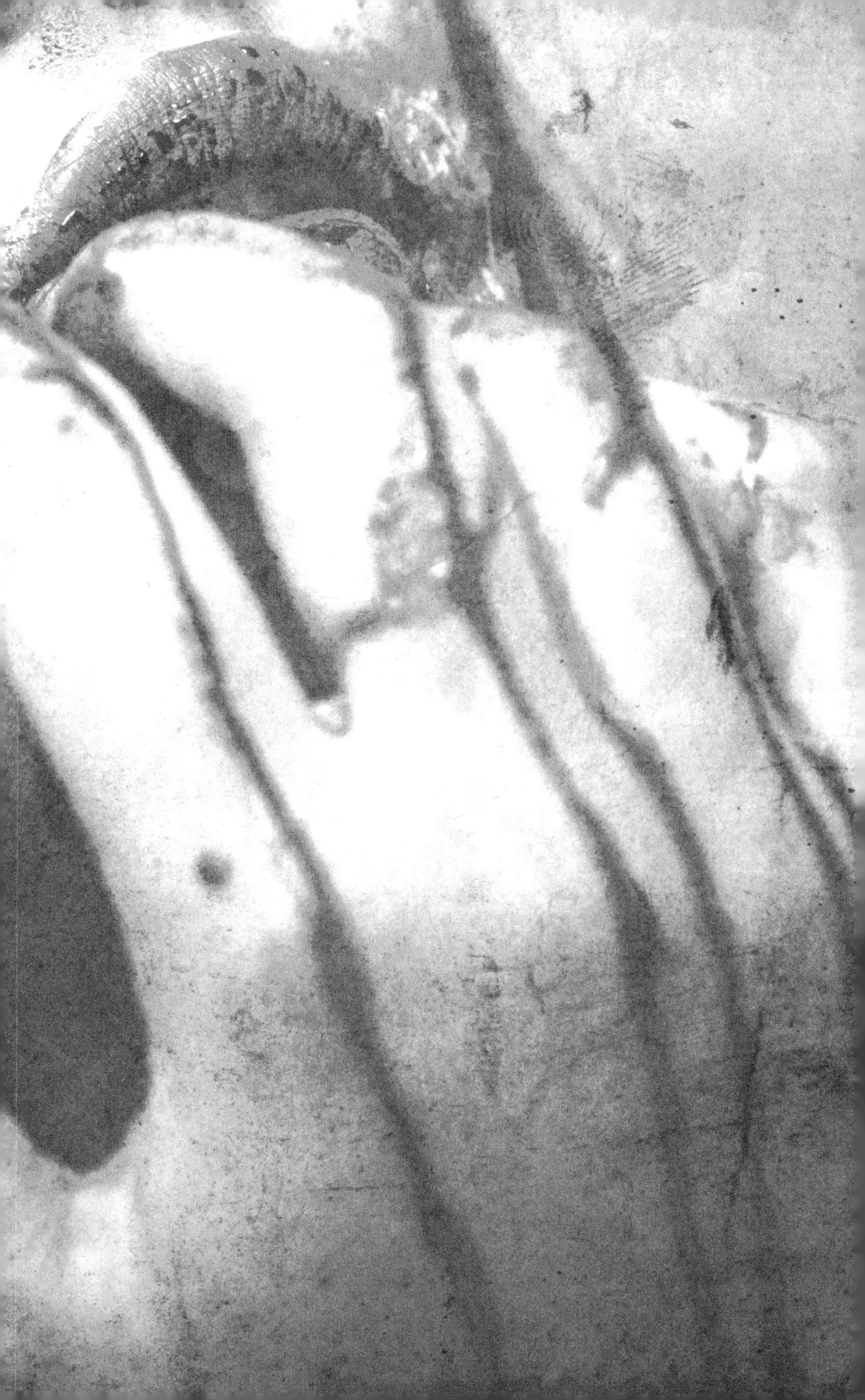

Chapter 6

Bekah

Of course the man I plan to murder would situate himself on the roof of this fucking building. And now, because of that, I have to climb fifteen flights of iron stairs quietly, *all* while keeping my fucking breathing under control. Except my lungs feel like they're about to explode.

"Fuck this bullshit," I growl on a whisper. "Whoever invented stairs, I'm gonna end their fucking lineage."

This asshole motherfucker better be up here or I swear to Satan himself I'll end it all.

Because there is no way I'm walking back down those treacherous stairs for at least another hour.

I squat down as soon as I reach the final flight of stairs. Taking slow, calculated breaths, I focus on on the need to calm my breathing and heart rate down as quick as I can.

All I need to do, is get up there without him seeing me, and I'll be fine. Slowly, I reach for the zipper on the right side of my backpack, pulling the silencer free. I twist the silencer to the edge of my firearm and secure it in place before gripping the yellow handle of the police issue taser that I moved to the back of my jeans waistband.

Once my breathing has gone back to normal, I peek over the edge of the broken-down granite leading to the roof, noticing Will pacing back and forth. A Sniper rifle clutched to his chest as though he was born with it. Luckily, my father hunts, so I know my way around guns and rifles. And at this kind of close range, it's useless.

Standing from my crouched position, I gradually move from my hiding spot, placing one foot in front of the other. I can't have him see me before I electrocute him with fifty-thousand volts, but also, I can't have him falling over the edge of the building and to his death. That's no fun at all.

Hopefully the others are right on schedule with subduing their targets within the walls and I won't have to worry so much about keeping him quiet. Raising both my hands, I rest my finger on the trigger and smirk before throwing a gentle whistle his way. The instant Will spins on his heel, I wink, before squeezing the trigger and sending every volt of electricity the gun holds, running through his body. And only when I think he's had enough do I pop my finger from the trigger.

Smacking the palm of my hand against his cheek, Will's eyes widen in shock, darting around before finally focusing back on me.

"Wakey, wakey, eggs and bakey." I snort at the ridiculousness of my statement. "I have things to get done, and I don't have time to fuck about waiting while you catch up on your beauty sleep."

Will thrashes at my feet, but he doesn't get too far, what with his arms and legs hog-tied behind him—looking around frantically in search of someone to save him.

"It's just me and you up here, dipshit." Squatting down beside him, I pull out the plastic sheeting. Grabbing the corners, I shake it out and lay it next to him. Smiling when I face him again. "Wouldn't want to make a mess up here. I hate cleaning."

"*Mmfm!*" he cries out behind the large red ball gag in his mouth. The plastic muffling his words –not that I care about what he has to say.

"Frightening when you're in the position you've had so many other women in before this, isn't it?"

I move to his left side, squatting down and reaching below his back and rolling him onto the plastic. The crackling sound it makes only serves to excite me further, knowing what's to come. Once I've positioned him right where I want him—in the middle of the synthetic tarping—I crouch down, sitting on his chest.

"*Mmfm! Mmmfm!*"

I roll my eyes, pulling the knife from the sheath attached to my thigh and groaning. "I'm not that heavy, and I find it quite rude you would insinuate I am. Anyway…" I wave my hand dismissively between us and place the hilt of the knife in my mouth while unbuckling his cargo pants. "Considering everything you've done recently, I figured I'd make this as painful as I possibly can, because why not." I shrug nonchalantly.

Dragging his trousers and tighty whities down as far as I can, I chuckle silently at the size of his puny cock.

"No wonder you're such an asshole, if you have to wake up with that every day. I'm a woman and my dick is bigger than yours."

Raising my hand, I thrust downwards, stabbing Will directly in the genitals. Over and over again with unyielding force. His muffled screams of agony do nothing to attract the attention of anyone else in the vicinity, and the more they turn from deep wails to high pitched squeals… the broader I smile. Blood spurts from every direction, coating my hands with sticky red fluid. I watch as tears seep from his eyes, and his cries for help become more subdued, weaker.

Everything about this man and his friends disgusts me. And the fact that I'm lucky enough to torture him like this while he's still awake fills me with a kind of joy I never knew existed. I wrap my fingers around his mutilated cock and tear it from the small fibrous tissue that keeps it attached, yanking it free from his groin. Will's eyes begin to flutter, telling me he's well on his way to death… or at least passing out.

"Oh, no you don't," I snort, unlatching the ball gag from behind his head and tossing it to the side. "Not before you choke on this!" I snarl. Thrusting his severed cock into his mouth and forcing it all the way down the back of his throat.

In a final bid to survive in his very last moments, he thrashes and fights with what little energy he has left. Pressing my hands to my knees, I push to stand and take the small bottle of lighter fluid from the side of my bag and squirt the contents all over him. It's then that I smile, taking in the scene before me and pull the lighter from my pocket, striking it to ignite the flame.

"Burn in pieces, cunt." I smile sweetly before tossing the lighter onto his chest. A loud *woosh* forces me back from his body the moment the flames engulf him. His garbled screams are unrelenting, piercing the space around us as gooseflesh prickles my skin, making the hairs on my arms stand at attention.

The plastic tarping singes and hisses while it burns. Will's once white flesh turns bright red, blistering while the fire continues to scorch it, his body finally halting of all movement while the flames crack and pop in front of my eyes. The walkie talkie attached to my waist cracks with static, and I pull it in front of me.

"Bekah?"

"I'm here," I respond instantly to my sister, not talking my eyes off the charred body, amber fires still roasting Will's carcass. "Are the others subdued?"

"Obviously," she snorts.

"I'll be down in a bit, getting up those stairs killed me." Elise chuckles as I step back from the body, taking a seat on the wall at the edge of the roof. "Oh, and just so you know, charred human flesh really does smell like bacon."

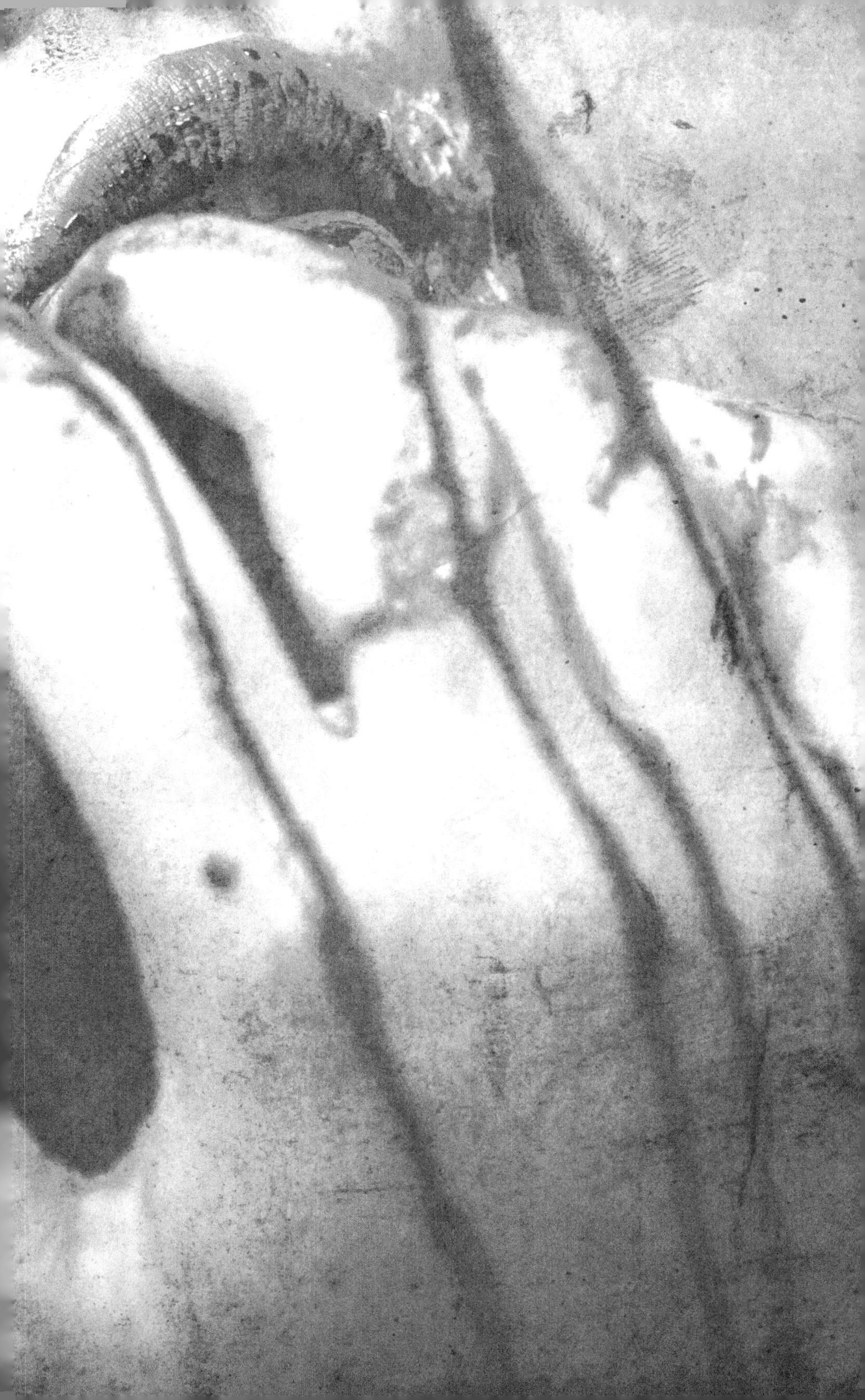

Chapter 7
Daisie

It's funny how things in life change in the blink of an eye. One moment you're hacking into the computer system of a bank just for the fun of it, placing a worm inside to syphon off small amounts of money without being noticed, and in the next, you're standing in front of a disgusting pile of shit like Ben Taylor. Rapist, murderer, and someone who watches child pornography on the weekends while his wife is at work, and he sits on his ass like a kept man.

Currently he's unconscious and bound to the steel medical table in the middle of the room I drugged him in. If the time on my watch is anything to go by then he should be waking up soon. The muffled howling of Robert Evans trickles up from the basement where Elise is. She's not killing him yet, just torturing him in the meantime while she waits for Bekah and I to finish with his friends first.

Propofol is a fast-acting anaesthetic. The effects are rapid too, usually within 0.5-1 minute and lasting anywhere from four to eight minutes of a single dose. That's all depending on the patient of course, but it gave me enough time to get him up on the table—with the help of Elise of course—and tied down.

Ben is face down, bent over the table with his ass and legs hanging over the edge. His wrists are secured at each corner with thick rope, and his ankles are tied to each leg, giving him a minimal range of motion. At the same time the alarm on my watch starts beeping, Ben's eyes begin to flicker, and his head starts to roll from side to side.

"Ben, so nice of you join me on this momentous occasion." I smile, rounding the steel table and running the tips of my fingers along the cold metal as I do. The balaclava over my face keeps my identity hidden for the time being.

He groans, opening and then squeezing his eyes shut to clear away the blur coating them. "Wh—" He breathes gently, rolling his head to the side. "Who…" He coughs, clearing his throat. "Who are you?"

"The question isn't who am I, but… what am I going to do to you."

Ben tugs at his restraints, becoming more and more flustered with the realisation he can't move, jerking his arms and legs, but the straps becoming none the looser.

"Is this really any way to talk to someone when you're tied up like a Thanksgiving ham? I mean come on."

"YOU FUCKING WHORE!!" The furious bellow of his words echo through the room, his eyes focused on me with hatred dancing through them and his teeth are grinding together so tightly they might crack.

I frown. "C'mon Ben, I haven't said anything bad about you and like… right off the bat you want to insult me. Rude much."

"You're fucking worthless!" Ben seethes. "Y'know that?!" Spit flies from his mouth and teeth. "If you think I'm going to fucking beg a womb carrier like you to let me go… then you're sorely mistaken." He barks out a laugh.

"Give it time." I smirk, crossing my arms in front of my chest. "When you feel what I've got in store for you, princess, you'll be screaming for me to kill you."

"You don't have it in you! Women are weak, all you do is respond based off of your emotions. Men. Get. Shit. Done. And yet here you are thinking you can play our game?!"

Rolling my eyes, I walk out of his field of view. "Women have been playing our own game for hundreds of years," I respond, running my fingers along the steel tray situated beside him. "Doing everything we can to survive a man's bullshit. Because even when they say they're they good ones… they never are."

"Aww, was the poor little girl hurt by a big burley man?" Ben laughs at me.

I should've fucking gagged him.

"Hey, what's all the noise?" Bekah questions from behind me.

I turn to face her and groan, rolling my eyes back. "I didn't gag him, wanna help me a quickly before you go to help Elise?"

"Fuck it, why not."

I grin in her direction and walk over to the wooden work bench behind me, picking up a pair of forceps and some gardening sheers. "Think you can hold his head down for me? Keep his mouth open?" I shrug questioningly.

The moment Ben realises what I'm about to do, his eyes widen in complete and utter terror. With what little movement he has, Ben thrashes around, calling and shouting for someone to help him. Bekah doesn't waste any time, pulling her arm back and punching him square in the face.

Shaking her hand out, she groans, "Fuck, that shit hurt."

I giggle. "Pussy."

Frowning, Bekah flips me off before pressing all her weight onto Ben's head and holding it down, and with her free hand she grips his jaw and opens it. Sliding the forceps in his mouth, I grip his tongue and pull it nice and taught. Opening up the sheers, I place his tongue between it.

"You might be sicker than I actually thought." Bekah chuckles before the inevitable happens and I snip Ben's tongue off as close to the root as I can.

The shrill cry of agony that leaves his mouth is astounding. Blood sprays from the open wound, coating the steel table as it gushes from the inside of his mouth and turning his white flesh claret. I turn my head and look at the tongue still gripped between the forceps and grimace.

"*Eurgh.*"

"Pussy," Bekah snorts, so I thrust the tongue towards her, causing her to release a yelp as she jumps backwards, and I can't control the burst of laughter that falls from my lips. The sound of it working over Ben's scream of anguish.

"Yeah, *I'm* the pussy alright."

"Go fuck yourself, I'd never do that to you." She narrows her eyes, but I know she would in a heartbeat. I raise my left eyebrow, calling her bluff because she's a fucking liar. "Alright fine," she groans inwardly. "I totally would."

"Exactly." I turn my attention back to Ben, watching scarlet liquid gush from his mouth, and smile. Spinning on my heel, I saunter back to the table behind me, placing his tongue in a clear glass jar and screwing on the lid for safe keeping. "You can go see Elise; I'll be fine here. Just let her know I won't be too long."

"No problem, call if you need anything."

I peek over my shoulder, nodding at her in agreement but also knowing that there's no way I'll be needing anyone's help. Punishing Ben for his infractions won't take me too long, but I do plan on enjoying the act of his torture before I inevitably end his life.

Never in my life would I have believed I had something so deadly living inside me, yet hear I am getting excited over the fact that I get to kill a man for the first time in my life. Bekah's footsteps retreat, leaving me and a helpless, wailing Ben in a room where there are no windows and nobody around for miles to hear the screams that permeate this building. His garbled sobs are starting to irritate me, the sound of his distorted pleas for help bringing frustration to every inch of my body.

Stepping behind him, I wrap my fingers around the hem of his sweatpants, and he starts to thrash around with what little movement he has. "I've looked into you, Ben. Found all the disgusting things your lawyer father kept hidden from the world. Keeping them all tucked away so you can keep walking this earth." I yank his sweats down in one go with his tighty whities. "No surprise you wear white fitted briefs." I grimace at the look of thick black hair covering his ass. "Gross."

"Uhleasshhh," he sobs.

"Huh? What was that?" I cup my ear, pretending I don't understand that he's begging me again.

"Puh... Puheathhh."

"Please?" I question. "When the girls you raped pleaded... did you listen to them? Did you understand their pain and stop?" I growl, forcing the words through gritted teeth. "No, I didn't fucking think so. Because you were having too much fun taking away the control of all those girls, laughing and joking while your father wept it under the rug."

"I'm-m... suh-owhy," he cries again.

I reach back to the table and carefully open the box. "Too late for your apologies now, asshole." The tingle running through my bones when I lift the white cloth inside the box makes me grin enthusiastically.

"If you were really sorry… you wouldn't have sexually assaulted the first girl."

My fingers curve around the slightly corroded device and I lift it from the plastic sandwich box, flecks of black and orange rust drop from the tool and onto the wooden table. Ben continues to writhe and flail around, even though he is fully aware—by how tight the restraints are binding his body—that there is no way he's getting out of this, getting free from this situation.

Not alive at least.

"Do you know what this is?" I ask him, waltzing to the head of the table. I rest my forearms on the edge of it, holding the item in my hand. Ben shakes his head, fear-riddled eyes stare back at me. Blown out and red, tear-stained cheeks and blood red skin are what greet me when I finally focus my gaze on him.

"This is what's called a Pear of Anguish, Ben, or the *'poire d'angoisse'* as Palioly called it. A seventeenth century torture device that was used on such people as liars, thieves and" —I swirl my hand in front of me — "those who were guilty of sexual crimes against others." I tap the tip of the pair shaped device. "This part, goes in the orifice. Vagina, mouth…" I smirk. "Anus."

Realisation dawns on him on what is about to happen, squeezing his eyes shut as more tears thread through the thick blood caking the lower portion of his face.

"That's painful enough, but it's this part" —I tap the opposite end — "the thumb screw." I work the piece between my thumb and index finger, turning it clockwise over and over again. I watch as fear and understanding morphs onto his face, bringing a hearty expression across mine. Each of the tapered leaves begin to open, widening with every twist, silently clarifying that the pain he is about to feel, will be unlike anything he will undergo again.

"This won't be gentle, nor kind. I won't show you mercy when I torture you, it won't be quick." I stand twisting the thing closed. "But it *will* be painful."

I stroll behind him, placing the iron torture device on the table before shoving my hands into a pair of black latex gloves and picking it back up. Pressing my left hand firmly against his left ass cheek, I push it open, gripping the thick skin at my fingertips. Trying my hardest to keep it open while he thrashes about hysterically.

Ben's frantic squirming does nothing to put me off. I want him to suffer before I inevitably end his life.

"Sorry, I forgot the lube." I chuckle, before I push the tip to his hair-covered ring. Forcing it forward with as much strength as I have, closing my eyes with elation the moment his cries turn into a throng of shrill operatic screams. Blood pumps through my ears, swelling thickly to where it begins to drown out everything other than my own heartbeat thumping against my chest.

I watch as the iron begins to push past the resistance of his ring, gradually splitting the skin as it breaches Ben's back hole. Blood pumping through the membrane of muscle while he fights to resist its entry inside him.

"Arghh!" he yells, his pain flooding back the moment I thrust the final inch, plugging his asshole. "*Mnrgh!*" Ben's inaudible protests of agony being on a burst of laughter from my chest.

"Good boy. Look at how well you're taking it!" I cackle through amusement, but it's short lived. Nothing will prepare him for what comes next. I pinch the handle and twist, turning it with treacherous intent counting each twist of the key and watching, waiting for the inevitable to happen. There isn't an ounce of regret, no guilt or remorse for what I'm putting him through.

He deserves this.

What he did to those women… how he…. hurt them.

The wider the pear gets, the more the thin membrane of his taint ruptures, gushing with crimson liquid. Plummeting to the floor at my feet and coating my once white sneakers red. My eardrums and mind will be filled with the memories of his agony for years to come, and I welcome every dream I have from here on out. I pray that I never forget the way it felt to inflict pain and agony on a man that scarred so many women before this day.

Once the pear and skin are stretched to their full capacity, his shrieks of pain now withered to whimpers of sadness, I lift the hunting knife from the leather sheath attached to my thigh and effectively carve his ball sack away. The steel of my knife slicing through the skin like an orange rind. Effortless.

Gore coats my hands beautifully, and as I walk to the top of the table, looking down upon Ben with disgust and hatred, I open his mouth and shove his scrotum inside. Forcing the soft tissue and orbs into the back of his whimpering throat.

"Choke on them." When I raise my hand above my head, the knife is gripped tightly within my grasp, and the moment I arc my arm, realisation settles as his eyes widen with one final look of trepidation. The steel blade pierces his throat right at the carotid artery, blood splattering and pooling around his neck. Choked noises pour from the back of his throat as I wiggle and twist the blade penetrating his gullet.

I stoop to his level, my gaze meeting his, and as I watch the life drain from his eyes, the paling of his skin as he bleeds out, all I can do... is smile.

"Sweet nightmares, cunt."

Chapter 8

Elise

Everything has come down to this. Months of prep work to be able to reach a crescendo as large as this. No matter how many times I ran through it in my head, I never expected the feeling to be so calming. It's as though my mind finally has a chance to relax since everything came to pass.

Robert Evans.

The animal whose perpetual hate for anyone and anything that wasn't to his high standards. Using his voice for nothing but hate, fuelling the internal rage of fire in men around the world who were consumed with animosity towards women and anyone who didn't fit the *'straight'* agenda.

I haven't taken my eyes off of him from the minute I knocked him out. Robert is presently tied to a St. Andrews Cross in the middle of the basement. It took some time—and strength on my part—but I finally got there with sheer determination alone. When he woke up, his eyes were fixed on me with pure hatred and disgust. A man who not only hates women, but everything we stand for.

The ball gag in his mouth permits him from speaking coherently, his words garbled as thick drool travels from the corners of his mouth and down his chin, but none of that matters. Not to me anyway. I've been issuing him with tiny cuts all over his naked body for the past hour. Not deep enough to take his life instantly, no. What we're doing here is all about making them suffer in the most painful way possible.

Letting him slowly bleed out slowly using the Chinese art of Lingchi, is what has been keeping me going. Initially, my anger towards him was filled to the brim, but suffering is the only way forward. His shrieks of agony only spurred me on to continue his torture in silence. I didn't need to explain to him about the why. He knew why.

I didn't want to interrupt the garbled cries of agony that permeated the four brick walls of this room. All I needed was for him to understand that no matter how many times I pushed the blade into his skin, no matter how many gashes I gave him, it wouldn't change the outcome. Robert Evans was going to die.

Bekah saunters into the room and pulls out a partially damaged chair, taking a seat. "Next time we go on a killing spree, *you're* taking the fucking stairs."

I let out a brief chuckle, hoisting myself onto Robert's makeshift computer desk. My sister never was one for exerting herself beyond the necessary. "I thought it'd be good for you."

"Good for—" She groans. "Bitch, you try walking up fifteen flights of stairs and see how much energy *you* have to kill someone."

"Was D okay?" I ask, flipping the paring knife in my hand.

My sister shrugs, a smirk tugging at the corner of her full lips. "In my opinion, she's enjoying this a lot more than I initially expected."

Other than Robert's distorted words, the dilapidated warehouse has been silent for a while now, which can only mean that Daisie has finished with Ben. Delicate footsteps make their way towards the room me and Bekah are sitting in, and the moment I look towards the door, there's Daisie. Her blood-soaked clothing, red flecks of blood splatter adorning her high cheekbones, leading down the column of her neck. She looks beautiful.

"Sorry I'm late." She smiles sweetly, meeting my gaze before glancing over at the bloody mass that is Robert. "Cool." Turning back to me, Daisie places a chaste kiss to my lips before taking a seat next to my sister. "We're ready." She grins widely.

Nodding in her direction, I hop off the desk, swapping the paring knife for a Buck 120. The same knife used in the movie, *Scream*.

My favourite.

Robert is naked and spread-eagle on the cross before us. His flesh sliced to pieces. I wrap my left hand around his brown hair and tug his head forward, releasing the clasp at the back of his head and listening as the ball gag falls free and hits the concrete floor. A cold shiver of excitement runs through me as I check my watch, noticing that only an hour remains of tonight's Coursing test run.

I want these next screams of anguish to be heard for miles.

I pick up the paper bag of salt, tearing the top open and tossing it at him. It's almost instant as the pig squealing shriek releases from Robert's throat. The granules of salt seeping into the cuts on his body, stinging him and biting against the wounds I inflicted.

"P-please." Roberts weak expression fills the air. "I'm—"

"Sorry?" I finish for him, thrusting his head back and out of my grasp before tossing the rest of the contents over him, eliciting a further yelp of distress. He's lost enough blood to stop him fighting against the restraints wrapped harshly around his wrists and ankles, as well as the creases of his elbows and knees.

"Y-yes."

"Men like you are always sorry when it comes to receiving your punishment. You call us weak, but it is a sure sign of weakness when one is incapable of controlling themselves around others. You're not sorry for what you've done, you're just sorry you got caught. But it's okay." I tap his cheek, smiling up at him. "It will all end in a few minutes."

I crouch down, lifting the litre bottle of household bleach and twist the cap before tugging it off and tossing it aside. I move to the space beside him and lift the container above his chest, pouring the thick chemical liquid all over him. Thick, domestic grade peroxide gushes over him and then he uses what's left of his energy to fight the excruciating burn as it falls over his body. Robert screams with agonising intent, thrashing and fighting, desperately trying to rid himself of this experience and break free. But he never will.

The pungent smell of bleach scorching the raw flesh brings a sharp, acrid smell to the room. The once white slices adorning his body have now turned a stark white as the bleach scalds and blisters the raw incisions.

"It won't m-matter," he snivels, his gaze glaring. "There are… more of us." In his weakened state, he continues, "It won't s-stop h-here."

"Then we will kill as many of you scum-sucking road whores as we can. You won't stop?" I question, pressing the tip of the steel blade against his stomach. "Well, neither will we." I push further, staring down towards his gut. Watching as the knife pierces the thick white skin, disappearing inside of him. "When I was a kid, my father took me hunting, taught me how to gut a dead animal correctly so that there is the least amount of damage to the organs and hide." I look up at him then. "And that's just what you are, Robert, a dead... fucking... animal. Except this time... I don't give a fuck."

Stabbing forward, I encase the entirety of the knife within his stomach. Robert releases a bountiful shriek as I begin to carve the steel along his lower abdominal area. Carving and slicing from one side, all the way to the other. Cutting through the stomach lining and watching as blood pours from the wound, splashing to the floor and coating the gravel red.

Before his organs cascade to the floor, I reach inside his stomach—the warmth of his insides meeting my skin—and wrap my hand tightly around his intestines, yanking them free. He deserves pain, he deserves to feel the fear. Because it's only a small percentage of what we experience daily. I bring my hand to his open mouth, stuffing the intestines inside. As far back as I can before losing my hand.

"Nobody will miss you, and those that do will meet the same fate as you and your friends." I watch as his eyelids begin to flutter, telling me he's either about to pass out... or die. But not before I get in one last hit. "Death," I mutter as I lean in closer, "is only the beginning." When the final word leaves my mouth, I stab up and plunge the hunting knife into the underside of his jaw, and twist, piercing his skull and brain with the blade.

As Robert chokes on his final intakes of air, I step back. My eyes never wavering from his while I look upon a man who hates the very ground we walk on. Bekah and Daisie move to stand beside me, each taking one of my hands as we stand in solidarity within this moment. His head drops forward, and we finally release a united breath.

"What now?" Daisie asks softly.

Unable to answer her question, I simple squeeze her hand tighter. Silently telling her that all we can do... is stand together.

The End.

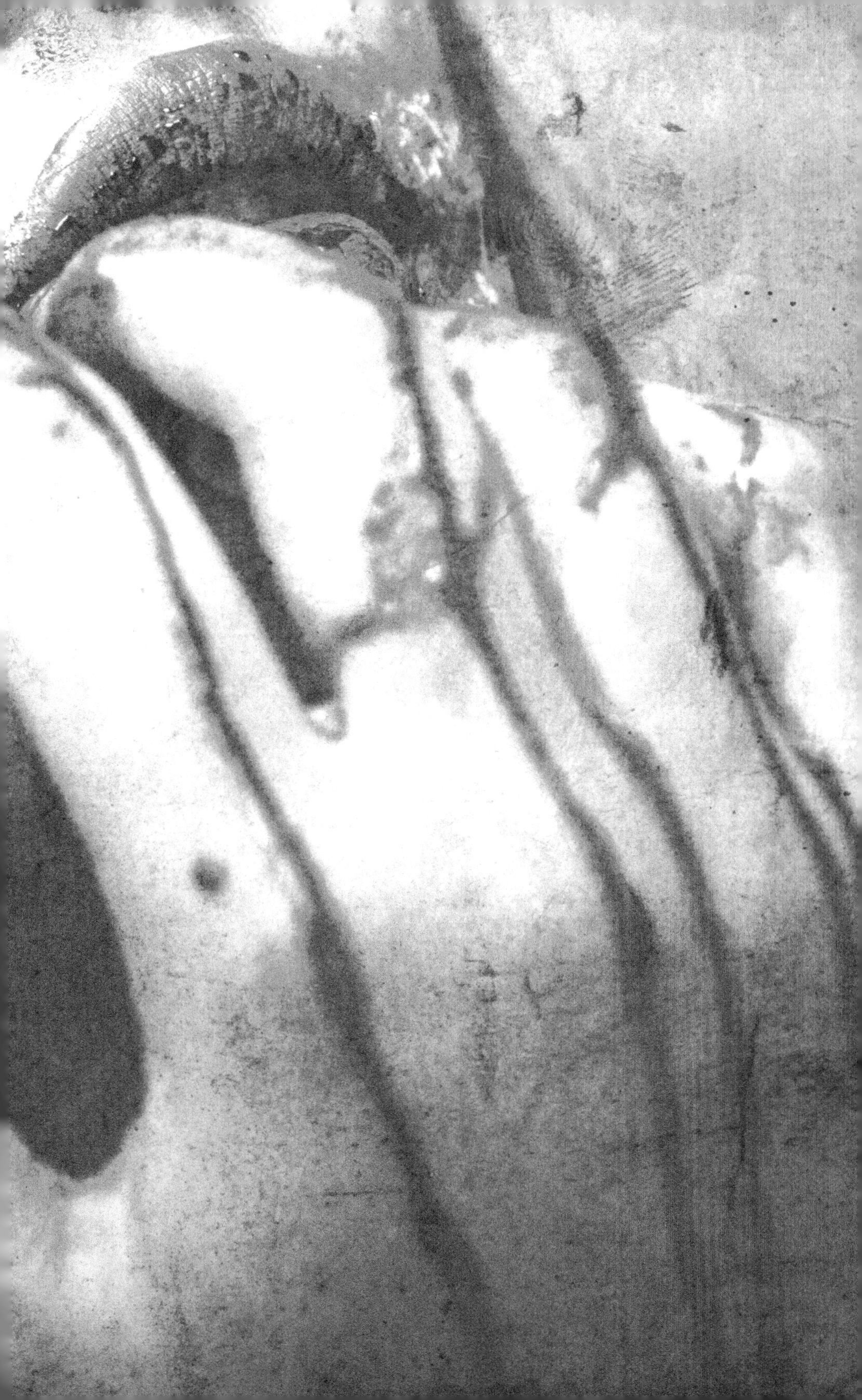

Note From CJ

Fear.

A sensation that women all over the globe feel on a daily basis. It's in the way we talk, how we dress, walk down the street. Even down to the way we conduct ourselves in public. We can't act or be the way we want to without shouldering all the blame for the actions of men and their uncontrollable need to destroy and devour us whole.

When we scream "all men" we are under no illusion that it is in fact not all men. However, when we walk down the street late at night, when we get out of our car in the dark and have to check our surroundings, when we have to remember not to pick up a drink that was left —for longer than a few seconds— on a night out, when we question our clothing before we step out onto the street… it's fear and concern that plunges our chests.

Continual worry if the steps we take in that moment will be our last. Or if something we say will set the nice guy off into a slew of abusive language that we have to defend. If questioning our boyfriend, husband, fiancé, on where they were last night—even though you know they were cheating—will be the final words we ever speak. Ever think.

It's the daily fight against what we want to do, against what we should do. It's taking away our rights. It's stealing our body autonomy. It's ridding us of a life we haven't even lived yet, because they deem nothing except power and constraint. It's the men who we trusted most that stole our innocence when we were children, the ones who took without permission and said, "You're being hysterical" or "You're crazy."

The gaslighting, the manipulation, the violence, the abuse. Being taught that women should be seen and not heard, and how we should shut up, put up, and put out. Even when we say no. even when we scream, and cry, and beg for salvation. It's our daily lives that force us to question every... single... move. It's being true to ourselves... even when it's frightening to do so. It's how we're the ones who have to forgive and forget. What were you wearing? How much did you have to drink? Did you say no?
No.
A complete sentence that so many ignore.

That is why we say all men. Because unfortunately, it's impossible to tell anymore. And if you as a man have to sit there and say, "it's not all men!" then you're part of the problem. You are the ones who sit by and let it happen. Because if you're not, and you stand with us, then you would know that not a single one of us mean you.

So, to those of us who recognise the dark times ahead. Who stand in solidarity with our sisters during this frightening and deplorable time in America, know this. We hear you; we fight with you, and though we might not be in the same country as you... or share the same blood, our strength and unwavering love will forever solidify our unity.

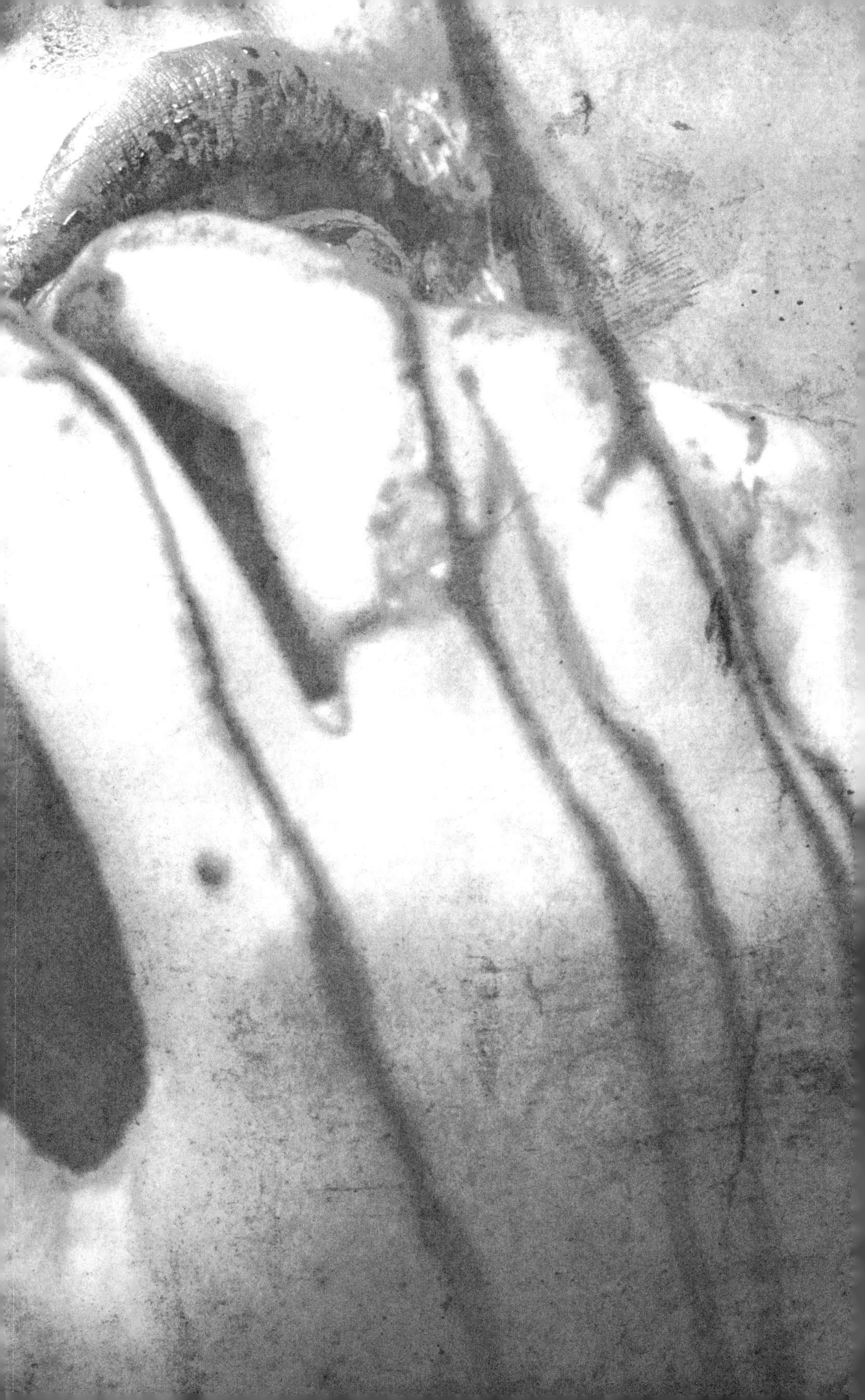

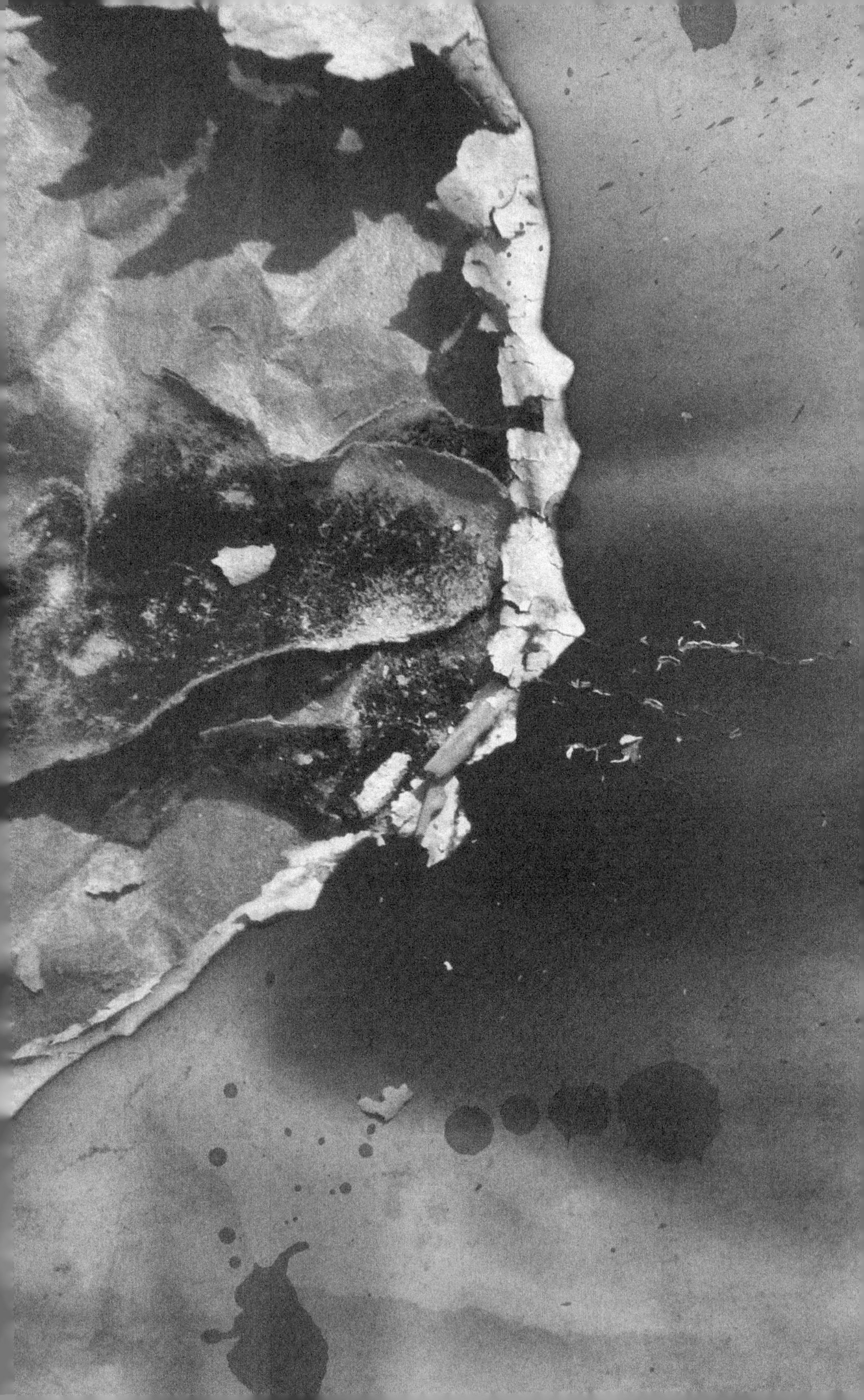

When Silence Screams

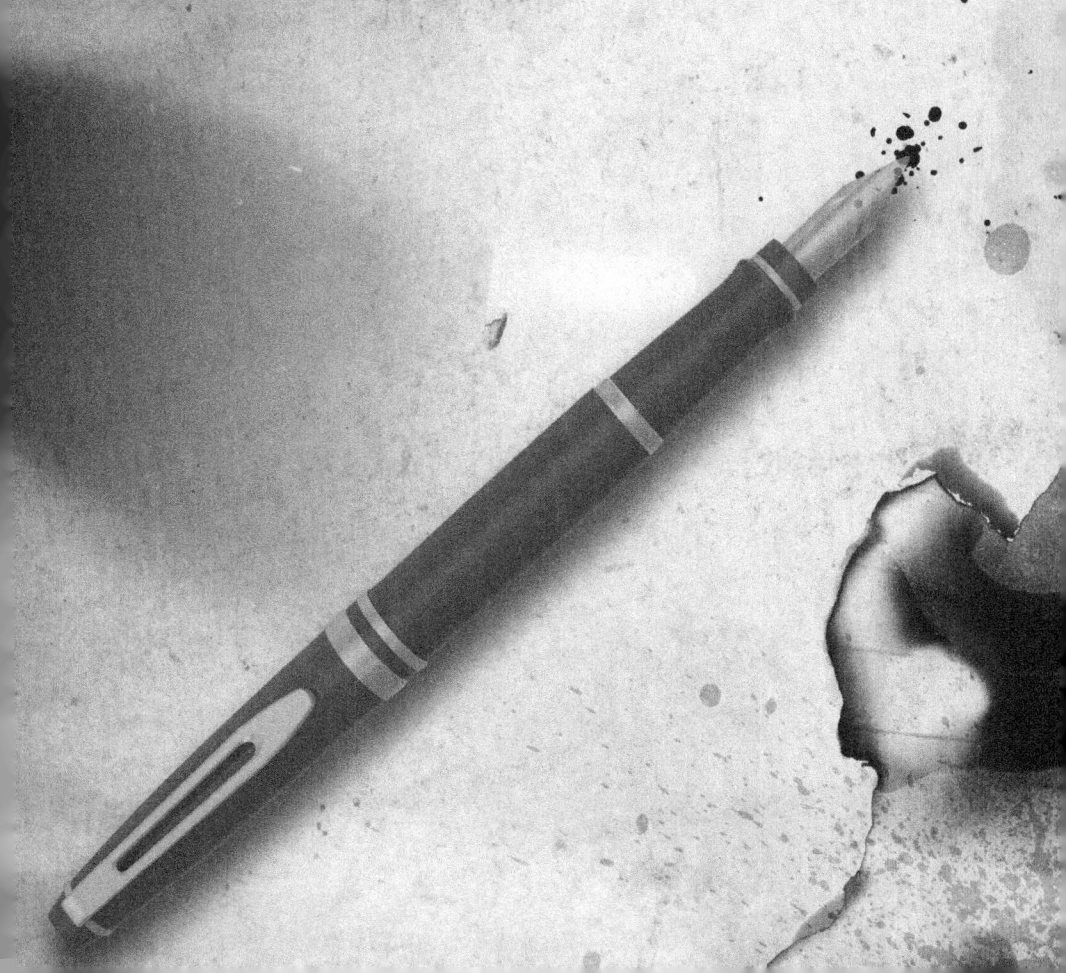

DK

Prologue

Ryder loved his wealth, especially his prized possession of sports cars. He loved to go fast, and he knew how much I hated it. We'd fly down the interstates, and while he would always have a big smirk on his face, I always had fear plastered on mine, begging him to stop. It was the fact that my life was in his hands, being controlled like it had been since I married him.

But luckily, I wasn't in the car when it flipped. That morning before he left for work, I was left feeling degraded, all because I didn't want to have a child. I wasn't ready. And as our marriage continued, I knew I'd never be. Not with him. I remember watching him drive down our driveway, going forty miles per hour, as I stood by our window, shaking my head, telling myself that those fucking sports cars would catch up with him.

When the phone rang, I had a gut feeling it wasn't good.

"Mrs. Vera? There's been an accident."

I should've been a sobbing mess. I should've had tears staining my cheeks as I drove to the hospital. But all I felt was freedom.

Ryder's funeral was a blur. His friends mourned him as if they just had lost a brother. Little did I know, my husband meant more to them because of the secrets they all shared. It wasn't until I was going through his office that I found the safe that left me with not a husband but a monster. Bank statements, photos of women, names, dates, keys, a location...

I should've called the authorities and had them take care of it. I should've just walked away. But where would the justice be in that? My husband gets a comfy coffin, while his best friends get a comfy cell because of their power and wealth? Fuck that.

I wanted their last moments on Earth to be what they thrived on—fear and pain. And when you meet a group of women who've been crushed under the weight of silence for too long, who've been broken and rebuilt stronger than they could've ever imagined...

You don't just get revenge. You get something only men fear. Because when women like us are done being prey, we turn into hunters. And by the time we're finished? Nothing is left but their destruction.

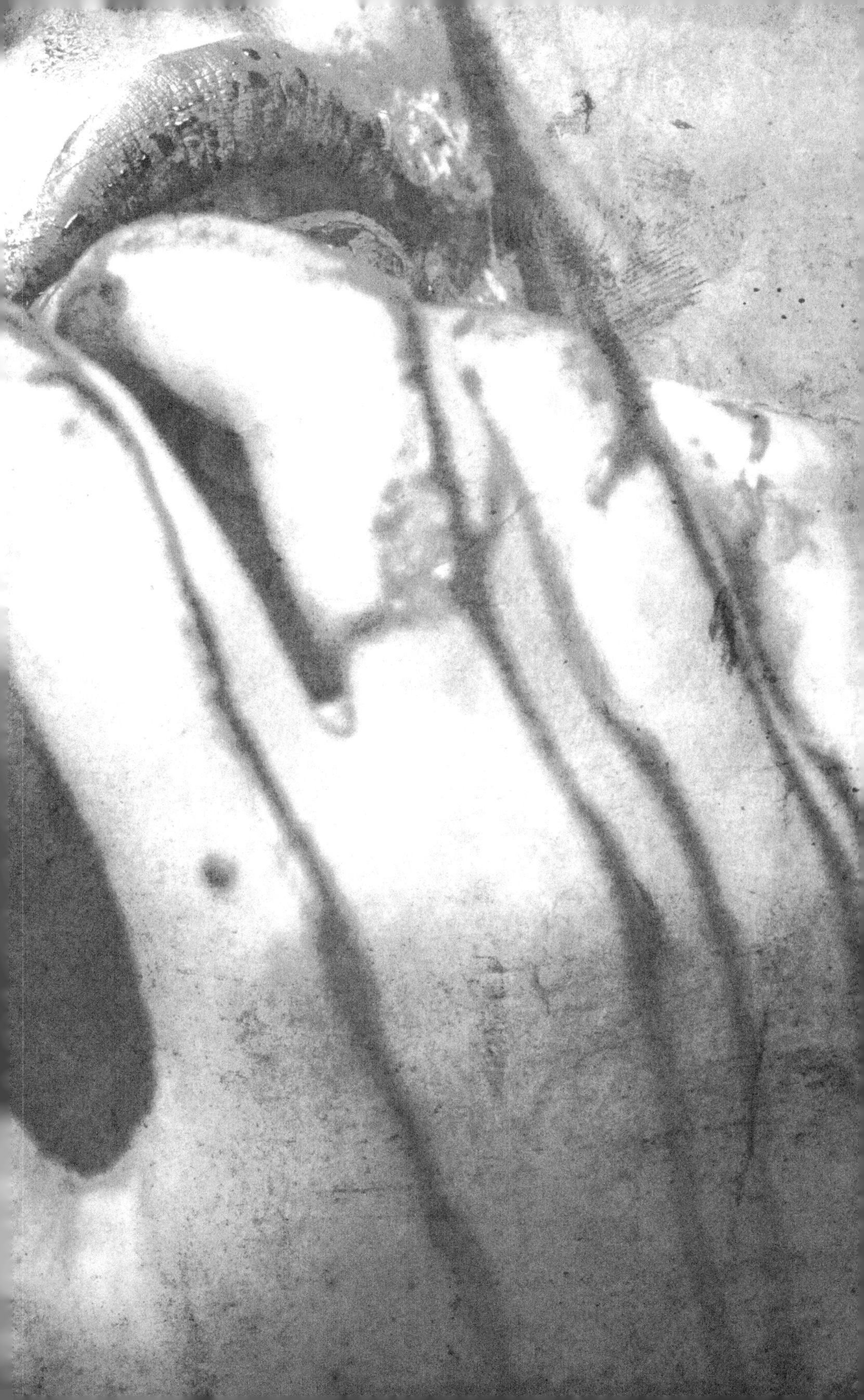

Chapter One

Tuesday

Discovering that your dead husband and his friends run their own personal human trafficking ring on a sunny Tuesday morning isn't ideal. Then again, I always did have a feeling Ryder was keeping secrets from me. I just wasn't expecting one this fucked. Ryder was too full of himself for me not to suspect his many affairs. The first time I found out, I demanded a divorce, and in return, he threw papers at me, showing me the contract I had signed the night before our marriage.

Back then, I was in love. Too eager and excited to start a lifetime of happiness together that would only deteriorate as time passed. I had no one. His family called me charity work—a basket case that only had my body to offer. I never showed that it got to me. I never showed how angry it made me because an angry woman is just mistaken for having hysteria instead of justice. At least in his and his family's eyes.

I stare at all the secrets and lies I laid out on his office desk. In one corner sits a pile of pictures of women, some dating back to two years ago when we first got married. The other corner is flooded with documents, and I've been trying to figure out what they all mean. And in the middle lays a set of keys to what the universe only knows where they belong to.

I sit back in the chair, looking at everything on the desk, not knowing what to do from here. Turning the chair, I look toward the safe when I notice a piece of paper just peeking out, not in the safe but under it. I quickly grab it, looking at the paper in horror. A blueprint of the barn

Ryder said we just "had to have" sits sketched on the paper. But within its design, where the stalls of the horses we never got it were supposed to be, lay a door. I flip the paper over as my heart is about to race out of my chest. A whole new blueprint has bile rising up my throat. Ryder didn't have that barn for rich horses. He built it as an optical illusion.

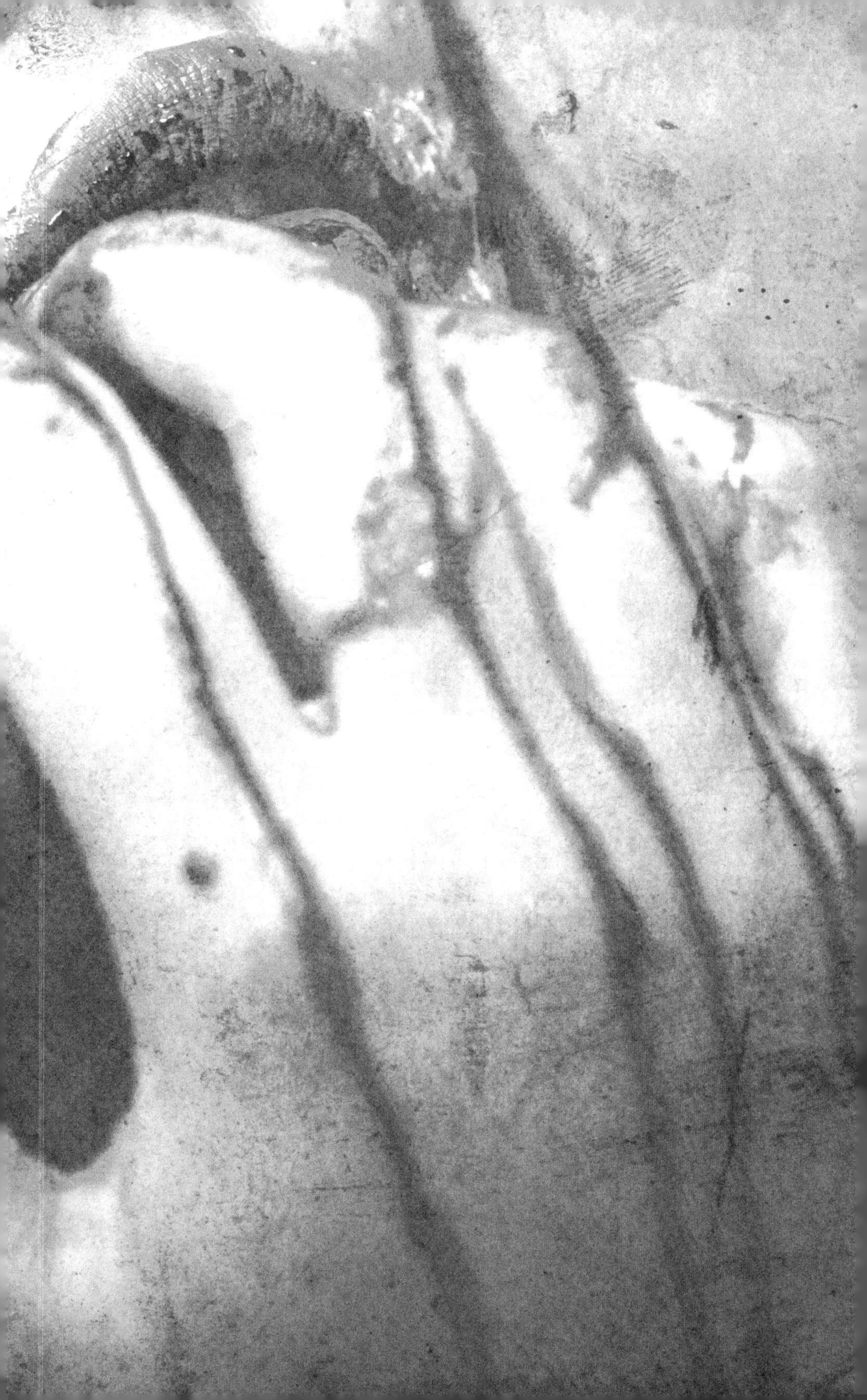

Chapter Two

Tuesday

I stand in front of the barn doors, throat tightening at what I hope isn't true. I always told Ryder it was a waste of money. That the barn would only be something else he forced me to take care of. I never understood why he insisted it be built in the very back of our property. You can't even see it from our house—which I have always thought was stupid since the bastard spent almost a million dollars on it.

With the keys in my hand that I found in his safe, I try the first one, and like clockwork, the barn doors unlock. I shakingly open them and am greeted by not just regular stalls. In each one sits one chair with one miniature-looking stage. As I walk deeper into the barn, I notice some stages have poles; others have chains hung up against the walls.

"What kind of monster were you?" I whisper, my body shaking. At the very back sits a stall that has black curtains hanging down. Taking a deep breath, I swing open the curtains, uncovering what I didn't want to be true. On the back wall stands a metal door with three sets of locks.

Moving with haste, I shakingly unlock them one by one. Welcomed by a set of stairs, I flip on the light switch and hear rustling from the bottom.

"Hello?" I shout, beginning to walk down. "A-Anyone down here?" I ask again. I reach the bottom and turn the corner, immediately gasping at the sight. A huge cell containing five women stands in the back corner, all shaking and terrified.

"Oh my god," I say, putting a hand over my mouth as tears flow down my cheeks. They all look at me with numb expressions as I run up to the cell, trying to find the key to unlock them. "I'm so sorry," I keep repeating as I continue crying, upset that I didn't come down here sooner.

Opening the cell, I walk into it, rage filling my veins by what these twisted men have done. "I promise they'll never lay a hand on y'all ever again." My voice shakes with fury.

One woman stands tall, taking a few steps toward me. "Where are they?"

"One of them died. The others are still out. The one who died was my husband, Ryder. I never knew anything until recently. I would've ended this much sooner."

"Then let's finish it," another woman says with a smile tugging at her lips.

I look at each of them, their eyes flooding with spark—*power*. These women have had their voices silenced. Their lives were stolen. But the one thing these men failed to take was the rage all women have. Nobody can ever take a woman's rage away. A woman's rage starts out as a small fire, building up over time until it's ready to burn—to destroy. Women who have been wronged let the fury guide them.

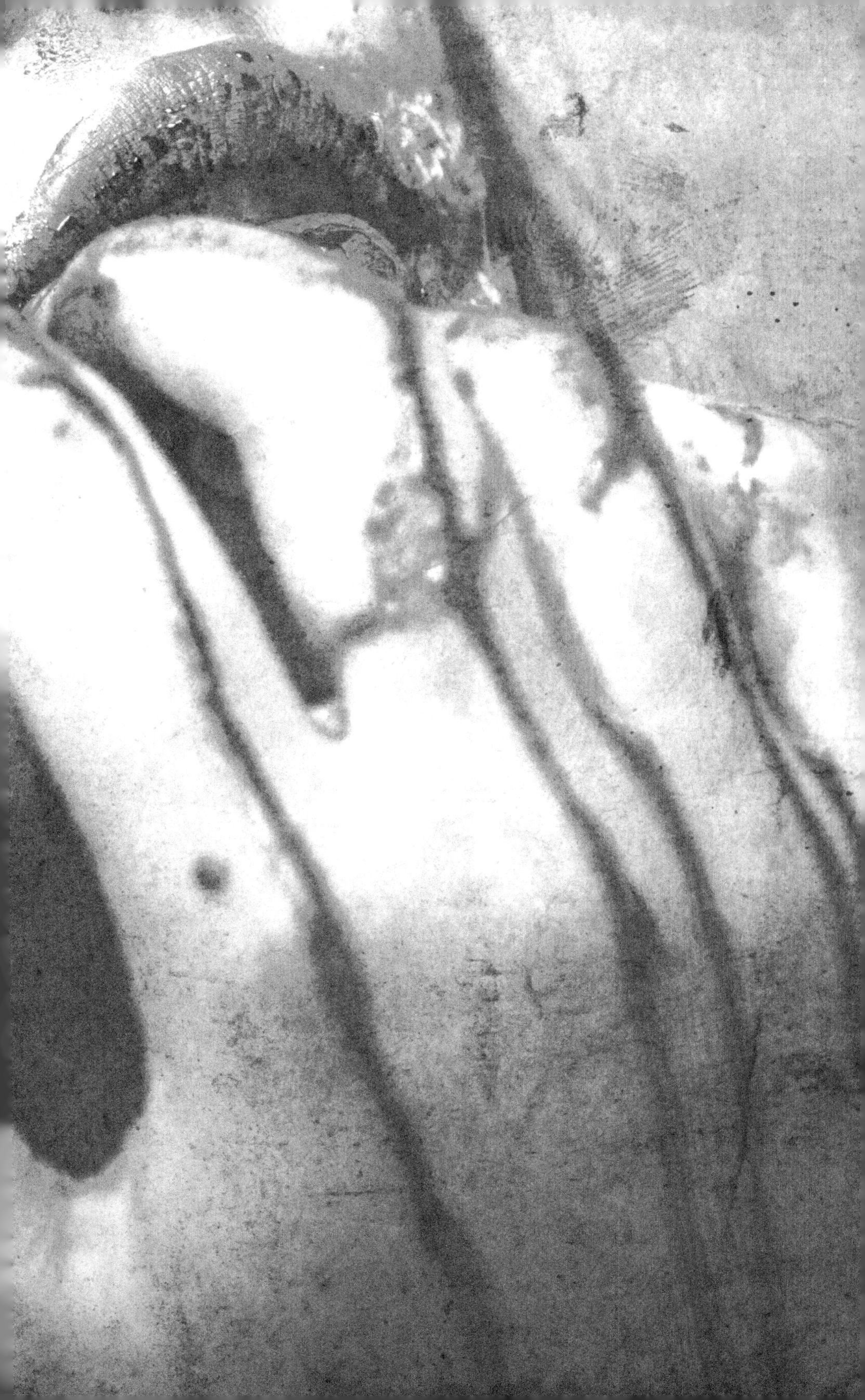

Chapter Three

Wednesday

It's no surprise a newly widowed woman is going through it. It's no surprise that she's wanting closure. But this type of closure is a little different. When I called Ryder's friends in a sobbing mess yesterday evening, asking if they'd come by tonight for dinner, I knew they'd come.

Maybe it's because they feel so bad for me. Or maybe it's the fact that I ended the conversation wanting to talk to them about his estate. After all, money talks.

The dining room is elegantly set, with all the food and wine you could possibly imagine. I need them to feel comfortable. I need them blindsided. I finish up my hair and makeup, adding a pair of diamond earrings Ryder bought me after I caught him with his first affair. The doorbell rings, and with one last glance in the mirror, I flatten out my dress and take a deep breath.

His friends, Vincent, Ethan, Jonathan, James, and Brian, all crowd the door with sorrowful smiles. I hug them all, greeting them through doors they'll never walk out of. "Thank you all so much for coming on such late notice. I've just been a wreck. I'm still getting used to a quiet home," I say as I walk them to the dining room.

Vincent puts a hand on my shoulder and says, "He always loved you." I flash him a smile, trying my best not to roll my eyes at his bullshit lie.

They all sit down, and I pour them some wine before bringing mine to the front. I lift my glass up, toasting to Ryder. Everyone takes a sip from their glass before Ethan asks, "How are you holding up?"

"Still getting used to things." I shrug. "I just thought this would help."

"Totally. Anything for you," he says with a smile, though I can see right through him.

The dinner is filled with nothing but fake laughter and forced conversations. Memories of Ryder that I never even knew existed just tell me more about a husband I never really knew. For a while, I sit back and watch as the five of them engage in conversation, acting as if I'm not there. I count their wine refills in my head, waiting for the perfect time to lure them in. And as wine bottle number seven quickly distinguishes, now is the time to make my move.

Clinking my glass with my knife, I get up. Their own conversations stop, giving me their attention. "Gentleman, as I told you, I wanted to discuss Ryder's estate. I know none of y'all have wives or children, but it doesn't feel right for me to be here. Which is why I want to sell it." I notice their shoulders growing tall, their eyes focused on not me but the offer they know is coming.

"This house is worth millions. I don't need millions, and I surely don't want it. Since you were all close with Ryder, I want to give you all a cut. But not without my own rules." They look around the table, confused.

"Your own rules?" James asks.

"That's right. I wanted to do it the fun way. And tonight, you all will be playing a game. Hide N Seek." I watch as they laugh it off.

"You can't be serious—"

"I am dead serious. But there is a catch. There are only five rooms you can go into. The rest I have already locked. You can't hide together, you can't move around, and you cannot go outside. They'll be prizes based on who stays hidden the longest." I smirk, wiggling my eyebrows.

"I'm game. Seems like something Ryder would come up with."

Which is exactly why I picked it...

I walk over to the dining room mantel and pick up a remote. "You all will have five minutes when the windows and doors close and lock."

Chapter Three

I press a button, watching and listening as all the windows become sealed shut with aluminum shutters. Each door of the house does the same. Their faces morph into serious, wide-eyed stares, but I only smile.

"Your time starts now, gentleman." They all get up, scattering like flies. For the first time in the night, I take a sip of my wine, watching the clock tick by.

Let's see how well they play when *their* lives are on the line.

Chapter Four

Five minutes go by, and their footsteps quiet down, taking their hiding positions. "Here I come," I yell, heading to the library, one of the rooms I've left unlocked. Books that sit on mahogany shelves line the walls from floor to ceiling, a grand fireplace burning in the heart of the room.

Two sets of reading chairs sit in the corner, and I notice a head poking through the opening.

I walk over, pulling the chair out from the corner, uncovering Vincent, who smiles and slumps his head in defeat. "Ugh, you found me!" He chuckles, thinking it's all just a game.

"I'm sure the women you trafficked said the same thing. Though I'm almost certain they weren't laughing and smiling about it." His face drops. Before he has time to react, I stab his neck, injecting the propofol. He stumbles forward until he fully collapses, going out of consciousness.

"Alright," I chirp, watching one of the women who were "his" come out from the hidden door. "How much time do we have?" Hailey asks.

"He'll be out for about ten minutes. Long enough to take him to the barn and get him situated."

I help her drag him out toward the back door, the only one I left unlocked. I make my way toward Ryder's bourbon room, startled to see Ethan just standing in the corner. *Fucker didn't even try.*

"Ryder always said you had a weakness for bourbon," I say, looking at him and all the bourbon bottles and barrels that take up the space. Chuckling, he says, "I could never say no to his bourbon."

"How many times did the women y'all kept in the barn say no? Did you ever stop when they were begging? Or did that only give you more of a sick and twisted thrill?"

He puts his hands up, taking slow steps back. "I never wanted to do it," he pleads.

I hear one of them hidden in the back start to laugh. His face whips in her direction. I make my move, injecting him, watching as he slowly falls to the ground.

One by one, they drop like flies. James and Jonathon practically begged and pleaded for forgiveness, their cries so beautiful I almost held off their sedatives just so the women and I could hear more. I head toward the only room left—Ryder's office. I knew Brian would hide in that one. They've been best friends since college, and in all the documents I uncovered, Brian's name was right next to Ryder's when it came to *business* matters.

Entering the room, I say, "You're the last one, Brian."

He comes out from under the desk, sighing in relief with a smile. "What's the first-place prize?" he asks.

"What do you want it to be, Brian?" I ask, approaching him and sitting on top of the desk. He looks me up and down, not missing how his tongue licks his bottom lip when his eyes focus more on my chest.

"What do you want me to have?" he whispers, placing a hand on my thigh, too high for comfort. I force out a soft smile. "What do you want me to have?" I repeat softly.

He leans closer, running his hands up to my hips. "Ryder always told me how good you were at satisfying him. How good you were at shoving him in the back of your throat while those pretty little tears ran down your face…"

"Oh yeah?" I ask, leaning into him. Our breaths fan each other. "You want me to suck you off? Choking, swallowing, crying over your cock like a good little widow?"

He nods his head slowly.

I kiss the top of his neck, softly biting his ear when I whisper, "I'm not here to satisfy you, Brian." I reach under my skirt, grabbing the last syringe. "I'm here to end you." I inject the sedative, watching him collapse on top of me.

I shove him off, calling in the last woman. The two of us work quickly to carry him outside, throwing him into the trunk. Jumping into the car, we speed off, heading toward the barn. If only they knew that the games had only started.

Chapter Five

All of us women watch them stir awake. Their minds go straight into flight or fight mode, though that won't be of any use to them. Chained to each stall door, the very stalls they would force themselves upon innocent women, they all beg and plead for their lives.

"Gentlemen, there's no use for your cries. It's not like any of you cared if the women did," I say, looking at each of them with disgust. "Ladies!" I call out, watching them come out from the stalls, standing in front of the men who have wronged them. "Tonight, you will all get exactly what you deserve. Pain... death..."

"And then what? You all kill us and then go to prison? Did Ryder's death fuck you up that much?

Instead of just letting these women go and send *us* off to jail, you would all rather suffer in prison?" Jonathan asks.

"You think Ryder's death 'fucked me up'?" I ask in quotations. "How many times did I tell him that, one day, his gas and brake pedals would fail him? Ah, but he never did believe a woman with knowledge..." I shrug.

His face morphs into disgust. "You were the reason he got into a car accident?"

"Indeed I was. And I'd do it again. Enough about Ryder, though... It's y'all's turn to meet him in Hell."

Chapter 6

Hailey's POV

Vincent stripped me of the life I once had. For three months, we'd been hidden, compacted into a basement cell as if we were only the scum beneath their feet. We were forced no matter what it was. There was no point in trying to run. For if we did, we would only be captured and put right back.

I look at Maribel, who gives me an encouraging nod to begin. I turn to Vincent, whose eyes are filled with fake tears. The only reason he's crying is because he got caught, not because he's sorry. I open the switchblade knife, the shine sparkling off the serrated edge.

"I have nothing to say to you. No matter what I say, it's not like you'd listen anyway. You never did." He screams for help one last time before I plunge the knife into his throat—again, again, and again. I hear the other men start to scream, but their screams only make me stab more. His pleads are muffled by the blood spilling out. My skin is coated with not only blood but victory. I pull out the knife, winding back when the last stab goes right into his penis, keeping it there.

I control my breath, wiping the blood off my face with the back of my hand. I stand tall, looking at his lifeless body. I knew I was free when Maribel found us. But I just got back the power I had missed for so long.

Chapter 7

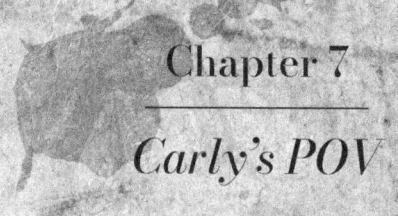

Carly's POV

Ethan was articulate with his evil game. He whispered lies into my ear that I fell so hard for. He promised me a lifetime with him. I just didn't know that meant spending it like this. Our second date was when he sexually assaulted me. I was barely conscious, remembering the pit in my stomach when I realized what was happening. Yet I could barely move, unable to speak.

When I woke up the next day, I was trapped in here. No matter how loud I screamed, I knew nobody would hear me. Especially not him nor the rest of them. But I never let that stop me. I never let him get the best of me. Instead, I've spent my time here fueling myself for the day I would be found. The women I met here I got close to real quick.

We promised ourselves and each other that we'd get our revenge. That one day, we would make them pay for what they did. I just never knew it would be Ryder's wife who would find us, and for that, I'm grateful. I don't look at her as our hero; I look at her as our reckoning.

"Ethan, Ethan, Ethan," I tsk, shaking my head.

"Please don't do this… I promise I'll make it right," he sobs.

"Your promises mean nothing to me. What matters most is making sure you will never be able to put your filthy hands on a woman ever again." I bend down, getting on his level.

"Maribel, can you hand me the knife, please?" I ask, smiling at him.

She walks up to me, setting down the knife. I pick it up, slowly tracing his fingers and then up to his wrist. "Good luck touching a woman ever again," I say as I slam down the knife into his wrist. I wind up again, listening to his cries. In three forceful slams, his wrist comes off, blood spurting like a holy fountain.

I do the same to the other, this time slicing to take my time. I look him in the eyes, seeing for once a man who lost his power. "I never want to look at you again," I grunt as I stab his eye sockets, spinning the knife into each one. I examine my work. No more eyes to leer. No more power to wield. Just another monster reduced to nothing, exactly where he belongs.

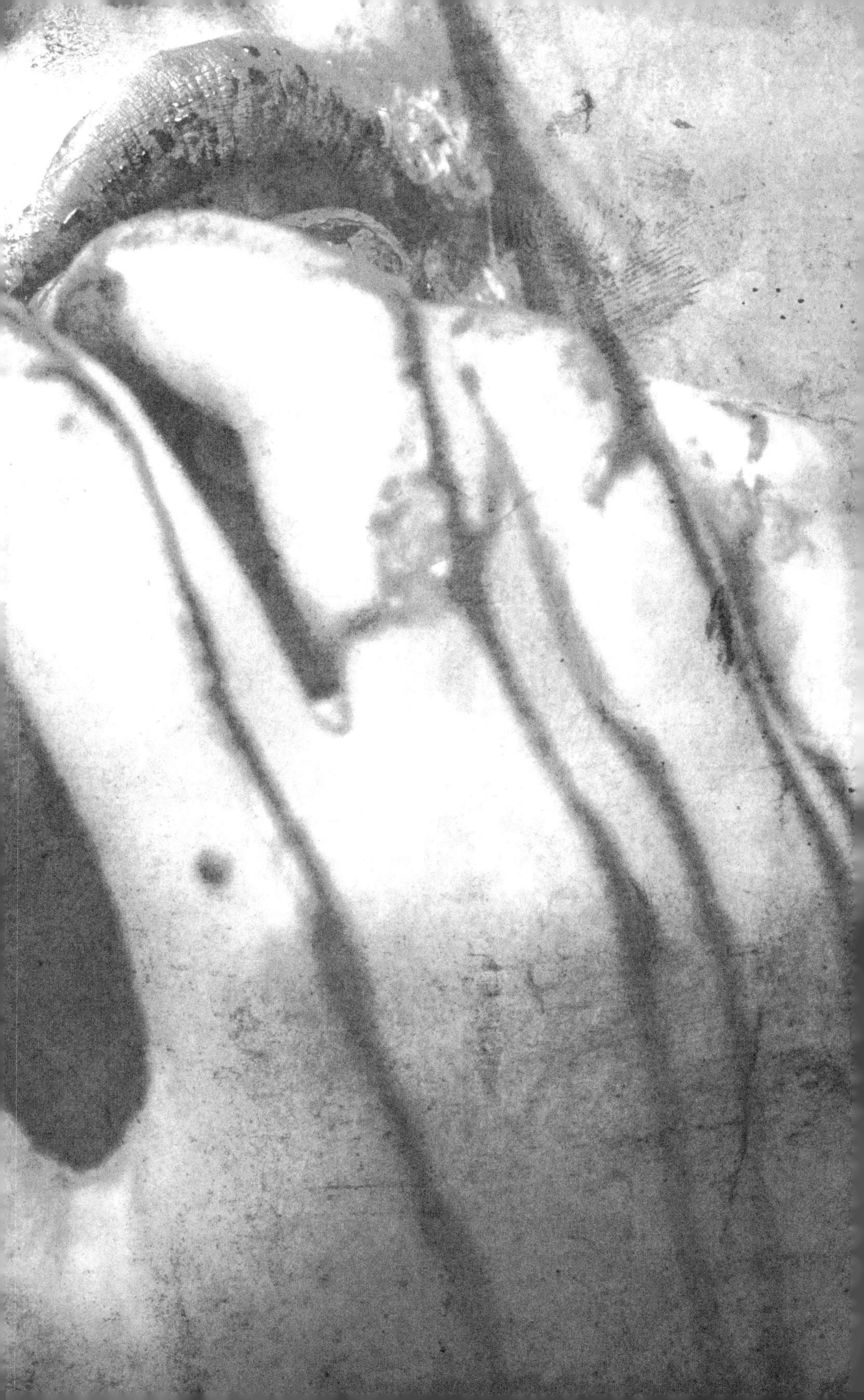

Chapter 8

Emily's POV

Jonathan told me he never wanted to do it. That he was only doing it because he felt pressured into it. *Give me a fucking break.* I could see the power fuel his body when he laid his hands on me.
Over time, I learned to dissociate myself from what was happening. At first, I imagined myself on a beach. Just me, myself, and I. But as time went on, my happy place was always me getting back at him. And now, it's finally a reality.

His body shakes, his breathing heavy. "Jonathan, do you remember what you told me the first night you raped me?" He doesn't answer—doesn't look up at me. Pulling out the dagger from my garter belt, I cut his shoulder, slicing through his shirt and breaking the skin. "Answer me!" I yell. He shakes his head.

"You told me it was going to be okay. You know why?" I ask. Shaking his head again, I bend down, holding his chin up with the dagger to look up at me. "Because you told me it was just the tip."

I undo his jeans, yanking them and his boxers down to his ankles. He thrashes, sobbing for help and begging for forgiveness. I look around at all the women, each of them giving me subtle nods with soft smiles. We've all been through hell and back; for a while, I was certain we'd never see light again.

"Emily, I promise that if you free me, I'll never tell a soul. Nobody will ever know about any of this. You want money? Fine. Say a number."

"You think money is going to help me or any of us gain what we lost? Men like you will never be sorry. The only time y'all are is when you get caught. Now…" I trail the dagger up his thigh, laughing while his body thrashes like a fish out of water, "…be a good boy and take the tip." I softly put the tip of the dagger at the entrance of his urethra, gently poking at it just to make him squirm more. To make his mind go crazy in the worst way possible.

"Count to five for me," I murmur. When he doesn't say anything, I press the tip of the blade harder.

"Okay… O-One. T-Two…" He stops, his cries taking up his breath and, frankly, my time. "And what comes after two?" I ask.

"Th-Three… then fo-four…"

I nod. "Mhm… good boy. Now, what comes after?"

"Five!" Just as he shouts, I press the dagger all the way into his urethra, watching as he tries to kick me away from him.

My laugh fills the air. I slowly take it out, only to slam it back in. I twist the dagger, hearing his screams slowly stop, knowing he's about to pass out. It's a beautiful mess, and I'm loving every second of this. I take the dagger out, quickly slicing through his penis and shoving it inside his mouth.

Barely conscious, he tries to fight it off with the little energy he has, but that only makes me shove it further down his throat. I watch him choke, having no other choice, just like the rest of us once had. But unlike us, he won't survive it.

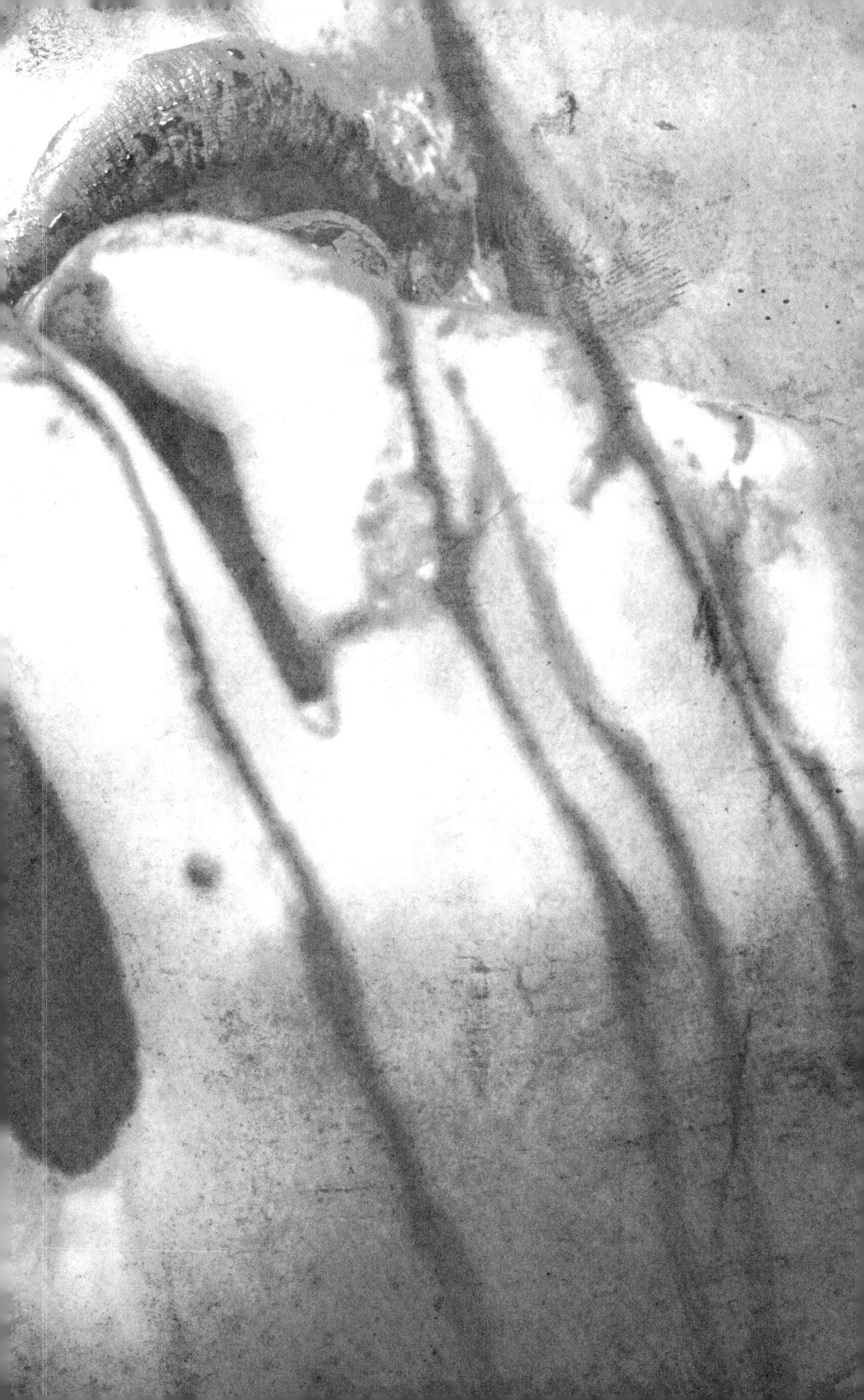

Chapter 9

Rebecca's POV

James has never heard me speak. I never let him have that privilege. I knew it was no use. I heard the other women scream and beg for their lives. But with their voices came only consequences. I figured the more I kept quiet, the higher the chance he would free me. It only made him more angry that I never fought back. I didn't want to let him win.

Even when I was working at my local bar and he'd frequently come in, I'd never say a word to him. I knew something about him was off. But now that the tables have turned, he's about to see what it feels like to be silenced.

"James." He looks up at me, almost wide-eyed that I actually spoke up. "You silenced me when I still had a voice." I take a step closer, gripping the sides of his face so he'll look up at me. I hold out my other hand, waiting for Maribel to hand me the gun.

She places it on my hand and whispers, "Loaded." Thanking her, I take the gun, gripping it firmly.

"But now, James? I'm the one who not only gets to decide when your voice gets taken away but also your life." Pointing the gun right at his mouth, I place my finger gently on the trigger. "I would take my time with you, but I hate wasting my time on someone who doesn't even acknowledge my existence, even if it's by force. You remember telling me that?" His eyes catch sight of mine, pleading for me not to do it.

Tilting my head, I pout my bottom lip before I fire the gun, his brain matter and blood popping like confetti. I always loved a good party.

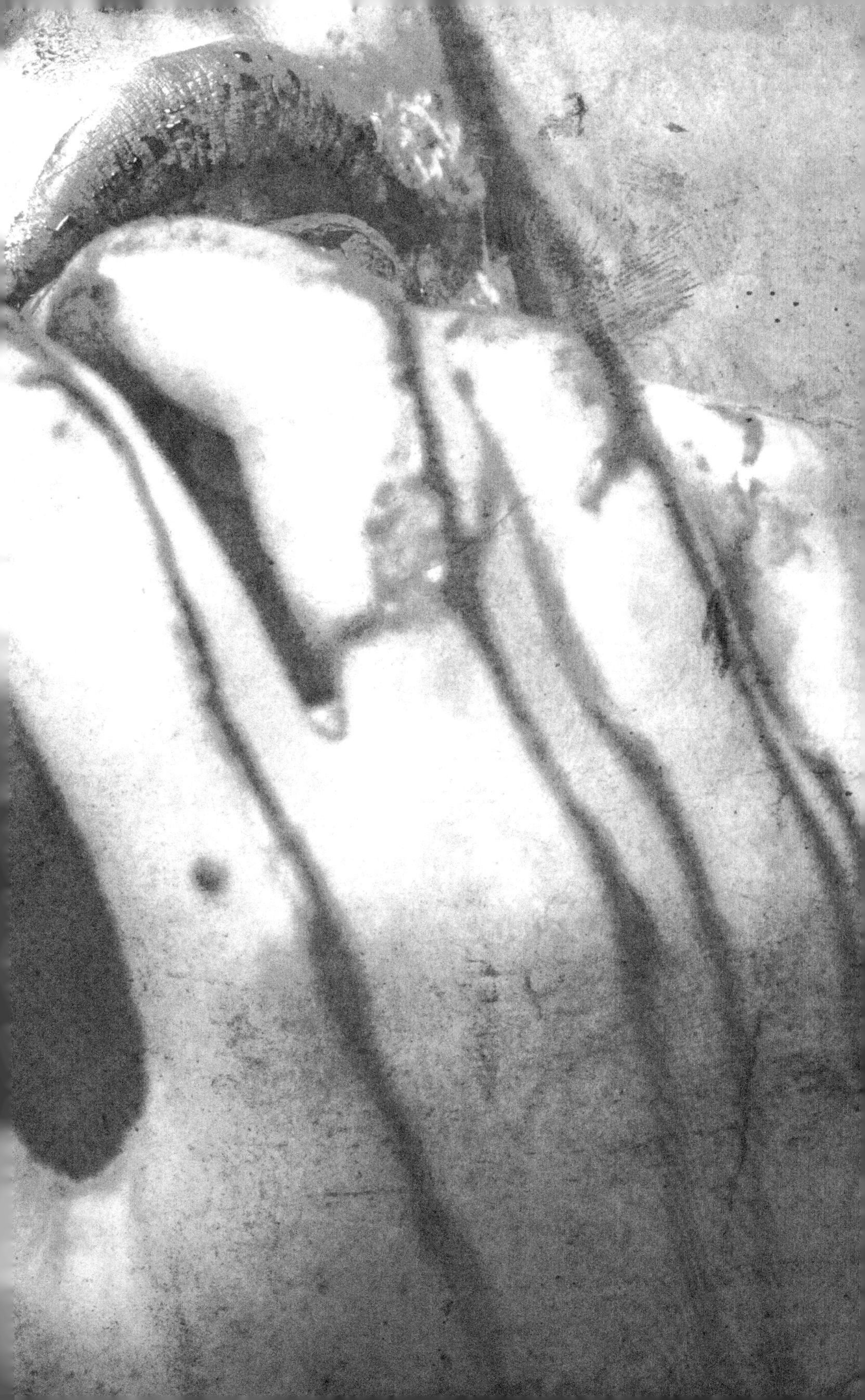

Chapter 10

Allie's POV

I was Brian and Ryder's, what they liked to call, "perfect two holes." I met Brian when I had just moved here. Who knew that something I was already running away from would come back and hit me ten times harder? I was quickly introduced to Ryder, and for a moment, I thought they were dating each other. When I woke up here to the both of them using me, I knew that I was a prisoner. Anytime they'd have their way with me, I couldn't help but stare at Ryder's wedding band, praying to myself that his wife would somehow see through whatever persona he was playing when he'd go back to his home, joining her in bed.

When I saw Maribel, I knew it was his wife who was not only coming to save us but also the look in her eyes, which was one we all have. Rage. Anger. A fire that only women have. When she told us Ryder died, relief washed over me, but Brian was still in the back of my mind. And now that I have him where I've always wanted him, I'm going to make sure he never steals from anyone ever again.

"Just you now, Brian," I sigh. I look toward all the women, all of them right by the barn doors waiting for me. Crouching down, I pat him on the shoulder and whisper, "You tried so hard to put out the fire that danced inside me. And now... you're about to be *in* one." His eyes look at me, but he still remains quiet.

Standing tall, I walk out with the women. Maribel hands me the lighter. "All yours, love. All yours." I flick it open, throwing it inside the barn. It doesn't take long for the fire to spread, the flames lighting up the night. We all hold each other tight, hearing the faint screams of Brian.

As the flames consume everything, I whisper softly, "Burn in the hell you created."

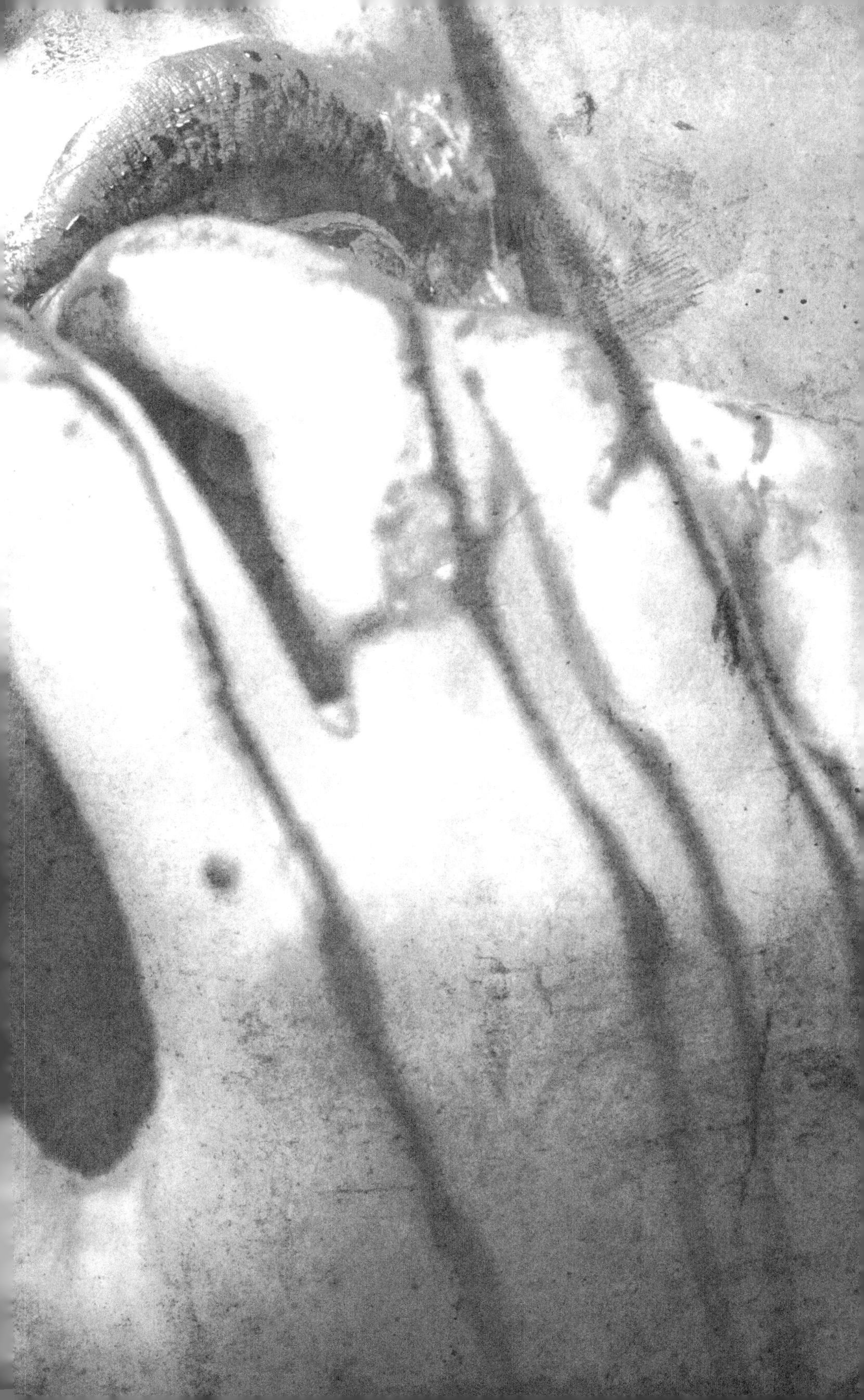

Epilogue

Maribel's POV

I stand at the edge of the ashes, the ground still warm beneath my feet, as the first light of dawn stretches across the horizon. Beside me, everyone stands tall, the same women who found themselves in the darkness and got back their voices.

"Do you feel it?" I whisper, my voice softer than I expected.

Nobody speaks, but I see it in their eyes. *Relief.* But also something far more dangerous—*power*.

The women watch in silence, their eyes reflecting the same quiet strength. They've endured unspeakable horrors, but they're still standing. And now? They're *free*.

"What now?" Carly asks, her voice barely above the breeze. I glance over at her, and for the first time in what feels like forever, I smile.

"Now?" I murmur, my gaze sweeping over the ruins of the barn, the place where their nightmares were born. "Now we take everything back. It's only the beginning." The men who caged us are gone. Burned. Forgotten. But us?

We're still here. *They're* still here. And we're not just survivors. We're *something more*. As the sun creeps higher, I take one last look at the ashes. I used to think I'd never be free of this place, but now I know better.

Nobody is trapped anymore.

We all turn away, walking toward a brighter future. The future may be unknown, but there are two things I'm certain about:

They'll never hurt another woman. They'll never silence them again.

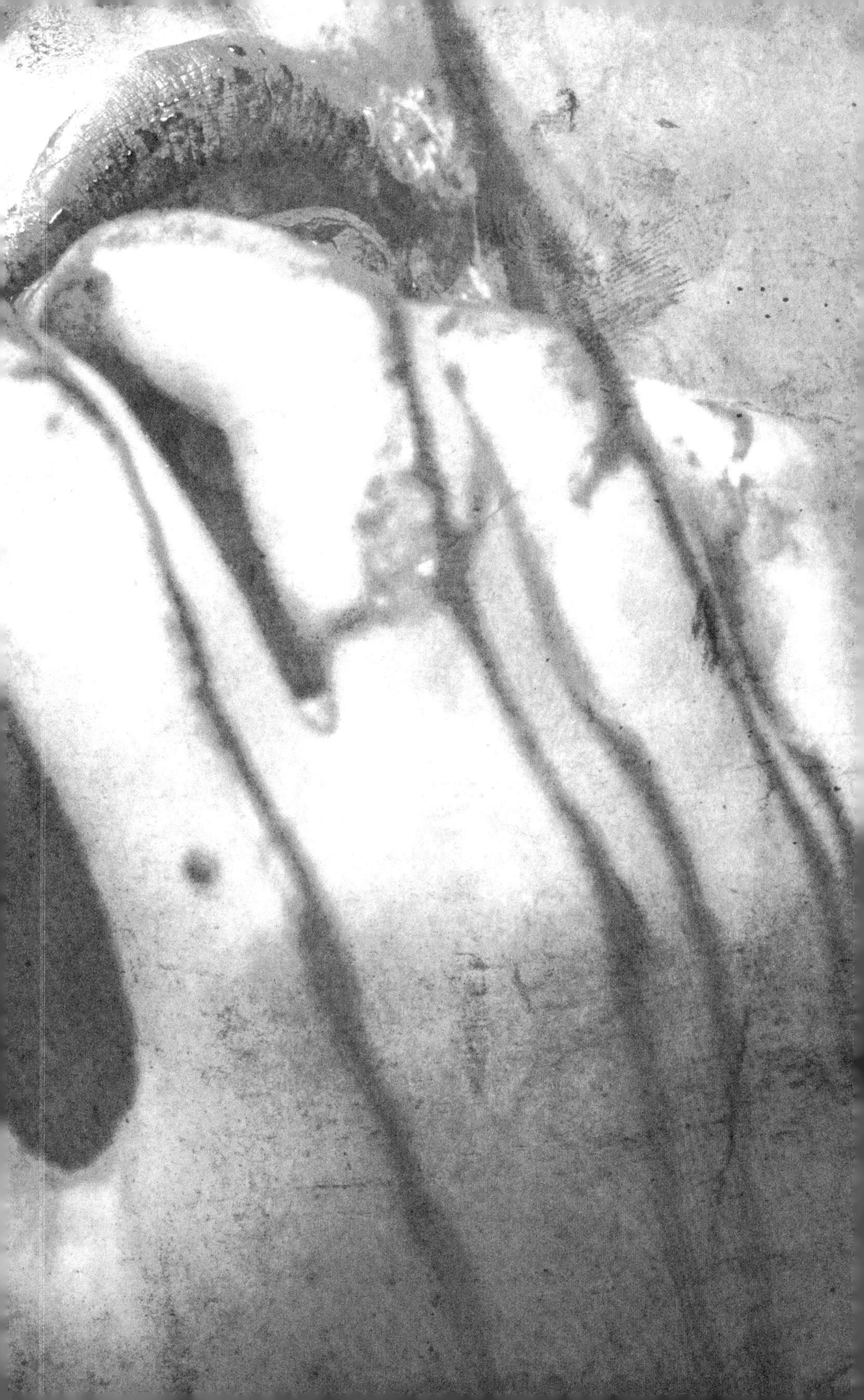

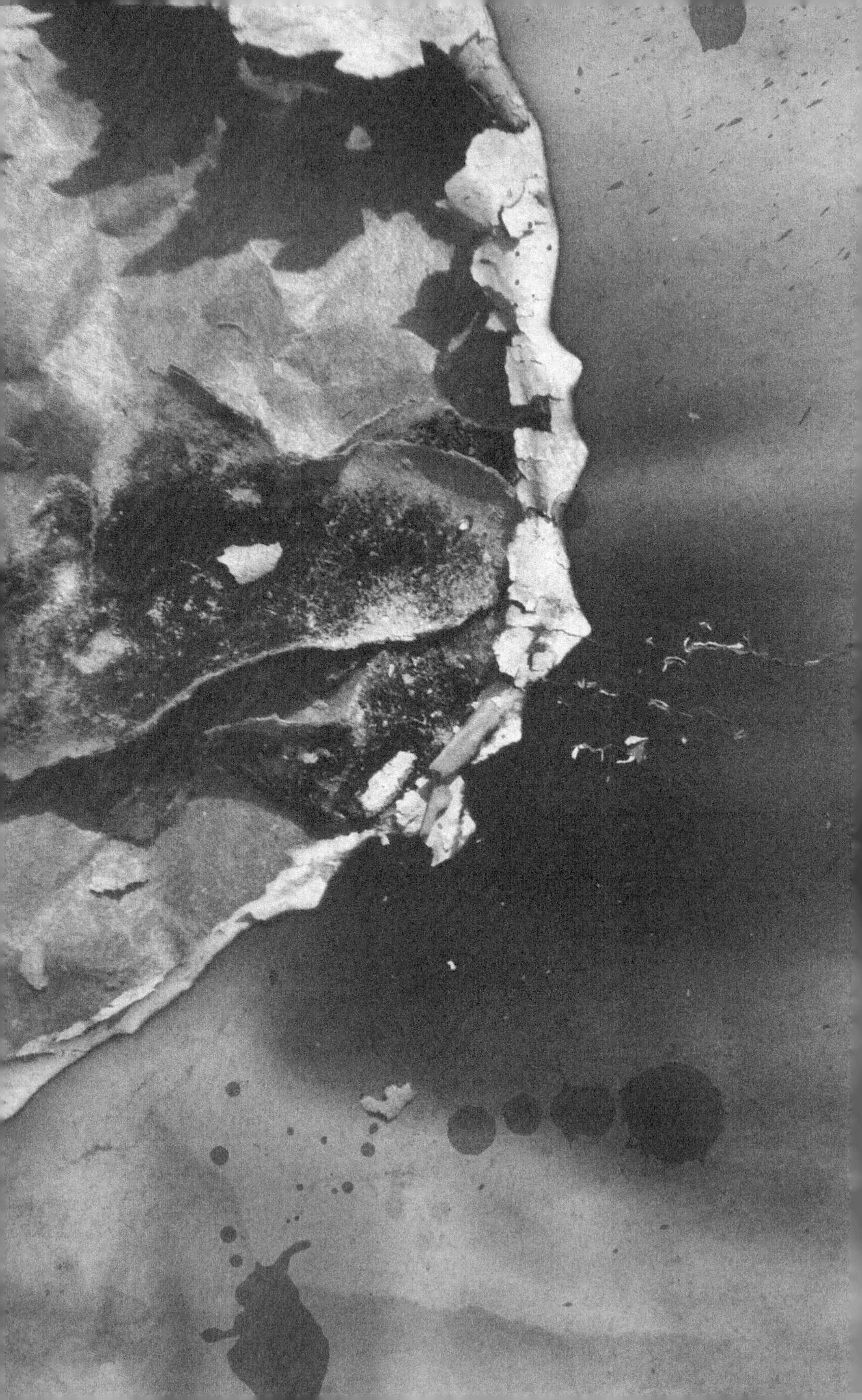

Stone

E. L. Emkey

Dedication

To all the girls who need a reminder that you are the hunter, the predator, and the thing that goes bump in the night. Don't let the prey talk you out of your next meal…

Foreword

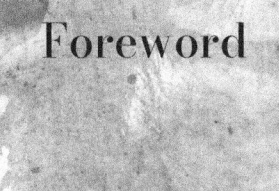

Kings have Honor.
Soldiers have Bravery.
Poets have Heart.
All I have is Rage.

Chapter One

October fifth.

A day just like every other day. Wake up. Stare at my reflection in the mirror—black hair, shit-brown eyes, and skin that could seriously use some quality sunshine. Shower. Brush teeth. Drive to Acadia Falls University in my busted-ass 2008 Ford Explorer and walk down the pristine hallway lined with lockers and trophy cases with posters meticulously displayed advertising the upcoming homecoming game.

Another mundane morning in a string of mundane mornings.

Professor Emerson discussed the story of Medusa during our Ancient Mythology lecture—the symbolism behind her snake-infested hair and the power of her petrifying gaze. Poseidon had raped her in Athena's temple. This sacrilege garnered the goddess' wrath, and she punished Medusa by turning her hair into snakes, cursing her so that if any man looked upon her, she would turn them to stone.

The tale resonated with me in a way I hadn't expected. Something about the injustice of it all—the woman violated and then punished for the crime committed against her. I felt sad for her.

As if reading my thoughts, Professor Emerson added, "Some scholars argue that Medusa's transformation was not a punishment, but rather a gift from Athena—a way to protect herself from ever being violated again."

I pondered his words as I walked out of the lecture hall. The more I considered it, the more I agreed with the scholar's interpretation. Perhaps Athena's curse was indeed a blessing in disguise—a way to empower Medusa and ensure that no man would ever hurt her again.

I went to the cafeteria, grabbed a pre-packed sandwich and a water bottle, and found an empty table in the corner. As I sat down, I noticed a group of guys a few tables over, their boisterous laughter echoing through the room. They were the typical jocks—tall, muscular, and oozing with confidence.

One of them, Felix Owens, blond, piercing blue eyes, resident heartthrob, and football team captain, caught my gaze. He smirked and nudged his friend, pointing in my direction. His friend and sidekick, Chase Maddox, gave me a smirk before turning to the other dipshits at the table and making some joke I was sure was about me. I quickly looked away, focusing on my sandwich. I could feel their eyes on me, their whispers and snickers grating on my nerves. I tried to ignore them, but their laughter grew louder and more obnoxious. Felix and Chase had a reputation on campus. They were the untouchable golden boys who could do no wrong. They walked the hallways like they owned them, their arrogance and entitlement seeping from every pore. Their daddies were some rich assholes on Wall Street, and they had an infinite amount of money to do whatever they wanted when they wanted. I had seen the way they treated girls like playthings to be used and discarded. They were the kind of guys who thought they could have any girl they wanted, and unfortunately, they were usually right. Girls fawned over them, eager to be in their arms, even if it was just for a night. But I saw through their charm and good looks straight to the rotten core underneath.

I glanced up, and Felix stared right at me with a predatory glint in his eyes. He said something to Chase, and they both stood up, walking toward my table. I felt a surge of panic. I didn't want to deal with their harassment today, or any day for that matter. I quickly gathered my things and stood up, ready to make a swift exit.

But Felix was faster.

He blocked my path, towering over me with a smug grin. "Where are you off to in such a hurry, *Briar?*" he asked, my name almost whispered.

How did he know my name?

I tried to sidestep him, but he moved with me, his broad frame an

Chapter One

imposing barrier. "I have class," I lied, trying to pull my arm away, but his grip only tightened.

"Come on, stay awhile. We don't bite," he said, his eyes gleaming with a predatory light.

I yanked my arm free, glaring at him. "I'm not interested."

His smirk faltered, replaced by a flash of anger, but he quickly recovered. "Playing hard to get, I see. I like a challenge."

I scoffed, shaking my head. "I'm not playing anything. I'm just not interested in guys like you. Please, just let me pass."

Chase laughed, a cruel, mocking sound. "Aw, come on, Briar. We just want to chat. No need to be so uptight."

My cheeks flushed with anger and embarrassment. I wasn't uptight. I just had no interest in being another notch on their bedposts. I knew their type all too well—entitled rich boys that thought their shit didn't stink.

"I said I'm not interested," I repeated, my voice firm despite the slight tremble I felt inside. "Now, if you'll excuse me."

I tried to push past them again, but Chase stepped in front of me this time, his tall frame looming over mine. "What's the rush? We're just trying to be friendly."

His tone was light, but an undercurrent of menace made my skin crawl. I looked around the cafeteria, hoping someone would notice my distress and come to my aid. Still, everyone seemed oblivious, too wrapped up in their conversations to pay attention to the unfolding drama.

"I don't want your friendship," I said, my voice rising despite remaining calm. "I want you to leave me alone."

Felix's grin widened, and he leaned in closer, his hot breath tickling my ear. "You don't mean that, Briar. I think you're just playing hard to get. But trust me, I always get what I want in the end."

His words sent a chill down my spine, and I felt a surge of genuine fear. "I said I'm not interested," I repeated. "Now, if you'll excuse me."

Shoving past Felix, my shoulder collided with his chest. He stumbled back a step, and his eyes widened in surprise. I didn't wait for his reaction. Instead, I hurried out of the cafeteria, my heart pounding in my ears and their laughter echoing behind me. I clenched my fists, my nails digging into my palms. I hated how they made me feel—small, powerless, like a plaything for their amusement.

I thought about Medusa and how she had been transformed into a monster to protect herself from men. I wished I had that kind of power. But I was just Briar. Plain, unremarkable Briar. I didn't have the power of a goddess or the curse of a monster.

I took a deep breath, squaring my shoulders as I walked to my next class. I sat down in the back next to my friend Sadie. As I slid into my seat, she looked up from her phone, her brows furrowing as she took in my frazzled appearance. "What's wrong?"

I forced a smile. "Just had a run-in with the dynamic duo."

She rolled her eyes. "Felix and Chase? God, those guys are such tools. What did they want this time?"

I shrugged, trying to act nonchalant. "The usual. Just being their charming selves."

But Sadie knew me too well. She leaned in, her brow furrowed with concern. "Briar, if they're bothering you, we should report them. You know they've got a reputation…"

I shook my head. "And have the whole school talking about how I couldn't handle a little harmless flirting from the dream team? No thanks. I can deal with it."

She looked like she wanted to argue, but Professor Larson entered, and the lecture began. A few minutes into the class, the door opened, and Sebastian Blackwell, the campus bad boy, stumbled in, nodding his head at the Professor, who continued with his lecture. Sebastian took a seat to my right and met my gaze. His black hair fell across his forehead effortlessly, and his green eyes held a mischievous glint. He smirked at me, a dimple appearing on his left cheek. I quickly looked away, focusing on Professor Larson's lecture on cellular biology, but I could feel his gaze lingering on me.

Sebastian was an enigma on campus. He had transferred to Acadia Falls last year, and rumors about him spread like wildfire. Some said he was a trust fund baby who had been kicked out of his previous school for getting into too many fights. Others claimed he was a genius who had hacked into the university's system and changed his grades. Some said he had a record, others whispered about a tragic family history. But no one knew the truth about him, and he seemed to prefer it that way.

Despite his reputation as a brooding troublemaker, there was something intriguing about him. His quiet intensity drew people to him even

Chapter One

as his aloof demeanor kept them at a distance. I had seen him around campus, clad in his signature black leather jacket—constantly alone, always with his nose buried in a book. Unlike Felix and Chase, who hid their cruelty behind a veneer of charm, Sebastian wore his darkness on his sleeve.

Today had been a weird fucking day with boys.

I glanced at him, wondering what he would do in a situation with Felix and Chase. Would he cower and run like I had? Or would he stand his ground, unafraid of their taunts and threats? As if he sensed my gaze, he turned, his eyes locking with mine. For the slightest moment, I forgot how to breathe. There was an intensity in his stare, a depth that seemed to see straight through me. I felt exposed, like he could read every thought, every fear, every insecurity.

The end of Dr. Larson's lecture broke the moment. I quickly gathered my things, avoiding Sebastian's eyes, and hurried out of the room behind Sadie.

"So, there's a party at Hangman's Bridge tonight. You coming with?" Sadie asked, hopeful.

I hesitated.

Parties weren't really my scene, especially the ones at Hangman's Bridge. The old, abandoned bridge had a dark history, and the remote location made it a prime spot for all sorts of illicit activities. It was a place where inhibitions were lowered, and bad decisions were made. There were rumors that several bodies were decaying in the deep, dark water below the bridge, victims of ritualistic sacrifice, now evil spirits that clung to humans, making them go mad.

"I don't know, Sadie. Nothing good comes out of going to Hangman's Bridge."

"That's the point, Briar." She gave me a mischievous grin. "Come on, it'll be fun. We'll make some bad decisions, maybe even summon a ghost or two. Live a little, babe."

I sighed, knowing she wouldn't let this go. "Fine. But if I end up possessed by a demon, I blame you."

She laughed. "Deal. I heard Sebastian might be there."

I frowned. "Why would that matter?"

She waggled her eyebrows suggestively. "Oh, come on. I saw how you two were eye fucking each other in class. There's some serious tension there."

I felt my cheeks heat. "Don't be ridiculous. I barely know him."

"Exactly! This is your chance to get to know him better." She winked. "Maybe even biblically, if you know what I mean."

I smacked her arm, rolling my eyes. "You're impossible."

She laughed, linking her arm through mine as we left the building. "You love me. I'll pick you up at nine."

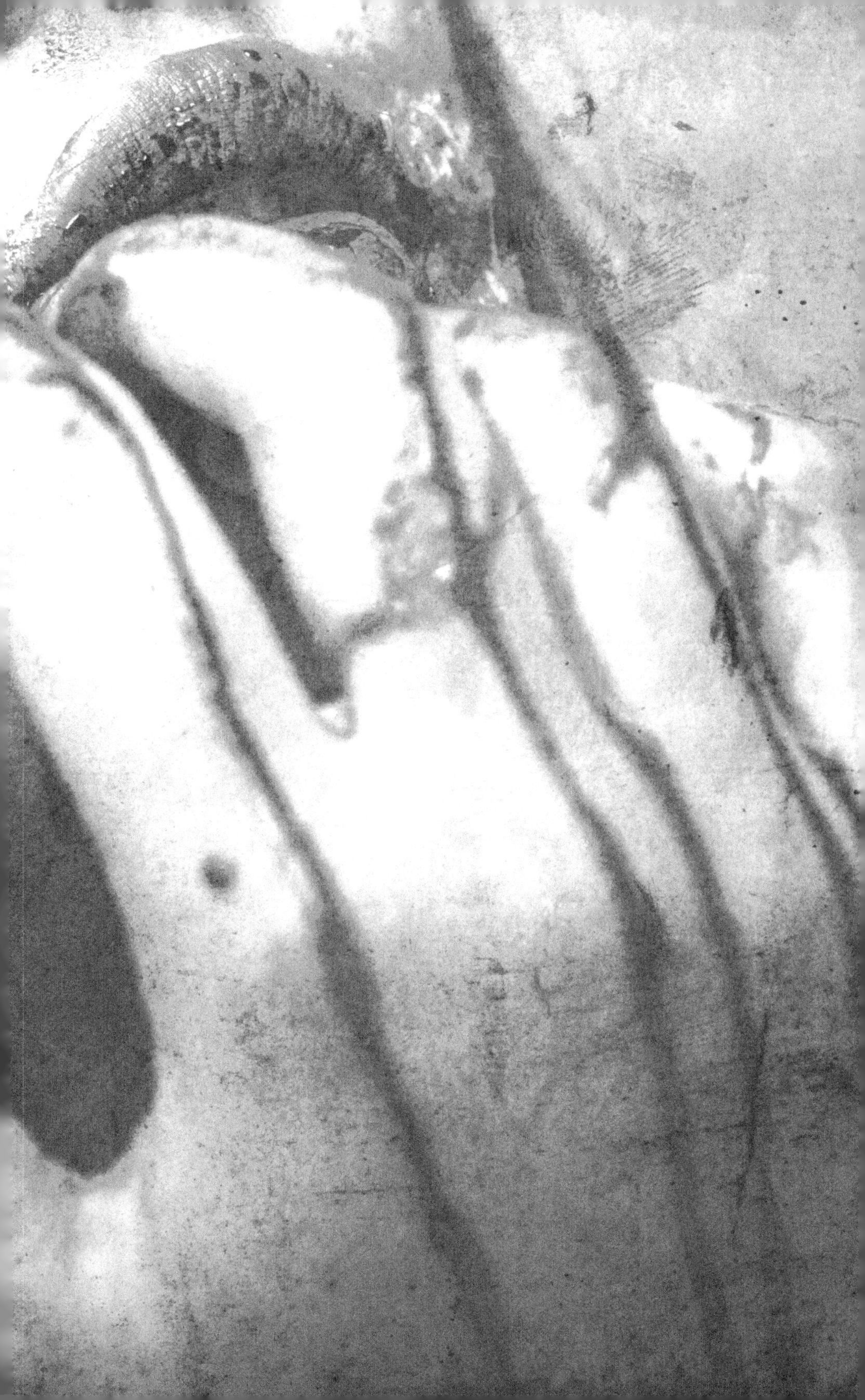

Chapter Two

The moon hung low and full in the sky, casting an eerie glow over Hangman's Bridge. The old, rickety structure creaked and groaned under the weight of the partiers as I walked across, Sadie at my side. The air was thick with the scent of cheap beer and cigarette smoke, the bass from the speakers thrumming through my chest. I tugged at the hem of my white sundress, suddenly feeling self-conscious. Sadie insisted I wear it and claimed my legs looked "killer." But now, surrounded by scantily clad girls and leering guys, I felt exposed and vulnerable.

I stood at the edge of the crowd, sipping from a red Solo cup filled with some noxious concoction Sadie had thrust into my hand. The bitter taste made me wince, but I welcomed the warmth that spread through my veins, easing some of my nerves.

"I'm gonna grab us some more drinks," she shouted over the music. "Linger with the locals. I'll be right back."

Before I could protest, she disappeared into the crowd. I sighed and leaned against the railing, staring at the dark water below. The river rushed by, with inky depths concealing her secrets. I turned to scan the crowd, my eyes landing on Felix, Chase, and their dum-dum posse. They were holding court in the center of the bridge, surrounded by giggling girls. Felix caught my eye and smirked, raising his cup in a mock salute. I quickly looked away.

"Not a fan of the dream team, I take it?"

I jumped to the sound of the voice behind me, turning to find Sebastian leaning against the railing, his green eyes glinting in the moonlight. He took a sip from his cup, but his gaze never left mine.

"They're not exactly my favorite people," I admitted, taking a swig of my drink for courage. The bitter liquid burned my throat but was a welcomed distraction from the intensity of the way he studied me.

He chuckled, a low, dark sound that sent a shiver down my spine. "I can't say I blame you. They're the worst kind of entitled pricks."

I nodded, surprised to find someone who shared my opinion of Felix and Chase. Most people on campus seemed to worship the ground they walked on, blind to their true nature. "They think they can take whatever they want, no consequences."

His jaw clenched, a flicker of something dark passing over his features. "Guys like that…they need to be taught a lesson."

There was an edge to his voice and a hint of danger that thrilled and unnerved me. I took another sip of my drink, letting the alcohol numb my growing unease. "And who's going to teach them? You?"

He smirked, and that dimple I secretly loved appeared. "Maybe. Someone should."

I studied him to gauge if he was serious or just posturing. A hardness in his eyes and a steely determination made me think he wasn't the type to make idle threats.

"Just be careful," I found myself saying. "They're not the kind of guys you want to mess with."

"Neither am I."

His words hung in the air between us. Part of me wanted to probe further, to unravel Sebastian Blackwell's mystery. But the rational part of my brain warned me to keep my distance. There was something about him, a darkness that drew me in and set off warning bells in my head.

I was saved from having to respond by Sadie's return, two fresh cups in hand. She glanced between Sebastian and me, a knowing grin on her face. "Well, I see you've found some company."

I felt my cheeks flush, but Sebastian just smirked. "We were discussing the finer points of campus politics."

Sadie laughed, "I'm sure you were." She grabbed my arm, pulling me away. "Come on, Briar. A game of truth or dare is starting, and we're playing." She turned back to Sebastian. "You too."

Chapter Two

I groaned and shrugged my shoulders apologetically at Sebastian. He shrugged and pushed off the railing. "Why not?"

We followed Sadie to a circle of people sitting cross-legged on the bridge, an empty beer bottle lying in the center. I recognized a few faces—Lila from my chemistry class, Asher from drama club, and Felix and Chase, who were whispering and snickering.

Felix's eyes lit up as we approached, a predatory grin spreading. "Oh look, everyone, the virgin girl and the school slut decided to join the fun."

I tensed, but Sadie just rolled her eyes. "Fuck off, Felix. We're here to play, not stroke your ego."

A few people snickered, and his grin faltered before he recovered. "By all means, join in. The more, the merrier."

We sat down, and I found myself wedged between Sadie and Sebastian. His leg brushed against mine, and I felt a jolt of electricity at the contact. I took a large gulp of my drink, trying to ignore how my skin tingled at his touch.

The truths and dares started tame enough—embarrassing confessions and silly stunts. But as the alcohol flowed and inhibitions lowered, the challenges became more risqué.

Felix spun the bottle next, and it landed on Lila. "Truth or dare, babe."

Lila giggled, her cheeks flushed from the alcohol. "Dare."

Felix grinned wickedly. "I dare you to make out with Chase for one minute."

Lila's eyes widened, but she nodded, crawling over to Chase, who leered at her like a hungry wolf. They kissed sloppily, all tongues and teeth, as the group cheered and wolf-whistled. This was precisely the kind of juvenile, degrading game I tried to avoid.

The bottle spun again, this time landing on Sadie.

"Truth or dare, Sadie?" Lila asked, wiping her mouth after disengaging from Chase.

Sadie smirked, never one to back down from a challenge. "Dare, of course."

Lila thought for a moment, then grinned. "I dare you to strip and run naked up and down the bridge."

Sadie laughed, already pulling her shirt over her head. "Easy."

I watched in disbelief as my beautiful blonde friend shed her clothes, tossing them in a pile beside her. The guys hooted and hollered as she stood completely naked, her pale skin glowing in the moonlight. She shot me a wink before taking off, her bare feet slapping against the wooden planks of the bridge. I admired her confidence, her utter lack of shame. I wished I could be more like that, comfortable in my skin.

She returned breathless and grinning, her cheeks flushed from exertion and excitement. She pulled her clothes back on and bowed as the group applauded her performance.

"Alright, my turn," she announced, reaching for the bottle. It spun in a blur, slowing until it stopped, the neck pointing at me.

Her eyes met mine and sparkled, and I knew she had nefarious plans for me. "Truth or dare, Briar?"

I swallowed hard, and my mouth suddenly dried. I knew Sadie, and I knew the dares she would make me do. The smart choice would be to choose the truth. But with everyone staring at me, expecting me to choose the truth, I found myself saying, "Dare."

A collective "ooh" went through the group.

Sadie's grin widened, and I immediately regretted my choice. "I dare you…" she paused for dramatic effect, "to kiss Sebastian for at least 30 seconds. And not just a peck, either."

My heart stopped. I risked a glance at Sebastian, who looked just as surprised as I felt. But there was something else in his eyes, a glint of curiosity, maybe even anticipation.

The group erupted in whistles and catcalls, Felix and Chase's jeers the loudest of all. "Looks like the virgin girl is going to get some action tonight!" Felix crowed.

"Come on, Briar. Don't be a prude," Chase taunted.

My cheeks burned with humiliation and anger. I met Sadie's eyes, silently pleading for her to take it back. But she just shrugged, a silent challenge in her gaze.

I turned to Sebastian, my heart pounding so loud I was sure everyone could hear it. He met my gaze steadily, a slight smirk on his lips. "You don't have to do this," he said quietly so only I could hear.

But I did. If I backed down now, I'd never hear the end of it.

"A dare's a dare," I said.

I leaned in, my lips brushing against his. They were soft and warm, and my lips tingled at the contact. What started as a chaste peck quickly deepened, his hand coming up to cup my cheek, his tongue teasing the seam of my lips. I parted them, granting him access, and he explored my mouth with skilled intensity. I lost myself in the feel of his mouth against mine. The catcalls and whistles faded into the background. His lips moved against mine with a hunger that took my breath away. He slid his hand into my hair, gripping gently as he tilted my head back, deepening the kiss. I clutched at his shoulders, my nails digging into the leather of his jacket.

Thirty seconds felt like an eternity, but it was not nearly long enough. When we finally parted, I was breathless and dazed, my lips swollen from his kisses. He looked equally affected, his emerald eyes dark with desire.

Someone cleared their throat loudly, and we broke apart, both of us breathing hard. I blinked as I came back to reality; my cheeks flushed with more than just the alcohol. The group stared at us, some with amusement, others with jealousy, and a few with disgust.

"Well, damn," Sadie said, breaking the tension. "That was hot."

"Who knew the virgin had it in her?" Felix laughed, his words slurred.

The group erupted into laughter and more catcalls. I ducked my head, my cheeks flaming. I couldn't bring myself to look at Sebastian, afraid of what I might see in his eyes. The game continued, but I couldn't focus. My mind kept replaying the kiss. The way his touch ignited something deep inside me. I snuck a glance at him and found him watching me, a small smile playing on his lips.

Ever the life of the party, Sadie grinned and picked up the bottle, spinning it with a flourish. "Truth or dare?" she cooed at Felix, looking him straight in the eye. The rest of the group fell silent, sensing the tension between them.

Felix smirked, clearly enjoying the attention. "Truth," he drawled, leaning back on his elbow and lazily draping an arm around Chase's shoulders.

"Okay," Sadie purred. "Tell me, Felix, how many girls have you actually slept with versus how many you brag about?"

The crowd gasped, and even Chase's smug expression faltered. Felix's composure slipped for a split second before he composed himself again.

"I'll let you find out for yourself," he countered with a wink, earning him a chorus of grossed-out noises from the group.

Sadie rolled her eyes, and Felix took his turn spinning the bottle. It landed on Asher from drama club, who reluctantly chose truth. "Alright," Felix said. "Tell us your most embarrassing hookup story."

A blush crept up Asher's neck as he shared a mortifying tale about a one-night stand that went wrong involving a flock of geese and a public fountain.

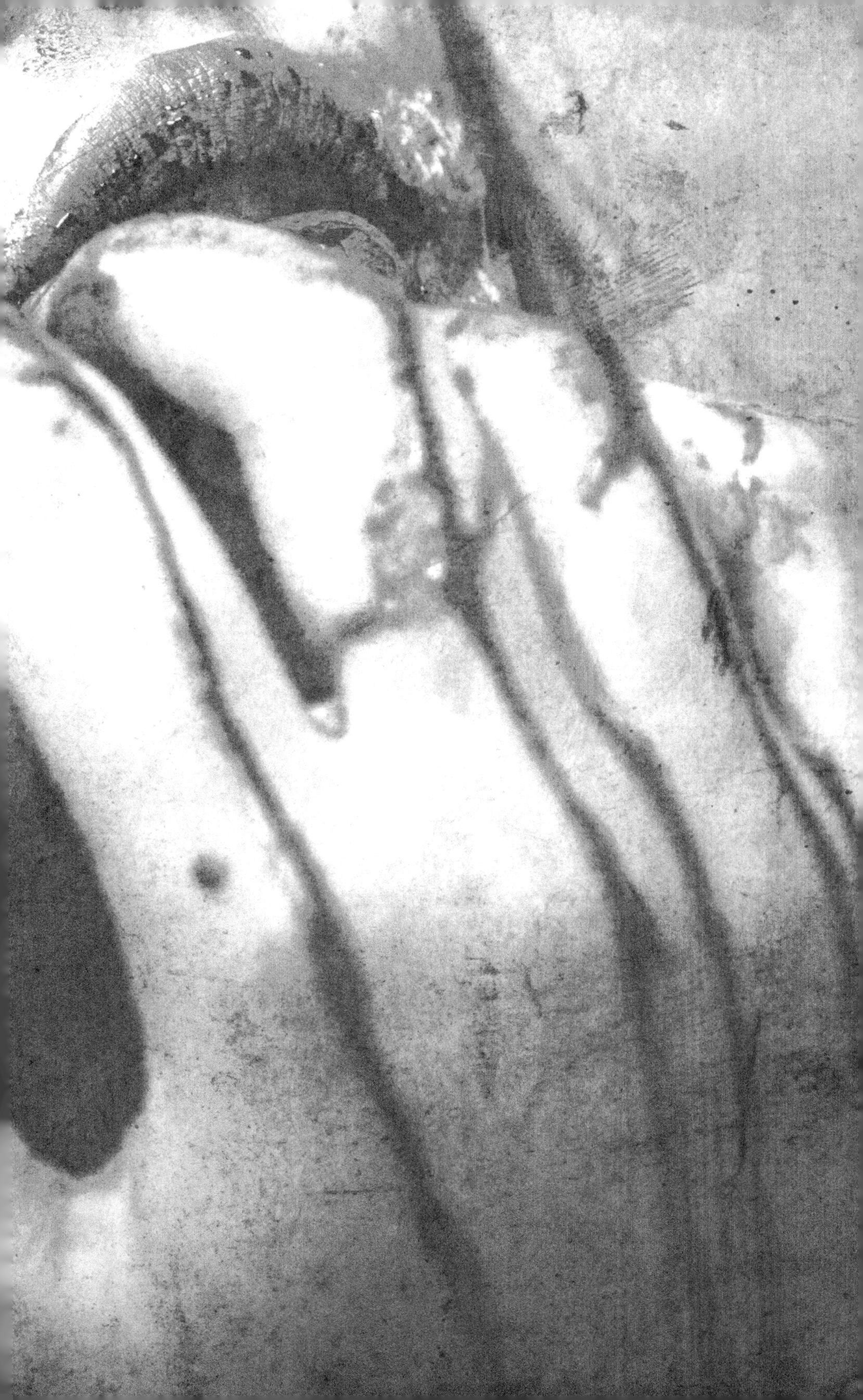

Chapter Three

The party was beginning to wind down, and only a few people were left, drunkenly stumbling toward their cars. Sadie had disappeared into the woods with Asher, and I needed to pee. Sebastian had disappeared somewhere, and I hoped it wasn't with another girl, but it's not like a kiss at a party meant he was mine.

"Damn it, Sadie," I cursed her and her vagina. But my scolding would have to wait. I needed to pee, and it didn't look like she was coming out anytime soon. I looked around, spying a trail leading down from the bridge to the trees.

I made my way down the trail, stumbling a bit in my slightly intoxicated state. The moonlight filtering through the trees cast eerie shadows, and I suppressed a shiver, wishing I had brought a jacket. The farther I ventured from the bridge, the quieter it became as the sounds of the party faded into the background.

I found a relatively secluded spot and hiked up my dress, squatting to relieve myself. As I finished, I heard a twig snap behind me. I whirled around, my heart leaping into my throat.

Felix stepped out from behind a tree, his eyes glinting with a predatory light. "Well, well, what do we have here?" he drawled, slightly slurred.

I quickly pulled down my dress, backing away. "What are you doing here, Felix?" I demanded, trying to keep my voice steady.

He stalked closer, a smirk twisting his handsome features. "I saw you sneak off alone. Thought you might want some company."

I shook my head, continuing to back away. "I'm fine. I was heading back to the party."

He lunged forward suddenly, grabbing my wrist in a painful grip. I cried out, trying to pull away, but he yanked me closer. "Don't be like that, Briar. We both know you want this."

His other hand groped at my breast, and I felt a wave of nausea. "Let me go, Felix!" I shouted, trying to wrench my arm from his grasp. But he was too strong. His grip was like iron.

"Come on, baby," he purred, his breath hot and rank with alcohol. "You can't tell me you don't feel the chemistry between us. The way you play hard to get...I know you want me."

"You're delusional," I spat, still struggling against his hold. "I've never wanted you. Not in class, not now, not ever."

His eyes flashed with anger, and his grip tightened, making me wince in pain as he bruised my arms. "Don't lie to me, you little slut. I saw the way you kissed Sebastian. If you'll open your legs for that freak, I know you'll do it for me."

Rage and disgust boiled inside me, overpowering my fear. "Let me go, or I'll scream."

He laughed, "Scream all you want, bitch. No one will hear you."

I opened my mouth to scream, but someone else's hand clamped over it from behind me, stifling my shriek. There was zero chance that hand belonged to someone other than Chase. I thrashed against their holds, but they were too strong. Felix grabbed my chin, forcing me to look at him. "You should have just been a good girl, Briar. We could have had some fun. But now, we're going to have to teach you a lesson."

I bit down hard on Chase's hand, and he yelped, his grip loosening just enough for me to wrench my head free.

"You bitch!" he wheezed.

"Help! Someone help me!" I screamed at the top of my lungs.

Felix backhanded me across the face. "Shut the fuck up!"

Tears streamed down my face as he shoved me to the ground, my head hitting a rock. Pain exploded through my skull, and my vision blurred. I felt his hands pawing at my body, tugging at my clothes.

"Hold her still," Felix snarled.

"I told you she was a feisty one," Chase growled, laughing as Felix groped me again.

Felix was on top of me in an instant, pinning me down with his weight. I scratched at his face, drawing blood, but he just laughed as Chase caught my wrists and slammed them to the ground above my head.

"I like it when they fight," he panted as he tore at my dress, the fabric ripping beneath his rough hands. I screamed again, thrashing beneath him, but it was useless. His eyes were wild, pupils dilated with alcohol and arousal. His free hand pushed up my dress, his fingers digging into the soft flesh of my thighs.

"Pl-please don't do this." I closed my eyes, a sob tearing from my throat.

But my pleas fell on deaf ears. He reached down, fumbling with his belt buckle. I squeezed my eyes shut, bracing myself for the violation, blood whooshing loudly in my ears. He rubbed himself against my entrance and thrust into me—not gently, not with love, but with pure wrath. I cried out as pain tore through me. Felix didn't care, however. Instead, he pounded into me, grunting with each thrust.

As his thrusts became more forceful, my cries mingled with the rustling leaves above us. He violated my body, ripping me apart, stealing what little innocence I had left. Tears streamed down my cheeks, mingling with the blood trickling from my split lip.

He smirked down at me, his eyes devoid of compassion or remorse. "See? I told you you'd like it," he panted as if the pain and humiliation I was enduring was somehow twisted pleasure.

I wanted to claw his eyes out, to make him feel even an ounce of the agony he was inflicting on me. All I could do was turn my head to the side, squeezing my eyes shut as I tried to separate my mind from the brutal violation of my body.

Felix's thrusts became erratic, his breaths coming in harsh pants. With a final grunt, he stilled above me. I felt his release inside me, hot and revolting. He collapsed on top of me, his sweaty body crushing mine.

"Fuck, that was good," he breathed into my ear. "I knew you'd be a great lay."

Then Chase took Felix's place. I lay there, motionless, silent tears streaming down my face as he panted above me, sweat beading on his forehead as he fucked me.

I remained still, unmoving like a corpse as Chase finished inside me, his grunts of pleasure a sickening contrast to my numb silence. When he was done, he pulled out, zipping his pants with a satisfied smirk. "Not bad for a virgin," Chase sneered, giving my bruised thigh a patronizing pat.

I didn't respond. I didn't move. I felt hollow. Numb. My body aching and defiled. I stared up at the white flowers near the water. *Cicuta maculata*...Water hemlock. A beautiful plant often mistaken for a fragile flower, but inside, it was poison.

My mind focused on the petals as it tried to separate itself from the broken shell of my body. I wanted to scream, to cry, to beg for help. But no sound escaped my lips. It was as if they had stolen my voice along with my innocence.

They stood up, adjusting their clothes while I lay there in my torn dress, my thighs sticky with their come and my virgin blood. I heard them whispering to each other, contemplating whether or not they should return to the party.

"We can't leave her here..." Chase whispered, "...she'll tell everyone."

"I'll lose my scholarship..." Felix hissed. "Kill her...throw her in the river."

I heard their words, but they sounded distant, muffled as if I was underwater. The river...they were going to throw me in the river. A spark of fear ignited in my chest, breaking through the numbness. I had to move, had to run. I tried to shift, to crawl away, but it was too late. They were going to kill me—silence me forever.

Felix straddled my body and wrapped his hands around my neck.

"Please...don't..." I managed to whimper.

His hands tightened around my throat, cutting off my air. I clawed at him, my nails leaving bloody scratches on his skin, but he only squeezed harder. Black spots danced in my vision as my lungs burned for oxygen. This was it. This was how I would die—raped and murdered, my body dumped in the river like trash.

"Why won't the bitch die?" Felix grunted as he slammed my head against the rocky ground.

Pain exploded in my head, my lungs screamed for air, and my vision was starting to turn black. I was dying, and no one was coming to save me.

Would Sebastian cry for me? Would they have a memorial at school in remem-

brance of the little virgin girl who disappeared like so many others at Hangman's Bridge?

And just like that, everything went dark and silent.

Chapter Four

The sound of rushing water and heavy footsteps pulled me out of the darkness. I could hear Felix and Chase mumbling, but I didn't dare open my eyes. If I played dead, they would leave me, and when they were gone, I could run and get help. I just had to lay here and try not to breathe. The cold, damp ground seeped through my clothes, chilling my skin. *No!* It was *wood* underneath me. They had brought me back to the bridge. And that sound of rushing water sounded just like it had when we were playing truth or dare.

I fought the urge to shiver, knowing even the slightest movement could give me away.

Someone's heavy boots shuffled closer, and I caught a whiff of sweat and stale cigarettes. A sharp kick to my side with a steel-toed boot took every ounce of willpower in me not to flinch or cry out in pain. My heart pounded in my chest, and I prayed they couldn't hear it over the sound of their heavy breathing.

"We gotta get out of here," Felix urged, his voice rising in panic. "If anyone finds out what we did…"

"Shut the fuck up!" Chase hissed. "No one's going to find out. We'll dump her over the side and pretend like none of this ever happened. Now tie a square knot and attach the end to this cement block," he instructed Felix.

Fuck.

The rope snaked around my ankles, its rough fibers biting into my skin. But I forced myself to remain perfectly still, not even daring to breathe.

"Hurry up," Chase growled impatiently. "Stop being such a pussy and get it done."

"I'm trying, okay?" Felix snapped back, his voice shaking. "It's not exactly easy in the dark."

After what felt like an eternity, the rope tightened around my feet, the weight of the cement block tugging at my legs. This was it. They were going to toss me over, and I would drown, my body sinking to the depths of the river, never to be found.

Tears threatened to spill from beneath my closed lids, but I blinked them back. I couldn't give up now. When they tried to lift me, I would fight with everything I had left. It was my only chance.

"Alright, on three," Chase said, grunting as he grabbed my shoulders. "One, two—"

I opened my eyes and slammed my head back into Felix's face, who was lifting my shoulders. His nose made a sickening crunch, and he stumbled back, howling in pain, clutching his nose as blood gushed between his fingers. I didn't waste a second. Ignoring the agony shooting through my body, I thrashed and kicked, my bound feet connecting with Chase's groin. He doubled over, cursing viciously. He lost his grip on my feet, and I fell to the ground, landing hard on my side.

Ignoring the searing pain, I rolled onto my back and kicked out with my chained feet, catching Chase in the knee. He howled in agony and dropped to the ground, clutching his leg. Using the momentum, I rolled to the side, narrowly avoiding tumbling over the edge of the bridge. The cement block teetered precariously, threatening to drag me into the churning waters below. Desperation fueled my strength as I clawed at the wooden planks, splinters digging into my fingertips.

Felix recovered first, his eyes blazing with fury above his blood-smeared face. He lunged for me, but I lashed out, my nails raking down his face, scratching his eyes. He reeled back, howling in pain and rage. Chase, still hunched over, fumbled for something at his waist. The glint of a knife caught my eye, and my heart seized with terror.

I had to get free. *Now.*

My fingers frantically clawed at the knots around my ankles, my nails tearing and bleeding as I struggled to loosen the rope. Chase's heavy footsteps thundered closer, the knife glinting menacingly in his hand.

"You stupid fucking bitch," he snarled, his face contorted with rage. "You're dead."

I kicked out wildly, my bound feet connecting with his shins. He stumbled back, cursing, but quickly regained his footing. Felix joined him, blood still pouring from his nose, his eyes promising vengeance.

My heart pounded so hard I thought it might explode. I had to get free. I had to survive. With a burst of adrenaline-fueled strength, I yanked at the ropes, ignoring the searing pain as they cut into my skin. The knots loosened slightly, giving me a glimmer of hope.

Chase lunged forward, the knife slashing through the air. I rolled to the side, the blade missing me by mere inches. The cement block tipped over the edge, and the sudden weight nearly wrenched my legs out of their sockets. I screamed in agony, my fingers scrabbling for purchase on the rough wooden planks.

Felix grabbed my hair, yanking my head back. I could feel his hot breath on my neck; the stench of his sweat and blood filled my nostrils. "Just let go," he whispered in my ear. "It'll be over soon."

The sharp pain in my scalp from his hold on my hair and my muscles screaming in protest as I fought to hold on was unbearable. I could feel my grip slipping from the planks, and I saw the look in his eye when he realized *he* was the reason I hadn't plummeted into the water below. And it was a look I'd never forget. With a wicked smile, his fingers released their hold on my hair, and the cement block pulled me down. The icy water engulfed me, stealing the breath from my lungs. The weight of the cement block dragged me down into the murky depths, the current tossing me around like a discarded plaything. Panic consumed me as I struggled against the ropes tight around my ankles. My lungs screamed for oxygen, but there was none to be found—only the suffocating embrace of the river. I clawed at the ropes, my movements growing sluggish as the icy water sapped my strength. Again, my vision blurred, black spots dancing before my eyes.

This was really it. I wouldn't make it out this time. I was going to die. Alone, in the depths of the river, at the hands of two fuck sticks. Betrayed and forgotten. The darkness closed in around me, the faint moonlight filtering through the water fading away. The last remnants of consciousness slipped away, and I disappeared into the inky blackness surrounding me.

OCTOBER FIFTH.

The day I died.

But also the day I was reborn. Pulled from the dark, icy depths of the river under Hangman's Bridge. A glimmer of light—faint, flickering, like a distant star in the night sky. At first, I thought it was just a trick of my oxygen-starved mind, a hallucination conjured up by my dying brain. But then a shadow moved within the light, growing larger as it approached—a voice called out to me.

"Briar, breathe. You have to fucking breathe."

Lips on mine. Air in my lungs. My eyes flew open, and I gasped, choking and sputtering as water spewed from my mouth. Strong arms cradled me, holding me to a solid chest. I blinked rapidly, trying to clear my blurry vision. A familiar face came into focus above me—dark hair plastered to his forehead, olive green eyes filled with relief.

"Sebastian?" I croaked, my voice raw and hoarse.

He nodded. "You scared the shit out of me."

I struggled to sit up. My body felt heavy and sluggish, my limbs refusing to cooperate. Sebastian helped me by supporting my weight as I leaned against him. The ropes around my ankles were gone, and in their place were angry red welts, the skin rubbed raw and bleeding. I winced as I tried to move my legs, pain shooting through my muscles.

"Easy," Sebastian cautioned, his arm tightening around my waist. "You're hurt."

I shook my head, gritting my teeth against the pain. "They killed me."

His jaw clenched, his eyes hardening with rage. "I know. I saw them dump you over the side. By the time I got to you…"

"Thank you," I told him.

"What do you want to do? I can take you to the police."

"No. You know just as well as I do their daddies own the police chief."

His lips thinned into a hard line. "We can't let them get away with this."

"*We* aren't doing anything. You can't be a part of what's next." I met his gaze.

His brow furrowed. "What do you mean? What's next?"

"*Revenge.*"

I don't know what fucked-up higher power gave me a second chance, and honestly, I don't care. All that mattered was that I was alive, and this time, I wasn't wasting a single fucking moment. I'd seen what's on the other side, and let me tell you, it ain't pretty. Death is just a vast, empty void. No pearly gates, no fiery pits, just an endless expanse of fucking nothingness. And it had been at that moment I understood Medusa's curse—the power to turn men to stone, to protect herself from their violence and cruelty. I survived that icy grave with the idea that my rage would be witnessed by the men who poisoned me with it in the first place.

I closed my eyes.

Something inside of me changed. I could feel this rage growing inside of me. I felt strong. Uninhibited. Primal.

Yes. Revenge is exactly what I would get.

But first, I would live.

Chapter Five

Sebastian brought me back to his place because I didn't want to go anywhere near mine. I didn't know if they were going to come by and make sure I was dead. Or make it look like I had left town in a hurry. When I cornered them, I wanted to do it my way.

On *my* terms.

When they least expected it.

Sebastian lived in a cabin in the mountains, nestled in a dense forest overlooking a serene lake. The winding road to his secluded retreat was treacherous, deterring unwanted visitors. The farther we got from the city, the more I felt like I could finally breathe. When I stepped inside, the warmth of the fireplace greeted me and cast dancing shadows across the walls of the dark, rustic interior. He locked the door behind us and drew the curtains.

"Go warm up near the fire," he said, gesturing toward the living room. "You'll be safe here," he said before heading into the kitchen and brewing a pot of coffee.

I stood near the fire, feeling the heat slowly penetrate my chilled bones. The crackling of the burning logs and the smell of burning wood filled the room, punctuated by the occasional pop and hiss. Sebastian returned with two steaming mugs of coffee and handed one to me. I wrapped my hands around it, savoring the warmth and the rich aroma.

"Do you want to talk about what happened?"

I let out a humorless laugh. "Honestly? I don't know."

"Well, I'm here if you want to talk. Why don't you take a shower? You can sleep in my room. I'll take the couch."

I followed him up the creaky stairs to the second floor. He showed me to his bathroom, a quaint space with a clawfoot tub and a small window overlooking the forest. "Towels are in the cabinet," he said, pointing to an antique armoire in the corner. "Let me know if you need anything else."

I nodded and watched him leave the bathroom. I turned on the faucet, letting the hot water fill the tub. Steam began to rise, fogging up the mirror. I undressed, letting my tattered white dress fall to the ground. My skin was covered in bruises on my neck, back, arms, and legs. Between my thighs was blood—now dried and dark red. I stepped into the clawfoot tub, the scalding water stinging my battered skin. I winced as I lowered myself down, the heat enveloping my aching body. The water slowly turned a murky reddish-brown as the blood and grime washed away. I scrubbed my skin raw in an attempt to clean any trace of those dicks off my body.

After turning into a prune, I emerged from the tub. My skin was pink and tender, but none of *them* remained in or on me. I wrapped myself in a soft, oversized towel and padded into Sebastian's room. He'd laid out a clean T-shirt and a pair of sweatpants for me. I put them on, savoring the feeling of soft, dry fabric against my skin. I crawled into the bed, pulling the covers up to my chin. The sheets smelled like him—a comforting scent of pine and woodsmoke.

I closed my eyes, but sleep wouldn't come. Flashes of the events that led me here played behind my eyelids—the faces of my attackers, their cruel laughter, the searing pain as they violated me. They had overpowered me, leaving me broken and bleeding on the cold, hard ground before they decided to dump me in the river like a bag of trash. A sob escaped my lips, but I quickly covered my mouth, not wanting Sebastian to hear.

Several days passed, and Sebastian stayed close in case I needed anything, like my guardian angel. But tonight, I couldn't stop tossing and turning in bed, the sheets tangling around my legs. I felt restless, like my insides were on fire, aching for something, anything to make the feeling that I was crawling out of my skin go away. I needed to move, to do something…anything to quiet the screaming in my head. Being violated and then killed changed me. The old me was gone, shattered into a million pieces that could never be put back together. But in her place, a new version of myself was emerging from the ashes—a phoenix rising from the flames of trauma and pain. And the new me needed a release.

I slipped out of bed, my bare feet padding softly against the hardwood floor as I went downstairs. Sebastian was stretched out on the couch, one arm over his eyes and a worn quilt over his legs. He stirred as I approached, lifting his head to look at me.

"Can't sleep?" he asked, his voice gritty and fatigued.

I shook my head and walked to him. I wasn't sure what I had planned on my way downstairs, but when I saw him, I had one thing on my mind. I stopped in front of the couch, and he sat up, his brow furrowed with concern. "What's wrong?"

I didn't answer.

Instead, I straddled his lap, my knees sinking into the cushions on either side of his hips. His eyes widened in surprise, but he didn't push me away. His hands instinctively came to rest on my waist, his touch gentle but hesitant.

"What are you doing?" he breathed.

I leaned in, pressing my lips against his in a desperate kiss. He hesitated momentarily before responding, his mouth moving against mine with growing intensity. His hands slid up my back, tangling in my hair as he pulled me closer. We kissed like we were starving for each other like we needed this connection to survive.

I shivered as his fingertips rubbed gentle circles on my bare thighs, and his lips trailed down my neck. My hands slid under his shirt, tracing the hard planes of his chest and abs. He groaned softly against my skin, his grip on my hips tightening.

"Are you sure about this?" I could hear the strain in his voice, like it was taking everything he had in him to stop touching me.

In answer, I rose on my knees and positioned myself over him, slowly grinding my hips against him, rubbing against his hard length beneath me. A low moan escaped his lips as I trailed kisses down his neck, nipping and sucking at the sensitive skin. His hands slid under the oversized T-shirt I wore, caressing the bare skin of my back and then moving over my ribs and higher. I gasped as his thumb brushed over my nipple, the bud pebbling under his touch. He tugged the shirt over my head and tossed it aside, leaving my upper body naked to his heated gaze.

"You're so beautiful," he murmured, reverence in his tone. He dipped his head, taking one aching peak into his mouth. I threaded my fingers through his hair, holding him to me as his tongue swirled and teased.

My skin felt electrified, every nerve ending humming with need. His touch was like a balm, soothing the jagged edges of my pain. I arched into him and pressed my breasts farther into his eager mouth. I was desperate for more contact, more friction, more of him.

I tugged impatiently at his shirt until he pulled it off, letting it fall to the floor. Reaching between us, I fumbled with the drawstring of his sweatpants. He lifted his hips, helping me push them down along with his boxers, freeing his straining erection.

I wrapped my hand around his length, stroking him from base to tip. He groaned, his head falling back against the couch. "Fuck, that feels good," he rasped, his hips bucking into my touch.

I positioned myself over him, rubbing his tip through my slick folds. We both moaned at the contact. I barely hesitated before I sank down on him, taking him deep inside me. I stilled for a moment, adjusting to the sting and how he stretched and filled me. He was twice the size of Felix and Chase, filling me and touching places I didn't know existed. He waited to see if I was okay, and I appreciated that, but I was more than okay. The aching feeling inside me was slowly disappearing as I began to move, rising and falling on his thick shaft. He met me thrust for thrust, our bodies moving in perfect sync. The only sounds were our ragged breaths and moans of pleasure, punctuated by the slap of skin on skin.

He sat up, wrapping his arms around me as he drove deeper, hitting a sensitive spot inside me. I clung to him, my nails digging into his shoulders, my cries of ecstasy muffled against his neck. Heat coiled tight in my belly, my inner muscles clenching around him. "Sebastian," I gasped, my voice strained. "Something is happening. I'm going to…"

"Let go, baby," he urged, finding my sensitive nub and rubbing tight circles. "I've got you."

His words pushed me over the edge, and my climax crashed over me in intense waves, my body shuddering against his. He followed right behind, his hips snapping up as he buried himself deep, spilling his warmth inside me with a guttural moan.

We stayed pressed together as we caught our breath. He stroked my back soothingly, placing soft kisses on my shoulder. For the first time since that night, I felt peaceful. A sense of control and calmness settled over me, and it felt good, powerful even. I felt re-energized, like a switch had been flipped inside me. The haze of trauma and fear that had been clouding my mind began to clear.

He must have sensed the shift in me. Pulling back slightly, he searched my face, possibly looking for any hint of regret in my eyes. "Are you alright?"

I met his gaze steadily and smiled. "That was exactly what I needed."

His brow furrowed slightly. "I hope you don't regret this. I feel like I took advantage of you…"

I silenced him with a finger to his lips. "You didn't. I wanted this. Needed it, even. Before they violated me, I walked through life cautious and afraid. I thought being a virgin was what I had to be because anything else would be seen as something negative. I wasn't alive before. Now, I feel different…awake. Being with you, having control over my own body, is something they didn't afford me. I don't feel ashamed. Fucking you made me feel alive. And I would never regret that."

His expression softened as he listened to my words. He brushed a strand of hair from my face and tucked it behind my ear. "So, you're saying you used me?" he teased.

I grinned mischievously. "Maybe just a little bit. But you didn't seem to mind too much."

He chuckled, pulling me closer. "No, I definitely didn't mind. In fact, feel free to use me anytime."

I playfully smacked his chest before reluctantly climbing off his lap. The fire had died down to glowing embers. He pulled his clothes back on while I retrieved my shirt and curled up against his side, resting my head on his shoulder. He draped an arm around me, holding me close. We sat in comfortable silence, watching the flames dance in the fireplace.

"Sebastian," I said quietly, lifting my head to look at him. "I'm going to make them pay, and I'm not sure you'll want to be a part of what happens next."

"What do you mean?"

I took a deep breath. "I'm going to hunt them down. And I will make them suffer the way they made me suffer. The moment they decided to violate me and leave me for dead, they created a monster. And now that monster wants blood."

He was quiet for a moment as he processed my words. "I'm not going away," he said firmly. "Whatever you're planning, I'm with you."

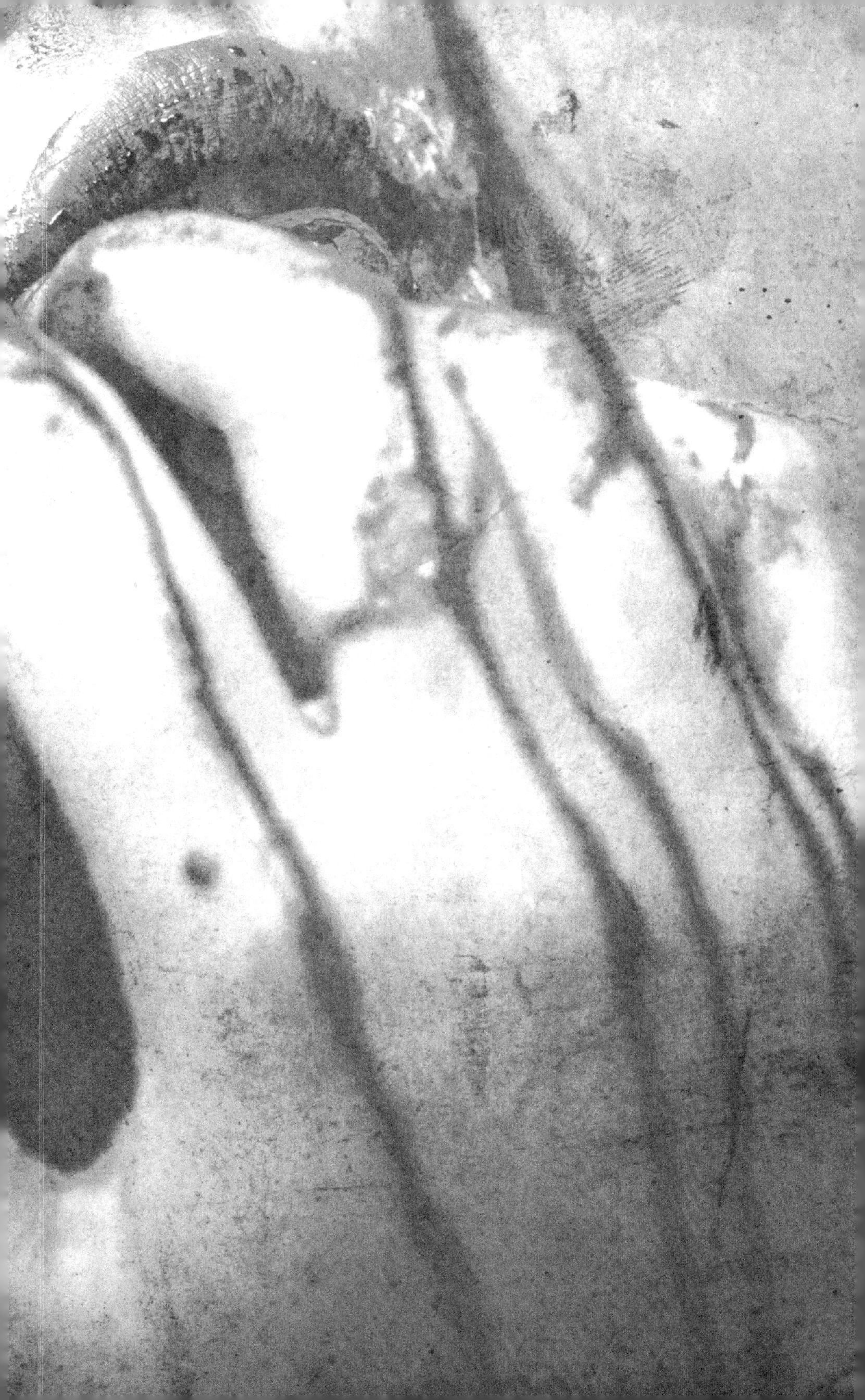

Chapter Six

I removed the flowers from the water hemlock I had picked and squeezed the cicutoxin from the stems into a small glass vial. The thick, brownish liquid shimmered with a faint amber hue as I held it up to the light. It was odorless and tasteless, precisely what I would use to get revenge. It had been two weeks since that night, and I had remained out of school to prepare, but I was ready. It was time.

"Are you ready?" Sebastian wrapped his arms around me and kissed my neck.

"I was until you started doing that."

"Hm, you mean this?" he whispered against my ear.

He traced a line of tender kisses down my neck as his hands slid under my shirt, caressing my skin and sending shivers rippling across my torso. I set the vial of poison down and turned to face him. I shoved him backward onto the bed and crawled on top of him, straddling his hips. My long, dark hair cascaded around us as I leaned down to capture his lips. His hands roamed hungrily over my body, digging into my hips and then pulling me flush against him. I grabbed his wrists and pinned them above his head as I bit his bottom lip.

He moaned in my mouth as I ground my hips against his hardness. His breath quickened, and his eyes darkened with lust. In one swift motion, he flipped us over so that he was on top, pressing me into the mattress. He ripped my shirt open, sending the buttons flying, and began kissing a trail of fire down my chest.

"Sebastian," I gasped, arching into his touch as he nibbled at my nipples. His hand slid down my stomach and deftly unbuttoned my jeans. I lifted my hips as he tugged them off, along with my lacy underwear. He gazed down at my naked body, eyes roaming hungrily over every curve. "You're so beautiful."

Then, his head dipped between my thighs. The first stroke of his tongue against my most sensitive spot made me cry out. My hands fisted in his hair as he licked and sucked. My eyes rolled back, and my toes curled as that fucking skillful mouth of his drove me higher and higher until I thought I might shatter. Just when I couldn't take anymore, he pulled his dick out of his jeans, crawled back up my body, and thrust into me with one hard stroke. He didn't fuck me gently—he knew I liked it rough. I craved it. I discovered many things about myself in the past weeks, and he let me use him however needed. I dug my nails into his back as he pounded into me, the headboard slamming against the wall with each thrust. I felt the stickiness of his blood caused by my nails, but he only groaned and fucked me harder.

"Harder," I begged him, nipping at his earlobe. "Make me come."

He obliged like the good boy he was, slamming into me with a force that pushed me across the bed, my head dangling off the side. The intensity built and built until my entire body tensed and quivered. With a few more deep, forceful thrusts, he sent me hurtling over the edge. I cried out his name, my inner walls clenching around his throbbing cock. He groaned, burying his face in my neck as his release overtook him. His hips jerked erratically as he spilled himself deep inside me.

With great reluctance, I pulled away and slid off the bed. I grabbed a maroon dress from the closet—since Sebastian ruined my shirt—and started getting dressed. He propped himself up on an elbow, watching me with an inscrutable expression.

"If you keep looking at me like that, we'll never make it to the school."

"Would that be such a bad thing? I'd rather stay here and fuck you until you can't walk."

I chuckled darkly as I slipped the dress over my head and smoothed it over my curves. "As tempting as that sounds, it's time."

After fixing my tousled hair and touching up my makeup, I grabbed my bag and the vial, tucking it safely into an inner pocket. Sebastian drove us to school, his hand resting possessively on my thigh the entire way.

As we walked through the front doors, heads turned, and whispers followed us down the hallway. Did they know the truth about what happened that night? Or had lies and speculation filled the void?

"Briar?" I heard Sadie gasp when I walked into the first period as if no time had passed. "Where the hell have you been? I've been calling and texting you for weeks. I thought something happened to you. I went to your house, and you weren't there. What the fuck?"

I figured she would be angry with me. But my absence was necessary, and I had already planned a lie to tell her to protect the reason I disappeared. Putting on my best apologetic facial expression, I hugged her. "I'm so sorry, Sadie. I had to leave town to visit my aunt in the mountains. I had no cell service, and it was rather urgent. I should have texted you, but it was just a whirlwind with planning the visitation and the funeral." The lie slipped easily from my lips, just as I had practiced.

"Oh my god! I didn't know your aunt died. Were you close?"

"Close enough," I answered.

Her eyes softened with sympathy as she squeezed my hand. "I'm so sorry for your loss. I had no idea. I feel terrible for being upset with you now."

"It's okay, you didn't know. I should have found a way to tell you. It just happened so fast after the party." I gave her a reassuring smile, even as the lie sat bitterly on my tongue. But there were far worse things I was about to do than deceive my best friend. Things that I had to protect her from, and if that meant telling a white lie about my whereabouts, then that's what I would do. I was securing my spot in Hell—no need to bring her along with me.

The day dragged on, each class blurring into the next. Sadie grilled me on my new coupling with Sebastian, and I gave her as many juicy details as possible because it seemed to perk her up, and she loved to hear about how her best friend got her cherry popped by the sexy bad boy. Even if it wasn't him who took my virginity, I still considered him my honorary cherry-popper. And this was my story now, fuck the truth.

"You look so different," Sadie said when I caught her looking at me.

"Different, how?"

"I don't know. More confident ... sexier? Like how you did your hair and makeup. That outfit is just killer. I love those boots."

I smiled at her compliment, "Thanks. I guess death changes you. Oh, and having sex with Sebastian Blackwell does wonders for a girl's confidence."

She giggled and playfully smacked my arm. "God, you're so lucky. He's like, the ultimate fantasy."

If only she knew the dark reality behind my 'lucky' situation.

The end of the lecture signaled lunchtime. I gathered my things and followed Sadie out of the building toward the campus cafeteria. Sebastian was waiting for me outside the doors, a cigarette dangling from his lips. He pulled me in for a kiss, and I tasted the smoke on his tongue. "I missed you," he murmured against my mouth. "I can't wait to get you alone later."

I nipped at his bottom lip, desire coiling low in my belly. "Keep talking like that, and we won't make it to later."

"Don't tempt me, Briar. I'll fuck you right here on the lawn in front of everyone if you keep looking at me like that."

Smiling, I took his hand and pulled him toward the cafeteria. "Later," I promised with a wicked grin. "Come on, I'm starving."

He nodded, his green eyes glinting dangerously. He knew the plan and his role. We headed to the cafeteria together, Sadie trailing behind us, still gushing over how hot we looked together. If only she knew the monsters lurking beneath our exteriors.

We entered the bustling cafeteria, the din of chatter and clattering trays assaulting my ears. My eyes scanned the room until they landed on my targets—Felix and Chase. They were sitting at their usual table, but this time they weren't surrounded by their loyal entourage of jocks and cheerleaders. The sight of their smug, entitled fucking faces made my blood boil. I had spent the past two weeks meticulously planning every detail of my revenge. Before long, I would get the satisfaction of watching them take their last breaths.

Sebastian's hand slid reassuringly to the small of my back as we approached the table. Felix looked up first, his eyes widening in shock, before he nudged Chase, who shared in his surprise. Their faces paled as I confidently walked to their table, and they looked me up and down like they were seeing a ghost. But they quickly recovered. It's not like either could say, *'We thought you were dead. How'd you survive us throwing you over a bridge with a cement block tied to your ankles?'*

"Well, well, well. Look what the cat dragged in," Felix sneered, trying to cover his unease with bravado. "We were starting to think you transferred schools...or ended up in a mental ward."

Chase snickered beside him, his gaze raking over my body in a way that used to make my skin crawl. Now, it only fueled my fire. "Damn, Briar, being a crazy bitch looks good on you. That body is even hotter than I remember."

I smiled coldly at them, every fiber of my being screaming to lunge across the table and wrap my hands around their throats. But I maintained my composure. After all, revenge is a dish best served with calculated precision.

I slid into the seat across from Felix while Sebastian settled next to me, his arm draped casually over my shoulders in a clear display of possession.

Felix's eyes narrowed as he took in our joined hands. "I see you've been busy. Sebastian. Finally managed to seal the deal with our resident ice queen, huh? She must be a wildcat in the sack to have you on such a tight leash already?"

Chase leaned forward, a malicious glint in his eyes. "Tell me, Briar. Is his dick as big as they say? Or were you too drunk to remember, just like at the party?"

I forced on a sugary, sweet smile. "Oh, trust me, it's even bigger," I winked, squeezing Sebastian's hand. "But I do remember that night perfectly, Chase. Every. Single. Detail." I let my words hang in the air, heavy with unspoken meaning. "But anyway, I just thought I'd stop by and see how you both were doing since the party. You look like you might be coming down with something, Felix." I gestured toward the dark circles under his eyes. "You should try getting some sleep."

Felix shifted uncomfortably in his seat, his gaze darting away from mine. "I'm fine. Just been busy with football practice and shit."

I tilted my head, feigning concern. "Are you sure? You look a little...under the weather. Both of you do, actually." I turned my gaze to Chase, who was picking at his lunch with a frown.

"We're good," Chase snapped. His eyes flashed with annoyance.

I held up my hands in mock surrender. "Hey, I'm just looking out for my fellow classmates. We wouldn't want anything bad to happen to either of you, now would we?"

Sebastian chuckled darkly beside me, his fingers trailing along my collarbone. "Briar's right. You two should take better care of yourselves. Eat your veggies, stay hydrated, and get plenty of rest. You never know when your health might take a turn for the worse."

Felix and Chase exchanged an uneasy glance, clearly unsettled.

"Fuck off," Felix spat.

I smiled. "Suit yourself." I stood up, smoothing my dress. "Enjoy the rest of your lunch. It was good seeing you both. We really should catch up."

I turned on my heel and sauntered away from their table. Sebastian's hand rested possessively on my lower back as we made our way to an empty table in the corner. I could feel Felix's and Chase's eyes boring into me, a mixture of confusion, unease, and barely concealed hostility.

Good.

Let them stew in their paranoia, but this was only the beginning of what I had in store for them.

As we sat down, Sadie joined us, her eyes wide with curiosity. "What was that all about? Since when have you all been buddy-buddy with Felix and Chase?"

I shrugged nonchalantly, picking at my salad. "Oh, you know, just catching up. Making sure there are no hard feelings after the party."

Her brow furrowed. "Hard feelings? What happened at the party that I missed?"

I waved my hand dismissively. "Nothing important. Just a little misunderstanding. But it's all water under the bridge now." I punctuated my statement with a pointed look at Sebastian, who smirked.

She looked like she wanted to press further, but thankfully, she let it drop. We ate our lunch, chatting idly about our classes and upcoming events. But my mind was elsewhere, running through the final details of my plan.

Felix and Chase were scheming the rest of the day, wondering what I was up to or if they were crazy. I knew it in every fiber of my being. They would war between being paranoid, I would turn them in, and what they should do about that. They couldn't let me walk around, fearing I would ruin their lives forever. If I were correct, they would finish what they started. Which meant they would come for me.

And I would be waiting.

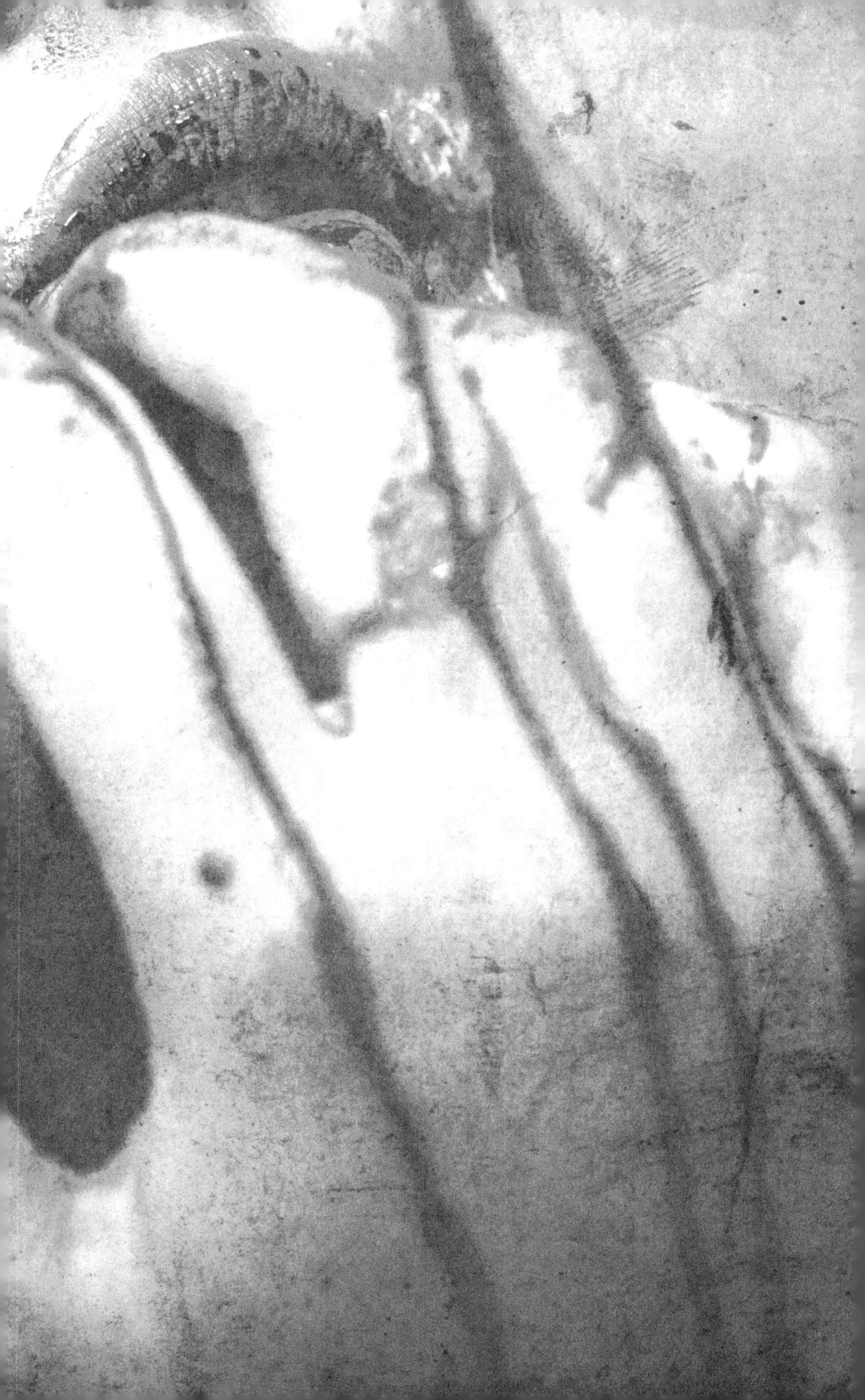

Chapter Seven

The sun had set behind the trees, and a chill had set in the air. Fog swirled through the trees, weaving an eerie tapestry of mist between the gnarled trunks. Felix and Chase had tailed us as we drove to Sebastian's place, staying back far enough that they thought we wouldn't have noticed. As we pulled up to the cabin, I glanced in the rearview mirror and saw Felix's headlights turn off and idle at the end of the lane. We pretended not to notice we had been followed and entered the house like usual.

I carefully set the scene, knowing it wouldn't be long before they came for me. They were weak, pathetic men who preyed on women—who took it as an affront to their manhood that they couldn't finish what they started. They would have to rectify it, especially when I had been so emboldened to show up, alive, taunting them with innuendos and hidden meanings.

For my plan to work, I had to make it look like I was alone because they were cowards. They wouldn't make a move if they knew Sebastian was around. Which meant I had to convince Sebastian to leave me long enough for them to come inside.

"Are you sure you want to do it this way?" he asked as he wrapped his arms around me from behind.

"No," I sighed and turned around to face him. I wrapped my arms around his neck and met his concerned gaze. "But there's no other way.

Felix and Chase will never make their move if you're here. I don't want to look over my shoulder, waiting for them to jump me. I saw the desperation in their eyes. They are scared, and they want to get rid of me as quickly as possible before I wake up and turn them in."

"I don't like the idea of using you as bait. What if something goes wrong? What if they overpower you before I can get back?"

I forced a reassuring smile. "I'll be fine. I'm not worried because I know you won't be far. Once they're inside, they'll be playing right into my hands. Trust me, this is the only way to end this once and for all."

He exhaled sharply through his nose, clearly wrestling with the decision to leave me. He searched my eyes for a long moment before finally nodding. "Alright. Promise me you'll be careful. Don't take any unnecessary risks."

"I promise." I pressed my lips against his, savoring the feel and drawing strength from his presence.

With great reluctance, he pulled away. He grabbed his coat and headed for the front door, pausing to give me one last look. "I'll be close," he said again as if to convince himself as much as me.

I nodded, not trusting my voice. The door closed behind him with a soft click, and suddenly, the cabin felt much larger and emptier.

I poured three glasses of whiskey and sat on the couch, watching the fire flicker and crackle in the fireplace while straining my ears for approaching footsteps.

It didn't take long.

Less than twenty minutes had passed when I heard the unmistakable crunch of gravel, and then the doorknob slowly turned. The front door creaked open, inch by inch, and the floorboards groaned under the weight of their footsteps as they crept into the room, believing they had caught me unaware. I kept my eyes fixed on the fire, my hand casually resting on the arm of the couch.

"Well, well, well," Felix's voice slithered through the air like a venomous snake. "If it isn't the one that got away."

I turned my head slowly, meeting his cold, predatory gaze. Chase stood slightly behind him, his eyes darting nervously around the dimly lit room. They moved around me with exaggerated caution.

"Felix. Chase," I greeted them calmly as if we were old friends. "Care for a drink?" I gestured to the glasses of whiskey on the coffee table.

Felix's eyes narrowed. "Cut the bullshit. You know why we're here."

I raised an eyebrow. "Do I?"

He took a step forward. "You should be dead."

I let out a humorless laugh. "I am dead."

Chase shifted uneasily. "Let's just get this over with, Felix. I don't like this."

"Shut up!" Felix snapped, not taking his eyes off me. "This bitch has caused us enough trouble."

I sat calmly, taking another sip of my drink. I watched Felix pace behind the couch, shifty-eyed, as he watched me.

"What's the matter, Felix? I thought you'd like me drunk, just like last time."

His eyes flashed with anger and something else—fear, perhaps. He stopped pacing and gripped the back of the couch, his knuckles turning white. "You think you're clever, don't you? Toying with us?"

I swirled the amber liquid in my glass, feigning nonchalance even as my heart pounded. "And here, I thought we could have a civilized conversation. You know, clear the air between us."

Chase let out a nervous laugh that sounded more like a whimper. "She's playing games with us, man. Let's just do what we came here to do and get out of here."

Felix ignored him, his gaze fixed on me. "You expect us to believe that it's all just a big coincidence you're here, in this cabin, waiting for us?"

I shrugged, taking another sip of whiskey. The burn in my throat steadied me, fueling the fire of my resolve. "Believe what you want, Felix. But I'm not the one who looks guilty right now—sneaking into a woman's home uninvited, with murder in your eyes. What would the police think of that, I wonder?"

His face contorted into a snarl. "The police will never find out because there won't be anything left of you to find. We'll make sure of that this time."

He stalked toward me, pulling out a knife, the blade glinting menacingly in the firelight. Chase shifted nervously, glancing between Felix and me. "Maybe we should just go, man. This isn't worth it."

"Shut up!" Felix growled, his eyes never leaving mine as he rounded the table. He shifted his gaze to the whiskey bottle on the table, keeping his knife trained on me as he grabbed the bottle and took a big gulp, the brown liquid dripping down his chin. He thrust the bottle behind him. "Drink this and stop being a pussy, Chase," he said, and once

Chase grabbed it and started gulping, he wiped his mouth with the back of his hand. "We're finishing this."

I remained seated, my posture relaxed, even as every muscle in my body tensed, ready to spring into action. Felix took another step closer, the point of his knife now mere inches from my throat.

"Any last words?" he sneered.

I met his gaze unflinchingly. "Just four."

He grabbed me by my throat and threw me to the ground. The air rushed out of my lungs as my back slammed against the hardwood floor. Felix loomed over me, his eyes wild with a crazed fury. He pressed the knife against my throat, the cold steel biting into my skin.

"Let's hear them then," he snarled. "Your last words before I slit your pretty little throat."

"You're. Too. Late. Felix."

Confusion flickered across his face for a split second before it twisted into a mask of rage. "What the hell are you talking about?"

Behind him, Chase began to sway on his feet, his eyes growing unfocused. The whiskey bottle slipped from his fingers, shattering on the hardwood floor. Felix whirled around at the sound, his knife lowering slightly. "Chase, what the f—"

Chase projectile vomited and stumbled forward, clutching at his throat, a choked gurgle escaping his lips before he fell to the ground, convulsing.

Felix stared at him in shock, then slowly turned back to me, realization dawning in his eyes. "You…poisoned the whiskey." He lunged at me with a roar and kicked me in the stomach. The blow of his boot knocked the wind out of me, but I fought through the pain, rolling to the side just as the knife plunged into the floorboards where my head had been a second before.

I scrambled to my feet, adrenaline pumping through my veins. Felix yanked the knife free, splinters of wood flying through the air. He advanced on me, his eyes glinting with rage.

"I'm going to gut you like a fish, you bitch."

But even I could see his strength waning as the hemlock started to take effect. I circled the couch, keeping it between us as he pursued me with unsteady steps, the knife trembling in his grip. His face had taken on a sickly pallor, a sheen of sweat glistening on his brow.

"You're not looking too good, Felix," I taunted.

He lunged at me again, but his movements were sluggish and unco-

Chapter Seven

ordinated. I dodged his clumsy swipe, and he stumbled, crashing into an end table. The lamp toppled to the floor with a crash.

Behind him, Chase had gone still, his eyes staring sightlessly at the ceiling. He was still alive but frozen.

One down.

Felix pushed himself upright, his chest heaving with labored breaths. He fixed me with a venomous glare, hatred burning in his bloodshot eyes. "You're dead," he rasped. "You hear…me? Dead!"

He charged again, but his legs gave out halfway. He fell to his hands and knees, the knife clattering to the floor. I kicked it away, sending it skittering out of his reach.

Felix crawled toward me, his fingers clawing at the hardwood. "I'll kill you," he wheezed. "I swear I'll—"

His words cut off as a violent spasm wracked his body, and he, too, vomited his stomach contents before he collapsed onto his back, his limbs jerking and twitching as the poison ravaged his system. Foam flecked his lips as he gasped for air, his eyes bulging in their sockets.

I stood over him, watching impassively as the life drained from his face.

"You shouldn't have come here, Felix," I said softly. "But I'm so glad you did."

He tried to speak, but only a gurgling moan escaped his throat. His hand grasped weakly at my ankle as his fingers spasmed. I stepped out of his reach, my lip curling in disgust.

In the distance, I heard the sound of tires crunching on gravel. Sebastian, right on cue. I glanced at the clock on the mantel. He had given me just enough time.

Felix's body shuddered and then went still, his sightless eyes staring at the ceiling. His chest was still rising, but it was faint.

The front door burst open, and Sebastian rushed in, his eyes wild. He took in the scene before him—Chase's motionless form, Felix's, the broken glass, and the overturned furniture. His gaze landed on me, and he crossed the room in three strides, pulling me into his arms.

"Are you alright?" he asked urgently, his hands roaming over me, checking for injuries.

I nodded. "Everything went according to plan." He touched a cut on my neck from the knife, and his face darkened. "Mostly."

"I shouldn't have left you alone."

I placed my hand over his, gently pulling it away from my neck.

"I'm fine, Sebastian. It's just a scratch. We needed them to think I was vulnerable, remember? Everything is fine. I'm fine."

His gaze drifted to Felix's and Chase's still forms. "Are they…?"

"Not yet," I said. "The hemlock will keep them paralyzed while I finish this."

Stone.

He nodded grimly. "We can't let them live. They'll come after you again if you do."

"I know."

I walked over to Felix's paralyzed body and crouched down beside him. His eyes were open but unseeing. I could see the rise and fall of his chest, shallow and labored. The hemlock coursing through his veins rendered him helpless, at my mercy just as I had been at his not so long ago.

I leaned in close, my lips brushing against his ear. "How does it feel, Felix? To be powerless, unable to move or speak while someone stands over you, deciding your fate?"

A strangled noise escaped his throat, a futile attempt at a scream or a curse. I smiled coldly.

"Shh, don't strain yourself. It'll all be over soon." I stood up and turned toward Chase, who lay paralyzed a few feet away, his eyes wide with horror. I knelt beside him. "What's the matter, Chase? Isn't this what you wanted—to get me alone, finish what you started that night?"

His eyes were bulged as he tried in vain to speak or move. I patted his cheek mockingly. "Don't worry, you'll get your turn. I want you to watch what happens to your friend first."

Rising, I walked to the kitchen and opened one of the drawers, searching for the right tool. I dug through the spatulas and mixing spoons until I found it.

A pestle.

I returned to the living room, where Sebastian stood nearby. His arms were crossed, and he watched me impassively. I pressed the tip of Felix's dropped blade against his throat, applying just enough pressure to dimple the skin without breaking it. "You know, I thought about killing you the same way you tried to kill me. Choking the life out of you, feeling your pulse fade beneath my fingers. It would be poetic, don't you think?"

I increased the pressure slightly, and a thin trickle of blood welled up, stark red against his pallid head, a gurgling whimper rising in his throat.

"But that would be too quick," I continued, easing the knife back. "Too merciful. After what you put me through, I thought I should return the favor."

I walked over to Chase, each step deliberate and measured. His terrified eyes tracked my movement, pleading silently for mercy he knew he didn't deserve. I crouched down beside him. "You always were the follower, weren't you, Chase? Never had the guts to stand up to Felix, even when you knew what he was doing was wrong."

A tear leaked from the corner of his eye, trailing down his temple and disappearing into his hair.

I felt no pity.

"Raping me was bad enough. You could have stopped him from dumping me into the river that night. You could have helped me. But you did nothing." My voice was cold, devoid of emotion. "And for that, your punishment will be equal to his."

He made a garbled sound, a pathetic attempt at an apology or a plea. I neither knew nor cared which. I rolled the pestle in my hands, feeling its satisfying weight. Behind me, Sebastian watched silently, his face an unreadable mask. But I could feel the tension radiating off him, the coiled energy of a predator waiting to strike. He would let me take the lead on this, I knew.

This was *my* revenge to exact.

My demons to put to rest.

"Help me get their pants and briefs off."

Sebastian stepped forward, and together, we roughly yanked down Felix's and Chase's pants and underwear, leaving them exposed and vulnerable.

I gripped the pestle tightly and knelt between Chase's legs. "You took something from me that night. Something I can never get back." I leaned down and whispered, "Now it's my turn to take something from you."

Felix made a strangled sound behind me, to which I said, "Don't worry, Felix, I'll be with you soon enough."

I gripped the pestle tightly, my knuckles turning white as I pressed the blunt end against his puckered hole. I pushed the pestle in hard, feeling a grim satisfaction at his choked scream, muffled by his paralyzed vocal cords. I was relentless, driving the stone instrument deeper, grinding and twisting. Crimson blood began to pool around the base.

I withdrew the blood-slicked pestle and stood up, breathing heavily. Chase had tears pouring out of his eyes, and his legs twitched spasmodically, his breaths coming in ragged pants. His lips were blue, and I knew it wouldn't be long until he took his last breaths.

Breathing hard, I turned to Felix, who lay there urinating on himself in mindless terror, knowing he was next.

"Your turn," I said coldly. I knelt between his splayed legs. "If you could speak, I imagine you'd be begging for mercy. But you showed me no mercy when you held me down and took turns raping me. When you strangled me and tossed my body in the river like garbage. You destroyed my life that night. You killed the person I used to be. I remember every detail, Felix. And, now, I'm returning the favor."

I positioned the pestle and drove in hard, feeling flesh and cartilage tear and rupture. I continued the assault, panting with the effort, ignoring the warm blood splattering my hands and arms. I kept going until the pestle met resistance, and I was sure the damage was irreparable.

He lay there, frozen; his bladder had released, and the acrid stench of urine filled the air. I wrinkled my nose in disgust. "Look at you," I sneered. "Not so tough now, are you?"

But I wasn't done.

The rage inside me gave me the strength to punish him for myself.

For all the women who had ever been violated by men who used their power and control to destroy us. Just because they could. For every woman whose life was ruined. For every scream ignored, every plea for mercy laughed at.

This is for them.

This is for me.

I raised the pestle high and brought it down with brutal force between his legs. There was a sickening crunch, and his body jerked. If he could have screamed, it would have been ear-splitting. And again. Pulverizing flesh and bone with cold, methodical fury until Felix's genitals were an unrecognizable mess of gore. He made hideous gurgling noises, choking on his blood as it bubbled up his throat. His eyes had rolled back, showing only the whites as he finally passed out from the unimaginable pain.

I stood up, my arms aching from the exertion. I stared down at their broken, bleeding bodies dispassionately. Chase had gone still, his eyes staring blankly at the ceiling. Felix clung to life, but barely.

They would never hurt another woman again.

The thick, coppery scent of blood permeated the air. The pestle slipped from my numb, gore-slicked fingers and clattered to the floor. My legs buckled, and I would have fallen if Sebastian hadn't caught me, pulling me against his chest. A raw, primal sound tore from my throat—half sob, half scream. The floodgates opened, and I wept, great heaving sobs that wracked my entire body.

For the girl I used to be.

For all that had been ripped away from me.

For the stain on my soul that would never wash clean.

For the monster they created.

Chapter Eight

"It's over," Sebastian said quietly. He stroked my hair and murmured soothing words I couldn't quite make out. I clung to him, my fingers digging into his back as if he was the only thing keeping me tethered to the light, not letting me drown in the darkness. He didn't try to hush me or tell me it would be alright. He let me grieve for all that I had lost, for the innocence that had been ripped away, and for the part of myself that had died that night in the river.

When my sobs finally subsided into shuddering breaths, he gently tilted my chin up to meet his gaze. His eyes were soft with understanding and … desire.

Desire that I felt, too.

I pulled his face down to mine and kissed him fiercely. Hungrily. The salty taste of my tears mingled with the metallic tang of blood on my lips. He returned the kiss with equal fervor as his hands roamed over my body. I pulled him down on top of me, and our hands tore at each other's clothes with desperate urgency, buttons popping and fabric ripping in our haste to feel skin against skin.

He knew I needed to feel something visceral and primal and alive. He touched and kissed me with reverent intensity, worshipping my body with his hands and mouth, slowly piecing me back together with each caress. Blood had pooled underneath us from the carnage I had inflicted on Chase and Felix, but neither of us cared. The orange glow from the fireplace illuminated the blood splatters and handprints that covered us both now.

When he finally entered me, I cried out, arching against him. He stilled, cradling my face between his hands, his thumbs brushing away the remnants of my tears. "Look at me," he whispered. "You've never been more beautiful than you are now. Stay with me."

I met his gaze, losing myself in the depths of his eyes, the slick slide of blood and sweat on our skin as he thrust into me, claiming me, branding me as his. I raked my fingernails down his back and urged him to go deeper. Harder. His touch grounded me, pulling me back from the abyss. As he drove into me again and again, the chill that had settled in my bones disappeared. Sebastian's touch, his body joined with mine, was like a baptism, washing away the stain of Felix's and Chase's violation. I was reborn, forged anew in blood and fire and flesh.

Our gasps and moans mingled with the crackle of the fire, and then all the horror and pain was replaced with searing, cleansing ecstasy. I shattered apart, crying out his name. His body tensed above me, his breaths coming in ragged pants as he neared his peak. With a final thrust, he buried himself deep inside me and groaned, spilling his warmth into me. I clung to him, my release cresting over me in waves, my inner walls clenching around him. For a few blissful moments, there was no pain, no blood, no death. Just us, joined as one, breathing each other's air as he buried his face in the crook of my neck.

The room was silent now except for our ragged breathing and the soft pop of embers in the hearth. Sebastian pressed tender kisses along my jaw, my cheeks, my eyelids—each one a silent promise. We lay tangled together on the blood-smeared floor, limbs entwined, hearts pounding in sync. The fire had burned down to glowing embers, casting the room in a soft, muted light. Felix and Chase were two crumpled heaps nearby, their blood congealing in dark pools around them.

Slowly, reluctantly, he lifted his head and gazed down at me, his eyes dark with emotion. He brushed a strand of sweat-dampened hair from my forehead. "Are you okay?" he asked softly.

Sebastian pulled out of me and rolled to his side, gathering me against his chest. We lay there on the bloody floor, our limbs entwined, listening to the crackling of the dying fire. My mind felt clearer than it had in weeks, no longer clouded by the constant fear and dread that had haunted me since that fateful night.

Chapter Eight

"What do we do now?" I asked quietly, tracing patterns on Sebastian's sweat-slick skin.

"We clean up," he replied calmly. "And then we do whatever the fuck we want."

I nodded, a small smile tugging at the corner of my lips. Sebastian always had a way of making even the darkest situations seem manageable.

We carefully disentangled ourselves and rose to our feet, surveying the gruesome scene before us with detached practicality. The cloying scent of blood hung heavy in the air, mingling with the musky aroma of sex. Crimson footprints and smears marred the hardwood floor—a macabre Jackson Pollock painting. Felix's and Chase's corpses lay crumpled and broken, their faces frozen and discolored, a testament to the brutal justice I had meted out.

"I'll get some garbage bags and bleach from the kitchen," Sebastian said, his voice steady and reassuring. "You start gathering anything that might have our DNA on it—the pestle, the whiskey glasses, the lamp."

I nodded, grateful for his level-headed guidance. We worked methodically and efficiently, moving in sync like a well-oiled machine. I collected the incriminating items while Sebastian laid out the garbage bags and started wiping down surfaces. We stripped off their blood-soaked clothes and shoved them into a bag along with the rug, couch cushions, and any other fabric that bore incriminating stains.

Next came the bodies. Sebastian pulled their car to the front door, and we loaded them inside. He had everything all planned out. We would drive their car to the top of the cliff, push the car over the side with their bodies inside, and let them rot in the hundred-foot lake below. The night was pitch black, the only light coming from the cabin's windows behind us, casting eerie shadows across the gravel drive.

I slid into the passenger seat while Sebastian took the wheel. The engine roared to life, and we pulled away from the cabin. We drove through the dark, winding roads up the cliffside, the headlights cutting through the inky blackness. The car rolled to a stop at the cliff's edge, and Sebastian put it in park. We got out of the car and circled to the rear. Sebastian popped the trunk, and together, we hauled their lifeless bodies out, grunting with the effort. His face was half in shadow as he looked at me. "Are you ready for this?"

I gazed out to the black expanse of the lake far below, a sense of eerie calm settling over me. "I'm ready," I said quietly.

We put them in the front seat and buckled them in. The night air whipped through my hair, carrying the scent of pine and lake water. The keys dangled from the ignition, and the engine was still running. I took a deep breath, savoring the crisp night air. Sebastian put the car in drive, idling forward, slowly inching toward the edge.

Sebastian's hand found mine, our fingers interlacing. "Together," he said softly.

I nodded, squeezing his hand. "Together."

The car teetered momentarily, then tipped and plunged down the cliff face, metal screeching and glass shattering as it careened and bounced off the jagged rocks. We stood at the precipice and watched its fiery descent; the tail lights glowing like the eyes of a demon being dragged back to hell. With a final distant splash, the car hit the dark waters and slowly started to sink, bubbles rising to the surface as water filled the interior. Within minutes, it had disappeared entirely into the black depths of the lake, leaving no trace behind except the fading ripples.

For a long moment, the only sound was our ragged breathing and the faint lap of waves far below. Then Sebastian exhaled slowly, pulling me into his arms. I leaned into him, resting my head on his chest, listening to the steady thrum of his heartbeat.

It was over.

Truly, finally over.

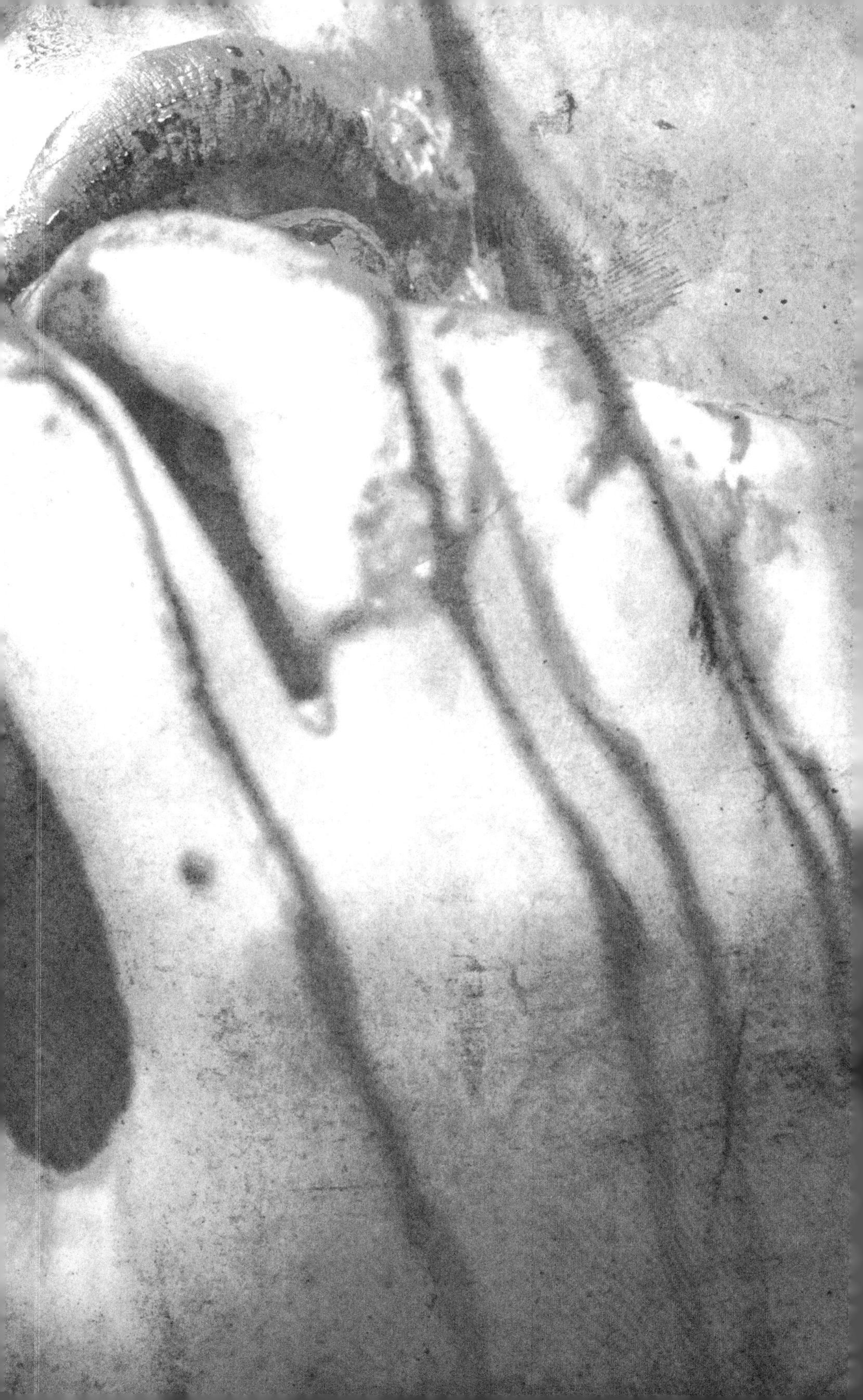

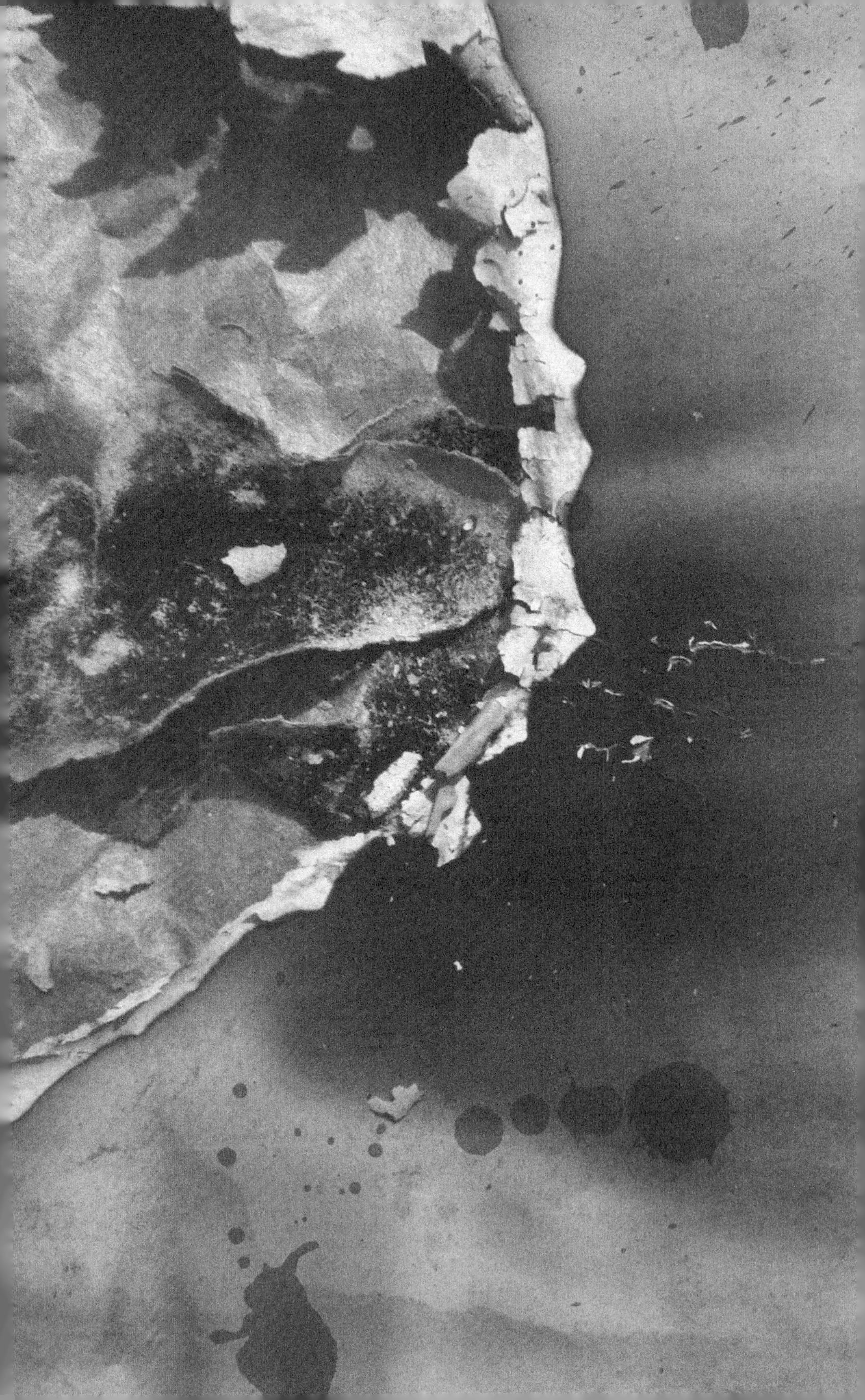

Silhouettes of Sin

Kamila Garaz

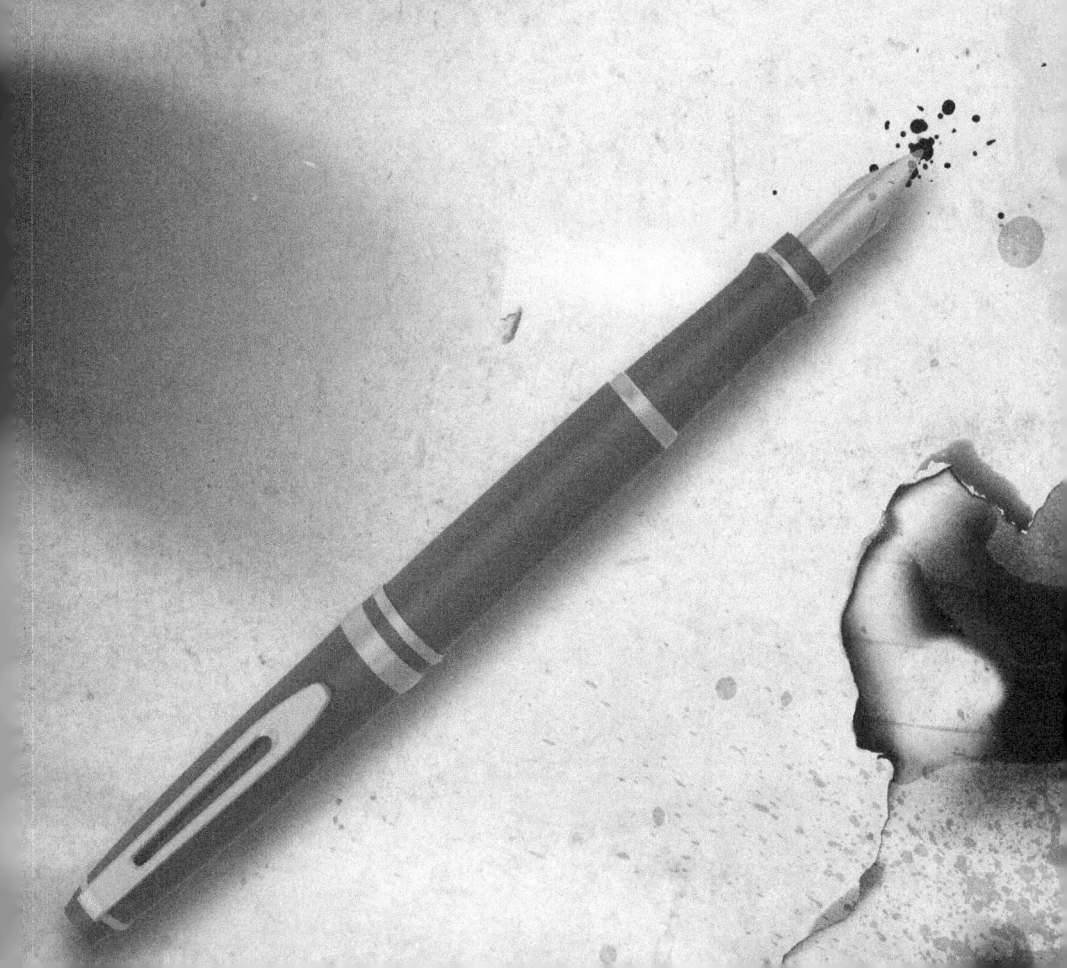

Dedication

To my vengeful women. Send that S.O.S.
Fuck men.
No body, no crime.

Code Name Key

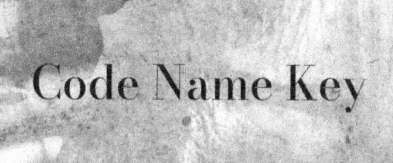

For Cris:
Queen from Jude
Mommy from Riley
Wifey from Frankie
Peaches from Blake
Reina from Noah

For Jude:
Pecas from Cris (Freckles)
Naughty Girl from Riley
Firefly from Frankie
Pixel from Blake
Sunshine from Noah

For Riley:
Wildcat from Jude
Estrella from Cris (star)
Trouble from Frankie
Rebel from Blake
Siren from Noah

For Noah:

Rebel from Jude
Bubbles from Riley
Mama from Frankie
Lovey from Blake
Muñeca from Cris (doll)

For Frankie:
Buttercup from Jude
Foxy from Riley
Esposa from Cris (wife)
Daddy from Blake
Shadow from Noah

For Blake:
Shortcake from Noah
Goddess from Riley
Supergirl from Frankie
Venus from Jude
Bebita from Cris (little baby)

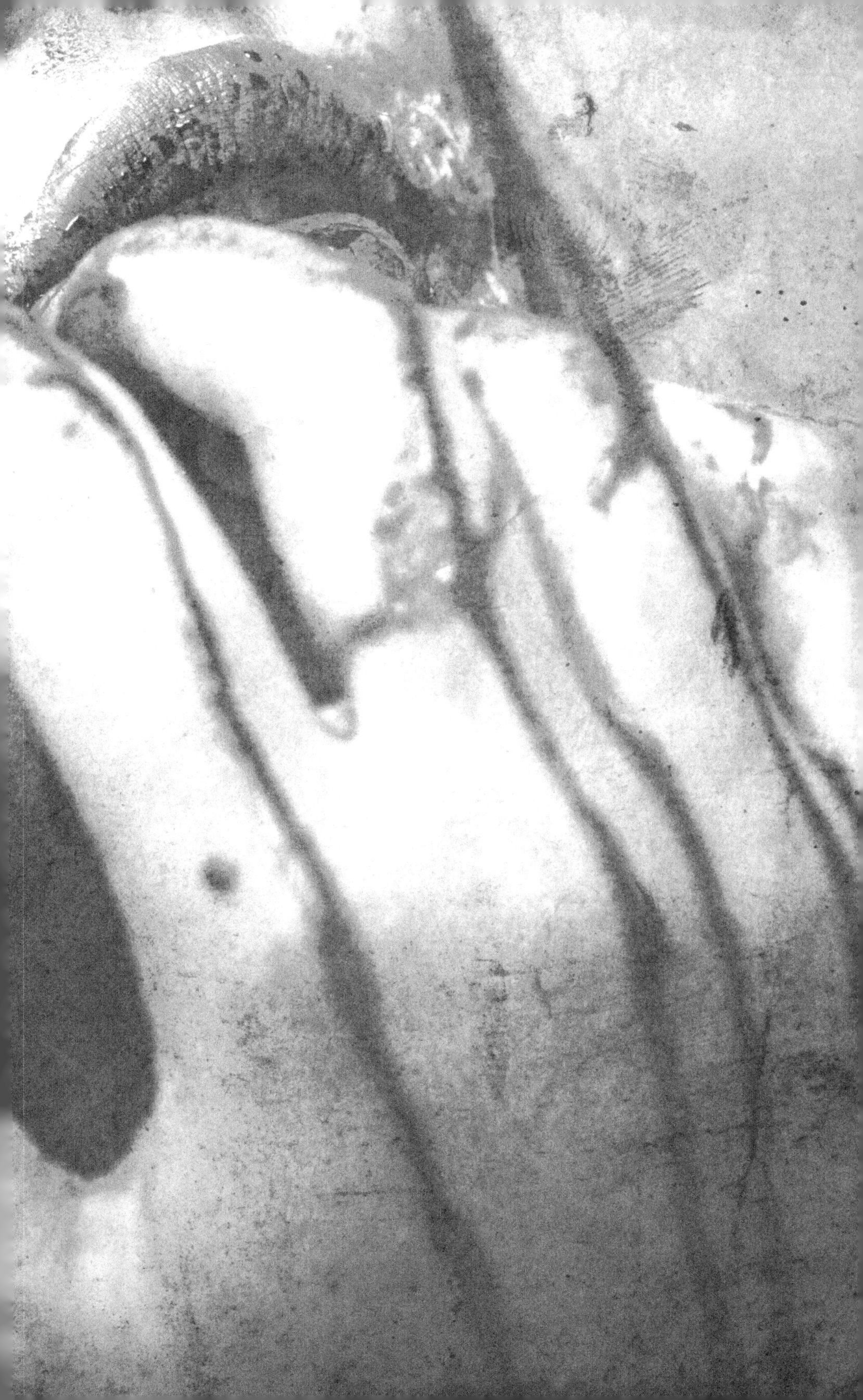

Prologue

It Takes A Bitch To Know A Bitch, Bitch

Blake

Three Years Ago

New York is loud, bright, and full of assholes. Tonight's no different — especially on this cold winter evening, when the cars honk in the distance, and the city lights illuminate New York.

The whipping cold air causes goosebumps to overwhelm my body as chills shoot through me. Opening the door, one last chill encloses me as I step inside for my next meet-cute.

Look at me — romanticizing trauma... Sue me for trying to make light of my work. But when you're newly eighteen and two years into high-end escorting, sometimes you've gotta laugh just to stay sane.

After-all, I must do what I can to get through the torment these disgusting men put on my body.

Making my way through the Sapphire hotel, my heels repeatedly resound against the marble floor, I head towards the bar, where I spot my client.

He's slouching over the counter, a drink in one hand and a lit cigar in the other, chatting it up with the bartender, who clearly couldn't care less. His dry, brittle blond hair is tied up into a low bun, sitting in his pressed silk maroon suit with his back toward me, the tips of his black plain-toe oxfords barely touching the floor.

Sighing, I stop to adjust my dress when a sudden movement to my left catches my eye.

A burly man dressed to the nines in black from head to toe leans against the front desk, his eyes pinned on me. I don't miss how his eyes wander up and down my body for several moments, and when his eyes meet mine again, the smirk on his face sends chills up my spine.

He returns his gaze to the receptionist as she finishes tapping on the keyboard, sliding a room key across the counter. The beautiful, petite woman, with her short black bob hairstyle and piercing dark brown eyes, bestows a panty-dropping grin that would make anyone fall to their knees. He picks up the key and executes exactly what is expected and returns a beaming smile, and she does something I know far too well.

There's a fast, visible twinkle in her eyes—one that screams she's got him right where she wants him.

I loosen my coat, showcasing more of my dress, and as I trek down the quiet lobby, I see that there are only two other men in here who are sitting at a nearby table beside the bar, looking like they are engrossed in a close, quiet conversation.

I turn my head, and my eyes meet the man who'll use my body for the next hour.

Jesus, fuck. He's hideous. Baring his not-so-million-dollar smile and showcasing his crooked yellow teeth.

You wouldn't know how massive he is while he's sitting down. Total catfish — nothing like the photo he sent me when we arranged this.

I usually prepare my purse with essentials I might need when I know someone is twice my size. I'm used to scrawny tech bros who want to get their dick wet for the first time and billionaire heirs who want to have sex without feelings being involved.

Jared, here, being my first time with a CEO of one of America's biggest banks.

He clutches my arms, bringing me closer as he leans in, whispering, "Hi, little red. You look incredible. How about we take this upstairs? I'm eager to take off all your clothes and make you mine."

He turns his head quickly and puts out his cigar on the ashtray beside his whiskey. I take that moment to shiver and scrunch my nose in disgust.

Jared reeks of a mixture of smoke from his cigar, whiskey, sweat, and the overwhelming spicy musk of his cologne. I fix my face into a big, bright smile and chuckle as I swat his shoulder.

"You're so naughty. I'd love to, sir," I utter sweetly.

Ugh, I hate that I need to pretend I'm interested like this.

"Come on, Little Red. The elevators are this way," he announces, entwining my hand with his. I roll my eyes at the insistent nickname he's going to keep calling me all night.

God forbid I'm short and have red hair. Come up with something original, idiot.

I'm so lost in thinking of how I could overpower him that I don't even see him press the button to the elevator. He forcefully pulls my body forward, almost yanking my arm out of its socket.

I yelp from the agonizing pain it sends up my arm, and tears form in my eyes. I look up, preparing to play it off and give him my best pouting face, but this motherfucker has other plans when a sinister smile plasters his wrinkly ass face.

That's when it hits me — I fucked up. Bad.

My eyes widen when I see the two men who were sitting at the table beside Jared, and the burly man I saw checking in with the receptionist. Oh, fuck. I'm in so much trouble.

Just as I'm about to scream, the men crowd me, and Jared covers my mouth to silence me. I bite down hard on his hand, and he hisses, quickly letting go and startling me when he swings his other hand, slapping me across the face so hard that I stumble to the ground and grab my face; the tears I was trying to hold in fall down my reddened cheeks.

"Feisty. We love that. You'll need that fire after we're through with you."

One of the men, a tall, scrawny man, clearly younger than the rest, lifts me up and throws me over his shoulder. The elevator doors open, and two more men await to escort us to a penthouse room to the far left.

303.

I'll remember that number for the rest of my life. Because I know today will change me.

Fuck. Fuck. Fuck.

Why did I not take precautions when accepting Jared as a client? I thought reviewing his background and status was enough, but if I didn't even know he was twice my size, there's bound to be more I missed.

Never again. Never will I make that mistake. If I somehow survive this, I will put my all into doing absolutely anything else. I've always loved science, and I'm good at it. That's it. I'll do that.

Just survive, Blake. Just survive, and you'll be a new person.

The door opens to an almost empty penthouse, and I remain quiet as this younger man takes me to the bedroom. He throws me on the crisp white sheets and removes my red stiletto heels.

Through the chaos of men entering the room, each ripping a piece of my clothing, and my willingness to close my eyes and let them taint my body, I almost don't hear the tell-tale sign of a room key being used.

"Oh, this bitch is perfect. You did such a good job getting us this one, Jared. I got you next time." I close my eyes, hoping that whoever has entered is here to save me from this hell hole.

The sound of heels clinks faintly against the penthouse floor, and I smile.

Women. Oh, hell yeah.

For the first time since this nightmare started, I feel something like hope.

Taking a deep breath, I smile subtly, ready for these assholes to get what's coming to them. With my clothes discarded and my naked body on full display, the door to the bedroom kicks in. My eyes flutter open, and two women stand side by side carrying guns along with knives strapped to their thighs.

"Well, it takes a bitch to know a bitch, bitch. Aren't you all a bunch of small dick whores who think they can take advantage of a young girl? Looks like everyone needs to be taught a lesson. What do you think, Noah?" a tall, curvy woman with olive skin says. Her long, dark brown wavy hair flows down just below her heaving breasts, accentuating curves under her skin-tight black satin dress adorned with killer red platform heels.

"I think they do, Cris. And look at them with their little noodles out for us to cut off. Dibs on the fucker with the greasy man bun and the little skinny twelve-year-old. We're going to have so much fun. Frankie will have her work cut out for her." I lock eyes with the beautiful brunette from the receptionist's desk, displaying a glimpse mixed with sympathy and strength.

"Listen here, sweetheart, we don't want to hurt you. How about you both come here and join in on the fun? Two whores like you look like you need a good fucking," Jared states as he turns around, advancing on them.

The receptionist—I believe the other woman called her Noah—chuckles and swiftly aims her gun with a silencer attached and shoots Jared in the kneecap. He grimaces in pain, doubling over and dropping to the floor with a loud thud. The other men immediately back away from me, tuck their cocks, zip their pants, and retrieve their guns from their backs.

They aren't fast enough. The burly man is down on the ground after a knife to the gut. Two more men take shots to the neck from Cris, while Noah has the skinny man in a headlock, putting him to sleep.

It's like I'm frozen, watching a movie I can't pause as I lie there watching these strong, ruthless women fight my attackers. Noah peers into my eyes as she lets go of the man, his body lax against the floor.

"Come on, Blake. Let me grab you a robe from the closet, and then you can step outside. Our girlfriend, Frankie, is waiting and ready to take you wherever you want. We'll deal with this, okay?" Noah opens the closet and retrieves a fluffy white robe with the Sapphire logo on the back. I hear voices and distant laughs coming from Noah's ear and realize she has an unrecognizable earpiece attached. Cris fights off one of the other men as he has her pinned by the throat against the wall, but she takes her knife and aims for the man's dick and pierces through, hitting an artery.

Lifting myself from the bed, I slide into my heels, my clothes ripped to shreds beside them. Tears well in my eyes, fearful of what could've happened if these two beautiful and caring women didn't step in.

"Here you go. Go outside, and we'll grab your things when we're finished. Don't worry about a thing." Lost in Noah's beautiful eyes, she slides the robe around my shoulders while I slip my arms through the holes.

She smiles, patting my shoulders and nodding for me to go. I match her nod and proceed to the penthouse door.

Opening the door, I block out the amplified voices, men's screeching, and blood gurgling and shut them behind me as I run into the hallway.

"Woah, woah, woah. Easy there, Miss Blake." My eyes dart up, and in front of me stands a woman covered in intricate tattoos that wrap around her neck, stretching across her chest and extending down both of her arms, not stopping until they reach her fingertips. They're gorgeous, almost as gorgeous as her.

She holds her hand in front of her, stopping me from running away, and says, "I'm Frankie. Do you want to wait next door before I take you where you need to go? Or do you want to go now? Your choice."

I don't know how to answer that. Am I curious enough to wonder what they do with those guys? Or do I feel so indebted to them for saving me from my life changing forever?

I think there's only one answer that makes sense at this moment.

"Next door. I'll wait next door."

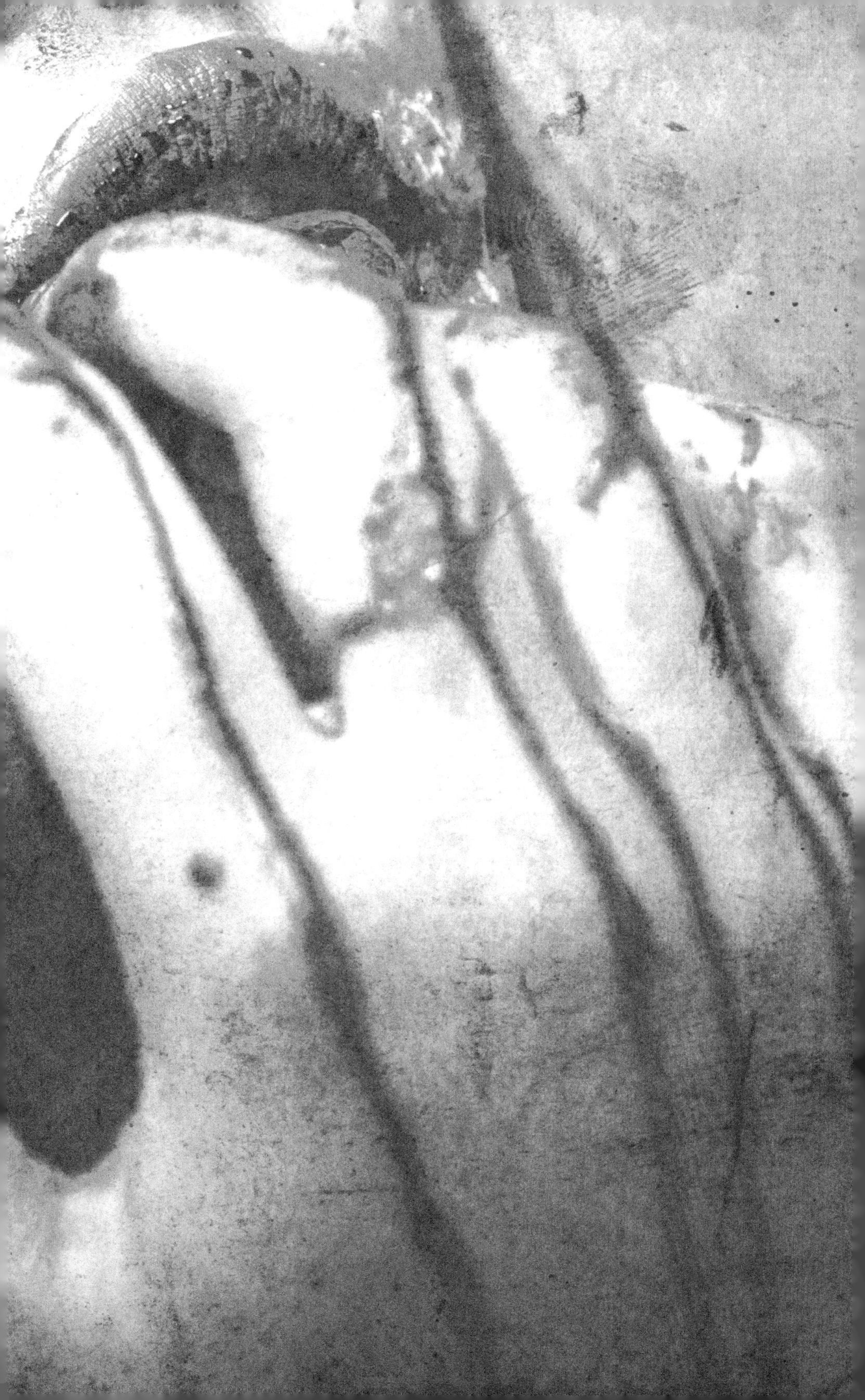

Chapter 1
Riding A Strap

Jude

Three Years Later

"Shh, you're going to get us caught, Wildcat. I'm supposed to be working here," I murmur, dragging my mini wand vibrator up and down Riley's puffy clit. Her fair skin glistens with sweat from the assault I'm putting her body through.

She came into my foxhole, her eyes beaming as she silently begged me to pleasure her. This is where I conduct my behind-the-scenes hacking and communication with those needing our help.

So, technically, if one of my beautiful girlfriends comes in here looking distressed, it's my duty to do whatever I can to help her — and if that happens to mean satisfying her sexually, then so be it. You'll never see me turn down a chance to see my Wildcat scream as I make her come.

This place wouldn't exist without Cris. Thanks to her, I not only have all the fancy equipment I could ever possibly need, but I finally have a purpose—a reason to use my self-taught skills for good.

Cris and I met after I saw her about to walk into an ambush once she killed a mutual target.

A known rapist congressman who I was trying to dig up dirt on as a source for blackmail. But after seeing Cris walk out of his room with blood staining her suede, nude trench coat and the swarm of security she was seconds from encountering as she made her way toward the elevator, I knew I needed to reach out to her.

I immediately ran her face through my facial recognition software, and just like that I pulled up her contact, and on the second ring she picked up. After brief hesitation, she followed my step-by-step directions and got out of that hotel without a trace.

Since then, we have joined forces, along with our girlfriends and built an underground hitwoman team. We specialize in killing high-profile men, ranging from congressmen, billionaire CEOs, domestic partners, and rapists. We call ourselves the Silhouettes of Sin.

The women who hire us need help escaping from toxic and unsafe situations, and we do just that.

Each of us has a specific set of skills, and while I mainly hang back in my foxhole, directing my team through everyone's earpieces, I am very much still a part of the process. It's become a part of me, and I'd do anything to keep it going.

"Yeah, busy working my pussy, naughty girl." My eyes meet hers, and a wicked smirk forms on my face.

"You know, I'd bet with your desk drawer filled with so many sex toys, you"—She gasps, the pleasure hitting her as she moans, her weak voice trying to finish what she started saying—"You"—her eyes roll into the back of her head as she inhales a breath—"must get so much 'work' done." Her eyes slowly open, and she gives me a wink, her face quickly morphing into one of otherworldly pleasure.

Rolling my eyes at her accuracy, I grin when a thought pops into my head. She wants to ridicule me for bringing myself and our girlfriends pleasure; well, I'll remind her exactly why she comes to me to make her come.

Every single damn time.

I slide my chair closer, my left hand holding the wand as I use my right to spread her legs further apart. Leaning forward, I inhale, and her sweet musk overtakes me. I slide my tongue vertically against her wet, slippery folds while maintaining eye contact with her baby blues.

"Holy fuck. *Jude.*"

Her voice is just above a whisper, and I continue pleasing my rebellious Wildcat. Riley may be as in control of her daily life as possible, but when we are together, she has learned to be in the moment.

To feel everything.

The pleasure. The release. The torturous torment. Everything.

I spear my tongue as far as I can go inside her tight hole, and she tightens her thighs around my face. Sliding my finger upward on the vibrating wand, I push the top button, increasing the speed. She jolts uncontrollably from the pressure, and I know she's about to come.

In. Out. In. Out. Up. Down. Up. Down.

Fuck, I could write code with how precise my tongue is moving.

Riley's body violently vibrates and expels a roaring moan, drenching my panties.

"FUCKKK! Jude. Baby. Just like that. I wanna see your face glistening with my cum."

Smiling, I continue devouring her pussy and feel her hand reach for my head. She grips my hair tightly, guiding my head to where she wants me.

I have no clue how much closer I can get, but whatever works for her, I guess. Riley falls backward across my desk, arching upward, and she's finally set off.

Quickly removing my face from her delicious pussy, I groan, "Mmm, that's my girl. You come so beautifully."

I raise my hand and slap her breast, causing her to yelp in pleasure. Her whimpers spur me to make her come one more time. But this time I'm going to do all the work. I want to work that sensitive clit and remind her what my mouth can do.

As she comes down from her haze-induced orgasm with her eyes closed and head thrown back, I make my move. Removing the vibrating wand, turning it off, and setting it beside her, I grab her thighs and place them above my shoulders.

Rising from my seat, I lift her carefully onto my shoulders, her pussy a perfect view in front of me. I trek to the nearest wall, allowing her to lean against it.

Slanting forward, I run my tongue across her slit, gather her juices, and suction her clit. She thrashes perfectly, and in contrast to earlier, she pushes my face away, but I don't let up.

Her cum is everywhere — on my mouth, my cheeks, my goddam soul — and I want more.

I want it injected through my veins.

Without removing my face from her pussy, I painfully squeeze her ass cheeks, making sure to leave a mark for all the girls to see. With another swat to her ass, I sense her breathing pick up, and I know she's going to come again.

"Yes. Please. I'm coming. I'm coming. *Jude*. I'm yours," Riley pants aggressively.

Groaning against her pussy, I bite her clit, and she releases a guttural howl I've never heard before. In the three years I've been with Riley and the girls, Riley has never come quite like this.

I beam with pride, and I feel her cum drench my face increasingly. I'm about to look shiny as fuck, and I couldn't be happier. Riley draws in a quick breath, trembling from the rapturous high of her orgasm.

Expelling from her delectable pussy, I slap her ass once more before sliding her body down mine, securing her legs around my waist. She yelps from the sudden movement and leans in, capturing my lips.

With her essence mingling on our tongues, I almost don't hear the blaring S.O.S. from one of my computers.

> S.O.S. Incoming...

My computer's voice-activated software loudly declares an incoming alert. Talk about a mood killer.

> Congresswoman Sonia Acosta initiated contact.
> Received sponsorship from former client Kayla Kane.

Oh, shit. I have to send an S.O.S. alert to the girls through our intercom about this.

Riley and I unravel from our kiss, and I peer up at her face and smirk as I see such giddiness in those baby-blue eyes. I know this new client is making my girl wet for what's to come. She's a little pistol when it comes to obliterating men, and I have to say it makes the sex that much better when she comes back off a fresh kill. It unleashes something so primal in the both of us and if I could get her fucking pregnant, she'd be swollen with my babies all the fucking time.

One last kiss, and I set my little Wildcat on her feet. Before I turn to leave, she grabs my hand and says, "Oh, we're not done here, naughty girl. I want you to ride my strap after this meeting."

Chuckling, I swat her ass, her long blonde wavy hair clings to her breasts as she sways toward my wardrobe, pulling out a robe. Her fair-toned skin showcases a tall and slender silhouette that I'll have burned into my memory for the rest of my days. She places her hands through the sleeves one at a time and ties it around her waist.

I click the keys on my keyboard, gathering information from the congresswoman and allowing it to filter my screens.

Pushing the intercom on my desk, I announce, "S.O.S., reconvene in my office immediately. It's for Congresswoman Sonia Acosta."

Looks like riding a strap will have to wait — it's going to be a long night of recon and data gigs.

Chapter 2

Dead Man Walking

Cris

There's nothing sweeter than a man begging for mercy right before he's about to die—the tears, the crack in his voice, the incoherent babbling, and the pissing of his pants is the most harmonious thing I've ever experienced.

Correction.

Frankie forcing my head against the wall and fucking me with her monster strap-on cock earlier has blasted its way to the top of my list. The way she slapped my ass, slid her tongue across my cheek, and pulled my hair back will be replayed on a loop the next time I need to come.

Snapping out of my daze, Frankie and I invade Jude's lair, where Riley, Blake, and Noah await. Riley is in a cozy white robe, Jude is in her usual cropped grey NYU sweatshirt and matching sweatpants, and Noah and Blake are adorned with similar cherry romper onesies, proof we were all up to something.

I chuckle as I grab one of Jude's black leather ergonomic chairs and slide it across the black and white speckled marble floor, setting it beside her. Taking my place, I observe the data that Jude has already compiled in just a short period.

We put it up on the big projector screen for everyone to see as I slide through the thick dossier, which is growing by the minute.

Jude's already pulled Sonia's entire digital trail — her husband Jason's movements, his searches. And let's just say I'm going to enjoy watching my girls deliver him a beautifully tragic death.

Who knows, maybe I'll grace them with my presence for this one.

Not only does this motherfucker beat Sonia, but he also dabbles in distributing revenge porn, and the nail in the coffin? He watches rape porn. What a fucking piece of work.

My nostrils flare as I scroll through each piece of new information, and I notice the girls are in equal states of rage.

"I call dibs on delivering the final blow to this piece of shit. I swear, I don't know how the congresswoman managed to stay with this fuck for so long," Noah snarls, her hands tightening into fists.

"Not everyone has the courage to leave, *Muñeca*. Let me remind everyone not to judge this woman or *her choices*. Sometimes, it takes a little time to realize that she can finally escape his hold over her," I reply.

Noah's eyes close, comprehending what she just spouted off, but joins the girls as they nod, agreeing not to chastise Sonia and her choices.

"Who's her reference?" I ask, glancing at Jude.

"Kayla Kane. We killed her serial cheater and rapist CEO husband —the one who searched the dark web for a hitman," Jude answers.

I bob my head in understanding and reflect on all that we have been through.

When I first created this group, I admit I didn't think these women didn't have it in them at first.

I met Noah and Riley while escorting, and I saw the killer inside them and drummed up a girl group who would kill men for a hefty price. We knew how to get men to surrender their control, and when they were vulnerable, we would go in for the kill.

On our first kill, we made a mess. A bloody one. Then Frankie walked in.

She worked as a cleaning lady, and when she came to clean our mess, she left the room spotless and didn't ask questions. That kind of discretion? Gold. We knew we needed someone like her, and after I promised to go on a date with her, she decided to join our group.

Two jobs after we met Frankie, Jude caught on with our mission when she hacked her way into a healthcare CEO's cameras and witnessed us about to get caught.

Somehow, she called my phone and spewed a quick rundown of what we needed to do, and we did it. After coming to our rescue, we told her to send us an S.O.S. text next time. That was the moment the mission got a name. And our group was formed.

The Silhouettes of Sin—Seeking vengeance for women that men have wronged.

It wasn't until we rescued Blake from those men three years ago that I realized just how difficult it is for women to break out of their norms. Blake went through the worst possible scenario to escape her routine and change course to a different world.

She didn't go through what some of our other clients did, but what happened to her? It was enough to carve scars deep.

Now, she doesn't talk unless she needs to, and we've come to a collective decision that that's how she needs to cope with her trauma. We respect it and don't expect her to break her silence.

"So, I'll make first contact with the congresswoman. *Pecas, por favor*, send a secure message for a meet-up at her office. I'll take an RF detector to sweep for bugs and hidden cameras," I order, glancing at Jude — my freckles girl.

She swiftly types across the keyboard, working through our encrypted and secure chat line, and sends an S.O.S. meet-up text. After it is viewed, it self-deletes, and I nod.

"Everyone knows their positions. I take point. Frankie and Blake stay behind with Jude as she provides overwatch. Riley and Noah bring in the long guns. Stay sharp for any unwanted contact. Clear?"

"Yes, ma'am," they shout in unison.

Well, minus Blake, as she nods eagerly.

"Okay, let's get some sleep. We're out the door t-minus seven hours at 9 a.m. sharp."

Noah, Blake, Frankie, and Riley vacate the lair, leaving Jude and me to talk alone. I turn to face her and bring her chair towards me.

Leaning in, I lazily kiss her and pull back, tasting Riley on her plump lips — sweat, salt, and sex. A glint of mischievousness fills Jude's green eyes, and I wink, acknowledging that I understand what she and Riley were doing earlier.

"I'll be here at 7 a.m. to pick up my earpiece, button camera, and RH detector. Is there anything else you need me to take?"

"No, that's perfect. I'll be here and set aside your Glock 19 and Balisong knife so you can strap up," Jude notes.

There hasn't been a kill that has me quite as excited as this one. Well, in a long time, that is.

Jason Samuels is a dead man walking.

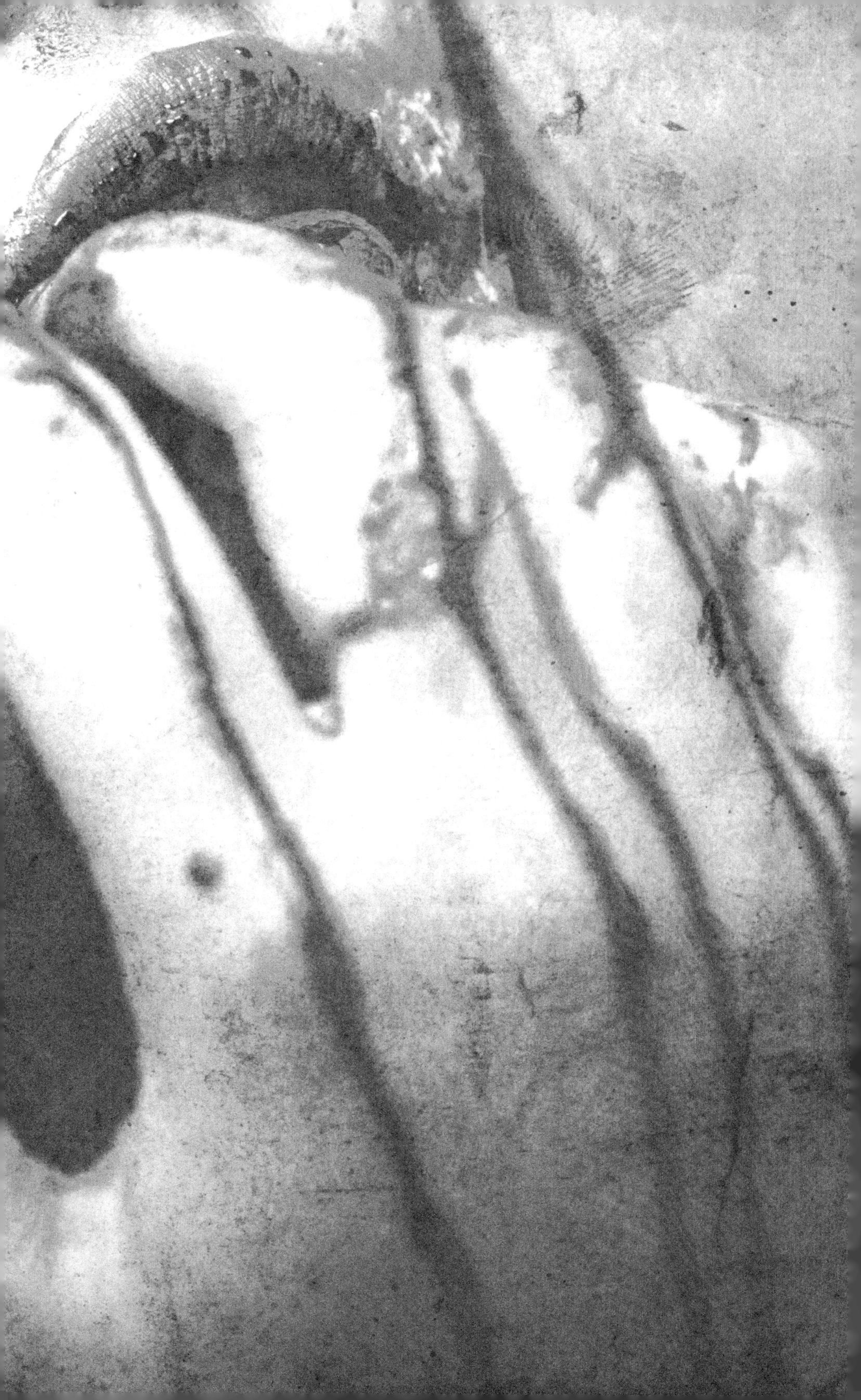

Chapter 3

Fuck You & Fuck Me

Riley

It's always smart to have a checklist before entering the belly of the beast that is a full-scale recon mission, from armed weapons, cameras, earpieces, infrared machines, and a full tactical search of the primary building and its surroundings.

When Cris dismisses us from Jude's lair, I swiftly make eye contact with Noah, and we nod in unison. Every time we are briefed with a new target, it's like a switch, and all I can think about is making this bastard pay.

"To the vault?" Noah and I chuckle in synchronization. God, I love her.

It's like we share the same brain, and I am so fucking excited to have someone who shares the same bloodlust I feel when I hear about these fucked-up men who think they can treat women with disrespect. I swear they'll hate to see us coming.

We approach the elevator in our apartment building and thumb the button with a 'V.' The doors open, and the bell chimes to indicate that we've reached our designated floor. We jog towards the locker room, change into loose clothing, and tape our hands.

"Five bucks, I'll knock you on your ass first," Noah snickers.

"Yeah, I highly doubt that, Bubbles. However, you're on. Ten, I have you pinned down in two minutes."

Noah shakes her head. We square up and take our stance. Sizing each other up, I jab forward, missing her face and landing a hit on her left shoulder.

"That's all you're going to land, Siren. Mark my words. You on your ass? Inevitable." Noah starts, and in a split second, she sweeps her right leg across my left.

One minute, I'm upright, and the next, I'm pinned down on my back with her arm across my neck on the padded mat.

Noah beams and leans closer, her mouth beside my ear as I catch my breath. Her breath warm, skin smelling faintly of sweat and sex. "Well, it looks like I was right. Just two minutes, and I have you pinned down on the mat begging for mercy, baby."

My heart pounds rapidly in my chest, and I attempt to catch my breath. I maneuver my right arm upward and push a strand of hair behind her ear. She leans her cheek into the palm of my hand, smiling brightly, and I take that moment to snake my hand around her delicate neck and squeeze firmly.

Her eyes dilate and sparkle with a tinge of neediness, and I know what I need to do next—perhaps letting loose before our mission isn't such a bad idea. Noah must see my thoughts reflected on my face because her lips lift into a slight grin, and I know she's game.

"Wanna roll around before we strap up?" Noah suggests.

"Strap up? Now, why would you mention that when we don't have any straps down here?" I chuckle as she shakes her head and rolls her eyes at my cheekiness.

"Shut up and listen, my little Siren. You are going to fuck me with those beautiful fingers and choke me at the same time. *Is that understood?*" Noah prompts, removing her arm from my neck.

"Anything you want, Bubbles. There's that spark I know and love. Remove those shorts and straddle my hips. Let me make you feel good."

Noah makes quick work of removing her shorts along with her lacy black thong, and I watch as she climbs over me, situating herself on my hips. She hovers as I slither my left hand up and secure it around her neck. I then take my right hand and slide my middle finger through her slit.

Gathering her slight wetness, I take my ring finger and repeat the same action, making sure both of my fingers are slick and ready to take my girl's tight pussy. Slowly, I inch my fingers forward and lightly tap her pulsing clit. Noah squirms and moans so sweetly as she instinctively rocks her hips back and forth against my fingers, drenching me with her essence.

"Dripping for me already, huh?" I smirk. "Someone was hungry for attention, wasn't she?"

"Fuck you and fuck me," Noah grunts.

Chuckling, I work my fingers toward her dripping pussy and insert two inside. Slowly, she aids in taking them further by sliding down and swallowing them whole. Her pussy clenches around my fingers, and we groan simultaneously.

"Holy fuck! I need you, Riley. Fuck me. Please," she begs.

I slap her bare ass and tighten my hold around her neck, distracting her as I guide my fingers in and out leisurely. Her delicious moans fill the training ring, and her eyes roll to the back of her head as she tilts it back. Not stopping, I plug her hole and move in and out, drowning in her overwhelming wetness.

Noah is in desperate need of more as she fiercely rides my fingers. Her angelic, curvy body moves up and down as her greedy pussy clenches around me tightly. I know her body like the back of my hand, and I know she's about to come.

I take my thumb and circle her engorged clit painfully slow, ramping up her need to fall over the edge. Her moans increasingly become more vocal as she chases her euphoria. Tightening around her delectable neck, Noah gasps as her eyes roll to the back of her head.

"That's it. Take it, Bubbles. I know you can do it. Ride my fingers like the greedy whore I know you are."

"Fuck. Riley. Fuck, I love you," Noah breathes as her pussy clenches one last time, and her cum drips down my hand. I gradually ease my thumb off her clit, and her body vibrates from the continued contact. God, I'll never get tired of this.

"I love you too, Noah. So fucking much. You're my girl. You know me inside and out, and I'll always love you for understanding exactly what I'm thinking," I reply.

Her eyes flutter open, and I carefully remove my hand from around her neck. She lifts her body slightly, and my fingers slip from her wet pussy.

I swiftly bring my fingers to my mouth and slurp her juices, basking in her taste. She's an absolute dream. I am in awe of how much I love these women.

They are there for me when I need them, love me even when I become slightly psychotic, and understand my need for killing because they feel the same way. We each share that need to kill men and torture them in the most gruesome way possible.

It is our purpose.

Our mission.

And we will stop at nothing to accomplish it *every single time*.

Noah, Cris, Frankie, Blake, and Jude are my everything. I can't imagine my life without any of them.

AFTER WHAT FELT LIKE A QUICK NAP, SIX HOURS LATER, NOAH AND I proceed to the vault's arsenal and gear up with our favorite sniper rifles.

I pack the infrared thermal portable handheld imager, extra magazines filled with 300 Win Mag cartridges, two first aid kits, and my AI AX50 sniper rifle with a suppressor. Glancing at Noah, I catch her gathering the same items, trading my rifle for her Counter-Strike AWM.

When we load the Sprinter van, we pack fast and clean while Blake, Frankie, Jude, and Cris situate themselves inside. Jude and Blake usually stay behind in the van while we do our thing, but today, Frankie will join them on the mission, providing extra assistance with Jude's monitors.

"Let's go, let's go, let's go! We are 40 minutes ahead of schedule," I shout, closing the door behind me as I sit beside Noah and our gear.

Adrenaline's already burning in my veins. "We need to set up and do two circles around the perimeter."

"I'm almost ready; I just need to secure my earpiece and button the camera to my coat. Does everybody have their earpieces? Let's do a quick comms check," Cris declares.

"Testing. This is a test. You look so fuckable, wifey," Frankie purrs. Cris rolls her eyes and throws Frankie a kiss while the rest of us chuckle at how cute they both are.

"Thank you, *esposa*. Let's go," Cris answers. Frankie puts the van into drive as we exit our apartment building's garage and watch as the gate opens and closes behind us.

After circling Congresswoman Acosta's office building, we pull into an alleyway that hides behind the back of the building, opposite the meeting place. Frankie lets us out, and we rush up the stairwell, eight flights up, not stopping to catch our breaths until we reach the door to the roof.

Noah grabs the doorknob, but I stop her. I need to get one last look before our focus is pulled in many different directions.

Leaning in, I softly graze my lips against hers, our breaths panting from the trek up. We stare deeply into each other's eyes, conveying all the love and our hopes to stay safe. We nod, and I grab her face, pulling her in closer before I kiss her gorgeous lips fiercely.

We pull apart, and Noah opens the door, leading the way across the rooftop. Noah marches with her gear to the left, while I depart to the right and unpack our rifles from our cases. I crouch down as I readily assemble my gear and situate the infrared imager on the ledge of the rooftop.

Mounting my AI AX50 sniper rifle with my suppressor attached, I view my surroundings, making sure not to get caught as I set up. Noah sets up camp 50 yards away from me with her Counter-Strike AWM sniper rifle, and I am so turned on at the fact that she looks so hot handling such a big and heavy gun.

Most men might underestimate us with our guns, gear, and ability to demonstrate such cruelty, but being able to keep up with the best of them just goes to show that we aren't fragile creatures.

I lie on the gravel rooftop, my left leg in line with my body and my right leg 20 degrees parallel to my rifle. My black cargo pants and black ribbed turtleneck chalk up gravel as I situate myself in position.

Leaning to the right, I rest my cheek against the stock and focus my right eye, peering directly through the scope where I spot Mommy Cris 500 yards away, infiltrating the congresswoman's building. My pointer finger ghosts the trigger as I place it against the bolt handle.

"In position," I whisper.

Cris enters the office as I receive a visual from the infrared scanner. I then spot two guards and a receptionist outside the Congresswoman's door.

"Hi, Sonia. Write it down, slide it across the desk, and await my command," Cris states.

"In position. Movement to the right side of the target's rooftop," Noah mutters. I lift my scope eyeline and spot another sniper lying on the target's roof with their rifle pointed at our Sprinter van.

Fuck. The girls.

"Firefly. Move the van now. Sniper. Target's rooftop. Now!" I shout through the earpiece, panicking and throwing all my training out the window, seeing my girls in trouble.

"Now. Go, go, go, go."

Frankie puts the van into gear, and the tires burn out against the asphalt, and one split second of lost focus costs me pain I've never felt before.

"Fuck. I'm *hit*." I sink to the floor, slowly crawling backward to take cover as I grip my left shoulder, trying to stop the blood from draining out of my body.

"Just my shoulder. I'm good. Keep going," I groan, blinking in and out of consciousness.

"No, she's not. Fuck. *Reina*, in and out. We need to move. Shadow, round the block," Noah commands, her voice blaring through our comms.

Holy fuck, I'm feeling woozy. The persistent throbbing of my left shoulder stings while I peer as the sniper boxes up a black case and throws it over his shoulder.

A man. A man is the last thing I remember before everything goes dark, and my mind reverts to the five most important people in my life.

My girls. I'll fight like hell to come back to them.

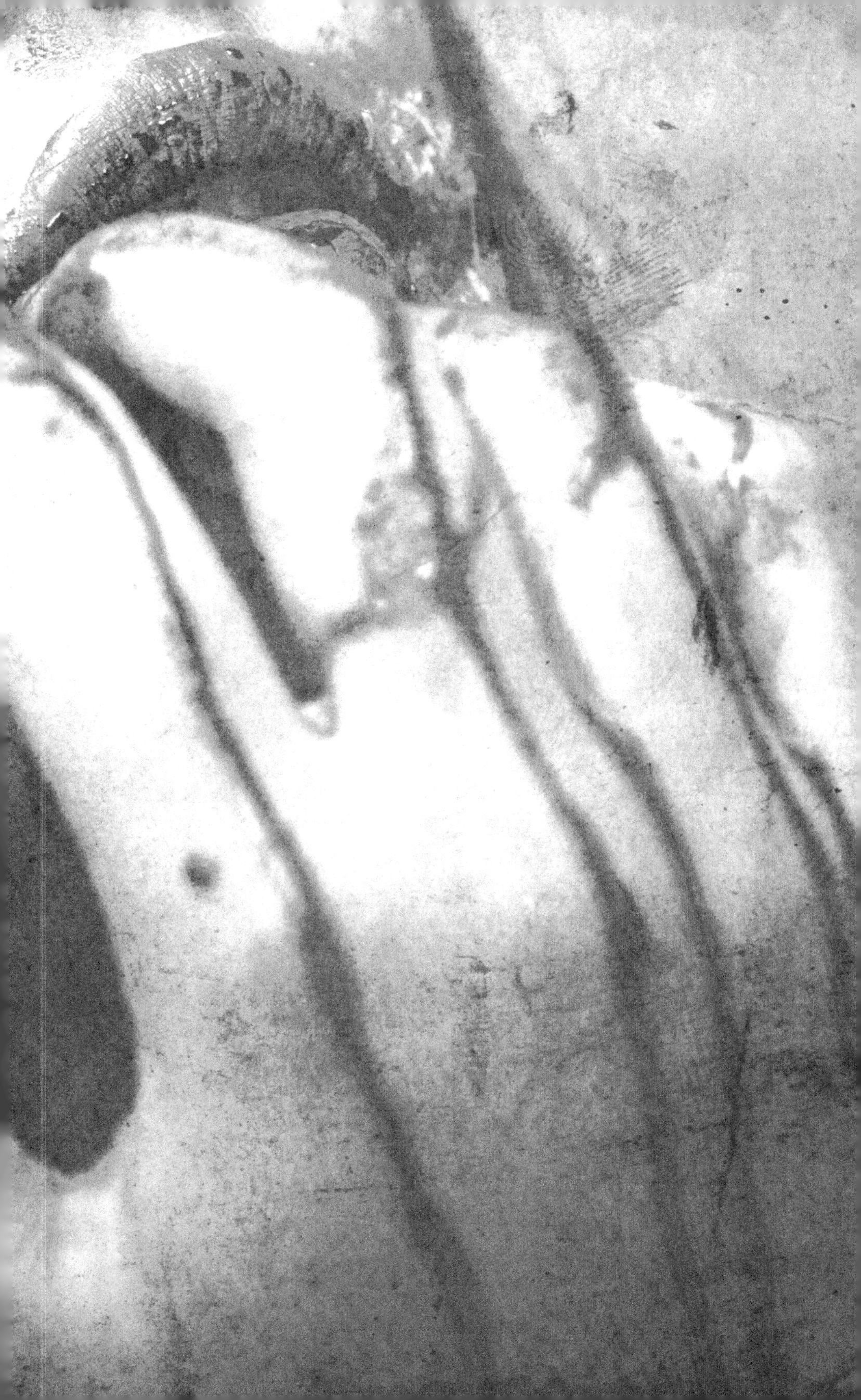

Chapter 4

To Save You

Noah

It was supposed to be a clear mission: set up across the friendly's building, have an in-and-out conversation, and then return home to go over the next steps to execute the mission. However, we didn't foresee this obstacle. And now Riley's bleeding out.

If something happens to Riley, I'll never forgive myself. We should've been more careful. The Congresswoman is a high-profile asset, but they weren't aiming at her. That man had to know we'd be there. Something is not right, and after we patch Riley up, I'll have Jude do a sweep of our communications.

"She's down. Fuck. I need backup. Shadow, come up now. Back stairwell. I'm using the first aid kit for a temporary patch. Firefly, call the doc. I'm carrying our stuff and our girl down the stairs."

I shut out all the chatter through my earpiece as I rapidly dismount, disassemble, package my rifle in its case, and haul it over my shoulder. Glancing toward Riley, I notice her going in and out of consciousness as she slowly tries to pack her items.

Ugh.

Of course she's still trying to pack. My stubborn siren.

She's hit and still pushing. Of course she is. And it's fucking terrifying.

"Will you stop, baby? Put that down and let me help you," I chastise, grabbing her rifle and placing it in its case.

Riley mumbles something, and I recognize her wobbliness, causing me to move faster and catch her in my arms. I open one of our first aid kits and some gauze and tape. Placing them aside, I rip her sleeve and see the bullet is still lodged inside her arm.

Fuck. She's going to need surgery. It's a good thing I told Jude to call the doc.

After I apply the gauze and tape it down, I swiftly toss her over my shoulder as Frankie opens the rooftop door. She quickly scans the rooftop and spots us before jogging toward our position.

"Here, take the rifles. I got Riley," I yell.

Frankie obliges, carrying the rifles, and grasps the infrared imager Riley placed on the ledge in her hand. I wait a beat until she has everything, and then we make our way down the stairs.

"We got you, baby. Stay with us. We'll do anything to save you," I whisper, moving a strand of hair behind her ear. "I'll do anything to keep you alive."

Blake greets us through the back entrance with the door to our Sprinter van open. Jude creates space for Riley, and I lay her across our makeshift gurney. Frankie hops into the driver's seat with Cris in the passenger seat as Blake closes the door behind us.

"What's the damage? Where did she get hit?" Cris asks. I move toward the front of the van and let Blake take over as she places pressure on Riley's wound.

"The bullet is still lodged in her arm. Medora and Esper should have no problem taking it out. I think she passed out from the blood loss, but she should be fine," I answer, shaking my head at how we missed seeing someone on the Congresswoman's rooftop when we circled the block.

"She'll be okay. She's too strong not to be. What did the Congresswoman say?" Frankie probes, driving like a maniac and approaching our garage after a swift turn.

"She gave me the method in which she wants it handled and said it was urgent. So, after Riley heals, we must form a plan to execute as soon as possible. You might need to take point," Cris declares, glancing my way.

"Got it." I nod, not thinking too much about that now. I'm more worried about Riley in this moment.

Frankie swerves into our garage, where Medora and her girlfriend Esper await us. Medora has been our on-call doctor and friend since we started this group. Her girlfriend, Esper, is a nurse, and when Blake needed a special touch all those years ago, she joined us. She has been a great help in teaching us the basic needs of caring for ourselves while on a mission.

The van comes to a halt, and Blake quickly opens the back door.

"What do we got? A through and through, or is the bullet still lodged inside?" Medora asks, climbing inside and carrying Riley in her arms.

Okay.

So, I don't like that, and by the look Jude, Blake, Frankie, and Cris are imparting, it looks like we're all on the same page.

"This one time only, Medora. Never lift her in your arms again," Cris growls. Yup. That tracks.

Medora's eyes widen, and she swiftly glances toward Esper. I laugh to lighten the tension and usher Medora to hurry up and go fix up our girl.

"She's not joking, but it's all good. Just go ahead and do your best work on our girl."

Esper bursts through the doors of our lower-level apartment building and climbs into the elevator with the rest of us on her tail, stabbing the button to our basement's surgical suite. It feels like the longest fucking elevator ride, and Riley still hasn't woken up.

Charging through the elevator doors, we reach the surgical suite, and Esper closes the door behind her.

I bang on the door, begging them to open it, but Blake takes my hands immediately, easing my nerves and causing me to slump into her dainty arms. Not where I usually end up, but today? I need it. I inhale her sweet strawberry scent and close my eyes as I think about the different outcomes this mission could've had.

I should've been the one to get hurt. I hate seeing any one of my girls hurting, but I know she'll be okay. She has to be.

And we wait. Wait for the possibility that she'll never be the same again.

After my minor freakout, Blake, being the little science nerd she is, decided to check in with Medora and Esper to check on Riley's status.

It's been thirty minutes, and from what I can tell, everything is going well. However, my heart stops when Blake exits the suite, tears welling in her eyes.

"What's wrong, Shortcake? What happened?" I yell frantically. It's the only nickname she ever let me get away with so it stuck.

She wipes her tears as Jude embraces her, and she snappily signs the letters O and K. I exhale a breath, my shoulders drop from the heightened tension, and I rapidly turn my head when Esper and Medora exit the suite.

"She's going to pull through. The bullet didn't hit any major arteries. She lost consciousness due to the blood loss, but we gave her a blood transfusion, and she should be up and out of bed in a couple of hours. She's lucky. A few inches to the right, and it could've been fatal."

Cris leads Esper and Medora to the elevator, thanking them for everything and discussing Riley's plan of care for the days to come.

She's gonna hate it. I don't care. Even if I have to force her to oblige with sex; I'll do it. She just needs to focus on getting better.

I tune out the chatter, and Frankie stands beside me, taking my hand in hers.

"She's going to be okay, Mama. Riley's a badass. You know this won't keep her down," Frankie whispers, attempting to console me.

"I know. I just can't think about anything other than how someone could have our location. Like Jude would've seen something, right? And if she couldn't, what does that say about our security? I don't kn—" I ramble as Frankie grasps my hands, encircling them around her slim body, and leans in, silencing me with a kiss. I never spiral. But this? This is too fucking close.

I lose myself in our kiss, temporarily taking my mind off Riley. Fuck. I love how she knows exactly what I need right now.

Arms circle my waist behind me, and I feel Cris's body press against mine. I know her arms like the back of my hand, and her warmth radiates all over my body, sending chills up my spine.

Frankie breaks our kiss, and I open my eyes, chuckling when I see the wicked grin she displays. I know what she's after, and she knows it's just the distraction I need.

They both do.

"Upstairs. The purple room. *Now*," Cris whispers as she playfully bites my earlobe. I hiss from the pleasurable contact, and my pussy drips with arousal.

I smile and say, "Let me say a quick goodbye to Riley before we go."

She'll feel me there, even if she's out.

They nod, and I disentangle from their hold and walk toward the surgical suite where my Siren resides.

The distant beeping of the monitor blares louder as I focus on my girl lying on the surgical table with a wrapped shoulder and wires coming from her body. Leaning in, I grab her hand and kiss her beautiful but messy blonde locks.

"I love you, my little Siren. You scared the shit out of me. Never do that again, okay?" I whisper, before leaving a soft kiss to her dry but full lips.

Letting go of her hand, I cling onto one last look and see my girls waiting for me.

"Are you ready?" Frankie asks.

I nod and entangle Frankie's right hand entwined with my left while Cris's left hand entwines with my right. They drag me toward the elevator before Cris shouts a quick 'bye' to Jude and Blake. I giggle, and Jude and Blake smile in kind.

I can't wait to turn off my brain and feel their bodies touching mine. To let go and be one with them. I'm ready to give it all up. For them.

Chapter 5
Insatiable Little Slut

Frankie

As a group of raging lesbians who are all in a relationship with each other, we feel everything. Not just through love or lust, but through what each of us carries.

Studying Noah's panicked face as she watched Riley through the glass of the surgical suite, I knew and felt her pain, panic, and longing to be in her place instead.

It hurts me as much as it hurts her, but I know what Noah needs. Cris and I both do. She needs to relieve herself of the guilt and second-guessing spiraling through her mind.

Cris and I lead her to the elevator, each clutching one of her hands to make sure she knows we aren't going anywhere. I lift her hand and place a gentle kiss on the skin where her inner arm and wrist meet.

Her body trembles from the contact, but she then breathes in and out, centering herself from her thoughts. I quickly glance toward Cris, and she nods, our thoughts transcending like telepathic twins who know what the other is thinking.

We will give her everything.

We'll give her pain. We'll give her pleasure. We'll give her enough sensation to drown out her memory.

The doors open, and Cris drags us toward our purple room, where our shiny toys, whips, chains, and instruments of sin for pain and pleasure are displayed along the walls that enclose us.

"Come on, Mama. Let us make you feel so good," I whisper, closing the door behind us.

"Kneel on the ground with your palms resting on your thighs and your head cast down," Cris orders. Noah hesitates for a moment but executes Cris's command gracefully.

Awaiting our instruction, Noah shudders, her chest rising and falling with every bated breath. I smile inwardly, shaking my head with the filthy thoughts swirling through my mind.

Cris clutches my arm and guides me to the bed; leaning forward, she whispers, "I'll get myself off on the throne while you please her. Then, I'll jump in when she needs more. Understand?"

God, I love it when she gets bossy. My Wifey is such a crazy girl. She gives commands like nobody's business and does it so well.

I chuckle, and before I please our girl, I kiss Cris on her sweet lips, smacking her ass for good measure. As I look back, I bite my lip and see her roll her eyes with mischievousness at what's reflected off mine.

"You're a wild one, *Esposa*. Now get started so I can watch my girls play for me," Cris teases.

I approach our wall adorned with an array of sex toys, whips, chains, and a strap-on harness set for each of us. I take my time selecting exactly what my girl needs and take down a few items.

I glide my finger across the harness attached to my favorite monster dildo. Just the thing for our filthy little girl tonight.

I lift it from the hook on the wall and throw it on the nearby bed. I smirk and gather one of my favorites, along with a pair of wrist-to-thigh restraint cuffs, a red silk blindfold, a black riding crop, and a red rose clit stimulator that will send just the right amount of pleasure coursing through her perfect little body.

Lastly, I amble toward the attached bathroom and retrieve a bottle of Isopropyl alcohol, a couple of cotton balls, honey-flavored lube, and an extended lighter.

I know Noah has a thing for fire, and I'm all about giving my girl what she needs and wants tonight.

With everything laid out on the bed and the nearby side table, I slowly trek back to Noah on her knees. Raising her chin with my index finger, I smile and tap my thigh, commanding her to lay her head against it. She does as she's told, and I stroke her head to calm her nerves.

"Look at me," I order, her blazing glare pools with unshed tears. She's still thinking about Riley, and I need to do everything in my power to take the last hour and a half out of her brain.

"Strip for us. But give me your panties, mama. I want to smell you as I fall asleep tonight." I wink, and she cracks a slight smirk.

There's my girl. A little naughty time with her girlfriends will do the trick.

Noah lifts her long sleeve black dri-fit top revealing her perfect perky tits. Well, it looks like someone was in the mood to play. She then lowers her black cargo pants along with her red panties as I extend my hand and she places them gently onto my palm.

I bring my nose to her panties and inhale her alluring scent, making myself drip with how sweet and mouth-watering her arousal is as it invades my senses.

"You smell like… *Mine. Ours.*"

Noah beams, her beautiful brown eyes abiding my direction and hanging on for any semblance of pain and pleasure.

"Come on, Mama. Lay on your back in the middle of the bed with your legs up and ass on the edge. Now," I command.

Noah glides to the bed and I hastily observe Cris naked on the throne looking like a badass queen as she plays with her clit with one hand and tweaks her nipple with the other. I blow her a kiss and chuckle when she shakes her head at my antics.

Approaching the sturdy, black king-size framed poster bed adorned with red silk sheets, I hurriedly strip from my clothes, discarding them on the floor. I then snatch my harness with the attached dildo and secure it around my hips.

Before she gets impatient, I gather the wrist-to-thigh restraint and softly slide each cuff through her thick thighs, one at a time. Next, I take each of her wrists and secure the cuffs around them, keeping her nice and tight without a means for escape.

Her breath hitches slightly, and I stroke her supple thighs to comfort her.

"Okay, relax, Mama. I'm going to blindfold you to heighten your senses. Keep breathing in and out. But before we proceed, we need a safe word. Say it and everything will stop immediately," I instruct.

She nods and reveals her safe word, "Blue. My safe word is blue."

"Understood. Now let go and just feel," I exclaim, securing the red blindfold tightly around her pretty little head. I then clutch the black leather-bound riding crop in one hand and use my other hand to glide my strap-on through her slit.

Noah releases breathy moans that mingle along with Cris's heavy pants, causing me to roll my eyes to the back of my head and my arousal to drip down my legs. Chills overwhelm my body and I shake my head, reminding myself to continue my torment on Noah's body.

Running the riding crop up and down her body, I halt, imparting a smack onto her right breast, coaxing a thunderous moan. I follow up with a second strike — a present she can feel. She squirms, causing her cuffs to bite her wrists.

"Moan for me, Mama. Let me hear your sweet little pleas begging for pain."

Noah shifts and arches her back from the sheets, displaying her pebbled nipples so erect and begging to be adorned. I lean forward and suck one into my mouth while teasing the other with the riding crop.

Biting her nipple, she squeals and the squelch of Cris's soaked pussy resounds in the background, and it spurs me to release her glorious breast from my mouth. I torture her some more when I lift the riding crop and unleash multiple swats to her thighs and two to her delicate glistening little pussy.

Wack.

I slide my strap on through her wet slit and lather it with her juices. After teasing her pussy I slowly enter her puffy pussy.

Wack.

She groans, arching her back once more before exhaling beautifully, full and satiated. I take my free hand and circle her dainty throat.

A perfect little hand necklace for my girl.

"Frankie, oh fuck. Yes. More. Please," she begs, her voice raspy and just above a whisper. Her hands ball into fists, desperate for more pain.

Her tan, exquisite little body displays bright red splotches, and I know she wants and needs more.

Burying my face in the crook of her neck resting above my hand, I inhale deeply, reveling in her sweet scent. I then plant kisses from her jaw to her lips. Before granting her with more, I bite her lower lip, breaking the skin and causing blood to pool on her bruised lip.

I take the tip of my tongue to collect her blood and before swallowing, I glide my tongue in between her breasts and around her nipples. Her moans grow louder and I thrust harder inside her soaked pussy.

Deeper. Faster. Harder.

I don't stop pumping into her clenching pussy. Releasing my hold on her neck, I notice Noah is on the brink of her release.

Not so fast.

I expel from inside her and harshly slap her pussy lips before groaning and saying, "Not so fast, Mama. You haven't been tortured quite enough. You know better than to come without permission."

Her whimpers and pleading make me laugh as I discard the riding crop onto the floor and pick up the lighter, the bottle of isopropyl alcohol, and a couple of cotton balls.

I drench a cotton ball with the alcohol and immediately ignite the fire, running a straight line from Noah's breast to her navel in quick succession.

We've talked about this. She loves the sting. She trusts me to give it — and to stop.

Palming the cotton ball, I put out the fire, basking in the short sting it has on my hand. Noah moans and arches her back from the intense feeling of the fire on her body. It sparks something inside me and I repeat the motion, enjoying the way she is overcome with pleasure mixed with a little pain.

"Yes, Frankie. More. I need more," she pleads, her hands squeezing her thighs as her nails break the skin.

I perform continuous rounds of lighting the drenched cotton and spreading the fire across her body. The previous bright red splotches beam on her skin and I know she's had enough. It's time to edge my little Mama until she's on the brink of coming.

I'm proven right when I see a tear release from beneath the blindfold, and use the nearby trash can to discard the cotton balls and set the lighter on the bedside table.

"Do you need to use your safe word, Noah?"

"No. I'm fine. It's making me forget," she sniffs. I rub her body, reminding myself I need to drench her with salve when we are finished.

I view the toys beside me and raise the red rose clit stimulator before lowering myself in between her stretched thighs. Scooting face to face with her red, puffy, and wet pussy, I ignite the clit stimulator and set it on the lowest vibration directly against her engorged clit.

I spread her lips further, and as the stimulator does its job, I gather

her juices from clit to her gaping hole and travel down to her forbidden little asshole. It clenches as I spear my tongue inside, and Noah unleashes a guttural groan that has me stopping the vibration.

I will have her sopping wet and begging before I allow her to come. Her panting breaths slow to a steady rhythm before she whimpers for more.

"Please. Shadow, I need to come. Please, baby."

Oh, she thinks calling me 'Shadow' and 'baby' in the same breath is going to help? She's sadly mistaken. I plan to deny her just a little more.

I turn to face Cris and see her tightening her harness with its attached monster cock as she seductively approaches the bed. Her round stomach, heaving breasts, and delightful curves are on perfect display begging to be fucked. She slaps my ass knocking me out of my obvious perusal and I shift my eyes from her cock to Noah's mouth. She shakes her head and smiles, indicating she's caught on to what I want her to do.

"Lie on your back, *Muñeca*, and open that pretty little mouth for me," she commands, grabbing her girthy dildo in her left hand as Noah obeys her command.

I resume my position, slicking my tongue once again with Noah's essence and reviving the vibration on the clit stimulator. Noah's howls are cut off by what I can only assume is Cris forcing her dildo inside her extended mouth.

Noah's legs vigorously shake and I see that she's on the verge of coming. I turn off the stimulator once again and slither my tongue every which way along her pussy.

In, out, up, and down.

I collect her juices, my face wet and glistening, and I rise from my position to see Noah gagging on Cris's monster cock.

Fuck. It looks so fucking hot. Saliva pours out of her mouth and I have a nasty idea.

"I promise I'll allow you to come in a bit. Let Wifey here get my pussy ready before I give you what you really want, Mama," I state, shifting Noah's body up the mattress with enough room for Cris to position herself behind me. I toss the clit stimulator and spread Noah's legs further.

Cris withdraws her dildo from Noah's mouth and I lean forward, my face in between Noah's thighs, and eat my girl's sweet pussy.

I swirl my tongue around her clit and down to her waiting hole, gathering as much of her juices as I can before I suck my finger and insert it slowly inside her asshole.

"Holy fuck, I'm going to come. Please, can I come?" she growls.

"There's nothing holy in here, Mama. Beg for it. Use your words like the good girl I know you are," I mewl through the slurping and licking of her pussy.

"Please, make me come. I need it so bad. Make my head spin, Shadow."

That's all she needed to say as I move away from her pussy, uncuff her wrists, and spin her around on her knees with her ass served on a silver platter in front of my face. She yelps as I slap her ass before diving in and eating her pussy like a starved woman trying to satiate her appetite.

I clench my tight hole as I feel Cris nibble against my clit, and shiver from the deliberate attention she delivers to my pussy. On the edge of an orgasm, I shift my hips forward, coaxing Cris to remove her face from my pussy. She chuckles and slaps both my ass cheeks in swift succession as I groan against Noah's pussy.

"Fuck, fuck, fuck yes! Right there. Right fucking there, Frankie," Noah howls, slapping her hands against the mattress.

Her cum douses my face and I clutch her hips tighter, not letting her pussy leave my mouth. Not just yet.

As my tongue is deep inside of Noah's pussy, I hear the cap of the lube crack open and feel it drip down from my forbidden asshole to my pussy. I shiver in anticipation, and now it's time to run a little train.

—Choo-choo!—

Finally removing my face from Noah's pussy, I allow Cris to take her monster cock and steadily squeeze into my tight hole. I move my hand toward the back of Noah's head and unravel the blindfold. As it drops she turns, and I nod, signaling for her to remain in position.

After adjusting to Cris's strap, she pauses, allowing me to push Noah's head further into the mattress and penetrate her greedy pussy. We both moan in unison at the feeling of coming together as one.

There's nothing like it — being together, buried in each other.

Bending over, I clutch onto Noah's hips, and Cris and I move in tandem forward and back.

"Oh, fuck. Harder. Fuck me harder. I'm almost there again," Noah screams.

Cris takes her outcry and shoves her strap deeper inside me, and I weep with satisfaction. I lift my body from Noah's and grunt as I forcefully fill her pussy harder.

I then take my hand and encircle her waist to find her clit, making her sing with pleasure as I sway my fingers side to side against her clit.

"That's it, Wifey. Fill my fucking pussy. Fill your insatiable little slut," I moan, clenching around Cris's strap-on.

"Your body was made for us. You're a filthy little slut so fucking take it," Cris grunts, slapping my ass for good measure.

After a few more thrusts and circling of Noah's pussy. We moan. We groan. We come — all of us, together.

"Yes! Fucking hell," Noah growls.

Cris chuckles as she pumps two more times before sliding her cock out of me. I do the same and drive out my strap from Noah's. Quickly, Cris and I undo our harnesses before throwing ourselves back onto the mattress and relaxing beside Noah.

I kiss the top of her head and we cuddle, sweaty, satiated, and dirty, but we don't care. We bask in the powerful feeling of being one as we cling to each other, our arms tangled within one another.

"STAY STILL, *MUÑECA*. WE NEED TO TAKE CARE OF YOUR BODY WITH the salve," Cris orders her voice low, all business now.

After our momentary relaxation tangled in each other's arms, Cris and I carried Noah to the bathtub and soaked for a few minutes. She was so cum drunk with her mind far off in the clouds. Which is exactly what we wanted her to feel.

We move our hands across Noah's body, focusing on the areas I slapped and ignited with fire.

The door to the room opens and in walks Jude, Blake, and Riley, snickering at the sight before them.

"We're sorry to interrupt this little fuck fest, but Jude thinks she knows how she can catch the man who shot at me," Riley smirks, clearly still high on adrenaline.

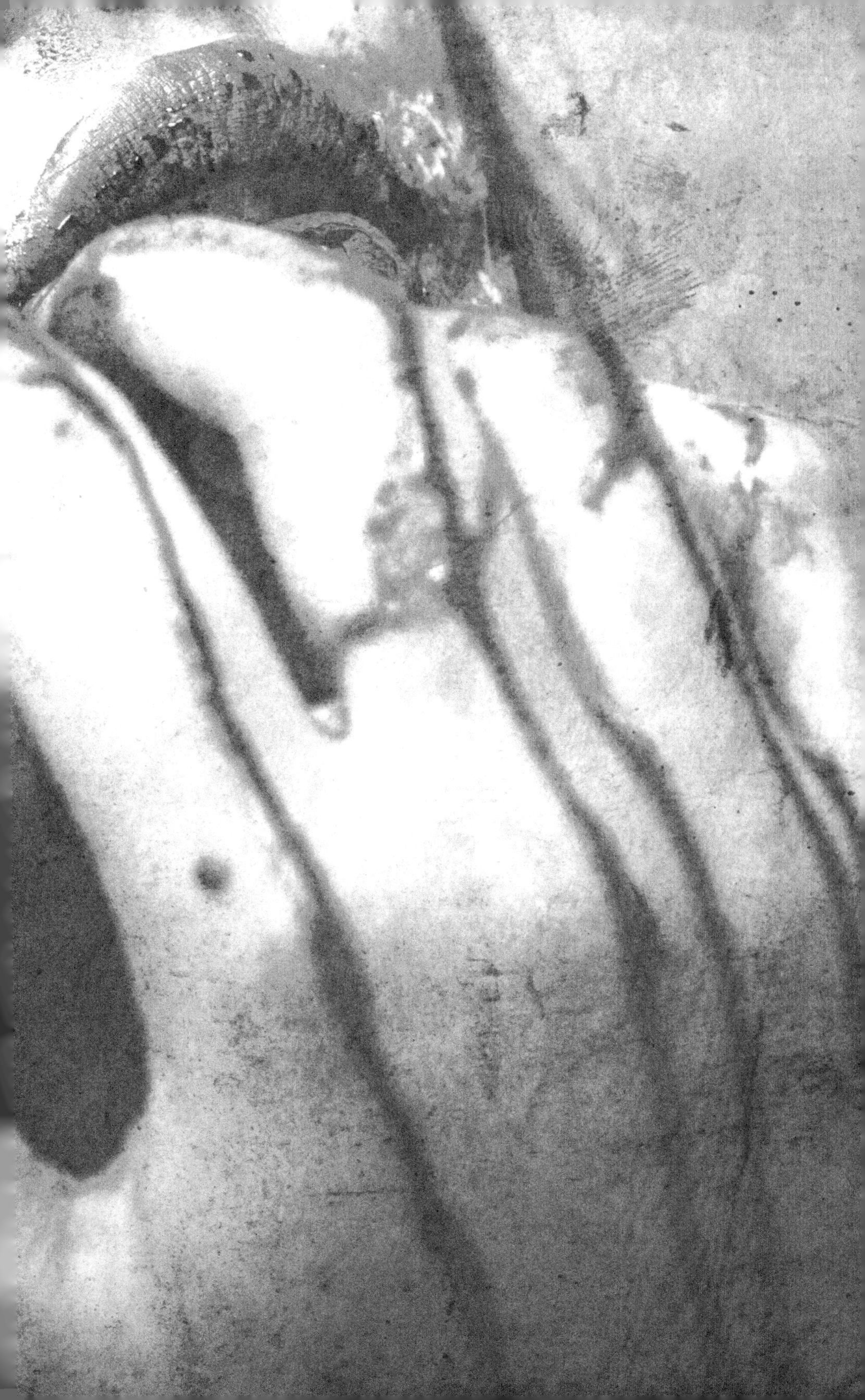

Chapter 6
The Texts

Blake

"Talk to me, *Pecas*. How could someone get through your firewalls?" Cris remarks as we settle on the black leather cushioned couches in Jude's office.

Jude huffs, and she types aggressively against her keyboard. Not responding, Cris walks toward her and places her hand gently on Jude's shoulder.

"I'm sorry. I didn't mean for it to sound like I was blaming you," Cris whispers.

"What? Oh, I'm sorry I wasn't paying attention. I'm trying to find out where he was able to hack into my firewall. There has to be a hole somewhere but I'm not seeing i-," Jude starts.

An alert echoes throughout the room as Jude quickly works to disarm it.

"I found it. It's here. How the fuck was he able to get through it. There's no way," Jude exclaims, her demeanor tense and exhausted.

I stand from my place on the couch and approach the tiny chair beside Jude, setting my hands on her lap. She closes her eyes as she takes deep breaths, then opens her eyes, showcasing a captivating smile toward me.

Her smile is so beautiful. It lights up her face, enhancing her gorgeous array of freckles, and making her green eyes sparkle.

"Thank you, Venus. I adore, cherish, and love you." Her words warm my heart, and a pang of hurt hits my chest — because she doesn't know what I'm keeping from her.

For them.

I'm keeping a secret…

A big one.

And I know that if any of my loves knew what I've been receiving, they'd chastise me for not telling them straight away.

I cast my gaze downward, unable to meet her eyes further, and close my eyes with a frown.

Riley, Noah, and Frankie's questions toward Jude and Cris fade into the background as I think about how I'm going to tell them.

What if the person who's been texting me for the past few months is the same one who hacked Jude's firewall? I can see she blames herself, and if it does have something to do with me, then I must come clean. No matter the outcome.

"What's wrong, *Bebita*?" Cris asks, lifting my chin with her finger.

I take a deep breath and take out my phone. I then type into my text-to-speech app.

After the attack three years ago, I haven't said a word. The trauma I went through left me shaking for days — I couldn't fall asleep, couldn't eat.

One thorough search of my background later, Jude came to me and asked if I wanted to stay with them until I got better. I said yes.

I felt safe with them.

They surrounded me with compassion and comfort through the first ninety days of shaking, crying, and the nightmares. I was a mess, but they stuck beside me through it all.

A couple of months later, the girls brought in an in-house doctor, who eventually diagnosed me with selective mutism. The induced anxiety and trauma froze something inside me, and I couldn't speak.

In some situations, I can call for someone if they aren't facing me — but usually, it's a grunt or a whisper of their name. The girls have been so patient. I adore them for that.

When I finish the text, I press the play button, and the text is read aloud.

"I've been receiving strange texts for the past few months," the automated voice reads.

The voice sounds calm. Too calm. I look down at my lap, ashamed of how loud my silence suddenly feels.

"What do you mean by strange texts? What do the texts say? Why didn't you tell us?" the girls ask at the same time.

I take a moment to draft another text, and they each crowd around Jude's desk, awaiting my response.

"I'm sorry. They said things like *'your day of reckoning is coming, and I will die for the bloodshed.'* The texts went from that to saying, 'here's another reminder you'll die soon, Little Red.'"

My hands tremble.

"I know I should've told you, but I just didn't want you to worry about me and have to save me once again."

"I'm sorry. It's my fault. What happened to Riley — it has to be my fault. I'm so sorry, Rebel," the voice speaks while my fingers fumble over signing my apologies to all of them. But especially Riley.

Jude is first, but then Riley, Frankie, Cris, and Noah surround me in a group hug. Their overwhelmingly shocking reaction brings tears to my eyes. I know I shouldn't, but sometimes I feel like an outsider, having met them after they established this organization. But seeing their initial response be so welcoming and empathetic. Now I know I didn't have to carry it alone.

I will never do it again.

"Wait, what did he call you?" Noah asks, expelling herself first from our group hug.

My eyes widen. That can't be right. The last time someone spit those words was Jared, and I know the girls killed him. It has to be someone else who was there and overheard at the bar.

I glance at the girls, and for the first time since that day, I whisper, "Little Red."

I haven't said or heard that name out loud in three years.

"It can't be. We killed all of them. There were three, right?" Cris presses, looking toward Noah.

I don't remember too much of that day, but I swear it felt like a lot more than three men in that room that night. Shuddering in place, Jude kisses my forehead before she gets to work typing away on her keyboard.

What if we missed someone? Is that even possible? I know I left the room, but the girls were there, and they'd know if someone had left the room too.

Right?

"Okay, so here are the pictures of the aftermath that Frankie took before cleaning up. Is there anyone you see that is missing?" Jude states, displaying the dead men and what the girls did to them on the overhead screen toward the left of her lair.

I sit beside Jude and keep my face down between my legs with my arms on my knees. Closing my eyes, I breathe in and out, taking myself back to that day. If I can't look at the photos, I have to go back in my mind instead.

I have to do something to make it up to my girls and the kindness they've shown me all these years.

After the girls view the array of photos, Jude combs through the surveillance of the hotel lobby and I lift my head to view the day my life changed.

I see myself come into the frame and my eyes widen as I see Jared talking to me while his crew is seated at the bar. Taking deep breaths, Cris grabs my hand and rubs slow circles across my palm with her thumb. I smile and ease the tension in my shoulders by exhaling exhaustedly, having to relive that nightmare.

"Everything is going to be okay, *Bebita*. We won't let anything happen to you, okay?" Cris reassures, lifting my head and kissing me gently. Her lips are soft. I sink into it — not because I'm ready, but because I need the anchor.

Our lips mingle, and the desperate neediness I feel to cling to her red silk robe is so compelling. I would freely let her use my body in whatever way she sees fit and enjoy it.

She breaks our kiss, my eyes closed, taking in the slight distraction as I exhale slowly, gazing upon her big brown eyes.

"You feeling a little better?" Cris inquires, pushing a strand of my hair behind my ear. I rapidly nod and sign 'I love you' to her.

"Look! How about that guy over there?" Riley shouts, pointing toward a man sitting beside the bar.

We focus our attention on the bar and see a man barely raise his head as I approach Jared. A faint twitch and Jude immediately pauses the surveillance footage to enhance the picture.

As she focuses on getting a clearer picture, I feel my phone vibrate on my lap. I use my face to unlock the phone and click on the newest thread.

I gasp, dropping my phone and unable to capture my breath from the clear threat that someone has sent me. Panicking, the girls lift me from the chair and lay me flat on the floor. I close my eyes, breathing in and out while counting five things that surround me.

My girls: Frankie, Jude, Cris, Noah, and Riley.

I repeat this like a mantra in my head over and over. Riley grabs my phone from the floor, turning it over to see the text I left on the screen.

Her eyes bulge, solidifying my panic attack and the fact that Riley's attack is my fault. I shed a tear, open my eyes, and see everyone's petrified looks plastered on their faces.

"What do the texts say?" Noah probes.

They wait on bated breath for Riley to reveal the text that will change everything for us. I don't know how we're going to catch this guy, but one thing I know for sure is that he is going to pay.

I'll even do something I've never done before.

I'll kill anyone.

For my girls.

Just like they've done for me.

About the Author

Want More? Find Me Here

Kamila Garza-
Instagram: https://www.instagram.com/authorkamilagarza_/
Linktree: https://linktr.ee/authorkamilagarza

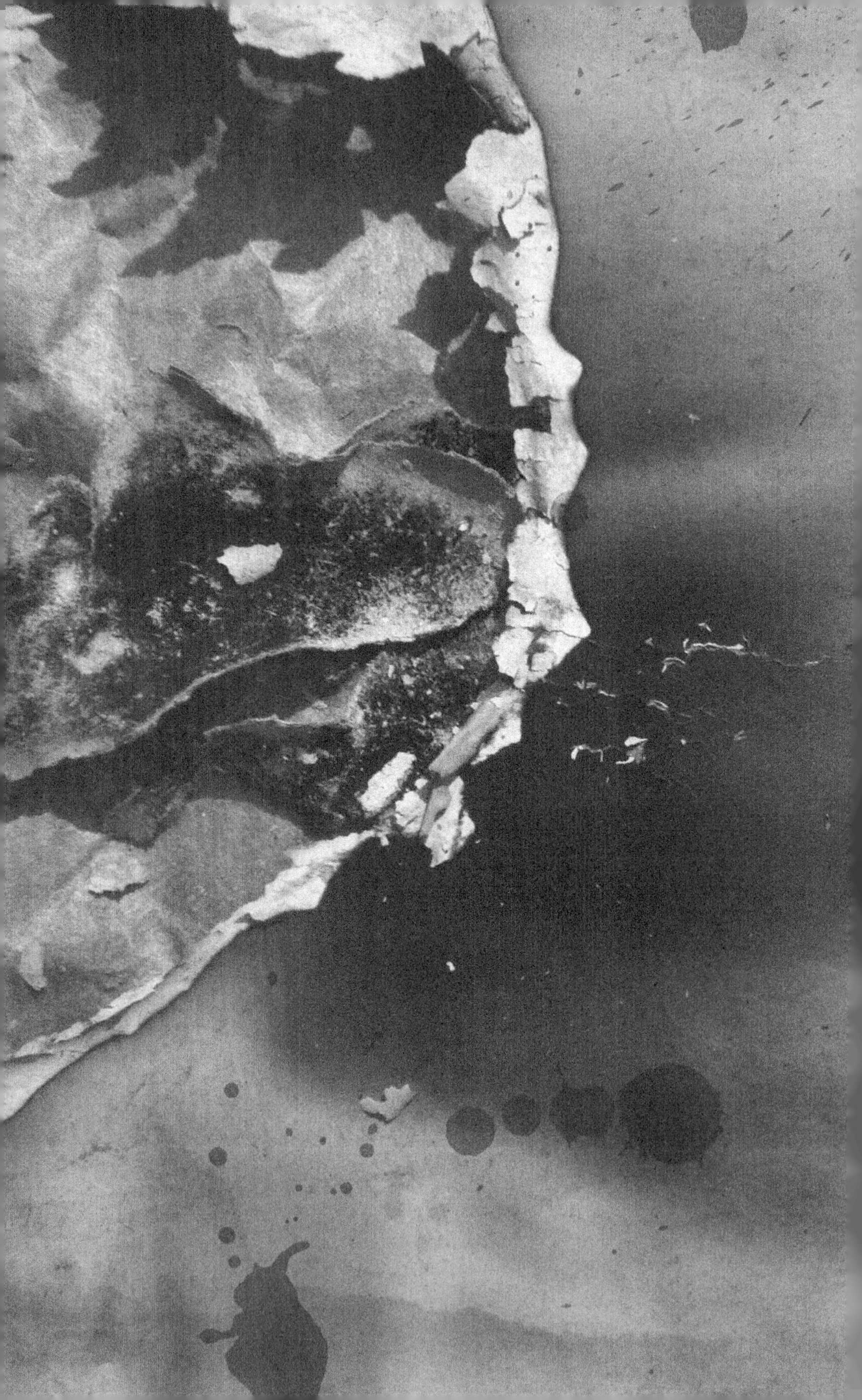

Your Worst F*cking Nightmare

KM ROGNESS

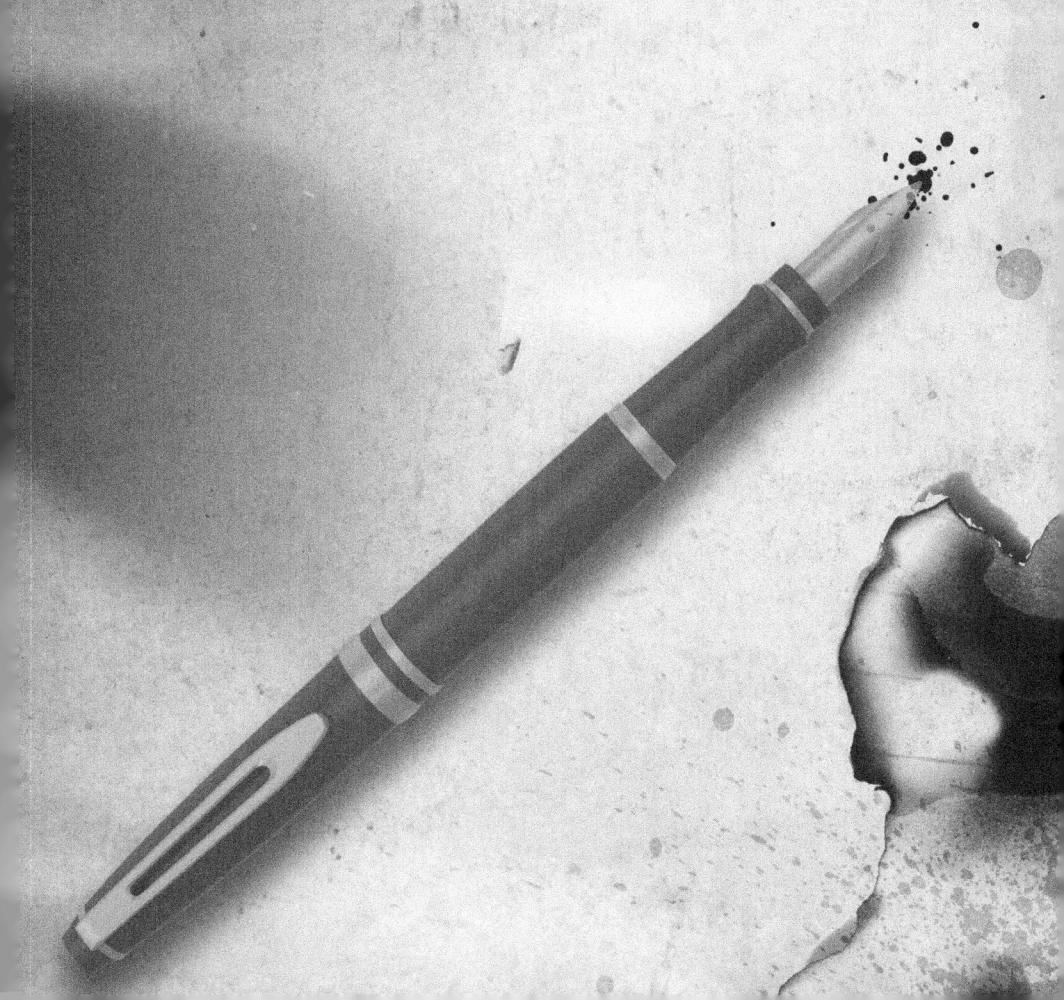

Dedication

For all of you who feel that burning rage, like fire flowing through your veins, go on and unleash it, fucker; it's going to be a beautiful fucking sight.

Playlist

Playlist Link: https://open.spotify.com/playlist/
2XxLIGdjYYwTUEZvL9C6eg?si=
RVTH6NOcRnSLHnLLqCA6oA&pi=JbMTjJU2TYiFN

Chapter 1

Flights and Flashbacks

Hot grains of sand swirl around us as we march in formation along the airstrip, the wind driving them straight into my eyes, burning and gritty. I attribute the tears filling my eyes to the discomfort rather than acknowledging the true source of my pain. I can feel the weight of countless stares boring into my back like daggers as we continue our procession. It's ironic, given that those very soldiers have already stabbed me in the back. Keeping my chin up and my shoulders straight, I concentrate on moving forward; I refuse to turn around and give them the satisfaction they crave.

I want to go home—to the familiar comforts of the good old U.S. of A., to my small city outside of Boston, where my twin stepbrothers eagerly await my return. There the autumn air is crisp, and the changing leaves are a vibrant spectacle, reminiscent of a postcard. I'm ready to leave Afghanistan behind, ready to escape the oppressive heat and the weight of my comrades' betrayals.

After eleven months, two weeks, four days, seven hours, fifteen minutes, and twenty seconds trapped in a relentless nightmare, I step onto the plane with my platoon, swiftly claiming the seat closest to the exit. Once buckled in, my bag securely kicked beneath the bench seat, I close my eyes tightly, avoiding any glance at the soldiers who deliberately sit across from me—the "fucked-up five," as I've come to call them. Once my protectors, once the brothers I admired, they're now nothing more than ghosts. I pretend they don't exist, even as the memory of their betrayal lingers, wreaking havoc on my spirit every day. I strive to appear strong and unflinching; I wear a mask, despite knowing it's painfully transparent.

The plane lurches forward, racing down the runway, jolting me from my thoughts and forcing my eyes open. I fixate on the timer on my watch, counting down each hour, minute, and second until I can find refuge from the harsh realities around me. No one is truly safe—not even those who think they are. They spent years coaxing me to let down my guard, only to shatter everything I had fought to protect. Just one night was all it took for my life to collapse into chaos, and that moment became the catalyst for their continued torment. I will carry the brutal reminder of their actions for the rest of my fucking life.

But they will, too. They won't just remember how they hurt me; they will remember how I fought back. They will feel my retribution until their very last breath. The thought ignites a smile across my lips for the first time in months, growing wider as I bravely glance at the "fucked-up five," watching the color drain from their faces.

I try not to fall asleep on the flight, knowing the darkness will come for me the second my eyes close, but it's inevitable, and before I know it, I'm transported back to that fateful night just months ago.

Flashback: 4 months ago

Sitting around the fire with five of my closest friends, we share memories of our lives outside of the military, as well as a bottle of Jack Daniel's that goes down smoother than usual. After a few rounds, I pass on my turn, feeling a bit woozy as the liquor flows through my body, creating inner turmoil with my mind and my stomach.

"It's not like you to pass on a drink, Black," Conrad says, a cocky little laugh following his observation.

"Shit ain't sitting right with me tonight," I mutter, the flames from the fire multiplying right before my eyes.

Brayden puts his arm around my back as I start to sway in my seat, and Patrick rushes up to my right to support my other side as I begin to lean.

"I think this is the closest you've ever let me get to you," he says laughing, the others joining in and bringing chaos to my ears.

"That's because I don't want you to get close to me," I snap, grabbing my head and putting pressure on my temples, just wanting the pain to stop.

Everything is loud and distorted. My head pounds and a blinding pain travels behind my eyes. Never in my life have I felt this way while drinking, and I instantly become paranoid, feeling myself start to freak out on the inside.

"Why don't we get you inside to lay down?" Ryan offers, suddenly appearing in front of me, blocking the glowing flames and bringing the smallest sliver of peace to my eyes.

"I can go by myself," I assure them, pushing their hands off of me as I try like hell to stand up and not bust my ass in front of them. "You act like I'm this fragile little thing, but don't forget I've beaten your asses numerous times."

I manage to get to my feet and stand on my own, still feeling my legs shaking and like my knees are about to buckle, but I push through it as I flash them one last smile.

"Why you gotta keep rubbing that shit in, Lailah?" Sebastian asks, a hint of embarrassment in his tone.

"Because it's fun, Bash," I laugh as I turn around, giving them a final wave as I make my way back to base alone, knowing deep down that something isn't right.

But I don't make it. Somewhere before the door, I collapse, and although my eyes are closed, I can hear their hushed whispers as I'm lifted into Brayden's arms, his strong Old Spice scent giving him away. I push against his chest, trying to tell him to put me down but no words come out. My eyes reopen but my body feels paralyzed, and as I'm brought into a room that isn't mine, panic begins to consume me, especially when the other four follow Brayden in and lock the door behind them.

As I'm laid on Bash's bed, I stare at my friends as they look at me with evil in their eyes. The sinister smiles that grace their lips turn my blood cold even though my body feels consumed with heat.

"Put something over her eyes. I can't do this shit with her giving me that look," Patrick says, a look of shame swirling in his eyes as he quickly undresses.

I try to move but I can't. I try to scream but I can't. Everything I try to do doesn't work, and that's when it hits me: I've been drugged.

"No, I want to see the look in her pretty eyes when she feels me inside her," Bash says, leaning down and brushing his lips across my cheek as Brayden and Ryan gently undress me, making sure my cammies are folded neatly on the desk near the window, a small act that reminds me how the military has molded our lives and turned us into their little puppets.

A wave of tiredness washes over me as Bash climbs on top of me, and thankfully, my eyes close and the darkness takes me at the perfect time.

When I wake up the next morning, I feel like absolute death. My body is screaming in pain, covered in bitemarks and bruises. I frantically sit up, breathing a small sigh of relief when I notice I'm in my bed, alone. But the damage has been done, and although I blacked out, I know exactly what they fucking did. And as I scrub myself raw in the shower, the water scalding hot, I promise myself I'll get my revenge on them. It might not be today or tomorrow, but it's coming, and they're going to fucking regret ever laying a hand on me.

Present

I wake up in a cold sweat, with my hands shaking and my heart thumping against my ribcage like it's trying to bust the fuck out of it. The cunning faces of the five guys who were once my best friends make me sick as I boldly stare back, refusing to let their intimidation attempt scare me away.

Thinking back on that night, I feel sick to my stomach knowing what took place after that. I found out the hard way that they recorded themselves gang raping me, passing it to the higher-ups whose pockets went as deep as the ocean. I couldn't report it to anyone because it seemed like everyone was in on it, and no one wanted to do a damn thing about it.

But a month later, even more bad news came, and it came in the form of a dozen pregnancy tests, all screaming positive right in my face. I felt even sicker knowing one of them got me pregnant than I did knowing that my five best friends drugged and gang raped me.

I didn't want the baby, but getting it terminated went against my beliefs. Not to mention, if the wrong people found out about it, I could get into some serious trouble with my command while the men who raped me wouldn't even get a fucking slap on the wrist—that's how the Marines dealt with shit, a quick sweep under the rug for the men, and most likely, a dishonorable discharge for the women who dared to speak out against them. I tried to hide it but I was showing quicker than I thought I would be, and soon the guys found out about my little secret. And what they did then was way worse than I could've ever fucking imagined.

I shiver, hugging my arms around my chest, anxiously chewing on my bottom lip as I recall the brutal beating they put me through. I was purposely pushed down the stairs by Ryan while Conrad, Brayden, and Patrick waited at the bottom, delivering vicious blows with their boots to my stomach. Bash was the one who carried me to the infirmary, claiming he found me after I had just taken a spill down the stairs. He stayed with me while I was there being treated, not because he wanted to make sure I was okay, but to make sure their little beating had done its job and caused me to miscarry.

The nurse, of course, was part of the group of Marines who knew better than to talk. My medical records were falsified since, after slipping her hush money, the fact that I was pregnant and lost the baby never made its way into my record. It was as if the rape and the miscarriage never happened. But they did happen, and I knew that they did.

That was when I finally understood how corrupt the military really was, and after enduring four years of training and deployments, I was ready to leave that part of my life behind.

Giving one last glance at the corrupt soldiers across from me, I maintain my smile as we descend the runway, anxious and ready to see the twins, but even more so to take back everything that was stolen from me.

Chapter 2

Rain and Romance

As I step off the plane and finally set foot on U.S. soil again, my heart races at the sight of Zander and Xavier waiting for me. A broad smile spreads across my face, mingling with joyful tears that stream down my cheeks. It's as if I'm in a scene from a movie, as I run toward them, letting my sea bag fall to the ground before leaping into their arms. I bury my face in the crook of Zander's neck, while Xavier wraps his arms around me from behind, showering my neck with long, overdue kisses. I'm home, exactly where I belong, and although this euphoric high may fade quickly, I intend to savor every moment.

I never shared the details of what happened in Afghanistan, but someone did. The twins were sent footage of my attack and had demanded the arrests of those involved, hoping for justice. Yet, instead of receiving the respect I deserved, I became a target of mockery; the incident that left me permanently scarred—both inside and out—was reduced to a cruel joke. Just another day in the life of a woman in the military. While I've learned to cope, the twins have struggled to come to terms with it.

As I gain my footing, Xavier picks up my bag while Zander scans the crowd of soldiers walking off the plane, likely searching for the "fucked-up five," but they only have a brief idea what those men look like, and I have no fucking intention of letting them find out here.

"Come on, I just want to go home," I urge Zander, tugging at the sleeve of his hoodie, his emerald green eyes blazing with the same anger I feel.

"Lailah, one of these days, you're going to tell me who those bastards are," Zander snaps, finally tearing his gaze away from the crowd to meet my eyes.

"There's no point; I can handle it on my own," I reassure him, winking as we start to walk away.

"Lay, not only are you not going to confront them, but you're definitely not going near them again," Xavier warns, a grin creeping onto my face as I link my arms through both his and Zander's, and we step out into the pouring rain.

"I understand where you're coming from," I say, glancing at them. "You both want to protect me—like brothers and boyfriends both—but I'm a grown woman and I don't need anyone's help." I clear my throat as we make our way to Xavier's sleek, black Lexus, its windows tinted as dark as its matte finish. "What I need right now is both of you, and nothing else. So take me home and fuck me like you've missed me."

Zander opens the passenger door for me, a playful grin spreading across his lips. "Now that we can definitely do, little soldier. That's a fucking promise."

I sink into the front seat, my fingers gliding over the luxurious leather. The familiar scent that I've longed for fills my senses, conjuring memories of our time together. Though our parents disowned us for it, the bond between the twins and I strengthened when I moved into their house after my mom's engagement was announced. What began as a friendship evolved into something unbreakable, even after we faced challenges like being kicked out. I once feared that joining the military might sever our bond, but instead, it brought us even closer, despite the distance.

PULLING INTO THE DRIVEWAY OF OUR HOME, XAVIER BARELY GETS THE car in park before I fling open the door and leap out. It's hard to contain myself after a year apart. I have needs too, and now that I'm finally home, it's time to fucking embrace them.

We don't even make it to the bedroom before our clothes are off, and Xavier pulls me onto his lap as he collapses onto the couch, his hands possessively gripping my hips as I rock back and forth on his cock. Zander gets behind me, brushing my hair to one side just so he can trail hot kisses across my shoulder blades and down my spine as he pushes his cock against my ass.

I can barely catch my breath, the sensations overwhelming as both of them take charge. Xavier's hands anchor me as he guides my movements, urging me to find the rhythm that drives both of us wild. My mind momentarily veers away from the shadows of my past, lost in the bliss of their touch. Zander's kisses send shivers up my spine, igniting a fire within me that I thought had been extinguished during my time away.

"God, I've missed this," I breathe out, my voice barely a whisper yet dripping with need.

Zander responds with a deep growl, his lips brushing against my skin, sending waves of pleasure coursing through my entire body. "So have we, baby. So have we."

"No more running, Lailah," Xavier murmurs, his voice thick with lust. "You're not fucking leaving us again. We'll do whatever it takes to keep you safe."

Zander chuckles darkly, his breath hot against my back. "And trust me, we know how to fight dirty, especially for you."

His hands find their place on my waist, his grip tightening as he aligns himself with me from behind, pressing against my body in perfect unison with Xavier. I throw my head back, ready to surrender completely to the moment.

"Then show me... show me how much I've been missed," I beg, breathing heavily as their touch sets fire to my skin.

It's a challenge, and they take it instantly, the heat in the room rising. With a sharp thrust from Xavier, pleasure floods my senses as he slams me down on his cock, followed closely by Zander's gentle but insistent pressure behind me as he slides into my ass, all the muscles in my body tightening then loosening with each thrust.

Together, they create a rhythm that resonates deep within my core, filling the empty void left by the recent chaos I've lived through. The worries and fears billow away like smoke disappearing into thin air; I'm suffocated by their presence, but in the best way possible as I run my palms up and down Xavier's fully tattooed chest, tracing his defined muscles with my fingertips. He smirks, digging his fingers deeper into my flesh until he finds my hip bones and holds me even tighter.

Feeling Zander's hand glide up and down my back, my entire body quivers in anticipation, and I put a slight arch in my back which allows his cock to slide deeper into my ass. He grabs the back of my neck while Xavier grabs the front, both of them squeezing as their thrusts become intensified as the three of us fuck to the sound of the pouring rain.

Every thrust, every kiss, builds the tension inside me until I'm on the edge, teetering between reality and a euphoric dream. It feels like I'm melting into them, becoming one with the heat, the love, the memories we're weaving together.

"Please," I moan, urging them for more, desperate for the release that feels so tantalizingly close.

With one last powerful thrust from Xavier, I feel the ripples of ecstasy crash over me like a tidal wave, dragging me under its intense pull. My body convulses—shattering, exploding—in a culmination of pleasure unlike anything I've ever felt before. And just as begin I ride the crest, Zander claims me fully from behind, pushing us over the edge as he joins me in the tidal wave of bliss.

Xavier pulls my mouth down to meet his using his tight grip on my throat, and our tongues duel in a fierce battle neither one of us wants to surrender to. While I'm lost in the kiss with his brother, Zander gently slides his cock out of my ass then brutally slams back in without warning, causing me to accidentally sink my teeth into Xavier's tongue. His cock throbs in my ass, pulsing rapidly with each spurt of cum he shoots into me. As he fucks me, fiercely and determined, hot cum drips out of my ass and slides down the inside of my legs, stirring something inside of me as I bounce up and down on Xavier's cock, desperate for my own release.

"That's it, my little soldier, bounce for me," he urges, thrusting his hips upward so the tip of his cock presses against the pleasurable spot inside of me that sends me over the edge once and for all.

Time seems to suspend as I lose myself entirely, caught in the storm of sensations that surround us. Gradually, the chaos begins to settle, and I find myself nestled between them—exhausted yet exhilarated—both emotionally and physically. Breathy laughs fill the air as Xavier brushes a damp strand of hair away from my forehead.

"Welcome home, Lailah," he whispers, and I can't help but smile even as my heart races in gratitude.

Zander leans in to plant a soft kiss on my cheek. "We'll always be here for you, but you need to promise us something." His expression turns serious, the supportive brotherly nature creeping back through his heated gaze. "You'll share what happened in Afghanistan when you're ready. No more hiding. We want to help, but we can't do it if you keep us in the dark."

As the rain falls hard against the rooftop, reminding me that I'm finally home, I lick my lips, deliberating over his words, but my heart knows the truth. "Okay," I finally say, my voice weaker than I'd like, "I promise."

The weight of the world seems heavier on my shoulders right now, but I feel a warmth radiating from their touch, a reminder that I won't have to carry it alone anymore.

As I look up at the faces of the twins—my twin flames, my unwavering anchors—I know that no matter what I've faced or whatever lies ahead, together we'll navigate the shadows, and in their company, I've never felt more ready to face the light.

Chapter 3
Rage and Revenge

Once I'm sure the twins are sound asleep, I slip out of our bed and quickly get dressed, choosing an all black outfit with my combat boots, making sure I'm ready for the chaos that tonight is going to bring. Armed with my gun and my knife, both tucked into my boots, I sneak quietly out of the house and blend in with the darkness as soon as I step outside.

The rain is still coming down, having turned into a heavy drizzle, with loud thunder and bolts of lightning that brighten up the gloomy sky. The entire walk down the familiar streets I grew up on, I repeat the address of the "fucked-up five" in my head, knowing that they all live together, and unfortunately, not too far from my house. I know where they hang out, the addresses of the girls they like to fuck, pretty much anywhere they go—I know about it. I've done more research in the last few months than I ever did in fucking school, but I'm prepared.

I pull a bandana over my nose and mouth, making sure the only thing they can see is my eyes. I want them to have to look directly into them when I take their fucking lives and they take their last breath. I want them to know it was me who took away their freedom and everything they loved, just as they took away mine.

Tonight, I know that Patrick and Ryan are home while Bash, Conrad, and Brayden are out celebrating their return to the U.S., so unfortunately for Patrick and Ryan, their first night home is also going to be their last.

Rage simmers beneath the surface, turning my insides to boiling as I approach the dimly lit house, noticing only the downstairs lights on. I reach down and pull my gun from my boot, cocking it so I don't have to waste any time doing so once I reach their door. Soaked from head-to-toe from the cold rain, I walk right up the steps and knock on the front door, a plan already concrete in my mind.

When the front door opens, Patrick's jaw drops and his hands raise in mock surrender, already knowing it's me beneath the mask. Pressing the gun into his chest, I push him inside and follow, quietly closing and locking the door behind me then turning off the porch light. Ryan comes walking by in nothing but a pair of sweats, dropping the bottle of beer he was holding in his hand once he sees the gun aimed at Patrick. Glass shatters across the hardwood floor and beer pools beneath his feet as he puts his hands up too, absolutely no color in his expression.

"Lailah, what the fuck do you think you're doing?" Patrick asks, almost in a taunting tone, as if he doesn't believe I can pull the trigger.

But I came here to do more than pull a lousy trigger, and they're soon going to find that out.

"You thought you'd get away with the shit you guys did to me? Thought I'd roll over and take it—the torment, the whispers? You fucking thought wrong," I bite, hearing the venomous rage in my tone as I guide them both to the basement, forcing them down the dark stairs where their lives are about to come to an end. "You thought wrong, motherfuckers. You shouldn't have fucking touched me."

"Jesus, we're sorry!" Ryan exclaims, his eyes wide with fear.

"Oh, now you're sorry? When you have a gun pointed in your fucking face, now you're sorry?" An unhinged sounding laugh escapes my lips, and the rage surging through me begins to intensify. "But you weren't fucking sorry when your ass was raping me, right? Or when you pushed me down the fucking stairs and beat the shit out of me to make sure I lost the baby, right? Do I have that shit right?"

"Relax, Ryan, she ain't gonna do shit," Patrick laughs, glaring at me with a challenging look. "And besides, if something does pop off, her ass isn't getting out of here alive, that's for damn sure."

I grip the gun until my knuckles turn white, the taunting pushing me faster over the edge of insanity. And when Patrick makes the slightest move, I pull the trigger, putting a 9 millimeter straight through his chest without flinching. As he drops to the cement floor, blood pooling beneath him, Ryan tries to make a run for it, but I shoot again, this time piercing his lower back with a bullet that goes through his stomach.

"I ain't gonna do shit, right? That's what you said, isn't it?" I bend down, pulling Patrick's hair to lift his head, grinning wildly as spit flies from my mouth as I talk.

Putting my gun down when I know they're both not a threat anymore, I pull out my knife from my boot, holding it up and watching it gleam in the moonlight streaming in the basement window. It's shiny, sharp, and clean... for now.

I get up and walk over to Ryan, ignoring both of their groans, pain clearly evident in the sounds slipping from their mouths. And fuck, they ring like music in my ears. I grab his arm and drag his limp body over to where Patrick lays, leaving a trail of blood behind. With both of them still barely alive, I try to hurry, wanting them to feel the pain that I feel every day.

"I remember you always wishing I'd touch your cock, Patrick, well, now you're getting your wish," I laugh, hearing how crazy it sounds through the smile gracing my lips, even though on the inside, the rage I'm feeling has never burned hotter.

I pull their pants down, just enough so I can get to their dicks. Holding back a gag and with my knife gripped firmly in one hand, I wrap my other hand around Patrick's cock and make a clean slice at the base, then do the same thing with Ryan's. Their screams pierce my ears, but I revel in them, and while their mouths are open wide, I take the opportunity to shove their cut off members down their throats, instantly silencing them.

But I'm not done yet. Grabbing Ryan by his hair, I lift his head, putting the blade to his throat. All it takes is a swift cut from ear to ear with some pressure, and his life is over instantly. Patrick begins to go into shock so I quickly slit his throat, then sit there watching both of them bleed out, with their cocks in their mouths and their heads pretty much separated from the rest of their bodies.

It's a beautiful fucking sight, and a small weight immediately lifts once I know they're dead and they can never hurt me again. But my mission isn't over. This was only two of them, there's still three more to go.

To keep my secret for just a little while longer, I spend the night methodically dismembering Ryan and Patrick's bodies, placing their severed limbs in thick, black contractor bags I found in the basement. I put their heads in the same bag, planning to take it with me to dump on the walk home. The rest of their body parts, I drag out into the thickly wooded backyard, along with a shovel and a bottle of vodka I stole out of their liquor cabinet.

I don't know how long I spent digging out there, but by the time I was done and the hole was more than six feet deep, my body felt like it did when I was put through boot camp. Muscles I didn't know I had ached like fucking hell but the vodka helped tremendously with the pain. Once the bags were thrown into the hole and I replaced the dirt and fallen branches, I turned my back and walked away as if nothing had ever happened. As if I didn't just murder two of my ex-friends and cut their bodies into pieces then buried them in their own backyard.

It didn't bother me one fucking bit. The only thing on my mind on the walk home was how sweet it was going to feel when I killed Conrad, Brayden, and Bash, the three I'd been closest to.

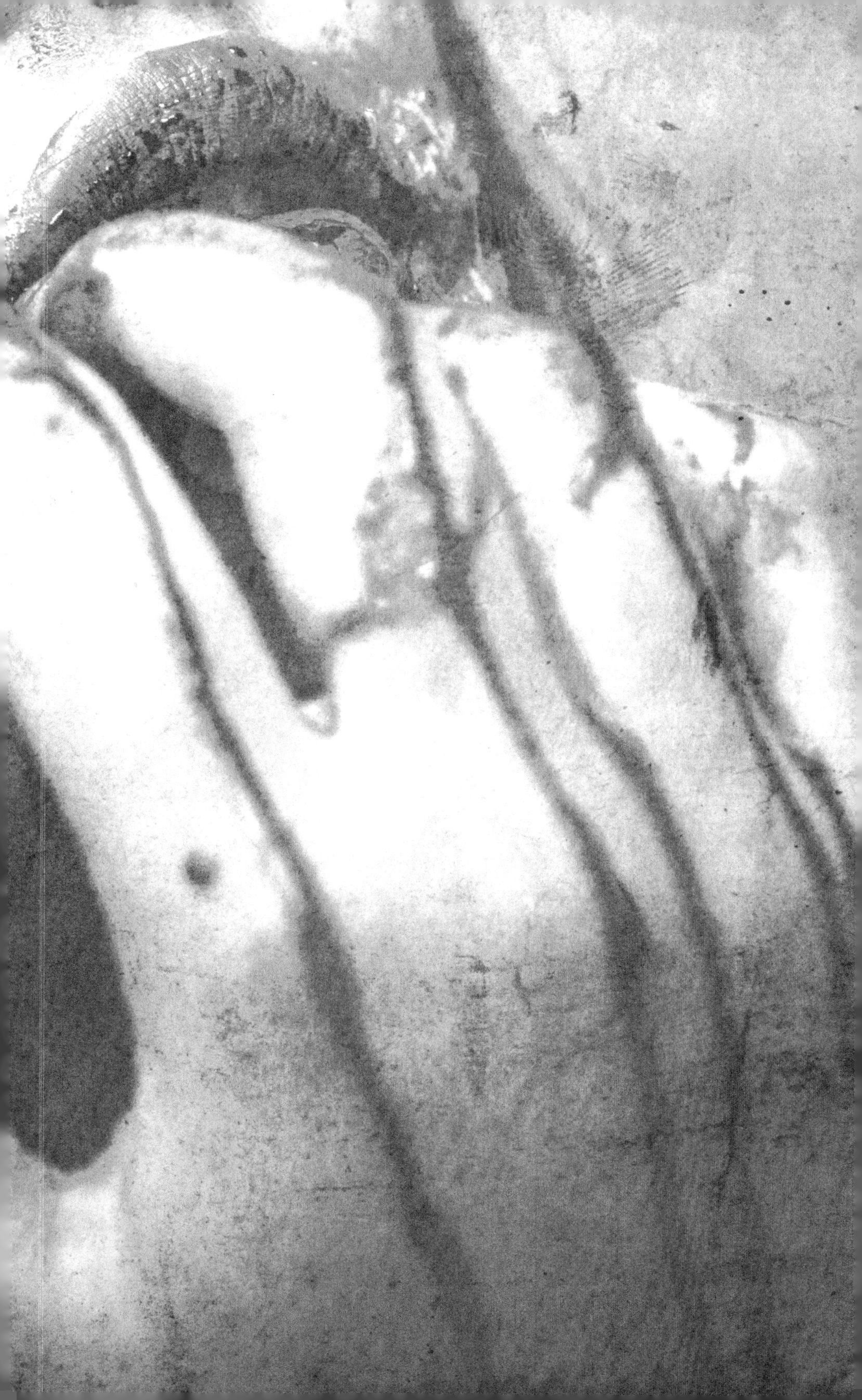

Chapter 4

Making Love and Murder

"Where the fuck have you been?" Xavier's deep, commanding voice startles me as I step into the dark house, the light flickering on to reveal him sitting on the couch in the shadows.

"I was out—I just needed some air," I reply, fully aware that he sees right through my lie.

"That's fucking bullshit, Lailah. Didn't me and Z tell you to stay away from them?" He rises, anger radiating from him as he backs me up against the front door, his hand tightening around my throat.

"It's my fight, X. Not yours," I counter, desperate for him to see my perspective.

They both know I can handle myself. Yes, I let my fucking guard down once, and it nearly cost me everything, but I won't make that mistake again. I understand their urge to protect me and take on my battles, but this is one I need to face alone.

"Did you kill them?" Xavier demands, his nose nearly brushing against mine, venom lacing his words as his grip around my throat tightens further.

"Two of them," I confess, a smirk dancing on my lips as my gaze flickers to his mouth. "There are still three left."

He shakes his head, a heavy sigh escaping him as he rests his forehead against mine, anguish clouding his eyes. As if drawn by an invisible thread, I slide my hands under his white shirt, caressing his chest and tracing the lines of his muscles, pulling him even closer.

No words pass between us as he lifts me effortlessly into his arms, my legs instinctively wrapping around his waist. Once more, he slams my back against the door, grips my throat, and captures my lips in a frenzied kiss—and I welcome it. In fact, I help him undress, pushing his pants down to free his cock, the thing I desire most. He puts me down, only to rip off my pants in a single, violent tug, then slaps my ass and cups it, lifting me once more.

His skin is warm against mine, and for a brief moment, the world outside fades away—just the two of us, lost in our desperate need for each other. I can feel the tension in his body, a mix of anger, fear, and desire. As he pulls away just enough to meet my gaze, I see the storm brewing behind his eyes, and it sends a shiver of thrill down my spine.

"Lailah," he breathes, his voice low, a warning wrapped in urgency. "This isn't just about you anymore. You can't keep doing this."

"Right now," I whisper, pressing my finger against his lips, "this is what I need."

I lean in, capturing his lips again, kissing him with a fierce intensity that leaves no room for thoughts of consequences. He reaches between our bodies and hastily pushes my drenched panties to the side, slightly bending his knees as he angles his cock so it eases right into me.

My back is slammed once again into the door as he thrusts hard, fucking me savagely against it so our bodies create a rhythmic thumping sound that I'm sure Zander can hear. He chokes me harder so I choke him back, sinking my teeth into his bottom lip as he sucks all the air out of my lungs. I ride him as best as I can for being held in the air, my pussy greedily gripping his cock as he tries hard to fuck me through the tight muscles that continue to clench around him.

It's a wild rush of passion and rage, a blend of emotions being exposed as we take our anger out on each other, both expressing our dominance and refusing to back down. His green eyes pierce into mine, holding my gaze as he fucks me even harder, ripping high-pitched whimpers from the depths of my throat.

"Why do you have to be so fucking stubborn?" he asks, panting and gasping for breath, his brows pinching in frustration.

I grin, bringing my other hand to his hair, fisting his silky black curls that are laced with his sweat. He growls against my lips while I'm still biting on his bottom one, refusing to let go. But when I do, it's only because the metallic taste of his blood hits my tongue, and I sensually lick along his jawline, trying to get the taste of his blood out of my mouth.

"You want to help me, don't you?" I ask breathlessly in between thrusts, the veins in his neck pulsing rapidly against my fingers as my grip tightens, pleasure surging through me like a fucking wildfire. "You want to kill the motherfuckers who hurt me, don't you, Xavier?"

His movements stop, only briefly, but the sudden shift in the air between us tells me everything I need to know. He drops me from his arms but catches me before my knees give out underneath me. Without speaking, he grabs my hair and drags me over to the back of the couch and bends me over it, delivering a brutal thrust into my ass that tenses all the muscles in my body. He reaches around to the front of my body, cups my breast, and then reclaims his place around my throat, cutting off all airflow almost instantly.

"You think this is a fucking game, little soldier?" he grunts, slamming his cock mercilessly into my ass and plunging his fingers into my pussy, fucking me with both in unison.

He nips at my ear and I shiver, pushing my ass back, desperate for more of him. "I'm not playing games, Xavier," I moan, throwing my head back against his shoulder. "But I want to hear you fucking say it. Tell me you want to help kill the motherfuckers who hurt me."

Just then, the sudden crash of glass shatters the intimacy. Instinct kicks in, and I'm off him in a second, adrenaline rushing through my veins. Xavier's expression shifts from desire to deadly seriousness, and I can feel the shift in the air. We're not alone.

"Stay behind me," he commands, his body taut like a coiled spring, ready to pounce.

Even though I'd be better at protecting him, I nod, moving back slightly, keeping my eyes on the darkened hallway where the sound came from. My heartbeat is deafening, echoing in my ears as I scan the sparse room for any signs of movement, my military training kicking in on instinct.

A figure emerges from the shadows, tall and menacing, the light catching a glint of metal—knives, several of them. The newcomer grins, twisted and cruel, and I feel Xavier tense beside me.

"You didn't think you could escape so easily, did you?" The intruder mocks, stepping further into the light, revealing a face I recognize all too well. A ghost from my past, someone I thought I had dealt with long ago.

"I thought I was clear." My voice is steadier than I feel. "You should have stayed gone."

"Oh, Lailah, you know better than that." His cruel smile widens. "You're the fight I need to win, and I always get what I want."

In that moment, I feel the white-hot surge of rage pulse through me, ignited not just by his words but by the fact that he's threatened everything I've built. With fierce determination, I step in front of Xavier, ready to fight like I've trained to do. This isn't just about survival anymore—it's fucking personal.

"This time, Brayden, you'll regret coming after me," I promise, adrenaline sharpening my focus as my pulse races.

"Is that so?" he taunts, flicking a knife in his hand, its blade glinting menacingly.

Without another word, he lunges forward. Instincts take over, and I dodge right, feeling the air whoosh past me as the knife narrowly misses my body. I pivot and counter, my own blade glimmering as it slices through the dim light, ready to reclaim my fight.

The room erupts into chaos, a whirlwind of limbs and adrenaline as I fight to regain control. Brayden's eyes widen for a fraction of a second with surprise; it's just enough for me to capitalize on. I lunge forward, determination fueling my every move, slicing the air with precision as I aim for his throat.

"Lailah, no!" Xavier shouts, but it's too late—Brayden is already reacting.

He twists to the side, narrowly avoiding my blade and countering with a kick that sends me stumbling back toward the couch. Just as I brace myself for impact, I feel Xavier's steadying hand on my back, pushing me forward, the instinct to protect surging through him.

"Stay back!" I yell, shaking off the moment of shock and snapping my focus back to Brayden, who's stalking toward us with a predatory grin.

"Did you really think you could try to take us down and not face the fucking consequences?" Brayden taunts, eyes gleaming with dark delight. He circles us like a shark, calculating.

"You're a fucking coward hiding in the shadows," I bite back, feigning confidence to mask the rising fear. "You think you can intimidate me with your pathetic attempt at whatever this is?"

"Pathetic?" He laughs, a sound that echoes off the walls. "You're playing a dangerous game, Lailah. But you know the stakes, don't you? I've taken everything from you before. What makes you think this time will be any different?"

"Because I'm not that scared little girl anymore," I growl, feeling the solid grip of my knife in my palm, its weight reassuring. "You can't hurt me anymore, Brayden—none of you can—but I can hurt all of you."

With that, I charge at him again, this time unleashing a series of rapid strikes, aiming not just to defend myself, but to push him back—back out of my house, back out of my life forever. Each move is fueled by years of hurt, loss, and rage, punctuated by the memory of every failure that led me to this moment.

He dodges and weaves, but I'm relentless, driven by the ferocity of my training. I duck under his flailing arm and thrust forward, my blade glancing into his side. I see the flicker of surprise cross his features as he reels back, blood soaking through his shirt, but the hesitation doesn't last long. Instead, he narrows his eyes, fury igniting his movements as he retaliates, swinging his knife toward me.

I barely manage to sidestep, the blade nicking my arm—a quick jab of pain that only heightens my awareness, sharpens my focus. It's a warning. I hear Xavier shout my name, but I barely register it, emotions surging—this is my fight, my chance to make things right.

I flip the knife in my grip, shifting my stance as I prepare to go on the offensive again. Brayden sneers, a twisted confidence in his stance.

"You're playing with fire, sweetheart. But fire burns out."

"Not this fire," I hiss, my blood boiling with every word, every thrust of my blade.

And with that, I attack again, forcing him toward the shadows at the edge of the room. Each thrust is more calculated, each movement carrying the weight of everything I've fought for. In the corner of my vision, I catch Xavier shifting closer, his own fists clenched, ready to jump in if necessary. The silent communication between us buzzes with an electric tension as I notice a flicker of hesitation in Brayden's eyes. I push my advantage, lunging at him, feeling the thrill of power surging through me.

"Fuck you!" I shout triumphantly as I drive the knife toward his upper side once more, only for him to twist the wrong way at the last moment, my blade sticking into his skin. He hisses in pain, wild eyes filled with rage and surprise, fury morphing into desperation.

"You think you've won?" he growls, backing away just enough to regroup. "I'm just getting fucking started!"

He lunges again, and I brace myself for impact, this time ready to counter him. I've been through hell; nothing can take me down now. As I sidestep his attack, positioning myself for the final blow, I feel Xavier's presence beside me, almost like a protective aura.

Reinforced, fueled by fury and the need for vengeance, I strike, my knife finding its mark deep in Brayden's abdomen this time. He gasps, shock written all over his face as he stumbles backward, collapsing to the floor in a heap of disbelief.

"Lailah..." he gasps, clutching his wound, eyes wide and desperate, the fight draining from him. "No..."

"Don't play the victim now," I spit, stepping forward to loom over him. "You brought this on yourself." I glare at him, feeling even more betrayed than before, and thrust my blade into his heart, viciously twisting the handle to inflict as much pain as I can.

As his breath grows shallow, an eerie stillness blankets the room. In that moment, I'm not the girl he terrorized. I'm a force to be reckoned with—a warrior forged through pain. I take a deep breath, adrenaline coursing through my veins as I lower my blade, turning back toward Xavier.

His eyes meet mine, concern mixed with pride, and for the first time, I can see the emotions swirling beneath the surface.

"You did it, Lailah," he murmurs, stepping closer, but there's something else in his gaze—an understanding that this is just the beginning of a much larger fight.

As we stand there, both panting from the adrenaline and tension, I know one thing for certain: this wasn't just a battle. It was a declaration. Brayden might have been a ghost from my past, but now he was nothing more than a reminder of who I am and what I'm capable of.

Three down, two more to go...

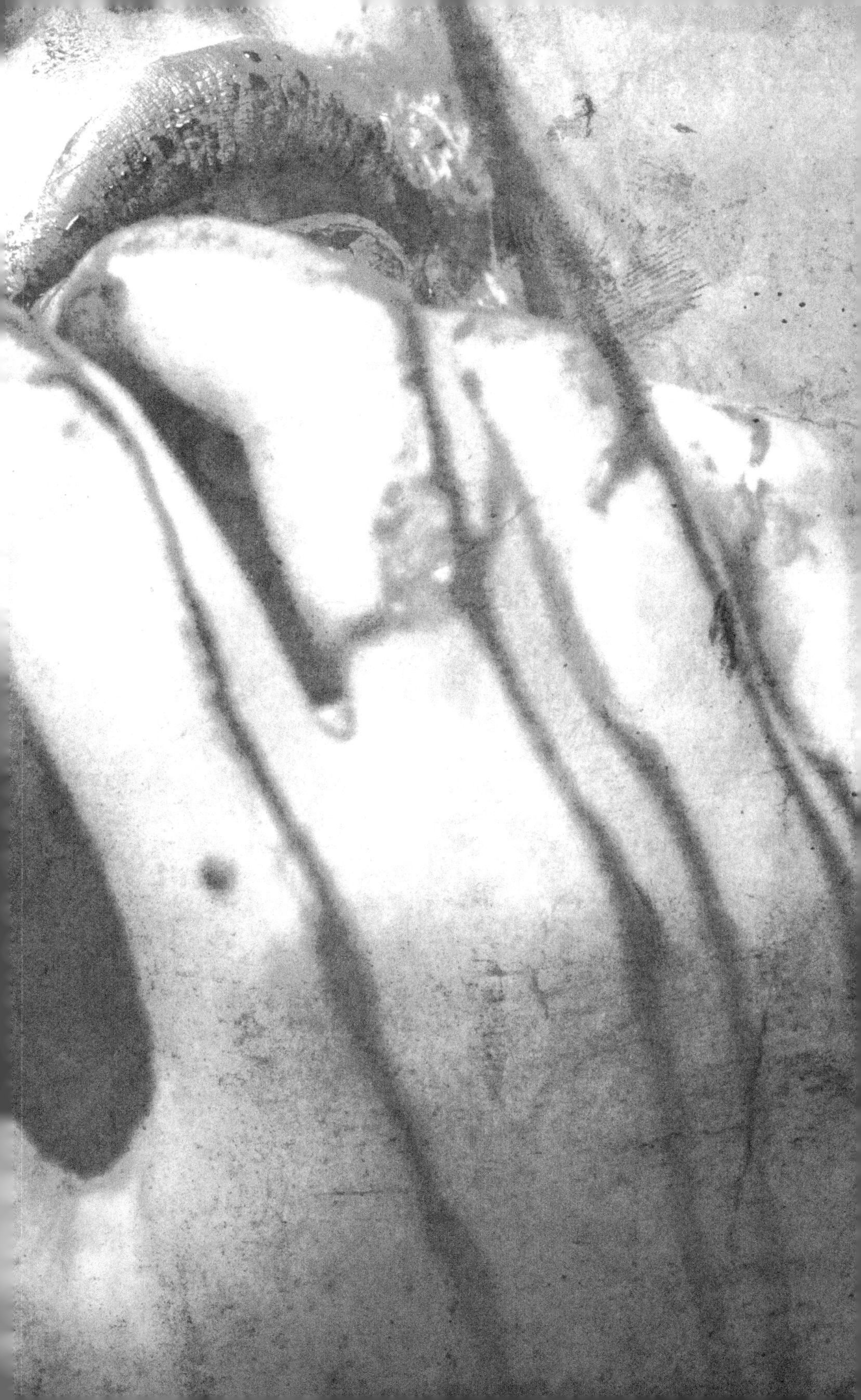

Chapter 5

Beatings and Betrayal

After waking Zander to assist with disposing of Brayden's body, Xavier drags me to the couch and tosses me down, glaring at me with frustration radiating off him. Zander paces anxiously, running his hands through his hair—both twins clearly at a loss for words. I can sense their anger, but Brayden's death felt almost like self-defense; he shouldn't have broken into our home with the intent to kill me. Still, I can't deny that he made things a lot simpler for me.

"Go ahead, let it out. Yell at me," I taunt Xavier, eager for him to vent so that I can finally take a shower.

He shakes his head, shooting a glance at Zander before replying, "I'm not mad at you, Lailah. He broke in and tried to kill you, so you did what you had to do."

The expression on his face suggests there's more to his feelings than he's letting on, but for some reason, he's holding back. I stand up, hands on my hips, focused on the two remaining threats I need to deal with. One look at Zander, and he sinks onto the couch where I had just been sitting, followed moments later by Xavier, who huffs, clearly displeased to find himself in this situation.

"You can either help me with the last two or step aside and let me handle it my way," I say directly, feeling the simmering rage rising to a boil inside me as thoughts of Bash and Conrad flood my mind.

"You obviously don't need our help, especially after what I just witnessed, but I can't let you go into the lion's den alone," Xavier replies, his voice heavy with resignation as he lowers his head.

"I feel like I'm missing something…" Zander suddenly interjects, glancing back and forth between me and Xavier, confusion etched across his face.

"Don't worry about it," I assure him, offering a reassuring smile as I settle into his lap and ruffle his already messy hair. "But get ready, because I'm set to go," I declare, my heart racing with anticipation.

Much like Xavier did earlier, I sit inside Bash's house in the dark, waiting for him and Conrad to get home. A yawn threatens to take me out, but I fight through it, clutching the pistol on my lap as my foot bounces anxiously. The sound of the rain still falling echoes in my ears, but my heartbeat thumps so loud it almost drowns out the sound of the rain.

I smile to no one, knowing the twins are hidden for their own protection but have weapons on them in case something goes wrong. But it won't. The moment I see headlights approaching, my stomach twists, and I stand up to begin my plan of attack.

Having never watched the video of my assault before, I cringe the minute I hear their voices come across the TV screen. I figured it would be poetic justice or some shit for them to watch the video of what they did to me while I kill them. This way the pain they caused me will be in the forefront of their minds while I return the favor to them, even greater.

I can hear the scoffing of the twins as the video plays, but I ignore it, taking my seat back on the couch, my pistol cocked and ready to fire upon their entrance. This is it. I'm not sure their deaths will solve anything, but as long as they can't hurt anyone else, then I'm happy. The damage to me is already done, and I just have to figure out how to live with it from here on out.

I take a deep breath as the key jiggles around in the lock, the door swinging open and their two drunk asses stumble inside. Frozen in the foyer from the sound of their voices, they slowly turn to face the TV screen, horror evident on their faces. They don't have to turn the light on to see me, not since the TV casts off a glow that lets them know I'm sitting on the couch.

"What is this, Lailah?" Bash asks, slurring his words as he leans against the wall to support himself.

"What do you think it is, Bash?" I ask calmly, my finger tapping the trigger, anxious to pull it.

"Are you here to kill us or something?" Conrad asks, laughing as if it's all some big fucking joke, reminding me of how Patrick and Ryan acted right before I killed them for the same thing.

Annoyed with him already, I raise the gun and aim for Conrad, ready to put an end to this madness. One shot is all it takes for the laughing to stop. He drops dead to the floor beside Bash, and I heave a sigh. Four down, one more to go.

"What the fuck, Lailah? You can't just fucking kill us!" Bash shrieks, checking for a pulse to which he finds none.

"I'm pretty sure I can, and I did," I spit, standing up to face the last of my attackers. "Isn't that what you guys did? You did whatever you wanted to and covered it up to save your precious reputations. Look how well that went for your friends," I laugh, suddenly caught off guard from a hard blow to my jaw.

I stumble backward, stunned, and put my hands up ready to fight, neither one of us holding anything back. Bash charges forward again, fueled by a mix of alcohol and desperation, but I sidestep him, backpedaling to create distance. I can feel the adrenaline coursing through my veins, inching me closer to the edge, and I'm no longer thinking about consequences. It's time to end this shit.

"Come on, you can do better than that!" I taunt, my voice dripping with challenge.

It's reckless, but anger is driving me now. The truth is, I've wanted this for so fucking long. I fantasized about this confrontation—how it would play out—but nothing could have prepared me for the reality of it. Feelings surge through me, and I channel them into my next move.

Bash rushes again, this time feigning left and swinging right with a punch that catches me square in the ribs, and I feel the air whoosh from my lungs. It's painful but brings me back into focus. The gun drops from my grasp, clattering against the wooden floor.

Dismissing the weapon, I pivot on my heel and deliver a kick to Bash's stomach that sends him stumbling back. He hits the wall, gasping for breath, and I seize the opportunity, lunging forward to tackle him down. We crash to the ground, a tangle of limbs, fury, and regret.

"Do you have any idea what you did to me?" I hiss, gripping his collar and bringing him close. "I'm not scared of you anymore!" I spit, feeling the heat of my words. It's a release; with each word, I feel the shackles of my past begin to loosen.

He grunts, his eyes darting around as chestnut hair falls into his face, preposterously asserting, "You think you're the first victim I've made? You're nothing, Lailah. Just a little girl playing revenge."

In that moment, something inside me snaps. I punch him in the jaw, feeling satisfaction as his head whips to the side.

"I'm not just some little girl," I yell, quickly swinging my fist again.

This time, it finds his nose. The crack resonates, almost drowning out the laughter of the twin echoes, and when blood splatters across the floor—hot and vivid—it feels like a cleansing.

"You took everything from me!" I scream, fabricating a fury that I hadn't known existed within me.

Bash tries to push me off, but my weight is too much for the weakened, drunken man. I straddle him, my knees pinning his arms to the ground, the taste of victory starting to seep in, intoxicating me far more than the alcohol he consumed.

"The darkness doesn't forget!" I glare, needing him to truly understand. In his eyes, I see flickers of fear—the same fear I felt when they took away my right to a peaceful existence.

"What do you want?" he pleads, voice tremulous, the mask fading as panic seeps through his bravado. "Lailah, please..."

"I want you to remember," I seethe, drawing back my hand fast and landing a final punch squarely on his cheek.

That finality buzzes through my fingertips, a spark of closure igniting as I back away, panting with the exertion and shock of what I've done. He groans on the floor, clutching his face, and I take a step back, collecting myself. The pistol lies just out of reach, but I don't care. I've left my mark, just as they left theirs on me. I take in the chaos I've wrought—the broken remnants of my own suffering laid bare before me like a gory art installation.

It would have been so easy to pull the trigger and end all of this in a violent swirl, but I wanted him to suffer. I wanted him to know the consequences of his actions because nothing could take back what they had robbed from me.

"That's it?" Xavier asks, stepping out from his hiding spot, shocked.

"Yeah, that's it. He can live the rest of his miserable fucking life knowing that he's the only one who got to live for something they all did." I shrug, feeling that alone is painful enough. Death would only relieve him of the guilt. This way, he's got to deal with it for the rest of his life.

I step over Conrad's lifeless body, the sense of power surging within, and head toward the door. Before stepping out, I glance back—Bash simply stares at me, a mixture of disbelief and dread washing over him.

"If I hear my name come out of your mouth for any fucking reason, I'll be back, Bash, and next time you won't be so lucky. Don't think I'm keeping you alive because I care about you—that shit is long over—because I don't anymore. I want you to live with the pain that I live with, the betrayal from someone who used to be your best friend. I bet you'll remember me now," I declare defiantly, leaving the house behind as rain continues to cascade down outside, washing away remnants of my former self.

As I drive away, the weight lifts from my shoulders, an exhilarating sense of release swells in my chest while new questions flicker to life—what comes next? But for now, I breathe deeply, feeling alive for the first time in so long, and finally ready to face whatever lies ahead.

Books by KM ROGNESS

Trick or Treat

Trick or Treat: The Alternate Ending

Breaking Boston

Drowning

The Killer Kids Thrillogy: Little Psycho, Psycho Boys, Psycho Killers

Unwrapping Ember

Touchdowns and Tinsel

Cupid's Curse

To find more of my work, visit my website: https://kmrogness.com

Find me on Amazon under KM ROGNESS, on IG as @darksmutauthor_kaseyr, or send me an email if you have any questions: darksmutauthor.km.rogness@gmail.com

Scan the QR code to my Linktree for everything else in one place!

Stay Dark, Stay Twisted, Stay Smutty

Kasey

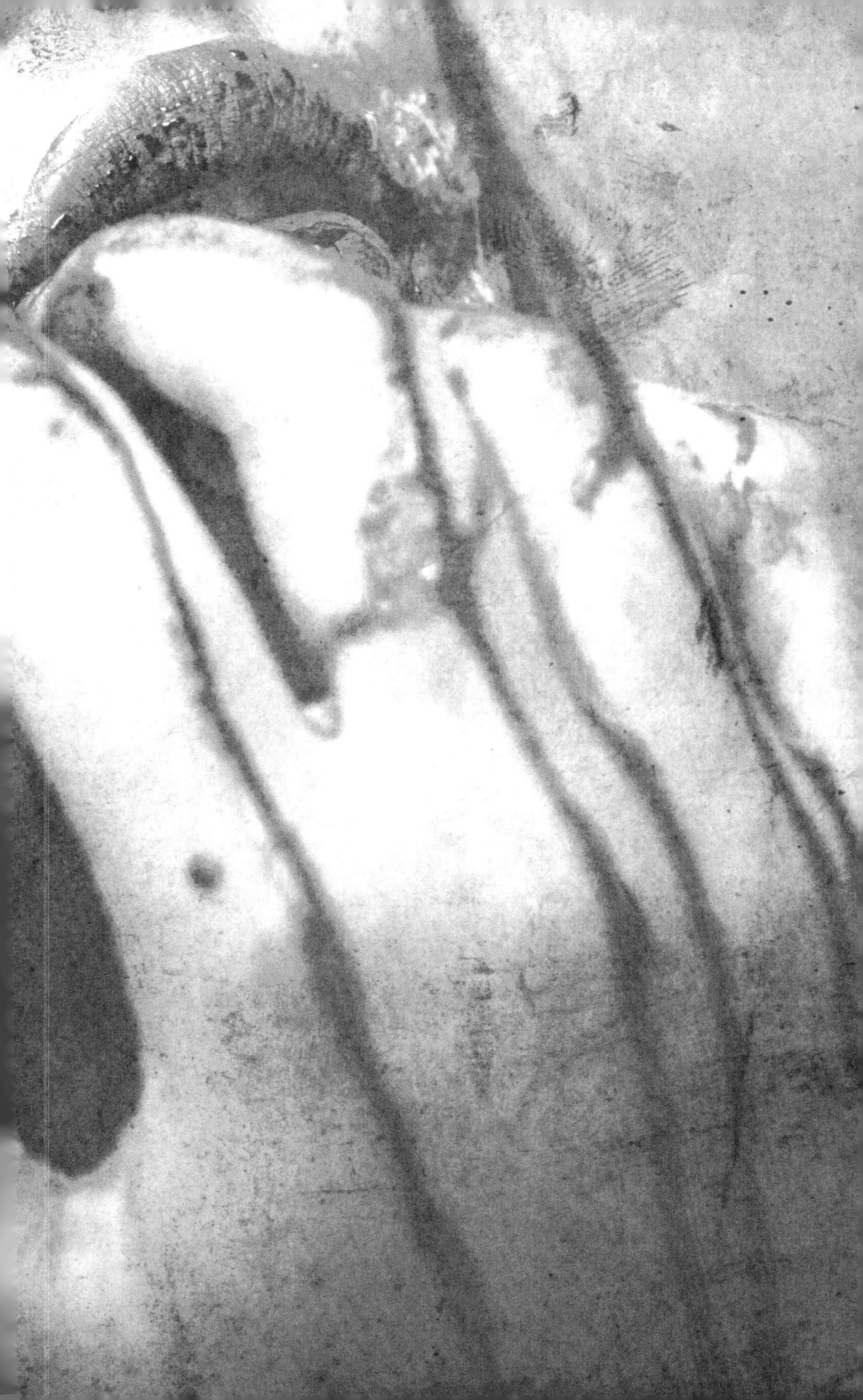

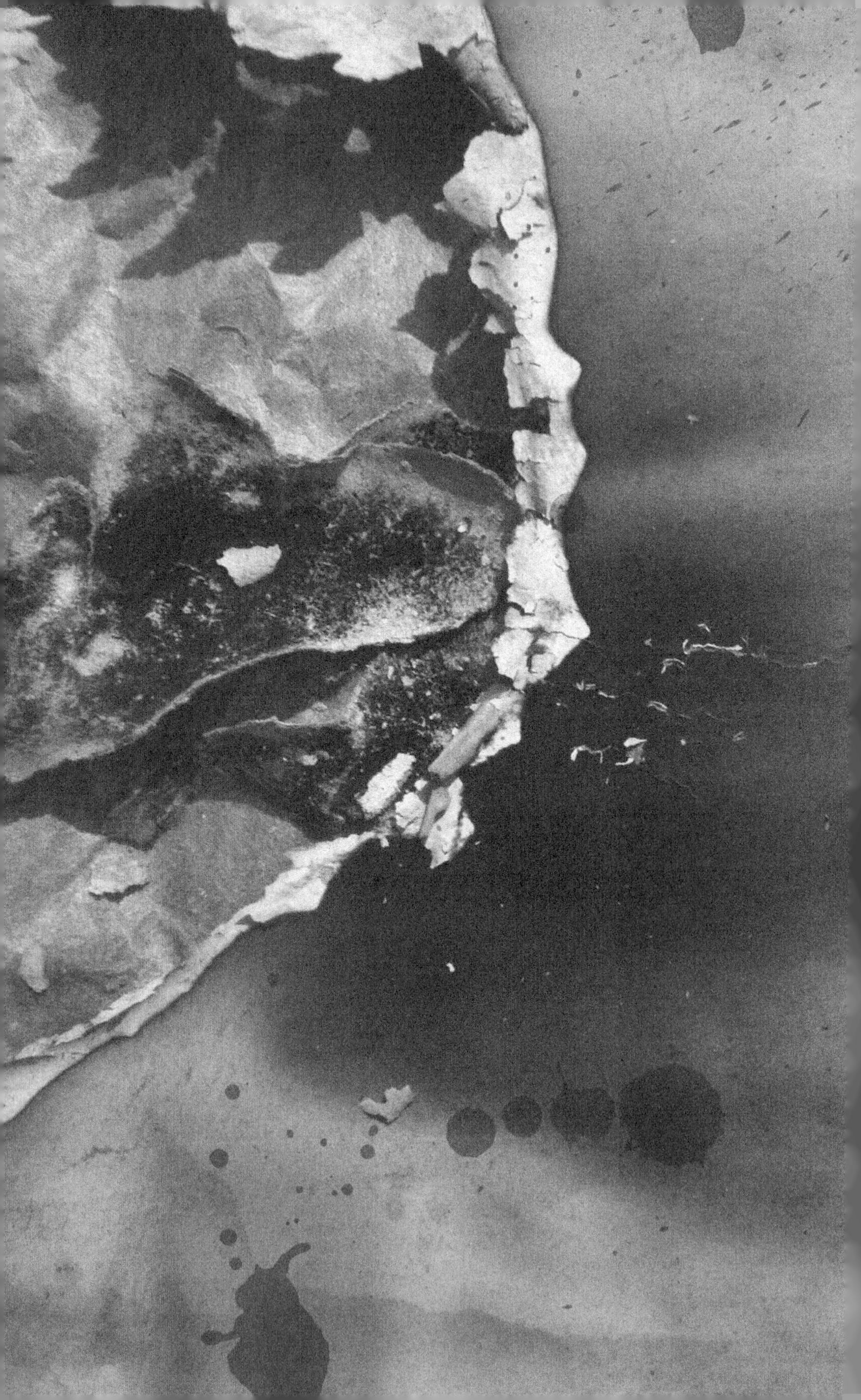

Soror Mortem

Lamia Lovett

Chapter One

Mothersound From First to Last

You know that sound when you're drowning? The muffled, barely audible frenzied screams of others as you sink further towards the bottom of a pool, awaiting your untimely fate. That's all I can hear right at this moment. The panicked screams that usually encroach on my nightmares are replaced by a high-pitched single note beep, a flatline, the one sound I dread to hear when I'm awake, indicating the end of yet another precious life.

The steady beep never falters as it crescendos, unlike the hitching of breath in my chest as I bring myself from the brink of panic and back to the present dire moment.

Tightly squeezing my eyes closed one last time, I brace myself for the painful sight that I know is going to meet me under the harsh fluorescent lights of the emergency room.

Vacant eyes stare at the tiled ceiling. Her body that was once so full of life now lies limp, covered in a sea of red and blue wires as nurses remove the endotracheal tube delicately from her throat. Her time of death is called out into the silent room of exhausted healthcare workers. Each one of us, bound by the law to stand by and watch as the deadly parasitic growth festers inside her womb, infecting her blood. Blood that now soaks our scrubs and paints our souls black against our will, damning us to hell. Against our oaths, and her desperate cries for help, we stand immobilized, watching a white sheet cover another avoidable death.

I have memorized all their names and held on to all their charts. Not that I could forget any of them. Their last moments forever burned into my memory and forever haunting my dreams.

Until we take a stand, my collection of innocent souls and sleepless nights will continue to grow.

A silent, rage-filled salty tear rolls down my cheek. I quickly swipe it away with the back of my hand. Forgetting the once blue nitrile gloves I'm wearing are now soaked in her now cold, hardening blood, it smears across my cheek, leaving an angry crimson streak in its wake. The anger bubbles deep within the pit of my stomach as I storm out of the trauma room, the doors slamming against the walls behind me due to the force in which I push them open. The unrelenting urge to scream makes its way up my throat as I remove the contaminated gloves from my shaky, sweat-soaked hands.

I fall against the nearest wall, sliding down it in the empty corridor, vacant of anyone else. Reaching into my pocket to retrieve my cell, I take a deep breath before pulling up the contact I know will help me. I take in my surroundings one more time before I hit the green icon, connecting our call.

She answers after the first ring, but I don't let her speak.

"I need your help," I say without explanation.

I swear I can hear the grin spread across her face like a cat who got the cream.

"I've been waiting for your call," she replies calmly. "I'll send you the location of the new hideout. Leave your cell behind."

"I know the drill, Bree," I responded to her with a clipped voice. My tone is not directed at her. "I'm sorry. I didn't mean for it to come out like that, I know. I know. You've taught me well," I ramble on.

"As I was saying…" She doesn't acknowledge my apology. "Bring everything you have. I'll see you soon."

She hangs up before I say goodbye. Bree may be a lot of things, but a person of many words isn't one of them. A ping comes from my cell immediately, no address, just GPS coordinates.

"Fuck sake Bree, you couldn't just give me a street name," I say to no one.

Chapter One

40.8042311
-76.34088766

I compose myself and pull myself up from my position on the floor to walk over to the unmanned nurse's station. Pulling open the web browser and entering the numbers into the search bar, I write down step-by-step directions in a short hand only I would understand if I were to be pulled over for any reason. It's been a while since I've had to use paper directions, but I know the importance of doing it this way. We must be careful and cover our tracks. I have helped Bree a few times when my skills have been required. She has prepped me well to make sure I leave no trace. I'll have to speak to Scott in security and get him to wipe the CCTV from the past hour or so...

Stuffing the paper into my soiled scrubs pocket, I ready myself for the remainder of my shift, praying to a god I don't believe in that I don't have to add another girl, woman or womb owner's name to my ever increasing, heartbreaking list.

Chapter Two

Street Spirit (fade out) Radiohead

Autumn has been battering our crumbling city. The orange and red leaves that painted the sidewalks are now a thick brown sludge, rusted from the bitter, relentless rain.

I battle against the Baltic wind that chills me to the bone. Ice cold rain drops slither their way down my spine, finding entrance beneath my tied up dark brown hair.

A shudder racks my body as I finally reach my blue Honda, that I left tactfully parked under a streetlamp. I round my vehicle, checking the tyres for punctures, and checking my windscreens and handles for distractions to lure me to absentmindedly leave the safety of my car.

Disappearances have been happening across the country—no, the globe. Anyone femme presenting, who is or close to childbearing age, is snatched from the streets, the supermarkets and even playgrounds. It's not safe for any of us as our birth rates continue to dramatically drop.

More missing person posters litter our communities daily. The authorities and news stations gave up reporting on the increasing number of missing people years ago; the counter constantly rising on our screens became too much for us to bear. These posters have been our only way to remember our cruelly stolen loved ones. Every photograph on aging paper overlaps, flapping in the wind on the overcrowded noticeboards, each face frozen in time, fighting to be seen by passerby, hoping to be found, begging not to become another forgotten smile. To not become a name never to be uttered again.

I DRIVE IN DEAFENING SILENCE TO THE LOCATION BREE SENT ME, constantly being mindful of my surroundings, keeping an eye out to make sure that I'm not being followed. The drive is out of the city and all the buildings and streets are derelict and run down. Old towns were completely abandoned and left to rot. The only sign of life are the weeds pushing their way through the cracks in the asphalt.

Rain batters my windscreen, the only sound blocking out my internal thoughts. I stare at the mountain of folders occupying my passenger seat. All the names of the girls who were once in my care that I will seek vengeance for.

I prepare the pitch of my plan whilst I continue towards the destination.

After driving for what felt like hours, I finally reached the abandoned-looking warehouse. To those who may pass by, it looks like every other run down building from the outside, but knowing Bree, what she's hiding on the inside is going to be a spectacular space.

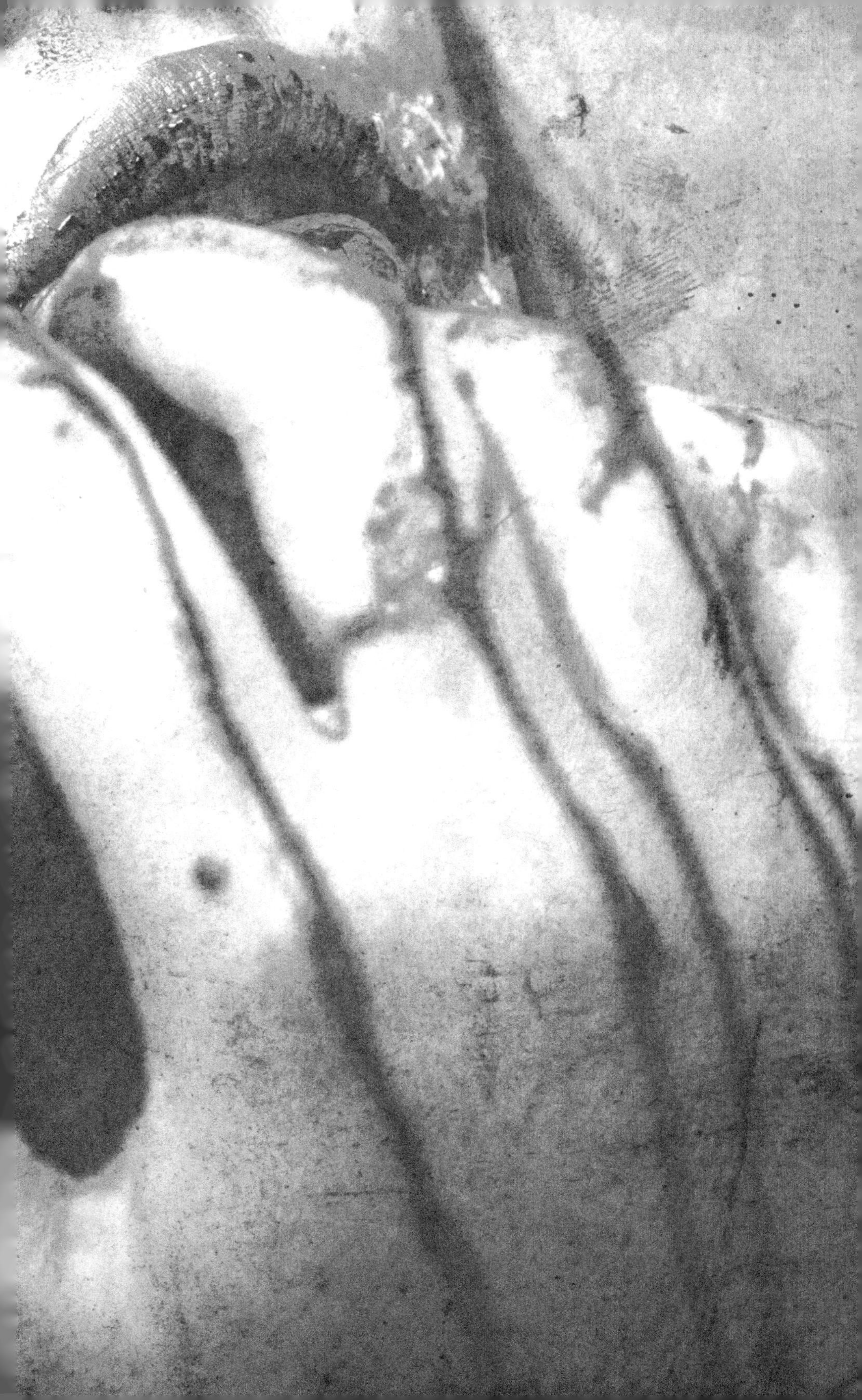

Chapter Three

Vermillion Pt 2 - Slipknot

Bree leans over the back of the wooden chair I'm occupying as I spread out the manila folders across the steel table. My hands tremble. The sight of their names has me reliving each of their final moments.

She covers my hands with hers, lowering herself into a squat position beside me. I look over at her, unaware of the tears streaming down my face. Her hands slowly meet my face, cradling it. I let out a deep sign as she dries the wetness with her thumbs.

We don't need to exchange words, just being in her presence calms my soul. Bree rises slowly, placing a singular kiss on my forehead. I've missed the feeling of her soft lips brushing against my skin.

"I've got you. You're not doing this alone. I promise." She reassures me whilst standing at her full height above me, one hand still on my cheek, I lean into her warm familiar touch.

I let myself forget for a single moment why I'm here in this magnificent, albeit frightening, warehouse.

Well, I'm not even certain how to describe the hideout: one wall is covered with monitors and screens from floor to ceiling, and the opposite wall hangs an array of painful torture devices and tools.

I remind myself to count my lucky stars that I'm probably one of the only people to see these walls and make it out alive, not that I'd ever be the type of person she seeks to maim and slaughter.

I clear my drying throat and focus back on the patient files. From the purse sitting on my tense lap, I pull out his name. The congressman in charge of our failing state, the one upholding the barbaric laws and legislation that have removed all our reproductive rights, leaving us nothing more than human collateral damage. Just targets with a price on our wombs and eggs. Our livestock currently has more rights than us. At least their carcasses can be sold for a profit and not hidden away in secret mass graves, disguising the actual truth of the destruction of our new world.

The picket lines and protests fell on deaf ears. Our screams for change labelled us rebels, and they locked us away to "protect" the community. They made us scared to speak out and fight for what was right.

I slap the piece of worn-out crumpled paper, his name scrawled in black ink, on the hard surface. Bree's face doesn't hide her delight as it lights up and her eyes widen.

"Oh Nance! You don't do things in halves, do you?" she exclaims, grabbing my head roughly and planting a quick kiss onto the top of my head.

"I'm so fucking proud. My baby is all grown up," she coos in a mocking tone, appearing giddy from the promise of watching a deserving man lose his life.

"We need to send a message. And I don't think we can find a better vessel to send it." I pause, taking in the magnitude of what I have planned for this piece of shit.

I scoot my chair away from Bree's proximity, the wood screeching against the hard concrete floor. Raising my face to meet her eyes, I continue,

"He's heavily protected. It's going to take some time and planning." I lower my gaze again in defeat, playing with the drawstring on my scrub pants, desperately attempting to rub off the dried blood that stains the once white fibres.

"Between my shifts, though, it's not something I can commit to or…"

Bree cuts me off, her fingers gently embrace my chin as she lifts my gaze from my twitching hands in my lap to her face

"Nancy, I said I've got you." I stare into her icy blue eyes. I see nothing but truth behind them. She's always been there for every person who needs her at the drop of a hat. I know she will absolutely do the same for me.

She hooks her foot around the leg of the chair I'm sitting on and pulls me closer to her, pulling my body up into a comforting embrace. Her muscular arms hold me in place against her hard torso, gently stroking my hair.

"I've got you," she repeats, instantly extinguishing the building panic I have in my chest. I melt into her arms, breathing in her comforting scent. A warming mixture of sage and vanilla.

I lay my face on her chest.

"I've missed you," I say, although a part of me inside hopes that the sound doesn't carry to her ears. I hate being vulnerable or seen as weak, but Bree gives me the space I need to drop my mask without any judgement. I feel safe to be myself around her.

Placing both her hands on my shoulders, she pulls me reluctantly out of her hold. Her gaze takes in every inch of my face, the way her eyes roam freely feels like she's seeing deep into my soul. Her eyes soften, and a kind, sympathetic smile, full of adoration, forms on her mouth.

"C'mon, I have a living area with a shower and a bed. We can go over this once you're clean and well rested," she says, motioning to the table beside us.

Grabbing my hand, she pulls me towards a well-hidden door. Behind is a large room, considerably different from the cold, sterile torture chamber we just exited.

Before I can take in the room and peek into Bree's carefully protected personality in its entirety, I'm guided into the bathroom.

Clinical, seamless white tiles cover every wall of the room, just like the torture room, it is void of any personal touches, free from ridges and imperfections.

Easy to clean, I say in my head.

Bree walks to the open cubicle in the corner, turning on the faucet. Housed on the ceiling behind a single pane of floor to ceiling glass is a large chrome shower head, water falls like heavy summer rain onto the hard ground below. The steam mixes with the cold air causing it to billow, fogging up the frigid air.

I stand motionless with my back against the hard sink countertop as Bree makes her way slowly back to me.

"Arms up, Nance. Let me help you," she gently demands, leaning into my ear.

Grabbing the hem of my scrub top, she lifts it up my body at a slow pace, her knuckles grazing their way up over my body, leaving goosebumps erupting over my skin in their wake.

Pulling it over my head, her hand finds its way to the base of my back, pulling me flush against her, her free hand loosening the band holding my hair in place. Tendrils of thick brown hair cascade down my spine as she runs her skilled fingers over my scalp, rubbing out the tension and worry from my head. Every moment melts and relaxes me. She doesn't once deprive me of her touch, her hands never leaving my skin. I close my eyes as she lowers herself on to her knees to untie my laces. I brace myself on the countertop, transferring my weight onto one leg as she removes my shoe and sock.

"Please, whatever you do next, just don't sniff them. I've just spent 14 hours on my feet," I say in a quick panic, ruining the moment entirely.

"I swear to God, Nance. One more word out of that pretty mouth of yours and I'll be stuffing it with your socks to keep you quiet."

Mortified , she brings the sock to her nose and inhales deeply, making a fake exaggerated retching noise.

"Yeah, you're right. That was fucking disgusting." She abandons her position on the floor along with the stinky sock.

Without warning, she grabs me by the waist. I let out a squeak, as Bree manoeuvres me onto the counter, lifting my remaining foot to her chest to relieve me of my footwear.

"You know, I was really enjoying having you on your hands and knees at my feet," I say playfully.

Her head snaps up to meet my gaze, her eyebrow raised questionably, as she pulls off the remaining shoe and sock in one quick movement, dropping it to the floor.

Her hands make their way along my calves, and at my knees, she pushes them apart. Spreading my legs to stand between them, her eyes never leave mine as her hands continue up to the apex of my thighs. I desperately lift my hips off the surface, pushing myself deeper into her touch.

"You know that's not how we play, princess," she smoothly says with a smirk as her fingers swiftly make their ways under the elastic of my pants, gripping the fabric tightly.

Chapter Three

Following her silent demand, I lift my weight onto my hands, allowing her to lower them over my ass and down my legs. The cold surface of the counter meets the back of my bare thighs. I'm left sitting in just my beige support bra and comfy briefs. My natural reaction is to cover my imperfections, to shield my round tummy with my arms, to hide my stretch mark covered hips and thighs, but the way she stares and takes every inch of me in melts all those worries away, in her eyes I can see that I am priceless art, worthy of being admired.

I'm gently pulled from the counter. The floor tiles are no longer cold against the soles of my feet as the hot steam from the shower wraps around us like a comforting blanket, sheltering us from the madness of the world outside of this room.

Hand in hand, we cross the room towards the shower. I abandon my remaining items of clothing and step under the steady water. I lift my face towards the cleansing heat and allow it to wash over me and wash away my sins from the demanding day.

I feel Bree step in behind me, sweeping my wet hair over one shoulder and peppering my neck with gentle kisses, her hands rubbing more warmth into my arms.

"I've missed you, too," she finally responds, her confession wrapping its way around my heart. She replaces her kisses with small bites, not hard enough to leave a mark, although I really wish she would.

Bree steps away, leaving me feeling alone briefly. In the split second she is gone, she retrieves body wash and a cloth. Turning to face her, I watch as she loads the cloth with thick fragrant liquid, working it up into white bubbly suds. The scent of sea salt and eucalyptus penetrates my nostrils as she sweeps the wet strands of hair away from my face and neck.

Working in small gentle circles, she starts just below one of my ears, her free hand supporting the opposite side of my face. Small murmurs of gratitude fill the comfortable silence between us as she repeats the same movements on the other side.

Her movements continue to glide over my collarbones, taking her time to cleanse every inch of my tormented shame, easing out the building tension I have yet to purge from my body.

Gentle hands make their way towards the curve of my breasts. She caresses them and adds in a careful, pressured pinch to my nipples. The contrast between the gentle touch and the welcomed pain ignites a fire within my belly that only she is able to extinguish. Her hands continue their journey south, towards my aching centre. I relinquish complete control, my body putty in her hands. I am at her mercy. My body is hers right now as she lowers herself to her knees to continue her silent worship, the flowing stream from the shower above us soaking her blonde hair, weighing it down over her sculpted naked form.

"May I?" she asks with a tap on the inside of my thighs, indicating I need to spread my stance so she can further rid me of the grime and sweat. Her meticulous and deliberate motion from the base of my leg raising to the crest of my thighs has me mewling with tormented, desperate need.

Leaning against the wet tiles, I lift my leg over her shoulders as she cleans my most intimate parts with a delicate teasing precision. Cupping the water running down my body to wash the remaining suds, her fingers continue between my folds, circling my sensitive and wanton centre. Without hesitation, her warm mouth hungrily latches onto my clit, pulling it into her wet mouth, her lustful moans vibrating against my fired-up nerve endings. Fingers enter me with ease, hooking upwards and pulling me further onto her face as if to devour me starting from the inside of my soul.

I throw my head back, my cries of pleasure echoing off the walls around us, our sounds mixing in a symphony of crazed and lustful desire. Our movements flow with a familiar ease, like a perfectly rehearsed waltz. The rocking of my hips matches the steady flow of her tongue and fingers as they dance against my core.

Our bodies are so blissfully in sync that I don't register her free arm hooking over my leg draped on her shoulder adding pressure to my pelvis above her masterful fingers, calling and coaxing out the rising orgasm that builds from my toes, exploding its way through my entire body in waves.

My screams ricochet as she draws out my pleasure, almost to the point of agony. My face prickles with a feeling of numbness and my sight takes a few moments to return to normal.

My satiated body turns limp in her arms, threatening to wash down the drain, along with the water dripping from our entwined bodies.

Bree holds me tightly as she rises from the shower floor. Staring deep into my eyes, she licks each soaked digit, savouring every drop of me.

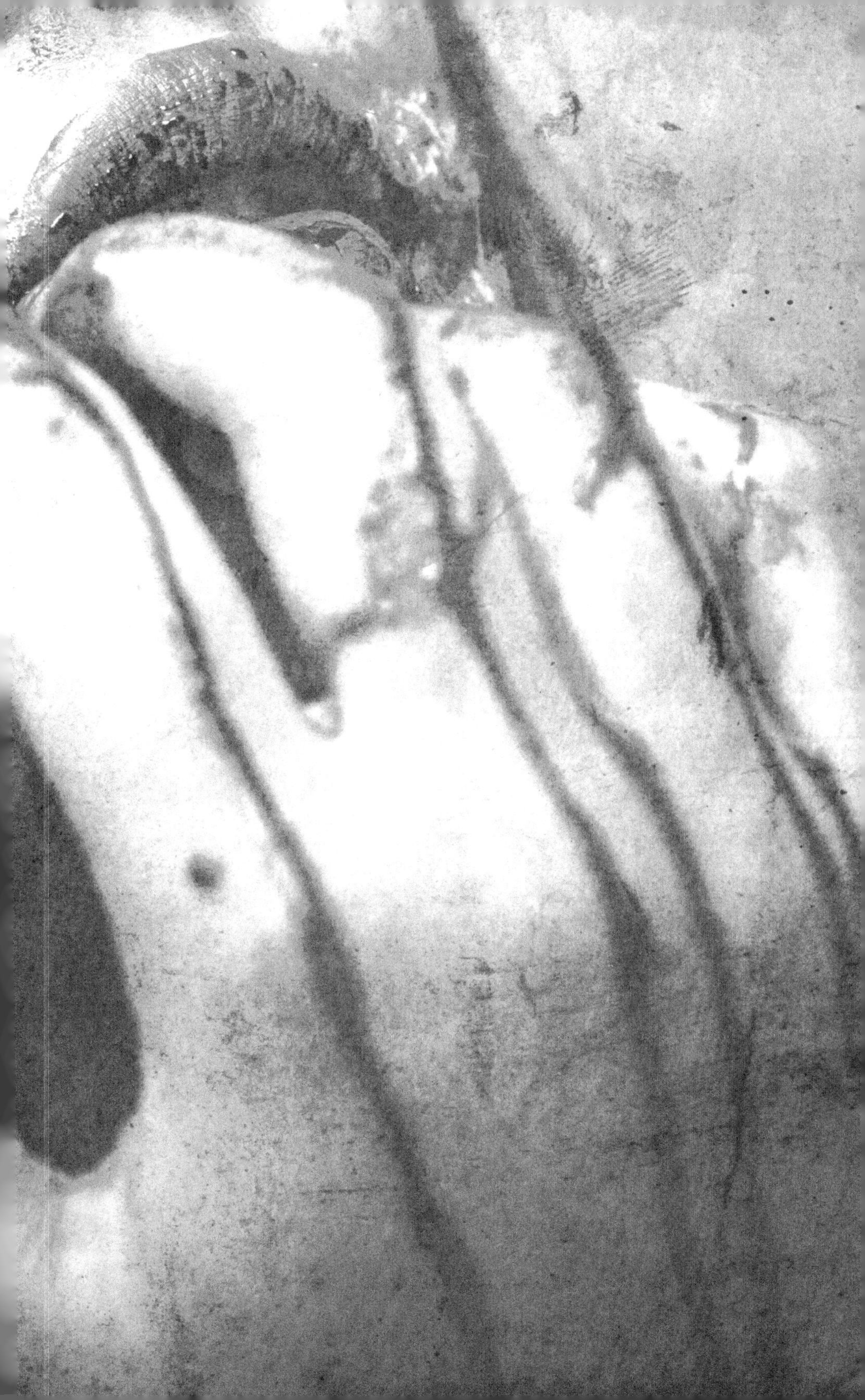

Chapter Four

VAN *Poppy ft Bad Omens*

It has been a tortuous four weeks. I have done my best to carry on as normal to avoid suspicion of the upcoming violence. I attend my soul crushing job at the multi-storey mausoleum disguised as a hospital. A place where we bring our sick and needy, expecting a miracle cure that will see them walking out healed and unscathed. In that short time, another 12 women's and children's lives have been unnecessarily lost. It's a senseless and avoidable pandemic of epic proportions. Loved ones that could return home if we still had the rights over our bodies. Scared women and children are forced to carry their abusers' babies, seeking out back alley terminations because of the government's warped idea of life beginning at conception and a "fathers" right to seek legally binding, forced pregnancies due to the ever-dropping birth rates we are experiencing.

Doctors are locked up and stripped of their licenses if there are even hushed whispers they are doing the job they signed up for before the laws changed. A modern day witch trial happened before our very eyes, a point in their direction without questions asked, and they were tied and burnt at the proverbial stake.

Behind the scenes, Bree has worked tirelessly with her extensive team. The collective she trusts consists of others who can naturally blend into the background. Trash collectors, postal service employees, wait staff, CCTV operators, plus many more, each with one objective, collect intelligence on a chosen target. Everyone has a role to play in the underground network that Bree has spent the past six years tirelessly building after her first kill changed the trajectory of her life goals.

After parting ways an agonising 29 days ago, I have all but chewed the skin around my nails down to the bone. To anyone on the outside, I'm calm and collected. My focus at work is unwavering and never falters. However, the moment my feet meet the grey concrete outside the sliding doors of the emergency department, the harsh reality of the bleak world around me sends shockwaves through every single nerve of my exhausted, but somehow restless, body.

Every time I return to the safety of my apartment, I stand immobilised, lifelessly staring at the blank wall in front of me. Electricity hums around me as dogs bark in the distance.

Every one of my senses is heightened, causing the short hairs at the nape of my neck to stand to attention at every minute sound, alerting me to the potential danger hiding behind the blanket of darkness and within its shadows.

There's a constant building pressure behind my excruciatingly tired eyes. An anger so incoherent it bubbles away just beneath the surface, begging for the opportunity to erupt.

My skin is on fire.

I'm on edge.

The plan whirls round and around my mind.

I play out every single possible scenario.

I plan everything that could go wrong.

The cogs never stop turning.

But what if it goes exactly as planned?

What if this is the start of the end?

What if this one seemingly dramatic demonstration of righteous violence gives others the strength and courage to enact their own form of retribution?

There are so many what ifs and hows. The moment they realise there's more of us than there are of them, and if we all band together, we can take anyone down, no matter their size.

They brainwashed us our whole lives with propaganda to be scared and to keep us from thinking for ourselves.

It's time to make them afraid.

My cheap burner chimes in my pocket. Pulling it out with a sense of urgency, I see the notification with the code phrase we decided on, marking that the plan is in full motion.

SOROR MORTEM

Sister Death

It's finally time.

It's time to make the congressman pay for the blood on all our hands.

For the first time in weeks, a sense of calm washes over me, and I'm full of the energy I've been unknowingly preserving all these long evenings I have spent paralysed.

Just like I've meticulously planned, autopilot takes over as I make my way across my silent apartment, towards the vacant room where my unmade bed lies. The brown wooden wardrobe doors are swung open as I dig my way to pull out the heavy black duffle bag that I spent the last few weeks filling with everything I need.

I have repeatedly checked the bag every evening, but I still take the time for one last check of my inventory, zipping it closed when I'm satisfied nothing has mysteriously gone missing or been forgotten.

Turning on the TV, I decrease the volume so it's just loud enough to be heard as a low hum to the other apartments surrounding mine. The screen will illuminate the room behind the drawn drapes, giving the illusion that I'm home to anyone who happens to pass.

I place all my electronics on their charging docks, keeping locations on when I leave them behind.

Leave no trace. Leave no tracks.

My brown hair is already brushed back off my face, firm gel applied to keep it in position, the length in a braid and wrapped in a tight bun. I lower a black baseball cap into place on my head, the brim obstructing the view of my face from above.

A gentle tap on the window to my back startles me out of my trance-like state. Slowly, I pull the drapes back and see Bree's beautiful face staring back at me. Panic sets in. This isn't a part of the plan. Something has gone wrong already. Is she backing out? What's happened? What's gone wrong already? My mind whirls with trepidation.

I slide open the pane of glass, the underwater feeling slowly creeping in, distorting the sounds around me. Bree's lips are moving, but I can't make out the words. A beeping noise starts to penetrate my ears like deafening feedback, and a sense of unfathomable dread builds in my stomach.

Bree snaps her fingers in my face, a look I've never seen paints her features when my focus is finally back on her. Quietly and gently, she informs me to take a step back so she can lift herself in through the opening, which she does with effortless grace.

Crossing the distance between us at a lightning speed, I'm taken tightly into her arms. She lifts and cradles me as she sits down on the mattress.

"Nance. Slow your breathing down. Everything is fine."

"Why are you here? What's gone wrong?" My words come out in fast short pants.

"Nance, please. I need you to take a deep breath in through your nose and out through your mouth. Can you do that for me?" she asks.

I nod and fill my lungs slowly with air. She mimics my breathing, guiding me from the edge and back to the comforting hold in her arms.

"I came here so you weren't alone. That is all. I'm sorry, I should have stuck to the plan. But I just wanted to be here with you right now." A look of something flashes momentarily on her face, something I can't place.

"Thank you." I breathe out into her neck as I hold on to her with a grip so hard I can imagine my knuckles are turning white.

Bree looks over at the black tactical gear next to my packed bag.

"Let's go collect this bastard."

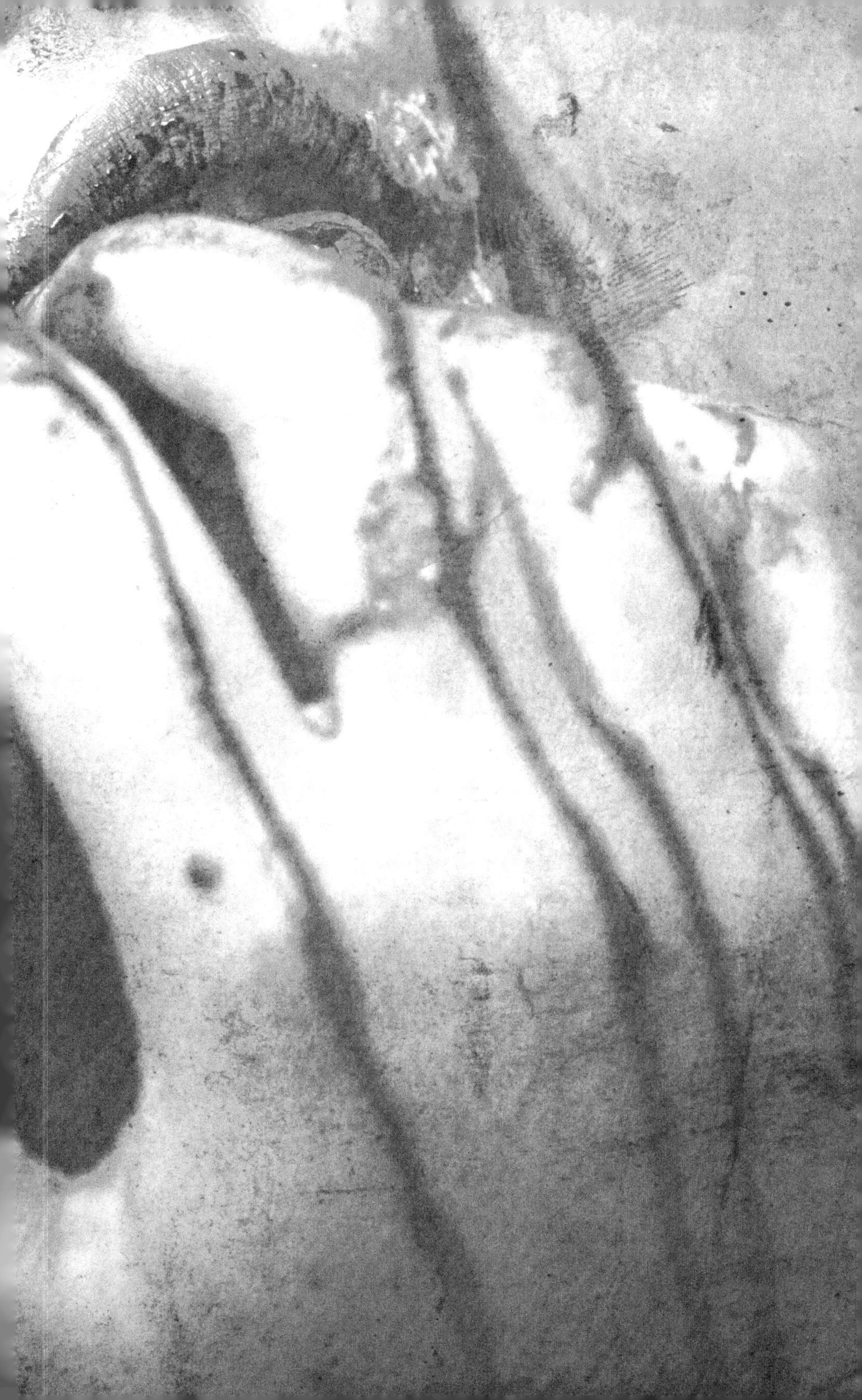

Chapter Five

Body Bag – I Prevail

Collecting the unsuspecting Congressman was surprisingly easy. Thanks to the network, we found a weakness in his protection detail when he visits one of his many mistresses one town over. I snuck up behind him whilst he was leaving the seedy, deserted motel. I was able to administer a fast-acting sedative, and menacingly loomed over his body as he hit the deck like the sack of shit he is. Bree pulled up beside us just as the sound of his skull hitting the ground filled the empty parking lot. The usually serious and stoic Bree let out the dirtiest belly laugh as crimson blood pooled under his unconscious body. The team was already on the sidelines, ready to clean up the bloody gravel and to wipe any CCTV footage as we tied up his body and threw him into the plastic-lined boot of the blacked-out SUV.

Unfortunately for him, he's not dead yet, just knocked out, although I'm going to make sure he begs for death when I'm done with him. It'll be music to my ears to hear him plead for me to put him out of his misery.

The wait for him to regain consciousness was agonisingly slow. I wasn't as prepared as Bree when she goes in and picks up her mark. She carries out extensive research to make sure any administered drug/poison and even venom is the correct dose for their body weight.

This brilliant woman was a straight A's science major with an overwhelming hyper fixation on reptiles and arachnids. I'll never understand why she chose to be a part of the police force after graduating college at the top of her class.

We are back at the hideout. A spotlight shines down onto the congressman in the centre of the room. He's been cut out of every item of clothing. Tape stretches over the ageing skin around his mouth. Shackles and chains hold him in place by the ankles and wrists. I've been pacing the room since laying out all my instruments. Not that I need anything more than a razor-sharp scalpel, however, I did make sure to bring adrenaline shots and a defibrillator. Bree sits in the corner of the room, her presence bringing me a sense of calm.

A muffled groan emanates from the centre of the room, followed by the telltale sign of a feeble attempt to pull against the restraints. The steel links clank and scrape against the metal table as the movements become more desperate and frantic. Oh, how I wish I could have been inside his head when it dawned on him that he is absolutely fucked.

I stalk over to the table. The congressman turned his head from the blinding light above his face, screwing his eyes shut as I silently stand beside him unnoticed, taking in every foul millimetre of this odious, pathetic man. Wiry, thick white hairs grow out from his ears and nostrils, his nose bulbous and clogged with grime. Dry flakes of skin sit in the creases around his eyes and broken capillaries redden his sagging cheeks. There is not one redeeming feature on him I don't find violently repulsive. I use the visceral reaction of merely being in the same room as him to throw fuel on the fire that is sizzling away inside of me.

"Nice of you to finally join us," I say, standing above him. His head snaps towards the direction of my unwavering voice. His reddened eyes adjusting to the lighting around him. I can see in his face he's trying to place me, trying to recognise me to make sense of the events that are unfolding before him. What he doesn't know is I'm about to make his worst nightmare feel like a walk in the park.

"You don't know me, Henry, and you never will. You're not here for me but for them." I point to the rows of patient files that Bree helped me display on the wall.

"You don't know them either, but you took away their lives. It may not have been with your own hands, but the ink on the signed legislation that allows their needless deaths came from your pen, Henry, and

I'm going to make sure you know every single one of them before I hand you over to the reaper."

Tears fall down Henry's face, but I know the tears are for him and not for his actions. Anger seeps from my pores and I tear off the tape on his mouth, the glue pulling at the fragile skin on his lips, blood making its way to the surface and coating his browning teeth red as he attempts to plead for his life.

"I…" Before he's able to whine out any further words, the back of my hand meets the side of his face. The sound of my skin slapping into his is quickly replaced by the sounds of his pathetic sobs.

I grab Henry's face, my fingers digging into his cheeks, turning him back to face me.

My calm demeanor has now been replaced by a rage so violent my body trembles, as I try to hold it back for just a little longer, a voice, unlike anything I've ever heard, passes my lips, full of strength and a power I wasn't even aware I held inside me.

"How dare you cry for you. How dare you think you are more important than they are. Killing you may not bring them back. But killing you might scare everyone else into making the right fucking changes we need so we don't lose anymore fucking people. I'm done with their blood staining my soul when they could have easily, easily been saved. I could have saved them, and you made it so I couldn't. I had to listen to every single one of them plead for me to step in to save them. To cradle them and smooth their hair as the infections take hold of their organs because I couldn't remove the thing growing in them, poisoning their blood. To watch them cradle their stillborn that they were forced to carry to term, knowing they'd never see them take a single breath. To hear mothers scream for me to save their daughters who tried to rid themselves of their abuser's vile, ungodly evidence of rape."

I push off his face, making my way towards the nearby tray housing all the surgical scalpels laid out at my disposal and the syringes full of adrenaline. The wheels of the heart rate monitor squeak as I pull it towards Henry. I grab the wires from the machine and attach them to his chest, my lip curling in disgust as my skin brushes his. Turning on the machine has the room filling with the beeping alerts. This will be our soundtrack for the torture, a sound I hope follows him to the afterlife, his erratic heart rate signifying the terror he's feeling. Good. I've barely even started. He has no idea what hell awaits.

I hold the sharp blade close to his face. Usually, the sounds from the machines fill me with fear, but this time the alerts are music to my ears as his body reacts to the danger in front of him. I press the blade to his cheek, dragging it across the surface. Henry takes in a sharp breath as the layers of skin split under its sharp edge, the white flesh slowly turning red as blood rushes to fill the gaping wound. I continue my movement down his neck towards his chest, not putting enough pressure to cause more than a superficial cut, but enough to watch his heart rate spike. Whimpers choke in his throat as he tries to hold himself still, as if not moving would make this less painful.

"I want them all hearing you screaming in unprecedented agony as I carve their names into your fucking skin." My free hand reaches out behind me, and within seconds, Bree is placing a folder into my waiting palm. I don't need this for me, as I remember them all, but for dramatic effect to add to the mental and physical torture, to really make him suffer.

"Jessica, 25. Came into the department complaining of abdominal pains and a high grade fever. It was discovered she was suffering from an ectopic pregnancy, and due to the laws that you didn't have to fucking enforce, we couldn't intervene past trying to treat the infected blood and not removing what was causing the infection. She was dying slowly of multi-organ failure despite our continued efforts until the pregnancy finally ruptured. Eight. Fucking. Days. Later," I shout in his face.

I lower the scalpel again onto his belly, pushing with force as I carve in the first letter of her name. His skin splits to reveal the yellow fatty tissue with each letter slowly following, blood flowing down his sides and gathering on the surface he lies on. His screams pierce my ears with every single new mark I etch into his body. He fights against the pain and the restraints, attempting to move away.

As I cut her name into his skin, I can hear her voice still begging me to help and how useless I felt standing by, being too scared to do anything. I wanted to help. I should have helped. I hate myself just as much as I hate him for not stepping in and allowing this to carry on for this long. I had just hoped, along with everyone else in the country, that it wouldn't get this far. We were all so stupid and naïve.

The sound of a flatline breaks me from my thoughts. This weak ass motherfucker is trying to crash out already. I grab the paddles from the already charged up defibrillator and apply them to his chest, sending an electric current into his heart, bringing it back into a normal rhythm.

He gasps in a ragged breath, his eyes frantically searching his surroundings, the look of hope shattering on his face.

"Oh, Henry boy, did you think I would let you off that easily? That I wouldn't bring you back every single fucking time until I decide we are done? You die when I say and not a moment sooner. We are in for a very long night."

Another folder slaps into my waiting hand. The smile on my face stretches as I turn back to Henry.

"Alison, 31… " I continue.

Chapter Six

Exit Music (for a Film) Radiohead

The floor is saturated with the blood from Henry's lifeless body. Not a single inch of skin is recognisable, a sea of yellow and red oozing from the tears I created. Empty syringes litter the floor around me as I attempt to give chest compressions. Exhaustion takes over my body and the pumping of my hands against his cold, sticky skin slows down. There is not a single drop of blood left to pump out of his corpse. The only sound left in the room is that steady beep, indicating the end of his worthless life. No one is there to respectfully cover his nakedness or call out his time of death.

My knees grow weak and my legs finally give way under me. I can no longer fight the tiredness as strong arms catch me before I fall and coat myself in the coagulating blood on the floor at my feet.

Bree lifts me and cradles me against her chest. I lean my head against her shoulder as she walks towards the hidden door that leads to her living space.

My eyes battle the heaviness as our bodies sway whilst she walks us towards the bathroom. She sits us both on the tiled floor of the shower fully clothed, turning on the water as she holds me tight to her body. The water soaks our clothes, the water staining red as it washes down the drain, the black fabric hiding the red of the spilled blood. I stare at my hands painted with his life and the frightening reality hits me like a train. I just willingly killed a man.

I start to tremble although the water is hot, the shock leaving me in emotional torrents as I cry into Bree's chest. She soothingly rocks me like an infant in her lap as she awkwardly unpins my hair from its bun with one hand, loosening the braid and the band holding it to my head. Her fingers reach into my hair, and I lean into her gentle touch, angling my face towards the ceiling, allowing the water to gently rain down on it. We stay like this silently until I fall asleep in her embrace, allowing me to forget about the corpse laying in the other room.

Bree let me sleep for an hour or so. We still needed to be somewhere before the sunrise. I woke up in a dry, warm bed and in one of Bree's t-shirts. My body, so exhausted from the day's events, I didn't even stir as she undressed me from my execution outfit. I was met with disappointment when I realised the bed was empty next to me. Sitting up, I took in the room for the first time. Little touches of Bree covered every surface. A weight bench and dumbbells lay neatly in one corner, and on another wall, beautiful vivariums stand, full of lush green plants and brown woods, their lights warming the entire room. I make my way over to inspect the animals she lovingly cares for, appreciating the shine of the scales wrapping around the stick in the corner of the tank.

Outside the room in the torture chamber, I can hear multiple voices chatting away. I make my way towards them and sheepishly open the door, very aware that at that moment I'm just in a t-shirt and a pair of briefs. Brees back is to the door as she talks to faces I don't recognise.

The floor now sparkles again, not a single drop of blood left after I drained Henry like a pig at the slaughter. Her clean-up crew is incredibly thorough at what they do. I look around the room, expecting to see the trolley with a body lying on it, but come up empty.

Almost as if Bree can read my thoughts, she turns to face me.

"He's in the van ready to be taken and displayed," she informs me in a calming tone.

"Let's get you dressed. You look really cute in my t-shirt Nance, but it's definitely not suitable for watching fireworks," she says with a wink. I bite my bottom lip to hide the smile that threatens to spread across my face at her small, but definitely there, compliment. She takes her thumb and reaches toward my lip, pulling it free from between my teeth.

Chapter Six

"Is it awful that I got really hot watching you kill a man?" she says, as she leans into my ear to make her whispered confession.

My eyes meet hers, full of lust. I open my mouth to speak, but she gets there before I do.

"If we don't get you out of my clothes and into some new ones right now, I'm going to take you in front of everyone, then probably have to kill them for watching."

I gasp as she drags me by the arm back into the room. A pile of clothes lie on top of the dresser, but I sit down on the bed and look at her with a pouty expression.

"I'm serious, princess. If we didn't have to be somewhere in the next 15 minutes, I would happily make you scream my name so loud you'd bring dear old Henry back from the dead." And with that, she picks up the pile of clothes, launches them playfully at my face, and exits the room.

BREE AND I STAND HAND IN HAND SAFELY IN THE DISTANCE, IN OUR sights, the bridge where his lifeless body hangs, drained of blood, displayed for all to see.

A calling card. An example. A warning.

A detonator itches in my palm. The timing of the explosion needs to be just right. Covered by the blanket of the night, we sit and watch the sunrise in front of us.

We use the burner phone to call every single news outlet and journalist in a five-mile radius to watch the spectacle that is about to unfold before their unsuspecting eyes. Photos of the Congressman have also been "leaked" on social media for all to see, the images immediately trending on all platforms.

Sirens begin to blare as the news travels around our sleeping city.

But my pounding heartbeat cancels out the growing noise as it whooshes around my skull.

This is it.

The blue and red lights reflect off the metal structures holding up the bridge suspended over the fast-coursing river.

News stations can be seen setting up their cameras and lighting behind a roadblock, keeping them away from the crime scene. A helicopter whirls overhead, shining its spotlight on the dangling body.

It's chaotic. You can feel the panic in the atmosphere as everyone scrambles towards the bridge.

I cast one last look towards Bree as she squeezes my hand, and we nod in unison. I take a long, deep, steady breath, and without any further hesitation, I trigger the detonation. Within seconds, the blinding blasts illuminate the remaining darkness in the sky. The force causing the glass in the nearby buildings to shatter and alarms on parked cars to wail.

Fire and flames fill the horizon, celebrating this new dawn.

Oh, how I can't wait to see what tomorrow will bring.

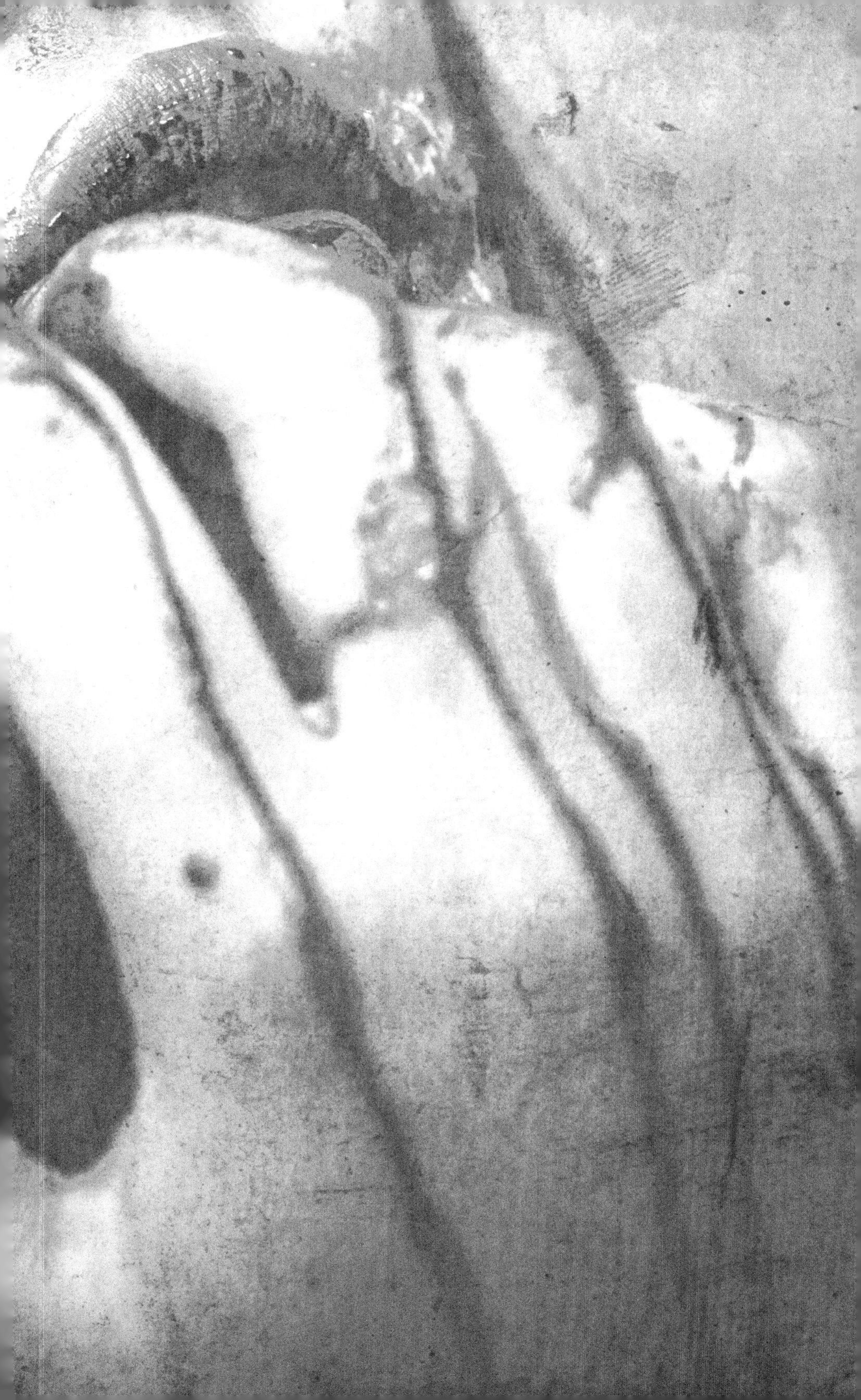

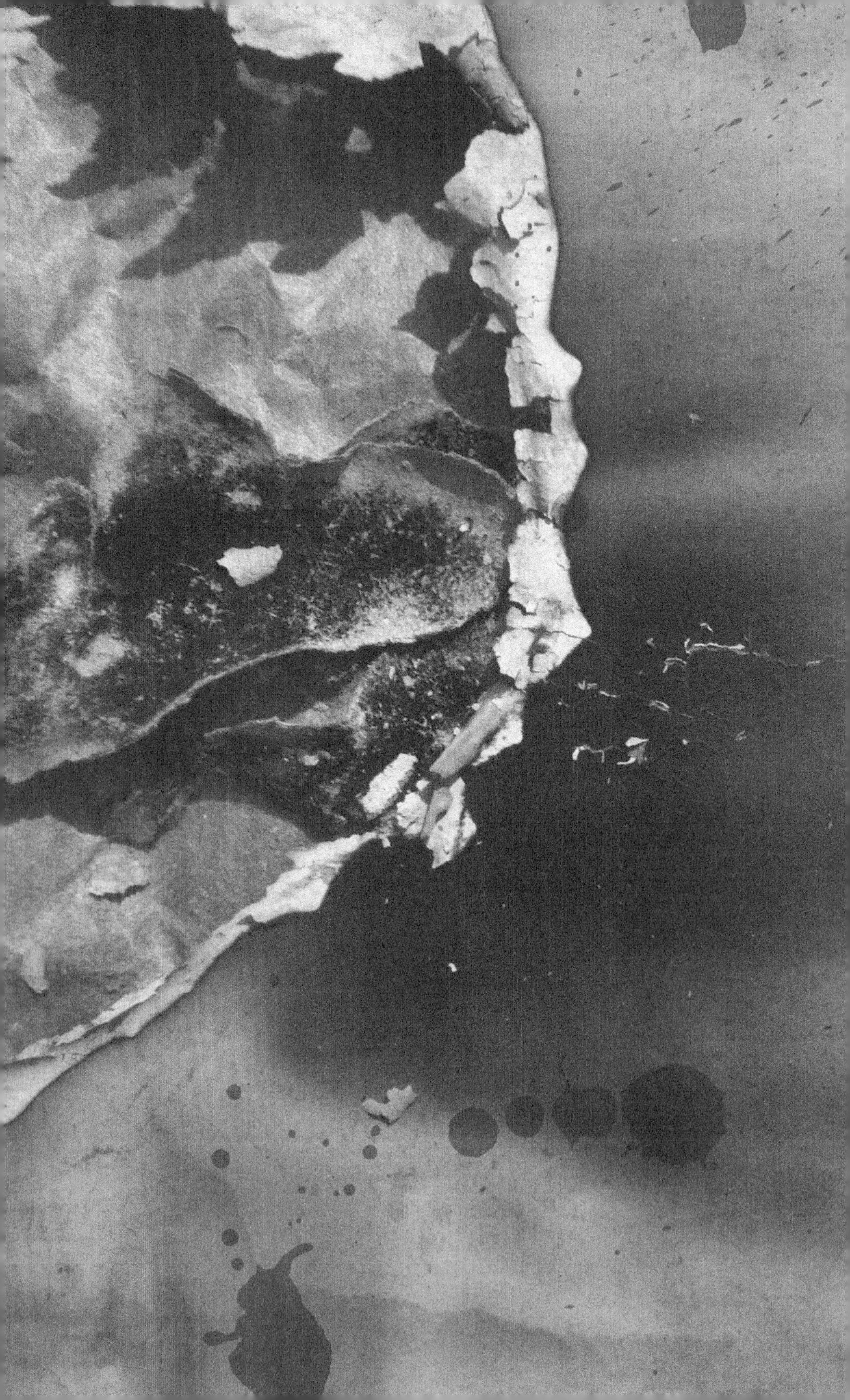

Fury

Nicole Banks

Dedication

To those who kept quiet because they knew the system wouldn't believe them.
To those who spoke up and the system still left them out to dry.
I hope you find comfort in these pages.
These characters believe you.
I believe you.

Chapter One

"Come on baby, we don't have that far to go." Hot breath coated Madison's ear as she stumbled, trying keep up with the man that was all but dragging her away from the bar. Her feet were killing her. The heels had been a bad choice, but Bob, Benny? No, Blake, maybe, had told her she had amazing legs and bought her all her drinks tonight.

She did have amazing legs.

She groaned when she stumbled again. Her world was spinning, and it made her queasy. "I don't feel good," she mumbled, though she wasn't sure he heard her. Her lips felt weird. "I thought you were putting me in a cab."

He laughed. "No, you're too hot to wait. This will be better."

'Too drunk' went unsaid.

"Don't worry, sweetheart, we're almost there, and we'll make you feel good." She stopped moving, but her blissful moment only lasted a second before she recoiled from an unwanted touch against her ass. A slimy tongue licked up the back of her neck and another hand grabbed at her right boob like he was trying to open a pickle jar.

"You're going to be a good girl for me and my friends, right?" Her shirt was ripped open, and she groaned. This was her favorite black top.

"Stop," she mumbled, pushing the hands off of her. The cool air hit her skin, and she shivered.

"We'll warm you up soon. God, you have great tits. Doesn't she look like the bitch we did two years ago, John?"

John.

"What bitch? All pussy starts to look the same with as much as we get." He laughed. "Right, Blake?"

Blake and....

"She does look familiar, but they all do." Blake's lips were on her skin. "All the hot and eager ones that need help giving it up. Also, cool it with the names, Rick. Shit," he cursed, realizing his mistake.

And Rick makes three.

She scanned the alley they were in. There was barely any light. They weren't far from the bar, but they were far enough that no one was going to come check if she screamed. They picked the perfect place for what they wanted to do.

"Stop." She batted hands away and tried to break out of their hold. "I don't feel good." She tried to move again, but the grip on her upper arms tightened.

"Bro, I don't want her mouth if she pukes." That had been Rick, laughing as his hand inched its way under her skirt. "Do you think she can handle all of us at once?"

Her body went ridged when he cupped her between her legs.

"She's not going to puke. She's going to be eager to show us if the carpet matches the drapes. You know what they say about redheads." Blake chuckled, going for his belt buckle.

"I want to go home," she protested, trying to push out of their hold. "Get off of me now," she snapped. She used her nails to cut into Rick's wrists. He hissed out a curse and ripped his hand off of her.

Good, I hope I broke skin.

"That wasn't very nice," Blake grabbed her chin. "I don't mind if you fight, but they do." He leaned in closer. His hot breath coating her lips made her want to puke. "I mean, you can fight me if you want to," his voice lowered, "I'll be sure to leave enough of you for my friends once I'm done."

Blake stepped back. "Make sure you hold her arms." He kicked her legs wider. "I'm getting what's owed. You think you can waltz away after you've been throwing yourself at me all night and making me by you drinks?" He laughed, going for his belt buckle again.

Chapter One

Entitled prick.

Madison abruptly laughed at the absurdity of it all. The sounded echoed around them and came off a little manic, which she was grateful for. Blake stopped what he was doing and whoever was holding her arms loosened their grip enough that she was able to break their hold. She cocked her elbow back hard, and she heard the satisfying crunch of bone breaking, followed by a high-pitched yelp.

She didn't stop.

She swung, aiming for Blake's nose, but he had been smart enough to back up, and she barely tapped his jaw.

Fuck.

"You're not drunk?" Blake asked. The disbelief in his tone made her want to bash his face into the brick wall. "You played me," he snapped.

She danced away from them, but it put her squarely against the dead end of the alley. It wasn't ideal, but she could work with it.

"I don't know if I should be offended or just straight up pissed off that you're mad I played you," Madison grumbled. "Especially when you brought me to a dark alley where your friends were waiting to...." She couldn't say the word.

It was silly that she couldn't say it, especially not to them. It had no power to break her, and yet saying it felt like it was giving them power over her. Her mind tried to flood her with memories at that exact moment—memories she tried to erase, but they were always there, waiting for her to let her guard down.

She could feel her heart racing and her breathing increased.

You are more than this. You are stronger than the world thinks you are.

She repeated the mantra in her mind, using it to steady her. She wanted to be all rage-filled and scary. She wanted to stand her ground, but sometimes she wanted someone else to fight the battles—at the very least to stick up for her and anyone else like her.

"I know you." Blake took a step forward, and she took a step back. "Your voice. I remember your voice." He looked her over, squinting his eyes, and she could see he was trying to place her.

"You do not." She attempted at an accent, but he didn't believe it. She fought the urge to check if her hair was still intact, though she doubted he'd know exactly who she was even if she showed up as herself.

"I'm sure I—" Blake's words were cut off at the sound of either Rick or John grunting and hitting the ground hard.

She tried to see past Blake's shoulders but could barely make out what was happening behind him.

Blake turned around, "Hey, man, what—" his question was cut off by a punch to the face.

Madison reached behind her to pull out her trusty knife—Sheila—she named all her weaponry. How Rick or John didn't feel it was beyond her, but she wasn't worried about that now. Her focus was on the newcomer who had easily dropped all three men on their knees. They were all groaning and slowly moving to stand, except one.

Fuck, is he dead?

If he was dead, that wasn't good. Too many witnesses, too much evidence left behind.

"What the fuck, man?" Blake struggled to get to his feet but was kicked back down but the newcomer.

"Didn't say you could get up." He sounded bored, but there was an edge to the way he spoke as he leaned over Blake. "I find it interesting that the three of you are in a dark alley with a woman who appeared to be too drunk to stand."

Madison's shoulders tensed. How long had he been watching them, and if he was paying attention, who else saw them?

Shit.

Blake opened his mouth, but the newcomer stepped on is dick, making him scream. "I don't care. You'll give me some bullshit excuse to make it sound like it was her fault, I'm sure." He took a step back and looked directly at Madison as if he just remembered she was still here.

Their eyes locked, his dark to her fake green—contacts for the win. His hair was cropped short to his skull. He had full lips that were pulled back into a smirk, and he was dressed in all black—including the gloves he wore.

"You should leave," he barked out the order, and she scoffed, crossing her arms over her chest.

"And why would I do that?" She wasn't going to let him have all the fun or ruin the plans she'd taken weeks to concoct and arrange.

"Not you, sweetheart." He chuckled. Goosebumps broke out across her skin—because she was cold, and not because of him. "I'm talking to dipshit one, two, and three." He put his focus back on Blake. "And I'd hurry if I were you. My patience is thin tonight."

She watched, annoyed at how quickly Blake and his buddies scrambled to their feet. They scurried out of the alley like little rats without so much as a backward glance. They never would have left her alone, but up against one man to their three they had zero problem tucking their tails between their legs and acknowledging defeat.

She was pissed.

"Did they—" his question was cut off by a curse. She launched her knife at his head, frustrated that he ducked out of the way, so it barely scratched his skin. "That's an odd way to say thank you. But maybe violence is your love language." He shrugged. "No judgment here, but you're welcome."

Madison laughed, full-on cackle that even she could hear sounded like she snapped.

And maybe she had.

Maybe it was the stress of the night, maybe it was finally tracking down Blake after all this time, or maybe it was how quickly her mind tried to trap her in memories she thought she had dealt with.

Maybe it was the fact that this guy had come to her rescue and that was all it took to get Blake and his friends to leave her alone because her 'no' wasn't enough.

It was never enough.

She did the only thing she could that made sense. She channeled everything she'd been feeling tonight and charged for her savior with fists swinging.

Chapter Two

The knife to the head should have been Andre's first clue to duck down and quietly back out of the alley. He did his good deed for the week. She was safe, and he should have just gone home. Instead, he was dodging hits from a hurricane that kept coming at him with all her force. He batted away two hits and an attempted knee to the balls. He didn't want to hurt her, but he didn't want to be a punching bag either.

"Sweetheart," he tried and got clocked for his efforts.

He pushed her back to rub at his jaw and spit the wad of blood he could taste pooling in his mouth. *Fuck*, she got him good. There was a lot of power—or anger—behind the swings. He wasn't sure when she'd run out of steam and did not need to get hit again. He wasn't entirely sure she wouldn't chase him down if he decided to run either, so getting her to calm down was his best option.

"Sweetheart," he tried again, and she came at him even harder.

All right, new tactic.

She swung at him, and he ducked under the hit. He used his palms to push her back with a little more force than he had before. It was just enough to get her to stumble, and then he was on her, gripping her wrists and pulling them down by her stomach. He pushed her back against the concrete wall and left enough room between their bodies so he wouldn't overwhelm her.

He wasn't sure how far the three of those assholes got with her, and he didn't want to seem like he only got rid of them so he could do the same to her.

"Let go," she seethed.

"Are you going to hit me again? Have any more knives on you I should be worried about?" He looked her over, using whatever lighting he could to take in her features. She had full lips and wore heavy makeup around her eyes.

Eyes he noticed were two different colors.

He looked over her red hair, noticing a hint of brown coming through the roots, and he didn't smell an ounce of alcohol on her breath.

Well now, that's interesting.

"Are you wearing contacts?" he asked. It could be heterochromia, but his gut was telling him that wasn't the case and that she wasn't as helpless as he thought.

"Let go of me." It was less of a threat this time, so he dropped his hold on her and quickly backed up with his palms raised.

"I'm not with them, and I'm not here to finish what they started. Those men are at the bar every week trying to take some drunk girl home." He felt the need to explain and hopefully get the look of death out of her eyes. He wasn't afraid of much anymore, but she still looked like she wanted to carve a piece of skin off of him and stuff it down his throat.

"So, you just wait at the bar to see who they take home and come in like a superhero to save the day?" she grumbled, pulling her shirt closed.

He smirked. He wouldn't call himself a superhero. He didn't think the law would either. "Not exactly, sweetheart." He saw the knife she'd thrown sitting by his feet, and he bent down to pick it up, not taking his eyes off her. She seemed to calm down, but that could be so he would let his guard down. "But something tells me we might have some similarities." He pointed the knife handle at her, encouraging her to take it.

She snorted. "I doubt it." Her gaze dropped to the knife, but she didn't move closer to him.

"Oh, really?" You're wearing contacts, your wig is falling off, and I don't smell an ounce of liquor on your breath, but I watched you stumble your way into the alley with them."

He'd seen her just as he made his way to the back of the bar. Most nights he parked his truck two blocks down and walked over so no one would mistake him or his truck for a regular. He needed to blend in—no one knew him here, and he wanted to keep it that way.

She cocked her head to the side, watching him like he just exposed a weakness. "You wanted a thank you for saving me, but you waited until I was in a dark alley surrounded by three men to come rescue me." She placed a hand on her chest, shimming her shoulders. "My hero, what would I have ever done without you?" She moved forward, snatching the knife out of his hands.

Even with his gloves on, the knife tore at the material and scratched his skin. "Ouch," he grunted, looking to see if the knife broke skin. "That's a little sharp, no?"

"Obviously, and for the record," she kept the knife pointed at him, "next time you want to be a good Samaritan, maybe intervene before it gets to this part."

"Duly noted." He smirked, realizing she completely missed his initial observation. "Piece of advice, since we're sharing and all." He took a step toward her, letting the tip of her knife touch his chest. He waited to see if she applied pressure, but she didn't. She didn't waver either.

"Next time you try and set a trap, make sure you don't get outnumbered, and if you do," he pressed closer, "make sure you have back up."

She smirked and leaned in. "Don't worry." Her eyes darted past his shoulder for a split second, and it was the only reason he knew someone had snuck up behind him—that and the press of a barrel to the back of his skull. Given how much crap was in this alley and the way he had kept checking to see if the idiots had decided to come back, he was impressed this person snuck up on him without a sound.

"She's got back up. She's always got back up."

Andre cursed when he easily recognized the voice behind him. She had been in his life for a long time, and try as he might, he could never forget the subtle hitch she made when she took quick breaths because sometimes she had flare ups from her asthma, which she swore she outgrew.

Randi Johnson.

Also known as his late little sister's best friend. They were thick as thieves until they weren't. He looked at the woman in front of him, now making out the features he initially missed. If his intel was right about her, that made the fake redhead Madison Arroyo.

Her girlfriend.

"I thought you moved to Chicago with your parents, Randi." He didn't see or hear any subtle shifts from either of them. They were good, he had to give them some credit, but not good enough because he could only imagine the reckless plan they had concocted for all of them to end up here tonight.

"Are we really going to pretend you don't know me, Randi?" he tried again. "Has it been so long that you've forgotten my voice?"

Among other things.

Neither one moved or said anything, and now he really wished he had stayed home. "Since this a party now, maybe we can put the knife and gun away? Or maybe just one?" He wouldn't begrudge them their need to keep a weapon in sight at all times.

"They both seem like overkill at this point." He could disarm Madison, but he wasn't sure Randi wouldn't pull the trigger by accident or on purpose. While his life had gone to shit, he still had things he needed to do before he met his maker.

Madison smiled, removing the knife only to place the tip of it under his chin. He sighed, but at least he didn't feel the barrel against his skull anymore. "You seem to think you know who's behind you, and yet we don't know anything about you."

Andre scoffed. "Randi does, and given how close you two are, I'm sure you do as well. It'll take a while to click, but let me help you out." He crossed his arms over his chest and leaned down onto the knife until he felt the sting of it, causing him to bleed. His smile matched Madison's, and he was impressed that she didn't flinch or pull away.

"My name is Andre. Nina was my little sister and Randi's best friend." He felt Randi's gasp on the back of his neck, hating how hot his body became.

She still sounds the same.

"I have a pretty good idea what you two are doing. But what I can't figure out is why and for how long."

"Good." Randi finally spoke and her voice only ignited the warmth in his body. She reached around him and grabbed for Madison who happily went with her. "You don't need to know why I do the things I do. You gave up that right a long time ago when you left." If she had hit him, it would have hurt less than hearing the accusation in her tone.

They started walking away from him, and he let them. Just like he let her go all those years ago. It was better this way.

Randi stopped when she reached the entrance, barley turning around to face him as she spoke. "Don't look for me, Andre. I'm not sure why you're here and not with your mom in Florida, but we aren't friends or exes looking to catch up. You made sure of that, and we're going to keep it that way."

Chapter Three

"Run, run, run, as fast as you can. You'll never get away, but it's fun watching you try."

John pumped his legs as fast as they would go, but given the way he was stumbling around, he wasn't getting very far. He didn't know where he was. It was dark and he was cold, and something wet trickled down his face.

"You're slowing down," the distorted voice taunted. "Don't you want a chance to escape?"

John tripped over something, and the ground was quick to greet him. The cold floor hurt against his bare hands and knees—where had his clothes gone?

It didn't matter.

He needed to escape.

He tried to crawl. He had to keep moving, but something hard hit his ribs, and he fell against what he thought was a wall. "Stop," he cried out, wrapping a hand around his torso. "Just let me go, please." He flinched when he felt a gloved hand against his shoulder. "Do you want money?"

A cold laugh sent a shiver down John's spine. "Money? You offer me the very thing you don't have? Tell me something, John. How many women were there?"

"Wh—" he yelped, when he felt something pierce his shoulder.

"Now, now," the distorted voice chastised, "this isn't the place to be coy and play dumb. You know exactly what I'm talking about. How many women was it? Did you ever do it on your own, or was it always with your friends?"

John's heart raced and he swallowed, trying to look around his surroundings for something—anything—to protect himself with. He couldn't remember how he even got wherever this was. The last thing he remembered was walking up to a group of girls trying to get into a bar. The redhead had smiled up at him, and that's the last thing he could recall.

"Ticktock, John. I hate wasting my time." The flash of silver had John's eyes widening. He tried to deflect the blow, but the shooting pain in his foot had him crying out in agony. He slumped over but was immediately pushed back up into a seated position.

"Stop bitching. It was a measly flesh wound." The voice laughed. "Are you going to tell me what I want to know?"

The flash of the knife was in the air a second time. "Wait!" John shouted. "I'll tell you whatever you want to know." He needed to get out of there. He wasn't sure what game this was, but he wanted it over and done with. "If you let me leave," he tacked on.

"Deal." The voice was still distorted, and John couldn't make out who was kneeling in front of him. They wore all black, a skeleton ski mask covered the bottom half of their face, and white color contacts covered their eyes. It was almost impossible to see the color of their skin with the low lighting. John couldn't tell if his captor was a man or a woman or if he even knew them.

"You don't," they smirked.

"I don't what?" He was confused, his mind was still foggy, and while he knew he needed to get out of here, all he wanted to do was sleep.

"You don't know me, but I know you." They held out their gloved hand as they rose to their feet. "Come, a deal is a deal."

John used whatever strength he had to lift his arm up and grab hold of the hand in front of him. He held onto it like a lifeline, and his pulse steadied a little as he got to his feet. He was getting out of there.

All he had to do was answer whatever questions this person had and keep one foot in front of the other—assuming he could with the room spinning and the throbbing in his foot. He felt nauseated as he took another step forward. "I don't feel good." He covered his mouth.

"Oh, you don't? Maybe you should lay down and rest for a while."

"No, I want to get out of here and go home," John protested but the words came out garbled.

"How many times have you heard the word 'no' and didn't listen?"

John's knees hit something soft and his body collapsed on itself. Was he on a bed?

"How many times have you heard 'I want to go home' and ignored it?"

John tried to push himself up, but he was knocked down hard. "You're not getting up, John." He flinched when he felt something soft caress his low back. "How many women was it, John? Do you remember their names? Their faces? Tell me or this is going to be worse for you."

The sound of a chair being dragged across the floor made him snap his head up, and that was a mistake. Everything around him spun so fast he puked.

"Ew, gross. I guess your mouth is off limits now."

"Please," John begged but was met with only laughter. "Please. Whatever you want, I'll give it to you."

"Tell me no. Tell me to stop over and over again." The distorted voice sounded far away, but it triggered a memory—the one time he and his two friends, Blake and Rick, had gotten caught.

"Are you remembering now? You thought you won." Cold metal wrapped around John's wrists, and he started to thrash against his binds, but his strength never returned.

"What did you give me? Who the fuck are you?" he seethed. His mind whispered who it could be, but he knew it wasn't her. She died after the trial, took her own life.

"I'm no one you need to worry about. But it's time to send a message to your friends." The ax flashed in front of his face. "I can't wait to hear you scream for me."

He was here.

Andre was here.

After three years, Randi thought she had finally gotten over the feelings she held for him and the heartbreak his sister Nina's death had caused. Hearing his voice a couple of nights ago proved that hadn't been the case. In fact, it had put her right back on her parents' front porch watching him get in a car and leave.

He was supposed to help her get justice for Nina. He was supposed to help her keep going, but he hadn't, and she lost her best friend and boyfriend in the same night.

"We're going to have to figure out how to get them again." Madison's shoulder brushed up against hers as they walked home from their daily run.

Randi hated running, but it was the only thing that kept Madison's nightmares at bay, and she wasn't going to deny her peace. She had already lost one person; she wasn't going to lose Madi in the same manner.

"We will, babe." She reached down and grabbed Madi's hand, giving it a tight squeeze. "We do what we've been doing. I still have tabs on all of them." she murmured, her mind slipping from past to present.

"You're leaving? Now?" Randi looked at Andre in disbelief. The trial had ended two days ago and all three of them had been found not guilty. The judge wanted to be lenient with them since 'it was their first offense.' It wasn't, but it was the only one that caused enough stir to get the justice system to do something. But it had been a waste because they didn't. 'It seems like such a waste to ruin your lives for something that can't be proven.'

She flexed her hands, trying to stem the rage burning through her body. The judge didn't want to ruin their lives, but what about Nina? Even if she managed to get past what happened to her, those scars lingered. Her life was altered, but theirs couldn't be? No. They'd pay.

If the system didn't do its job, she'd find a way.

"I have to, and I need you to look after Nina. She's...." He didn't have to say it. She knew. She was hanging on by a thread. Her only hope had been getting justice for what was done to her.

"Then stay, Andre." She reached out for him, needing him to keep her world from breaking, but he took a step back, shaking his head.

"Do you think they're going to go back to the same bar?" Madison questioned, pulling her back to the present. "It seems idiotic, especially given what happened."

Randi shrugged. "They're not smart. They just have luck on their side and enough money and connections to evade the system."

Madi scoffed. "Which means they think they're untouchable."

Randi nodded. Nina hadn't been the first they assaulted, and Madi hadn't been the last, but every time someone spoke up, it got swept under the rug. It wasn't just them either. So many men in positions of power used that power to exploit those they deemed beneath them. They were taught the world was theirs—something they could just take because it all belonged to them anyway.

So it was better to just shut up and take it.

"How you feeling?" Randi squeezed Madi's hand, as they turned down their block. "We didn't get to talk about what happened the other night." She hadn't wanted to send Madi in to deal with Blake and his friends, but she couldn't talk her out of it either.

"It was fine. I knew everything going in. You can't keep being the one to go into these things. Besides, I'm not sure how well you would have fared given who my knight in black armor was." There was amusement in her tone. "So that's the infamous Andre, huh?" She nudged her shoulder into Randi's.

"Nope. Not going there." Randi shook her head. When they started dating, the conversations of past relationships had come up. They both talked about their experiences. Madi never had her heart broken, but Randi had poured her heart out about her relationship with her best friend's brother and the guilt she carried for being with him the night Nina had been assaulted.

If I had been with her, I could have stopped it.

"Why not? He was a big part of your past," her voice dipped to a whisper, "of why we're doing what we're doing, too. You can't tell me that knowing he's back isn't bringing stuff up for you."

Randi abruptly stopped walking when they were close to their home and pulled Madi into her body. Her lips came crashing down on hers, pouring everything she felt for Madi into the kiss. The woman had brought her back to life, and Randi needed her to know that whatever lingering feelings had come up with Andre, it wouldn't change how Randi felt about her.

"Not that I'm complaining," Madi murmured against her lips, "but what was that for?"

"Reminding you that you have nothing to worry about." She looked at Madi, her heart in her throat, wondering how she got so lucky and prayed every day those scars she couldn't see didn't linger the way Nina's had.

Madi snorted. "I wasn't worried. In fact, I think he's kind of cute."

Her full lips pulled back into a smirk. "You didn't see him in action. It was hot. Hot enough to…." She waggled her eyebrows, causing Randi to cackle.

It wasn't out of the norm for them to open up their relationship. They'd been doing it as long as they had been together, so it wasn't an unusual request for Madi. But it wasn't happening. Whatever business Andre had here would not intertwine with her.

Andre was already forgotten, and Randi was going to ignore the way her heart sped up and her stomach tightened at the idea of sharing him with Madi.

"Put it away." She turned, tugging Madi toward their home. "Let's shower and grab something to eat so we can go over…." Randi stopped talking when she noticed a package by the door with lilies on top of it.

"Lillies?" Madi whistled. "As in your fave flower? Any guesses who that's from?" She pushed past Randi to grab the package. "There's a note addressed to you too." She handed over the white envelope while she used a key to cut open the box.

Randi ran a hand over her typed name before she opened the envelope.

I wanted to be surprised to see you the other night, but I wasn't.

I always knew you'd find a way to keep your promise. No matter how dangerous it is.

But know I did as well.

It seems we're on the same side of things, love.

Randi rubbed at the sharp pain in the center of her chest. 'Love' had been his pet name for her.

"Um, babe?" She heard Madi's voice, but she kept reading.

I left because of the guilt, and in doing so, you know what happened.

I learned I wasn't responsible for what happened. It was a hard lesson, but I hope you learned it too.

If you haven't figured it out, I'm sure this package will give you a clue.

And not that I have to tell you, but just in case you're feeling sentimental, make sure you burn this letter and bury what I've gifted you.

She felt Madison close the space between them. "I'm sorry to say this, well, not really," she smirked, showing Randi what was in the box, "but I love a man who gives us flowers and the hands of our enemies. It makes me want to do all sorts of delicious things to him."

Randi couldn't keep the shock off her face as she stared down at the severed hands. Something dark and delicious coiled in her stomach as she looked at the gift. Madison was right because suddenly she wanted to find Andre and show him her gratitude, even though a small part of her hated the idea. "Me too, Madi," Randi whispered. "Me too."

Chapter Four

Andre sat in the back booth of a twenty-four-hour diner. The place was pretty busy given how close to midnight it was. His gaze flashed toward the TV. The news was reporting on a dead man found near a park with his hands cut off and the word 'whore' carved into his chest. The sound was off but the subtitles—erroneous as they were—said they hadn't been able to identify the body, given how badly the face was bashed in.

Good.

Andre hid his smile behind his hand as he munched on the rest of the fries on his plate. This was the only real meal he had all day, and he wasn't sure when he'd eat again, especially because he had to go out tonight. He knew even without their friend showing up, Blake and Rick would still hit the bars. He wasn't even sure they cared their friend was missing—laying dead in a park. Their dynamic was that of a perceived king with two lackeys.

Blake was the ringleader—the one with the money and the connections. As long as he still ruled his kingdom, he didn't care about what happened to Rick or John.

Or the women they destroyed.

It pissed Andre off that, after all this time, no one put them down like the pieces of shits they were. Three years later and they still had free rein.

It would come to an end soon.

Andre drummed his fingers against the table next to his black gloves. He had to pull out a new pair thanks to the friend he made the other night. He still couldn't believe not only that had she'd thrown a knife at his head but also that she was with Randi. What were the odds?

My love.

He pulled at the collar of his black shirt and shifted in the booth. He wasn't going to look too closely at what he was feeling. It would just distract him. What he wanted to know was when she'd come back home. Any and all tabs he had on her said she was in Chicago—thriving with her girlfriend, Madison. He couldn't think of any reason for her to want to be back here in this hell hole, until he realized what she was doing.

"You won't help get justice for Nina. I will do it on my own. It may not be today or tomorrow. But they will hurt the way they made her hurt, and as her big brother, you should want that too."

"Coffee, sweetheart?"

Andre smiled, looking up at the newcomer. She looked different than she had the other night. The brown hair he saw peeking out of the red wig actually looked auburn under the diner lights. Her eyes were a dark brown, and her bow-shaped lip still looked pillow soft. She was in ripped jeans and a cropped hoodie and holding a coffee pot.

"Is it poisoned?" He leaned back, keeping his gaze on her while wondering how far Randi was.

She laughed. "Poison is too subtle for me." He nodded toward his empty cup, and she poured it to the top before sliding onto the seat across from him.

"Figured, considering you did throw a knife at my head," he moved the cup away from him, "after I saved your ass."

Madison laughed. "Did you, though? I had everything under control. If anything you ruined my night." She cocked her head to the side. She didn't do anything to hide the fact that she was looking him over—cataloging his features. He let her have her fill, still wondering if Randi was close by, listening in to their interactions.

"You've grown into your looks." She reached across the table for his coffee and took a sip. A smirk playing across her full lips. "Oh, and she's not here, so you can stop looking for her."

Andre licked his lips to hide his smile. "And who would that be?"

She swiped a fry off his plate. "Are we playing coy tonight?" She batted her eyelashes at him. "Interesting move, considering you're here because you knew I worked here and because of the gift you left Randi." She went to swipe another fry, and he pushed the plate toward her. He was finished eating anyway.

"Jealous?" he mused, even though he didn't think she was. He had to give her credit for putting two and two together. He had come into this particular diner because it had the best burgers when he was a kid —they still did—and because a little updated research showed him that Madison was a waitress here. Her schedule was harder to pin down, and while he didn't have time to sit around and wait, he hoped to run into Randi through Madison.

Showing up at Randi's house wasn't an option. He wasn't sure she wouldn't slam the door on his face, present or no present. When he left, he had hurt her twice. Once because it broke her heart, and after because she had to pick up the pieces after his sister's death.

"At least you came back for the funeral." He reached up to wipe away a fallen tear. She swatted his hand away and shoved him so hard he almost fell on his ass. "Don't. If you're not here to do what you promised, bye. I'll make sure Nina gets the peace and justice she deserves."

Madison laughed. "Hardly. In love? Maybe. As far as presents go," she leaned in, "that declaration was kind of hot, even if you're a couple of years too late."

He shrugged. "What's that saying? Better late than never. I do keep my promises."

"They will pay, Randi. But we need to be smart about this. It doesn't have to happen today. They will get what's coming to them eventually."

Andre shook the past from his thoughts as he stared at Madison. "I am curious." He grabbed the coffee and made sure to take a sip from the same spot Madison had. He enjoyed watching the way her eyes flared, but he tried to ignore it.

He had to.

"Are you scheduled to work tonight?" She shook her head. "Then why come in? I'm assuming Randi sent you, but A, how did you both conclude I'd be here? And B, why didn't she come with you?" He scanned the diner to make sure he hadn't missed her coming in.

When they were younger he was so attuned to her that he knew the moment she stepped into any space, even if he was in the middle of playing football. It was an awareness that wrapped around his chest.

He hadn't felt it at all when he was sitting here, and hadn't felt it in the alley before Madison made her presence known.

Maybe that awareness died when he left.

Madison sat back, her lips still pulled into a smirk. "She didn't send me here. In fact, she wasn't too thrilled with the idea." She rolled her eyes. "But I wanted to get a better look at you."

Andre chuckled. "Come to size up your competition?" The words fell from his lips before he could stop them and he mentally cursed. He wasn't competition. Whatever he and Randi had was ancient history, and he wasn't here for her—not in the sense of getting her back. He was here to keep his word, and the longer he sat here, the harder it was going to be to catch his prey, and yet he couldn't get his limbs to move.

He wasn't sure what it was about Madison that had him glued to the plastic booth. She was attractive—he had to be dead not to see it. But where Randi had been a soft beauty, Madison had sharp edges and claws. It didn't help that she had thrown a knife at his head and came at him like she would enjoy breaking him apart piece by piece before she feasted on him.

Madison's laugh was full-bodied and loud. Her smile widened as her eyes narrowed. He shifted, trying to quell the fire burning in his gut, threating to spread across his body. "You're deliciously cute." She ran her tongue across her top lip as if she could already taste his blood. It wasn't lost on him the way she kept a tight grip on the knife they left on the table. It was no sharper than a butter knife, but he didn't have a single doubt she would use it to flay him.

"To be competition you'd have to be an actual threat." He jumped when he felt her boot across his calf and moving up his leg. "You may have had her heart when she was younger, but it's my name it beats for now." Her foot continued to climb, even as he scooted back.

He'd done a lot of things in his life recently that had lessened his capacity to feel fear, but interacting with Madison was bringing that back at an alarming rate.

Along with an unhealthy does of arousal.

Madison's gaze swept over him again. "I see why she liked you." She hummed. "Tell me, Andre." The hand not holding the knife went to her throat. A small whimper escaped her, and the fire that had been burning in his gut spread through him. His cock pressed against his jeans, even as the hairs on the back of his neck stood up. The whispered warning was too low for him to heed. "Did you make him scream?" She licked her lips, keeping her eyes on him. Her foot stopped its little exploring between his legs, and his heart was a stampede in his chest. "Did you make him beg? Did you make him tell you 'no, stop' over and over again until he cried?"

Warning bells went off in his head. He cleared his throat. "I don't think this is the place to have this conversation." He glanced at the clock above the register and silently cursed. He was late.

He was late because…Madison was distracting him. His eyes narrowed on her. "Why are you here?" he questioned with a little bass in his voice. He left the 'and not with Randi' part out. The inferno he'd been feeling started to burn a little higher from the annoyance and anger coursing through his body.

"I need to go." He grabbed his gloves and stood, but Madison was up and in his face just as fast.

"You won't get there in time," she whispered, her lips too close to his skin. "We both thank you for taking out one, though." She reached for his hand, the one she had sliced. Her fingers trailed over the cut before she brought her soft lips to his skin and placed a gentle kiss on his hand that made his cock twitch. "All better," she murmured before looking him in the eye. "I know you think they're yours because of who they took from you, but they're not." She looked him over once more. "Stay out of it, Andre. I'd hate to see what would happen if you got in our way again."

Chapter Five

Randi smiled as Rick screamed, cried, and begged her to stop. The pain in his voice felt like warm chocolate on her tongue. "You want this, sweet boy," she murmured, cutting into his flesh. "Maybe you shouldn't have flirted with me in the bar while you waited for your friend." Another cut to his skin. "Maybe you shouldn't have worn that dark denim shirt. Only sluts wear those."

"Please," he whimpered.

"Please what?" she whispered, bringing her face to his. He had pissed himself twice, there was snot all over his face, and his cracked lips were bleeding from where she hit him.

Seeing him like this—weak, broken, pitiful—made her pulse race.

How many times had he and his friends walked around like they were untouchable?

How many times had they broken someone just because they could?

Because everyone was always on their side.

"Please stop," he sobbed when she brought the knife down on his dick. The urge to saw it off and stuff it in his mouth overwhelmed her.

"Why would I stop?" she purred. "You know you want it." She chuckled when he let out another deep sob.

Randi pushed his head and walked back over to her worktable. She ran a gloved finger down all her knives, debating how she wanted to display Rick's body once she was done with him. She and Madison had debated for a long time on whether to keep all three of them alive—keep their hearts beating while their bodies and minds broke.

Death was too easy for them.

There would be no suffering in death, and they had hurt too many people to go off into an afterlife peacefully.

Not that she was sure she even believed in an afterlife, but either way, she had wanted these three to suffer for as long as possible.

"But that's out of my freaking hands now," she grumbled, picking up a hunting knife she bought out of state with cash. They needed to keep any traces back to them as small as possible because the same people who refused to help her when they hurt Nina and countless other women will want to know who finally took them out.

"I'm sorry," Rick wailed. "I'm sorry for everything. I'll give you money. Everyone wants money."

"Money, money, money." Randi turned around, her grip on the knife tightening. "It's always about money with you three, isn't it?" She walked behind him, placing one hand on his shoulder. He flinched and it brought a smile to her face.

"You're apologizing. That's always a good start." She would have given anything to see these three show remorse, apologize to Nina, and take responsibility for their actions.

If she were a better person, Rick's tears and apology would move her to rethink this whole thing. But that person didn't exist anymore. She died when she had to bury her best friend.

Randi held Rick's head back against her stomach. "Ricky, Ricky, Ricky. You don't even know why you're saying sorry." She brought the hunting knife to his neck and slowly sliced across his flesh. He jerked in her hold and she laughed. "The mind and body are always so desperate to survive."

He grunted and flopped around like a fish out of water. It was his last-ditch effort to make it out of there. It was pathetic that he didn't know he was dead the second he found himself strapped to this chair.

"Shh, just let it happen, baby. Stop fighting it. You know you want it." Randi pushed his head again and then kicked the chair over. Her anger still needed an outlet. No matter how many lives she took, it never felt like enough.

The sound of the door opening had her turning around in time to see Madison strolling in. Randi let her eyes drink in the sight of her in jeans and a cropped hoodie, teasing the soft stomach she woke up kissing this morning. There was a smirk teasing her lips, and those eyes that helped heal her narrowed when they landed on Rick's form.

"Are you kidding me?" She threw her hands up. Randi dropped the knife and removed the gloves before closing the distance between them. "You couldn't wait fifteen minutes?" Madison's anger quickly faded when Randi pulled her in close and kissed her.

"Not fair," Madison pouted. "Andre got one and now you have one. You both better leave Blake to me."

"Sorry, Madi." Randi kissed her again, needing something to ground her. The killing was getting easier—leaving less marks. But being with Madi seemed to balance out the scales. It kept her human.

"You could have come to play," she kissed a path down Madi's neck. "But you went to play with someone else." She nipped at Madi's skin, causing her to shiver. It pushed the two of them closer.

The feeling of Madison's nails on her back made Randi's pulse race. It made her wonder what the quickest way was to peel Madison's clothes off without contaminating the scene any more than it already was.

"You sound like him," Madi whispered, pushing out of her hold. "Don't tell me you're both jealous." She crossed her arms over her chest, her gaze swinging toward Rick.

Randi tried to ignore the way her heart skipped at the idea of Andre being jealous. Whatever they had ended the moment he got in that car and left her to deal with Nina and her death.

"Where are we putting him anyway?" She nodded toward Rick. "The news already reported John's body, but they don't know who it is, yet."

Randi shrugged. "That depends. How did your talk go with him?" She hadn't wanted Madi interrogating Andre—or tipping him off to what they were doing. She made peace with keeping her promise, and she didn't want him to try and stop her or take out the marks on his own.

This was supposed to be Madi and Randi's crusade.

Righting a wrong that had been done to Nina and to Madi.

Andre was years too late. If he had stayed and helped her, maybe she wouldn't be so annoyed by his presence. Him getting to John first actually pissed her off. He was theirs. They had to make sure they got to Blake before he figured it out.

"I'm still obviously in love. A man who takes out who we've been hunting?"

Randi scoffed and rolled her eyes. Andre was always good looking, add to his little stunt and Madi had stars in her eyes.

And maybe me too, a little bit.

"I mean," she sighed, "yes, I'm a little annoyed I haven't taken out one of the three. Honestly, I feel like I deserve it the most. But…" she held her hand out, and Randi went to her, interlacing their fingers together.

Madi kissed her, nipping and sucking on her bottom lip. It enticed a hunger in her that had her pushing Madison toward the nearest wall. The little gasp Madison let out only fueled Randi more. She needed Madison as desperately as she needed her next breath.

"Hmmmm, you're distracting me." Madison's whispered words turned into a groan when Randi shoved a thigh between her legs.

"That's the point." Randi used her hands to move Madi's hips.

"I'm not complaining, but," her breath caught, making Randi smile, "I think we need to focus on the body behind us and…" her words died out. Her head fell back, and her eyes closed. Her hips moved faster and her breathing increased.

Randi smiled, watching the flush creep across her face. "There's my girl." She stretched her hand across Madison's stomach, slowly inching her way up beneath her cropped hoodie.

She tsked under her breath when her hand grazed Madi's bare chest. "You went out without a bra on?" She pinched Madi's nipples, earning her a soft whimper. "You sat close to my ex, knowing if he wanted to, all he had to do was put his hand up your shirt and he'd be touching what's mine."

"Oh," Madison cried out, her hips moving faster. Her breath hitched. "Don't stop touching me." Her command would have been more believable if the words hadn't come out on a groan.

"So demanding," Randi smiled, pulling the cropped hoodie up enough to expose her breast to the cool air. Her mouth watered, watching the way Madi's body moved—the wild desperation clawing at her as she chased her pleasure.

"Please," Madi's hands wrapped around Randi's wrist, tugging her closer to her body, "I need more."

Yes, she did. But Randi was a little too content to drag this out.

"You think you deserve more?" She blew a breath across Madi's puckered nipple. "Going out to meet with my ex." She ran her tongue across Madi's nipple. "Sitting close enough for him to tell you were bare underneath this hoodie. I bet you don't even have underwear on."

"I don't," Madi whimpered.

Randi's chuckle turned into a groan. "My filthy girl. Were you hoping he would stick his hand down your pants?" Randi pulled back, long enough to toss Madi's hoodie up over her head and onto the floor. Her hands went to the button on her jeans and slowly pulled down the zipper, shaking her head when she came up against bare skin again.

"What am I going to do with you?" she whispered.

Madi's hand grabbed her neck and pulled her in for a kiss. She bit down hard on Randi's bottom lip before pulling away. "You're going to make me cum," she kissed her again, "please."

Randi's body hummed. Her own pleasure sinking into her bones as she looked at Madi. The flush of her skin, the way her eyes were heavy, and the way she bit her lip made her own stomach tighten.

The urge to claim her after she spent time with Andre seemed to fuel her movements. She dipped her head, taking Madi's nipple into her mouth. She hissed out a breath when she felt Madi's nails in her shoulders.

"Don't stop," Madi chanted over and over again. Her hips moved faster and faster. She was close, going by the way her breath hitched between each word.

It was intoxicating. It made her drunk, tasting her passion—her pleas for more. The fact that there was a dead body only a couple of feet away from them made this hotter. The fact that Andre's presences seemed to linger in the air around them made Randi's skin sizzle. She tried to ignore it—needed to. But it drove her need to make Madi climax higher.

Make her cum for us, Randi. I want to see how pretty she explodes.

"Fuck," Randi moved her thigh from between Madi's leg and shoved her hands in her jeans. She was drenched. Randi slipped two fingers inside of her with ease and brought the heel of her palm against her clit piercing.

The low groan that left Madi's lips wrapped around Randi in a vise grip. Her own core throbbed as she felt Madi's walls close around her fingers. "You're close, aren't you, sweet girl?" Randi whispered against her skin. She moved to the other nipple, humming against the sweet symphony of Madi's chanting.

"I can feel you tightening around my fingers." Randi nipped at her flesh. "Cum for me, Madi."

Bring light into my darkness..

Madi exploded against Randi's hand, her body shook and her knees buckled, but Randi was there holding her up. She pulled back just enough to watch Madi's back arch off the wall. Her nails dug into her wrists, no doubt leaving tiny marks, which Randi would wear proudly. Madi's eyes were closed and her lips were slightly open as that familiar flush crept across her skin.

"So beautiful," Randi whispered, "so perfect."

Madi slowly came down, and Randi pulled her hand out of her pants, bringing her drenched fingers up to her lips. Randi hummed low in her throat, her own eyes closing as she let Madi's climax seep into her tongue and alight her taste buds.

"My favorite flavor," she smiled, looking at a sated Madi.

"I like getting welcomes like that. You should make it a thing every time I see you," she pulled Randi in for a kiss.

Randi melted into Madison, a content sigh leaving her mouth as she wrapped herself around the only person who kept her grounded.

"We need to go, babe," Madi murmured against Randi's lips. "As much as I want to strip you out of your assassin clothing."

Randi snorted out a laugh. Wearing all black did not make it assassin clothing, but she wasn't going to correct her.

"I thought for sure Andre was going to follow me back here, and since he didn't," Madi let out a sigh, "that means he's going after Blake and I want him, Randi. Maybe we can work together to catch him, but I want that kill to be ours."

Randi looked over her shoulder at Rick's body. They would have to work fast to catch up to Blake and Andre. If he hadn't followed Madison first, it might even be too late. But that didn't mean they couldn't try and stop what was probably already happening.

Blake's death was theirs and theirs alone.

"Then you, sweet girl, need to hurry up and get dressed." She patted Madi's hip. "We have to go hunting."

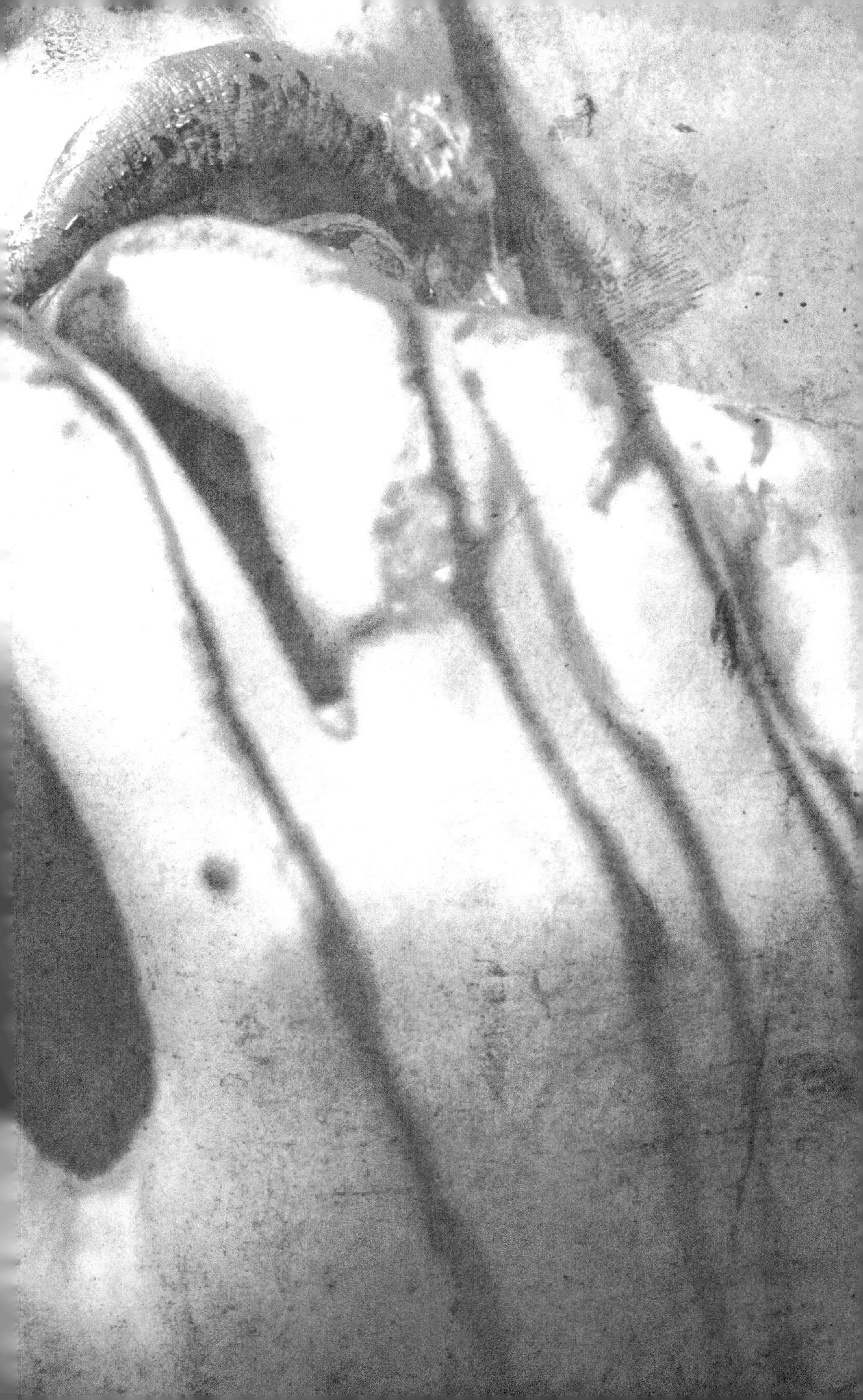

Chapter Six

Blake paced the length of his living room, pissed that his uncle, the police chief, practically grounded him and forced him to stay home tonight.

"Your friend showed up dead, and you can't get a hold of the other one," he snapped. "You don't find that suspicious?"

Blake had scoffed over the phone line. Rick and John were a means to an end. They were leeches he had no problem throwing under the bus when the time came, but his uncle had other ideas.

"If one is guilty, you all are guilty."

How was it possible for all them to be guilty when it was him who had the connections and power? He was untouchable. Who cared if John was stupid enough to die? That had shit to do with him.

Blake paused in the middle of his pacing and went to the window to pull back the curtains. He could see the unmarked car parked out front and all but rolled his eyes. He hated being kept under lock and key. It was a weekend. Did his uncle not realize he had women waiting for him?

"Man, fuck this shit." He dropped the curtain and made his way toward the back of the house. He wasn't about to be kept in his home like a toddler. Whatever was going on with Rick and John wasn't about him. They could piss anyone off, and that was probably what happened.

He grabbed his keys and phone and opened the back door, coming face to face with a woman in all black—her pants look painted on. She had brown eyes and long brown hair. There was something vaguely familiar about her, but when his eyes caught on the sheer black top she wore with nothing underneath, his cock immediately hardened.

Maybe I don't have to go out after all.

"Can I help you?" He leaned up against the door, taking his time looking her over again. He wondered if she was a screamer.

"I'm sorry," she looked over her shoulder and back toward him. His house sat on the corner, but because of its size, his front door opened up to one street while his back door opened up to another. He looked past her, not seeing an unmarked car watching him and he smiled.

His uncle didn't think of everything.

"I was just..." she stammered. "He was...."

"Come in, come in." He moved to give her room to step through the doorway. He had no clue what was chasing her, but vulnerability was easy to manipulate.

The relief on her face sent heat throughout his body. Tonight was going to be a good night for him.

"Oh, thank you." She walked into his home, and he kept his eyes glued to her ass. His palms were already itching to grab hold of her.

"Don't worry about it," he shifted, taking his hand off the door so he could walk in behind her. "Do you need to call somebody? Want water?"

She turned around, her smile warm and inviting. She crooked her finger at him, and he went willingly. Staying home did have its perks.

"Do you know what I want?" her voice was sultry, and he couldn't wait to see what sounds she made once he got his hands on her.

"What's that?" He reached for her, but she stepped back.

"For you to know what it's like to feel pain."

Blake didn't have a chance to react, something cold and hard hit him from behind and he dropped to his knees. His mind scrambled, trying to keep his body upright, but he slumped to the ground with his final thoughts on the woman in front of him.

He remembered her now.

Randi Johnson.

Nina's best friend and the woman who had threatened him all those years ago.

Fuck.

Chapter Six

"I THINK YOU HIT HIM TOO HARD." Randi stood over Blake who was still slumped in the chair they had tied him to.

"Personally, I don't think I hit him hard enough." Madison crossed her arms over her chest. She didn't want to stop at one hit. She wanted to keep swinging until his skull was caved in, but where was the fun in that? She wanted him awake for what she planned on doing to him.

"The smelling salts aren't working?" Madison walked around Blake, her eyes going over the furniture and appliances he had. Everything looked the same from the last time she was here, and she wasn't sure if that was comforting or not.

There were no memories beating down on the wall she built to block out what happened to her, so she was going to take that as a win.

Randi shook her head. "Kind of wish we could take him out of here too. But there's a car watching the front of the house."

Yes, his uncle no doubt wanted to protect his only living relative. Where Blake was oblivious to actions having consequences, his uncle wasn't. "We're going to have to be quick." Madi pulled out her trusty knife, Sheila. "And I hate that we have to be. But there's no telling who has keys to this place and who is going to waltz through either door."

As soon as she finished the sentence, the back door opened with an eerie creek. Madison lifted her hand and threw the knife without waiting for the person to fully step through the door.

There was a grunt followed by a low curse. "Are you fucking kidding me?" Andre snapped, and both Madison and Randi groaned. "What is with you throwing knives at my head?"

"It's always in the way?" Madison shrugged. She heard the subtle shift in Randi's breath once Andre walked through the threshold wearing all black. He looked larger than he had before. There was something menacing about him now—it was there the other night when he 'rescued' her.

Her stomach tightened watching him and Randi stare at each other. The energy in the room shifted, something dark and delicious coated the air, and it made Madison lick her suddenly-dry lips. She closed the distance between her and Randi, interlacing their gloved hands together.

Andre's gaze dipped to their joined hands, his lips pulling back before he looked at Randi again. "Go home. You shouldn't be here doing this." He looked at Madi. "Either of you."

"And this is why you get a knife thrown at you," Madi grumbled. She didn't mind working with him but only if he stayed in his lane. They got Blake without Andre's help. He was currently tied up and unconscious. The only thing they would need help with was moving the body if they decided to do that.

"You shouldn't be here." Randi's voice held steady. "You're trying to save me from the burden of taking a life, but you're a little too late," she whispered. "They weren't our first, and until the world changes, they won't be out last."

Because the world responded to power and power rarely was in the hands of women. This was their way of taking it back. Maybe it made them just like their perpetrators, but neither Madison nor Randi cared.

How many people never got the justice they deserved?

How many have stayed silent because they knew it wouldn't matter to the world?

The scales were severely unbalanced, and this was their way of tipping it back.

Andre pinched the bridge of his nose. "I'm going to regret this, I know it." He let out a breath. "I'm not saying I agree, but I get it. I don't want this to change you at your core and, trust me, it will."

Randi shrugged. "Maybe I'm becoming exactly who I need to be."

A groan had all three of them turning their attention to their guest. "Oh, goodie, he's awake." Madison let go of Randi's hand and made her way toward Blake who looked a little pale until his eyes met hers.

"I know you." His words turned into a growl when he realized he was naked and bound to a chair.

"You actually remember your victims? I thought all pussy looked the same to you." She knelt down, ignoring the feel of Andre's eyes on her. If he hadn't figured out her 'why' before, he just did now.

"You stupid bitch." He spit at her, and Madison scoffed, taking out another knife and slashing it across his chest.

"Rude." She stood up. "Not nice to start off this way. We had so many plans for you." She lifted the knife up and drove down on his hand.

The fuck screamed—louder than she thought he would—and she rolled her eyes. "You're being dramatic."

Andre was there, his gloved hand covering his mouth to muffle the sound. "Did you guys have an actual plan, or was this put together with stick figures?"

"We had a plan. You fucked it up twice." Randi closed out their little circle with a roll of tape in her hand. "So now this shithead is on protection detail, and we're improvising."

Andre backed up enough to let Randi put the tape across Blake's mouth, and Madison pulled the knife free. Blake still had a high-pitched scream, but it was muffled now.

"You guys are going to have to be quick." Andre's eyes scanned the room. "I can't imagine his uncle not having someone check in on him soon."

Madison wanted him to be wrong, but she wasn't stupid. They had pushed up their timetable, and as anticlimactic as all of this felt, there was a surge of giddiness making her blood pump faster. Especially when she looked down at Blake and saw the fear in his eyes and the pool of pee sitting below his chair.

He finally understood what fear felt like and it fueled her. "I'm going to slit your throat until I see what a coward looks like from the inside." She bent down till they were face to face. "You used to be scary. A monster in so many nightmares, and seeing you like this…," she ran the tip of her knife up his leg, breaking skin because he kept squirming. "You're pathetic," she murmured, fascinated when she could see the tears building in his eyes. "You've always been pathetic, and that's why you seek to take power from others."

She would have laughed if it hadn't been so sad. He had taken her power from her in a moment, and it took so long to reclaim. But how had she ever let him take it in first place?

He was nothing, and once she slit his throat, he'd be nothing.

No one would mourn or miss him. The stain he left on people would fade, and there would be no more people he could hurt.

"I couldn't figure out how to get you out of my mind and off my skin, but seeing you like this…small…," she drove her knife into his side. He kept trying to squirm away from her, but both Randi and Andre held him down and kept him still. "Weak," another stab, "pissing yourself and crying," another stab. "This will be the last vision of you I'll have, and when the news gets wind of your death," she brought the knife against his throat, "those you've hurt will be set free, knowing someone took your power away." She took the knife and slowly cut across his skin, savoring the satisfaction coursing through her. The sight of his blood made her feel light-headed, and her body hummed in anticipation.

When she was done she grabbed for Randi, kissing her and pouring everything she was feeling into her.

"We did it," Madison whispered against her lips, feeling giddy.

"Yes, we did," Randi responded, "And now—"

"And now we take on the rest," Madison finished. She turned her gaze to Andre who didn't bother to hide the heat in his gaze. "You coming with us, or doing your own thing?"

Andre shrugged. "If Randi says it's okay and you stop throwing knives at my head, yes, because you two can't plan for shit."

Randi scoffed. "We had a plan, and you ruined the plan. So maybe if you're gonna hang with us, you…I don't know…don't get in our way."

Madison laughed, wondering how they were going to survive each other, but one thing was for sure. They would find a way to bring closure to those who couldn't rely on a system to do it.

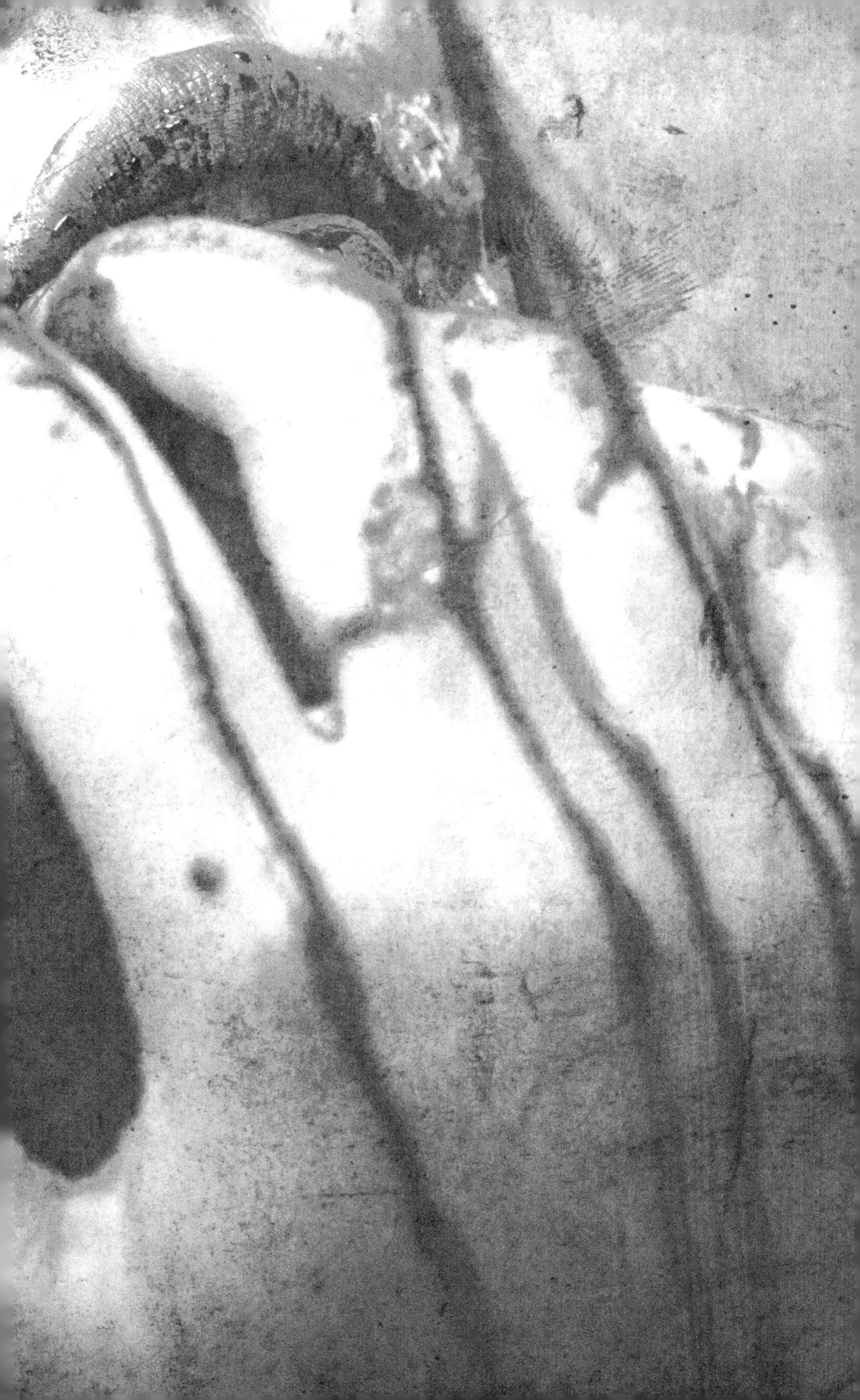

About the Author

Want to keep up with Nicole Banks?
Follow her on Instagram @_nicolebanks_
www.nicolebanksauthor.com

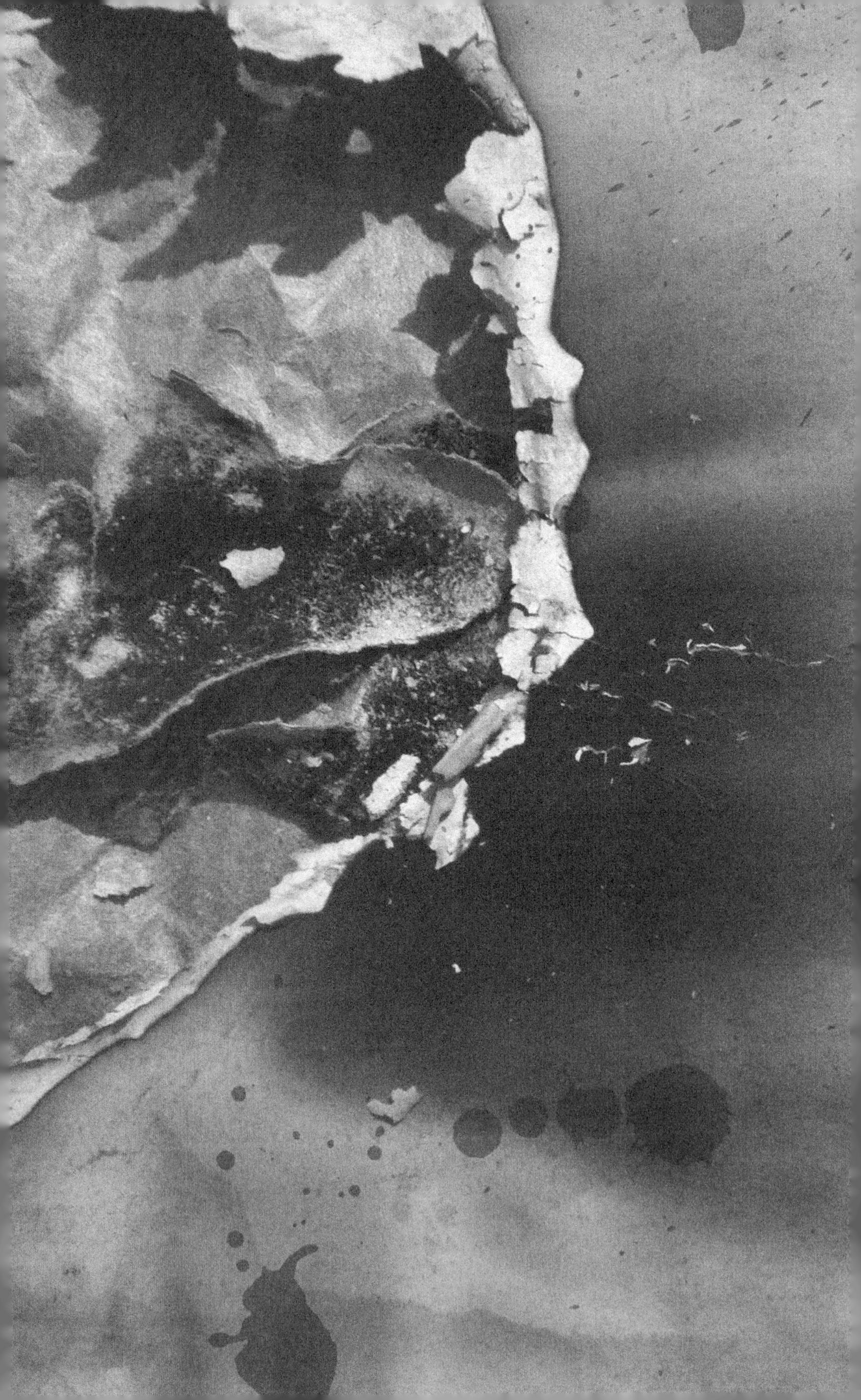

Maneater

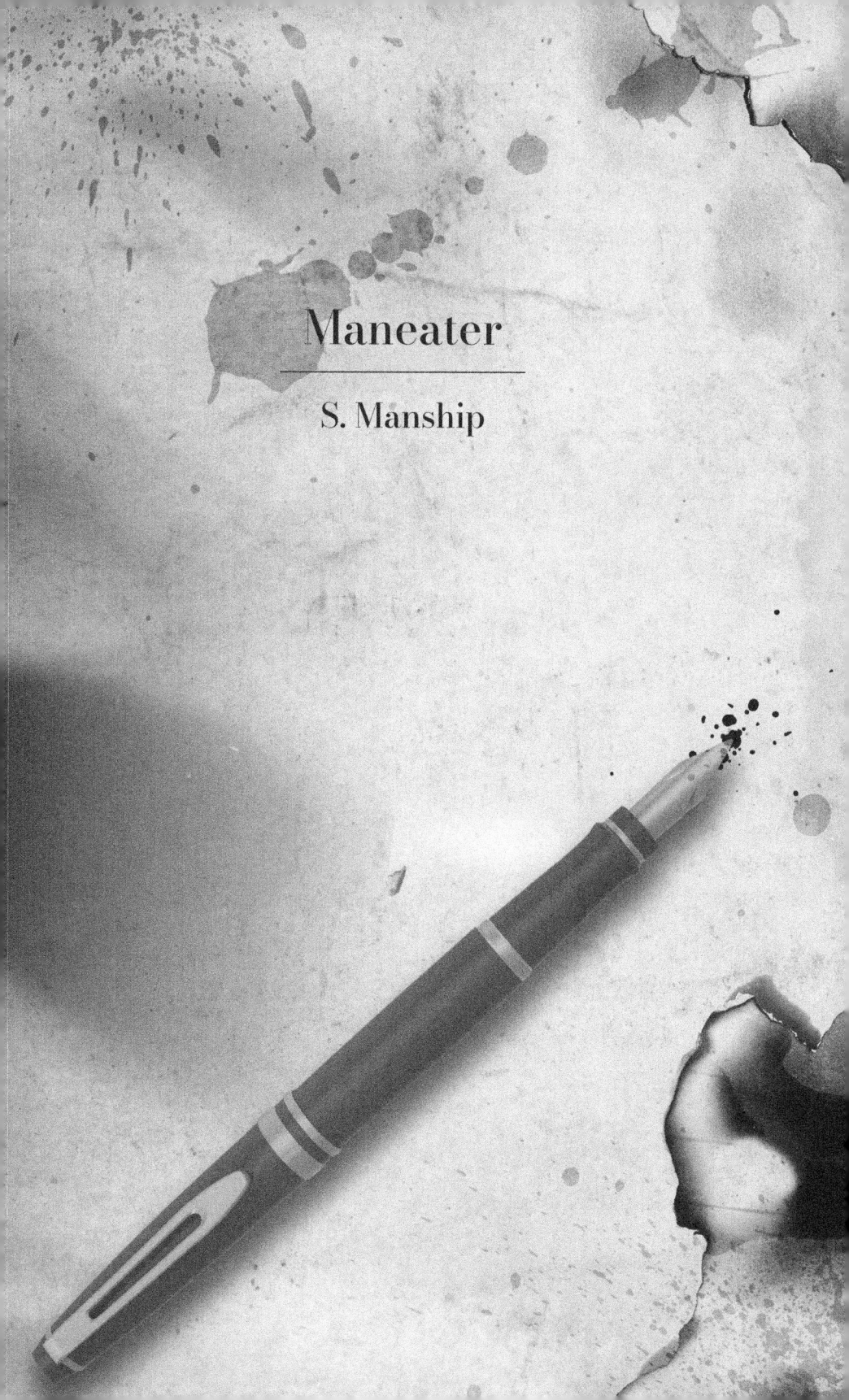

S. Manship

Chapter 1

The Start Of A Legacy

"He's a mute."

Angora makes the declaration as if she's commenting on the weather or the time of day, not declaring a person incapable of speaking. My eyes dart to the man standing behind her chair, anticipating a poor reaction. He looks perfectly at ease, as if the casual nature of the statement is something he expected. The idea any man could be so impervious to being perceived as "less than"—less than whole, less than perfect—is astonishing.

When I came to Angora, I told her I needed a quiet husband, one who wouldn't question my decisions or go against my actions. She seems to have taken me to the letter of my word rather than the spirit of the request.

"By choice or by force?"

She shrugs, not even bothering to turn toward the man in question before answering. "By birth, I believe."

My eyes snap to him again, only to find his startling gaze already focused on me. He's an unusual looking gentleman, with hair so blond, it appears white in the sunlight pouring through the atrium windows. His features are strong, a square jaw and straight nose, but his lips are soft and wide. The sudden quirk of those lips tells me I've been caught staring.

"He truly cannot speak?"

"Not a word."

"Well." I catch myself smiling for the first time in what feels like years. I hadn't expected a mute, but I should have known Angora would pull out all the stops. She's as invested in this as I am, after all. "That certainly fits the bill."

The skin around Angora's eyes wrinkles as she bites back her own amusement at the situation we've found ourselves in. "I thought he might suit."

Taking a sip of my tea, I allow my gaze to roam over the man. He looks healthy, strong, and admittedly more handsome than any man I dreamt to find through a service like Angora's. Even as a mute, I can't help but wonder what kept him from marrying. He must have another misgiving. An unpardonable relation, perhaps?

"What's his name?"

God herself couldn't have prepared me for the name that comes from Angora's mouth. "Apollo Vanderlee."

"Of the Hawthorn Vanderlees?" The man, Apollo, doesn't miss the shock in my voice. He attempts to cover the smile threatening to break across his handsome face with a soft clearing of his throat, but I see the twitch of his lips all the same. His gaze remains on me through it all, giving a small nod of his head in acknowledgement of my question.

Panic presses against the cage of my ribs, and I force my eyes away from his. "I cannot marry a Vanderlee."

"I disagree." Angora shrugs her slender shoulders, taking a sip of tea. She remains perfectly calm, wholly unrattled by the idea of bringing a Vanderlee into this mess. "I believe he's the perfect match."

"How could you possibly think that?"

Angora's sigh is the first outward indication she's not as collected as she's attempting to appear. "His name will protect you."

"His name will draw attention," I counter, but she waves me away.

"You didn't know his name until I said it."

It's true; I had no idea there was an Apollo Vanderlee, or that the Vanderlees had any available men of marriageable age left. I've certainly never seen him in any circles the other heirs tend to run in, though I am decidedly outside those circles myself.

"Apollo is not one of the Royal Vanderlees, nor one whose name is in the paper every other week. He bears enough to have connections but stays outside of the rest," Angora explains, raising one dark brow at me. "I thought you would know better than to judge someone on their relations, Legacy Kennaway."

Apollo seems to approve of her description, his shoulders relaxing the slightest amount even as curiosity wrinkles his brow. Those startling green eyes are on me again, dissecting in a way that makes me wonder what he knows of my family history.

"Yes, well," I murmur, attempting to drag my attention from his haunting gaze. Something in the sharpness of his stare tells me the answer to my question, but I must ask to be sure. "Is he addled?"

Apollo smirks, holding my gaze as he continues to stand silently at Angora's side. Her harsh laughter makes me jump. "Not at all. In fact, he's quite intelligent."

"Do you know why he cannot speak?"

Angora turns to look at Apollo for the first time since she called him into the atrium. Her eyes linger on his face, some unheard conversation passing between the two of them before she turns to me again. "He has all the correct anatomy, the mental faculties, and even the ability to make some sounds, but the words do not come."

"Does he communicate in any way?"

"He can write as well as any man."

"Then I would like to speak with him for a moment." I let my gaze drift between the two of them, eventually settling on Angora. There's a knowing look in her eyes, as if she has already won, despite the fact that I haven't agreed to give this ridiculous pairing a chance.

Angora stands with help from Apollo's outstretched arm, patting him appreciatively on the shoulder as she moves to exit the room. Another look passes between the pair, and he nods his head almost imperceptibly.

There's a moment of stillness as we watch her retreat. Something about being left alone together lends weight to the reality of what could happen. A Vanderlee and a Kennaway? An impossible idea in theory, but perhaps more plausible than I originally thought.

Apollo finally moves, reaching into his coat pocket and producing a pen and paper. He steps up to the table, one eyebrow raised in question. Straightening my shoulders, I gesture for him to take the seat Angora vacated.

He slides gracefully into the chair, leaning back and crossing one leg over the other as he waits for me to take the lead. I suppose the best place to start is at the beginning. Then, he can decide if this is something he wishes to align himself with or not.

"I am certain Angora informed you I am looking for a husband in law alone, but allow me to shed some light on what that truly means. I am in need of a man who will sign his name to purchase properties and holdings for my use and benefit, and most importantly," I add, stealing my spine for what's to come. "I desire a husband who will neither question me nor argue against my agenda. Do you believe you could fit such a bill?"

There's a long pause, made longer by the total lack of sound from the man sitting across from me. Eventually, he bends his head just enough to see the paper in his lap as he jots down a quick response.

I believe I can.

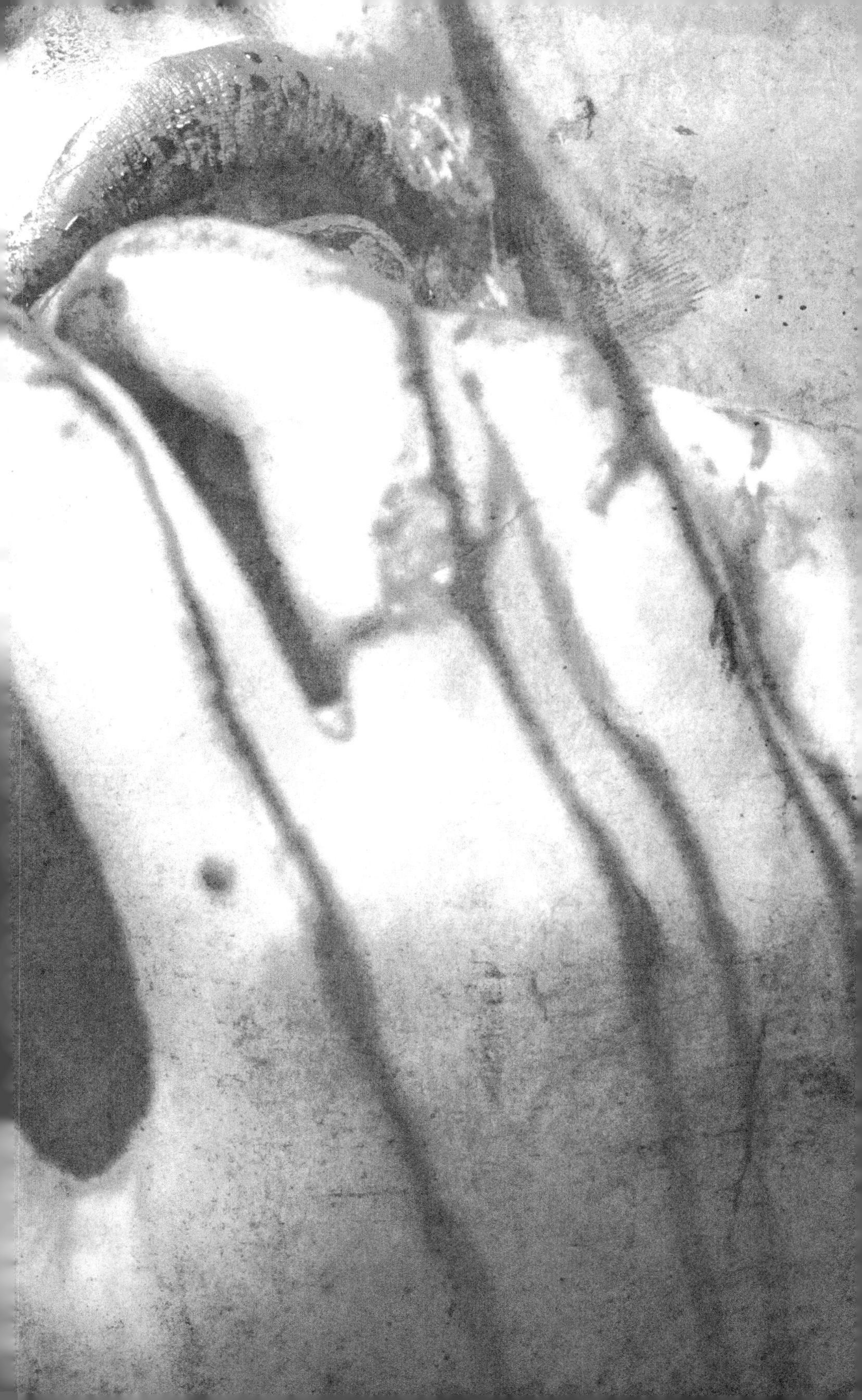

Chapter 2

Mary, Did You Know?

"A man?"

"Yes, Mary," Legacy sighs, bending to lace her fingers through the hands of the man lying between us. "I've already explained all of this to you."

"But…" I grip his ankles, straightening until I'm standing at my full height. If only I were taller or stronger; then, I could do this on my own without having to drag her into it every time. Legacy meets my gaze, adjusting her hold on his hairy wrists before nodding to show she's ready. I don't nod in return. "Does it have to be a man?"

Legacy laughs, a soft sound wholly out of place in this dank cellar. "In this world, it always has to be a man."

I'm not so sure that's true. We've been doing fine without a man up to this point. We have food, shelter, and freewill, so long as we don't step outside these walls. And we're together—safe and alive. That's all that matters to me.

"Just give him a chance." She huffs an impatient breath, shifting her grip on the man's wrists again. "I think you'll like him."

"Unlikely," I murmur.

She sighs her exasperation before pointedly glancing down at the man and back at me again. I give her a small nod, silently agreeing to focus on the task at hand for a moment. Legacy bends her knees, and I match the motion, listening for her soft count to three before we lift the man's body off the ground.

"At least try not to be outwardly hostile, please," she grunts, shuffling her feet across the dirt floor. We reach the table, shifting around until we can drop the man on the sheet laid out. Legacy releases a harsh breath, reaching up to brush the hair from her eyes with the back of one delicate wrist. "I need him to like us for this to work."

Her piercing gaze meets mine in the dark, and I know I've lost this fight. She's too beautiful, too perfect for me to ever tell her no. A wicked thought tickles the back of my mind, a selfish act to seal me that much closer to the woman I love. "Will you reward my good behavior?"

It's teasing, but we both know what I'm really asking. Legacy's dark eyes meet mine again, and she points to the rope in the corner. "Get him on the table."

The bedsheet pulley system was a stroke of genius on Legacy's part. We couldn't keep dismembering bodies on the floor—it was murder on our backs and nearly impossible for Legacy, who is almost always trapped in a corset. Unwinding the rope from its hook, I walk back until the man's body is suspended high enough for Legacy to push him over the table. Taking careful steps forward, I lower him until his weight is supported by the table rather than the ropes.

There's a long silence while we work to get the cloth out from between the man and the metal tabletop. The moment it's free, I fold the sheet around the ropes, storing it in the corner while Legacy begins cleaning the man's body. We already removed his clothes, picking out the valuables and burning the rest.

I don't normally interrupt her while she works, but tonight, I can't seem to leave well enough alone. "Is there something you're not getting?" Legacy stops with the scalpel an inch from the man's chest. Her brow is furrowed when she turns in my direction, genuine confusion lining her perfect features. "From me," I elaborate, walking around the table to stand at her side. "From us."

Legacy puts the scalpel down, turning to face me fully. "How could you think that?"

"Because you're marrying a man."

"Not by choice," she corrects, putting both hands on her hips, as if she's about to lecture me within an inch of my life. "I would rather light myself on fire than tie myself to a man, but that isn't how this world is built. Women can't own property, or vote, or drive. There isn't a thing I can do without a man's permission. First, it was my father, then my uncle; now, it will be my husband, and eventually, it will be my son. One man after another, picking out each piece of my life from birth until death."

Her all-too-familiar rant rings off the damp walls of the cellar, reminding us both of the lengths we've gone to just to survive in this world. But that's all this is: survival. With the right man in our corner, we could thrive. She could thrive.

"I understand." I nod my head, but my eyes won't meet hers. There's a dark stain on the floor next to her right foot, and I study it in the flickering candlelight. The candles were another idea of Legacy's. There's no fireplace in this room beneath her uncle's town house, so she created a lattice of candles on two of the walls. It takes a while to light them all, but they throw enough of a glow to clearly show the surgery table and tools sitting in the center of the space.

"Mary," Legacy sighs my name, stepping into my space until I have no choice but to look at her. We're almost the same height, my eyes a fraction of an inch higher than hers, but in this moment, I feel incredibly small. "No man will ever come between us."

"Except the one who will be in your bed every night," I correct, trying to keep the pain out of my voice. "The one you'll legally belong to, be forced to share marital relations with at his whim."

She takes a deep breath, squeezing my hands in hers. "Apollo isn't like that."

"You don't know him."

"Neither do you," she reminds me, her tone soft even through her conviction. "Give him a chance."

Her fingers brush against the inside of my wrist, and I lose sight of what we're talking about. It's always like this when she's close, when she touches me, like nothing else matters—nothing but her and me, what we mean to each other.

The realization we're alone suddenly hits me. There aren't many times we are truly alone. The house is always occupied by some nosy person or another, and when we sneak into each other's rooms late at night, we're forced to be quiet. We wouldn't have to be quiet this far beneath the house. There's no chance of anyone interrupting us, only a dead man and the spiders as witnesses.

Flipping my hand in hers, I pull on Legacy's wrist until she's pressed against me. Her mouth is inches from mine, those dark eyes widening for a moment. I let my hands drop to her waist, dragging my fingers along the outside of her corset before bunching the fabric of her skirt in my fists.

"What are you doing?"

"Reminding you of what you'll be missing with him."

"Honestly," she groans, but I cut her off with a kiss. She tastes like tea and honey, her soft lips molding to mine as I press her back against the surgical table. "Wait, wait, dead man," she gasps, arching away from the cold metal slab.

I use her involuntary movement to better position myself between her legs, dropping to my knees in the mystery stain I'd been staring at earlier. "Focus on me, Legacy," I command, smiling when she takes the skirts from my hand without being asked. "If you're very good and you keep your eyes on me," I begin, leaning forward to run my nose along the edge of the dark curls between her thighs, "then I promise not to murder and eat your new husband."

"Mary," she admonishes, but it turns into a guttural groan when I flick my tongue against her sensitive skin. "This is neither the time nor the place for this kind of thing."

"There is no time or place for this kind of thing," I remind her, running one hand along the inside of her leg. She wobbles slightly when I lift her knee over my shoulder, but she regains her balance by dropping a hand onto the table next to the dead man. "But you won't have to stifle your desire to scream my name down here."

Legacy lets out a small whimper in response, but her eyes stay locked on me as I lean into her space. My tongue runs along the softest parts of her, reveling in her taste as she bucks against my hold. A quick glance upward shows my perfect goddess still has those dark eyes on me, but her mouth is open, and she appears to be struggling to breathe in that damn corset.

"Do you need me to stop?"

"Don't you dare," she snarls, her fingers tightening against the fabric bunched at her hips until they turn white from the effort.

Chuckling, I lean forward again. This time, my fingers join my tongue in spreading her open and holding her hostage to my efforts. Legacy arches against me, rocking her hips as she chases her orgasm.

Pulling back, I run two fingers against her clit and chide, "I can't hear you."

"Please," she whines, bucking her hips hard against my hand. "I'm so close, Mary. Please."

Smiling at my victory, I lean forward again. Legacy's soft gasp at the first touch of my tongue against her clit is music to my ears. She sobs when I add the hand not holding her open, dragging my fingers through the mess she's making for me.

My name falls from her lips on a loop in perfect sync with the grind of her hips against my mouth. "I need more."

I will never deny this woman anything. Not my fingers, my mouth, or a man, it would seem. I press into her, groaning along with her when she squeezes around my fingers. She's so wet, so soft, so perfect for me that my body aches for her.

Legacy moans a plea, dragging her clit against my tongue as she fucks herself on my fingers. "Christ," she gasps, and I feel the pulse of her against my tongue. Her entire body melts as she comes, as if whatever strings were holding her together have finally snapped.

Licking Legacy clean is my greatest pleasure, and I take my time as she settles from her high. When I feel her fingers against my cheek, I meet her gaze again.

"We're going to be alright." I can tell she means it, but I'm not so sure. Regardless of my worries, I have told her I will be good, and I intend to keep that promise.

"I know," I lie, pulling the skirt and chemise from her grip and letting it fall to the ground between us as I stand. "Now, let's pick apart this man before he spoils."

Chapter 3

Apollo's Hancock

Blindly signing documents is never a good idea. That is the promise I made to Legacy, and I intend to keep it, though I begin to question the soundness of my decision when the fourth multi-page document slides across the table.

I press my notepad toward Legacy, pulling the document in front of me in exchange. She quickly reads my message, a soft chuckle escaping her lightly painted lips. "This is exactly how I imagined spending my wedding night."

She nudges the notepad back to the middle of the table, waiting with her hand outstretched while I scribble my signature on one last contract. This one is full of words like "non-disclosure" and "maritime law", which is concerning but not unsurprising.

Nothing surprises me anymore.

Legacy shuffles the papers, double and triple checking my signature is neatly sprawled across each line. Once satisfied, she drops the contract into the stack at her side, folding her hands together and turning that startlingly dark gaze on me. "The final question is where we are to live."

A husband in law alone. That's what she asked for on the day we agreed to be married. In this world, a woman is only as privileged as the man who speaks on her behalf. Since I am unable to speak for myself, much less anyone else, I decide to turn the decision over to her.

After all, a woman who enters a marriage with four detailed contracts would surely have steadfast opinions of where she is to live.

Leaning forward, I snatch the notepad from where I'd placed it in the center of the table and scrawl out my question.

Where would you prefer to live?

Legacy's head tips to the side as she reads my question. A single dark lock of hair slips from its perfect updo, dropping to rest against her high cheekbone. She truly is a beautiful woman. When Angora told me there was someone in need of a husband who didn't fit the typical mold, I was skeptical. The women I'd been introduced to in the past gave me little more than a passing glance once they learned I couldn't speak, and I'd long since given up on the idea of marrying in this life.

This woman is different, though. I can see it in her eyes, in the way she holds her shoulders tense but her hands softly in her lap, in the small wrinkle forming between her brows. She may be hiding something, but she isn't lying to me. Whatever her agenda is, it is for the greater good.

"I only bring it up because I am more than one person," she explains, shifting in her seat as if suddenly uncomfortable. "There is a boarding house full of women under my care, and they cannot afford to continue living in the manner they have grown accustomed to if I am not with them."

My pen moves across the top sheet of paper, the familiar scratch soothing in the silence of the room around us.

How did you come to be in charge of a "boarding house full of women"?

"I am," she hesitates, those dark eyes ghosting over my face again before dropping to the stack of paperwork in front of her. We are legally bound to one another now, and the reminder of that seems to loosen her up a bit. "I am involved in efforts including the housing and safety of individuals in need."

She couldn't have skirted any further around the truth if she tried. If I had to guess, the "individuals in need" she's assisting are women and children on the run from husbands and fathers who mean to do them harm.

The set of her jaw makes it evident she would rather eat the teacups sitting between us than expand on the nature of her work. Since I'm not in any hurry to alienate myself from my new bride, I decide to leave my theories alone for now.

Legacy is an unusual name.

The sudden change in subject surprises her, but she adapts quickly. One dark brow quirks as Legacy assesses me, her eyes sliding over my face in search of something. The way her lips purse indicates she has found me lacking.

"And Apollo is so common."

I shrug, giving her a canned response from a sheet earlier in my notes.

My father was obsessed with the Gods.

A derisive snort brings my eyes to hers again. They're so dark, it's almost unsettling to hold her gaze, but something hidden within the depths of her soul holds my attention far longer than I expect.

"Mine was obsessed only with himself."

Her response breaks my concentration, and I drag my eyes back to the notepad in my lap. I've carried this pad for as long as I can remember—ever since I first realized my voice couldn't be relied upon, since the first time it failed in my father's presence. Acid curls in my stomach at the memory, threatening to crawl its way up my throat as I scribble a reply on a fresh sheet of paper.

We should start a cult for children of narcissists.

I've grown to be something of a magician with my words, easily pulling attention where I need it so people aren't looking at the parts I would rather hide. Legacy gives a thoughtful hum, as if she's genuinely considering the off-hand remark, and I know I've managed to pull off the trick again.

"We'd end up with every man, woman, and child under our care."

I'm afraid you are correct.

I don't turn the page toward her immediately, something about the words not quite seeming to fit. After a moment's consideration, I scratch them out and write the question now pinging around my mind.

You're always correct, aren't you?

Something about the words spark that little light I saw so deep in her gaze. Legacy likes being recognized for her intelligence—her wit and cunning are clearly important to her. What else is important to a woman who has her life so wholly under control, she went shopping for a husband in Angora's atrium? I want to know everything about her, everything that makes her the unusual woman sitting before me.

"I am not often wrong."

She leans back just enough to adjust in her seat. The corset locked around her torso should make the movements difficult, but she pulls them off with a practiced ease. If I wasn't studying her so closely, I might not have even noticed the slight pinch to her brow. The corset appears to be paining her, though she's doing a valiant job of hiding it.

My mind slips, the image of her spread before me in nothing but a corset and stockings suddenly flooding my senses. The echo of Legacy's claim that she needs a husband in law alone shatters the fantasy. I tuck my disappointment into the furthest recesses of my mind as I quickly scratch out my next question.

Have you made your decision about where we shall live?

"Not necessarily," she admits, a small frown pulling between her brows.

The only light in the priest's office comes from a dying fire in the corner of the room. It had been brighter upon our arrival, so there'd been no need to light a lantern, but now, I'm wondering if that wasn't a mistake. I can't see her well enough to piece apart the subtle shifts in her eyes, the minute twitch of her lips telling me she's hiding something.

I've become a scholar on the planes of Legacy Kennaway's face, and having it half-hidden from my view eats at my patience. Legacy Vanderlee, I remind myself with no small amount of pride.

She shifts, bringing more of her features into the firelight's path. When she speaks again, there's a forced lightness to her voice that tells me this isn't her ideal solution. "You could live at the townhouse with us all."

Or, you all could live with me.

"We couldn't impose," she argues, that tiny frown forming on her face again. "There's a great many women who come and go sometimes in the dead of night. That's too much to ask of a Vanderlee."

Legacy holds steady, no shifting or fidgeting as she declares what is too much to ask of a Vanderlee. I watch her for a long moment, cursing the space between us. There's no reason this ancient desk should remain between us, not when the ceremony is over and the contracts are signed.

She doesn't jolt when I stand, but it's a near thing. Every part of my new bride tenses, and there's no relief to her taut muscles when I approach her side of the priest's desk.

You seem to be forgetting you are a Vanderlee now.

I hand the paper down to her, allowing Legacy to focus on something other than me as I settle against the edge of the desk in front of her. This close, I don't need the firelight to show me the movement of her gaze as she reads and re-reads the message.

"It would be too much," she repeats, but it has lost some of her earlier resolve. When her bottomless eyes meet mine, there's a question in them I cannot answer. I don't know what she's asking when she's still holding so many secrets to her chest.

What I do know is this; there's only one solution to our situation, and it is whatever one she chooses. If that means I am to live in a crowded townhouse with an undetermined number of women and children, then so be it. If she decides to move those women and children into my humble estate on the outskirts of town, the more the merrier. My only request is that we be together, regardless of the rest.

"Do you have room for us all?"

The question is so soft, so timid, and so entirely unlike everything

I've come to expect of my brave and bold new wife, I nearly laugh. Considering she's still holding my notepad against her chest as if it is her only lifeline, I choose to answer her question in a different way.

I move slowly, so slowly , she has time to pull away if she wishes. In fact, there's so much tension left in her shoulders and neck that when I do bring our lips within an inch of one another, I pause. My intention was only to wait until she relaxed a bit, anything to tell me she's not an unwilling participant in this kiss to seal our future, but she doesn't allow me that time. Legacy leans forward, sealing our lips together on her terms once again. And thus, with a kiss, I find myself wholly at her mercy. The gentle press of her lips against mine has every part of me tuned to her, begging for more and wishing for everything she's willing to give me. This is my life, my future, my wife, and I will give her anything she needs and everything she asks, until death do us part.

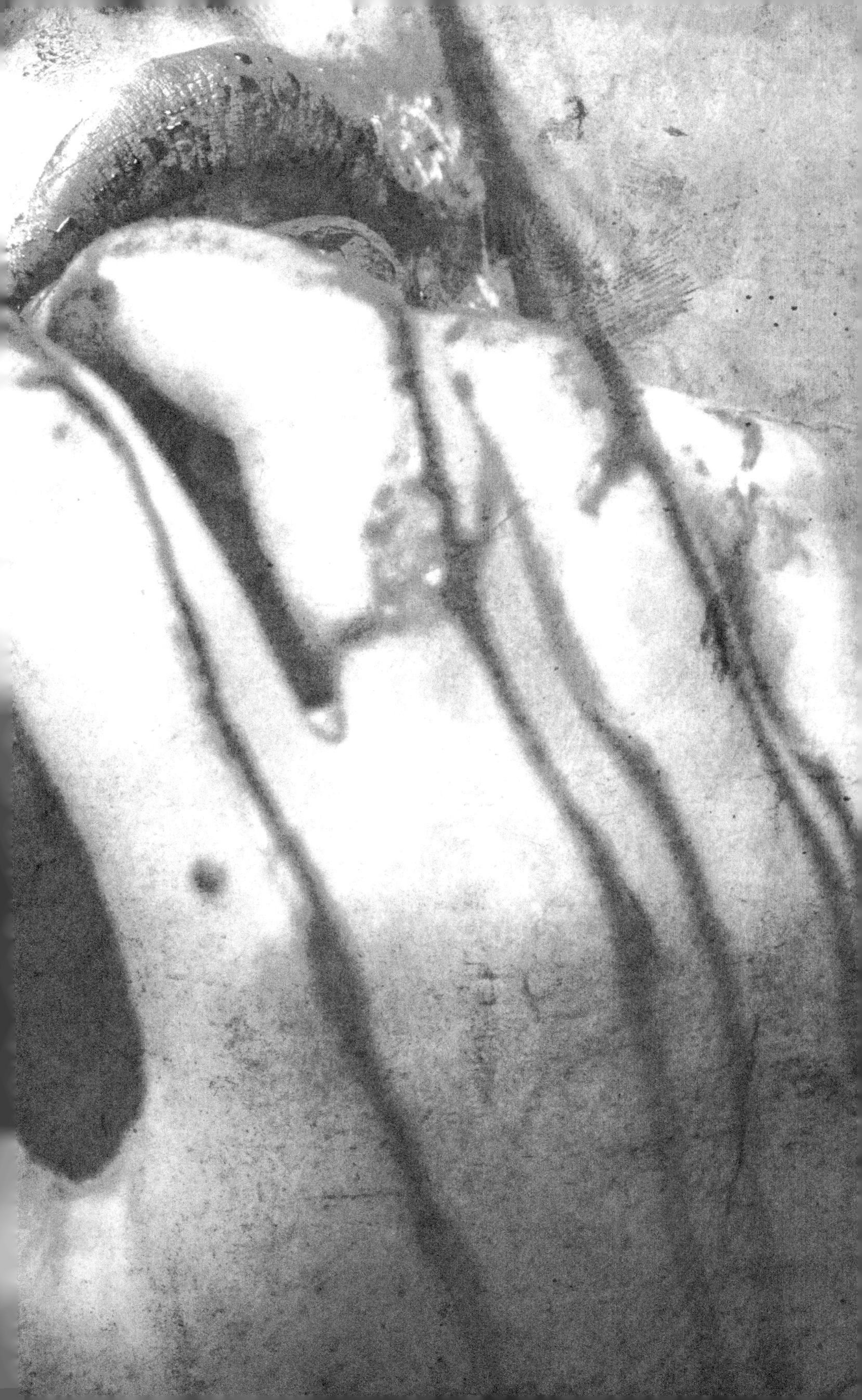

Chapter 4

Romeo, Juliet, And Apollo

My new wife might be a murderer... A murderess? A killer of...something or someone. Several someones by the looks of the fully stocked surgical table sitting alone in the center of her basement.

I'm not supposed to be here, but I took a wrong turn on the first floor and ended up in this nightmare fuel of a room with only the gas lamp at the top of the stairs to light my way. It's impossible to see into the corners of the room, but my imagination fills them with enough body bags and meat hooks to send a shiver down my spine.

Turning on my heel, I take the stairs two at a time until I'm safely back in the main lobby of the house. Shutting the door behind me with a definitive snap, I spot the lock that should have been securing this door from prying eyes. It's cracked open, the key still twisted in the mechanism, as if someone left the room in too much of a hurry to properly secure it.

Who that might be, I cannot be sure.

I'm suddenly quite grateful Legacy chose not to live in the townhouse. I thought the worst of it would be sneaking the women and children out in the dead of night, or maybe the forty thousand stairs I've traversed in a single afternoon, but that was before I saw the murder dungeon.

The sound of footsteps around the corner reminds me of the

conversation I'd had with my new wife just this morning. Legacy insisted we could not hire men to help us move, since any one of them could see or find something that might tip them off to the women hiding here. Now, I'm not so sure it wouldn't have been to our benefit to hire a crew and just have her dispose of them when we were done.

I can only imagine the horror on Legacy's face had I suggested that, particularly since I have no proof the murder basement is hers, so I keep that idea to myself.

Suggesting someone is a murderer—and even more, recommending she do some murdering as a solution to a trivial problem—isn't the best way to endear oneself to their new bride.

Though there doesn't seem to be much I can do to endear myself to her. Legacy insisted on moving all the people in her care on our wedding night, which meant hours spent driving from one side of town to the other, transporting as many women and children as my carriage would allow. The car would have been faster, but the smaller capacity and clear windows made it less practical.

While I was transporting strangers, my blushing bride spent her night coordinating with Mary, a petite blonde woman with full lips and a razor sharp gaze. It turns out, Mary is the other half of this organization—not a desperate survivor like most of the women who live here, but a fighter all the same. She's whip-smart and headstrong, just like Legacy, but unlike my unassuming wife, Mary is unapologetically not going to deal with anyone's shit.

As if the very thought of her conjures the woman from thin air, Mary appears at my side as I round the corner toward the stairs. We both know I should be in the room on the second floor right now, gathering another load to take to the carriage, but she has no idea I was sidetracked by a murder dungeon. Her immediate assumption of why I'm still on the first floor is unsurprisingly an unkind one.

"Struggling to keep up with her already?" She clicks her tongue in mock disappointment, moving past me as she takes the stairs two at a time. "You'll have to work on your stamina, Man."

I frown after her, watching as she disappears into the room Legacy has been cleaning out for the last half hour. That's the third time Mary has called me "man" as if it's my name. She evidently has some kind of chip on her shoulder when it comes to my sex, but there's something pointed in the way she directs her barbs at me. I've only known the woman for eighteen hours, yet I've managed to piss her off somehow.

Turning into the room, I find Mary hunched over a pile of things sorted and packed into boxes for the move. She's smiling at something Legacy has said, but the moment she spots me in the doorway, her mouth falls into a frown. I'm barely in the room before she's pushing past me toward the stairs again. I can't stop the huff that slips from my lips when she goes out of her way to knock her shoulder against my arm.

"You'll have to ignore her," Legacy sighs, still digging through the chest of drawers under the room's only window. "She doesn't like men."

I want to tell her I've noticed that myself, but the idea of wasting energy writing out a sentence when there are at least fifty more trips to make is an exhausting one. Plus, there's always the off chance Mary is the proprietor of the murder room, which means I'm better off keeping my opinions of her to myself. Reaching for the box Mary left, I heft it into my arms and start toward the door again.

I'm nearly through the opening when Legacy suddenly blurts, "She's not a bad person. She's just a bit…troubled. She'll come around, I promise. The two of you might even like one another someday. Maybe…"

Legacy trails off at the end, a hopeful lilt to her words but a deep frown pulling at her face. It's important to her that Mary and I get along, that much is clear, but the why is lost to me until Mary appears at the top of the stairs.

Her piercing gaze is locked on mine as she approaches, another dark comment about my lacking abilities on her tongue as she passes through the doorway. Yet, the moment she's within sight of Legacy, it's all smiles and laughter. I recognize the behaviour instantly; it's a physical representation of how I feel when Legacy is in front of me—the bone-deep desire to see her smile, to be the one to make her smile, already has a hold on me, and it appears I'm not the only one.

The true question is: are these feelings mutual? Or is Mary harboring a one-sided affection? And what lengths will the woman go in order to keep Legacy all to herself?

Chapter 5

A Familiar Legacy

"When you said he was a man of means, I didn't realize you meant," Mary trails off, gesturing broadly to the massive house in front of us. It's a beautiful white estate set in the center of several hundred acres of land. There's nothing but trees and rolling hills as far as the eye can see, and the eye can see a lot farther here than I ever imagined.

"It's not even that far from town," I whisper, turning in a circle again. The trees block any sign of human life, deadening the sounds of town to nothingness. It's as if we've stepped into our own world, completely separate from the rest of humanity. "It's perfect."

Mary snorts, giving me a rueful look. "I'm sure he'll be overjoyed to hear you're falling for his land."

"I meant for us," I snark back, meeting her steady gaze. "We could operate here."

"You've made it impossible for us not to," she reminds me with a pointed arch of her brow.

"I mean it," I grasp her hand, not daring to pull her any closer for fear of someone seeing. Even this far from civilization, we're not without prying eyes. "We could thrive here. The women and children have room to run, to be outside, to exist."

Mary isn't seeing what I'm seeing, isn't imagining the joy a place like this will bring to the newly freed. "And the men?"

The men are a different issue. "We can figure out the men."

"How? When? Where are you planning to—" Mary cuts herself off, turning away from the house when a figure appears in the doorway.

Apollo is watching us, his hair shining white in the midday sun. He raises a hand, waving us into the house with a smile broad enough to be seen from several hundred feet away. There's too much distance between us for him to hear my words, but I speak through clenched teeth and a fake smile all the same. "I promise you, we will find a place to take care of them."

It's two weeks before my promise is tested for the first time.

We've been settling into something of a routine in the new house. The days are filled with tending to the runaways while my nights are spent staring at a door that just. won't. open.

Neither Apollo nor Mary have tried to sneak into my room any of the nights we've spent under this roof, and I'm not sure which concerns me more. While I had expected, and more often than not dreaded, the idea of my husband coming to partake in his marital rights, it never occurred to me that I might feel disappointed when he ultimately chose to stay in his own room. Mary is simply being spiteful, but I know she'll come around.

At least, I hope she will.

Ultimately, when someone finally does make their presence known outside my closed door in the dead of night, it isn't with the amorous intentions I had anticipated.

"What do you mean he's dead?"

"I believe I mean exactly what I say," Mary hisses, bouncing from one foot to the other. She's dressed in her male attire tonight, the dark trousers and matching shirt hiding all sight of her feminine curves. "The man is dead."

"Why on Earth," I demand, reaching into the hall and grabbing her arm. Mary lets me pull her into the room, but she keeps her distance even before the door is shut. "Didn't you tell me you were going out tonight?"

"You were busy."

"I was not."

"And how was I supposed to know that?"

"You could have asked," I snap, rummaging through the dresser to find something more appropriate for creeping through the house than my simple nightdress. "But I suppose that would require you to speak to me for more than two seconds at a time."

Mary mumbles something under her breath. When I turn a questioning look in her direction, she audibly sighs. "I've been giving you space."

"I didn't ask for space," I remind her with a harsh snap of the dresser drawer. "Did I?"

"We don't have time to argue." She avoids the question, waiting until I've tied the dressing gown around myself. "He's rotting out there."

We move silently through the house, trying our best to avoid waking anyone else. It isn't until we're standing on the front porch in the frigid November air that I realize the extent of our predicament.

"What was the reasoning behind leaving him on the steps?"

"The horse got him this far, but I wasn't strong enough to get him..." she trails off, gesturing broadly to the front door and the darkened house beyond.

I nod, drawing the gown tighter around my waist. "And you were bringing the dead man into the house because...?"

"I can't exactly quarter him on the front lawn, can I?"

"You shouldn't be quartering him at all," I hiss, stomping down the steps toward the corpse. He's a massive man, easily twice her size, with a dark mop of greasy hair that does nothing to stop the sickening drip of blood from the gaping wound on his head. "Help me move him."

Mary's at my side in a moment, but she doesn't bend to grab the dead man's legs as I asked. "Where are we moving him?"

The urge to tell her not to argue is on the tip of my tongue, but she's right. We don't have anywhere to move him to, much less any of the supplies to clean and pack him once he's there. "Did we leave everything in the basement?"

"Yes," Mary admits with a sigh. "I could go back for it, but I have no way to get the table here by myself."

"Shit," I groan.

The man's clammy hands drop back onto the steps with a sick thud. We both stare at him for a long moment before Marry suggests, "The kitchen?"

"We cannot clean his body in the kitchen."

"Why not?"

"Because it's unsanitary," I deadpan. When she starts to argue that fact, I cut her off with an exaggerated eye roll. "Because it will get us caught, Mary."

She stiffens at my tone, her bright eyes narrowing in the moonlight. "Right, because your new husband can't know what you get up to in your free time."

I know she's speaking of more things I get up to than the one at hand, but I don't have the patience for that conversation at present. "No," I draw out, matching her crossed arm pose. "Because we can't let the women and children know we've been feeding them their husbands and fathers without consent."

Mary's shoulders drop as she clears her throat, looking thoughtfully down at the man again. The air has a distinct snap of impending snow, the wind cutting around the house and whipping the fabric of my nightgown. After a long moment, Mary's eyes catch on the movement of my skirt, an idea forming in her sharp mind. "It's going to snow."

"And?"

"What if we just bury him?"

My gaze drops to the man's body. He's surprisingly tall, his shoulders cresting the top step while his feet still touch the ground. I would imagine that the unnatural length of his body caused the biggest issue for Mary, who can usually carry a body around his weight over her shoulder without much issue. Digging a hole for a man this tall would take ages, even before the snow has frozen the ground.

"It would be a waste of meat."

"We don't exactly need the meat anymore," she reminds me, nodding toward the looming mansion behind us.

She isn't wrong in that assessment, but it brings up a whole slew of questions fighting for the right to leave my mouth first. "If we don't need the meat, why did you kill him?"

Mary shrugs, dropping her hands to her pockets. "He started it."

"Do I even want to know?"

"Probably not." She shoots me a half-smile that has me all but melting at her feet. I'm not sure how she manages to get under my skin with a simple look, but she never fails in that endeavor. "Let me bury him."

The way she suggests it feels like an olive branch—an apology and a solution all in one. She doesn't let me argue this time, leaning forward to place a kiss on my lips before she bends to grab the man's wrists.

Mary's dragging the man down the steps when something shifts in the air. There is no explanation for how I know it, but every part of me is suddenly certain we are no longer alone. My eyes dart around the forest, bouncing from tree to tree and back again. I can't see anyone, but I can feel them watching us.

"Mary," I hiss, my eyes still sweeping the treeline.

She looks up, a question on her lips, but it dies in a heartbeat. Mary drops the man's wrists, her eyes locked on the house as I watch the body slide down the steps toward the ground. The corpse is still in motion when I turn to see what has stricken such terror into my beloved killer.

Apollo is standing in the shadows of the porch, his white hair brilliant even in the depths of the night. He's looking right at us, those brilliant eyes taking in everything without giving anything in return. How long has he been standing there? What did he see? What did he hear?

"A-Apollo," I stumble through a greeting, pasting on a smile as if there isn't a dead man sprawled across the ground not five feet from where I stand. "This isn't what it looks like."

He steps out of the shadows, one blond brow raised in what I assume is a sarcastic question of what could it possibly be then? I'm still struggling to find an answer when he moves past me, taking the steps two at a time until he's standing at Mary's side near the base of the stairs.

She flinches away from him, bracing for a blow that never comes. Silently, Apollo points to a small shed near the back of the house, holding up two fingers then miming using a shovel. Mary slowly nods her understanding of what he's trying to communicate, but her wide eyes stay locked on Apollo's face, her feet immobile.

Apollo frowns at her for a moment before bending to heft the dead man over his shoulder. The movement is so simple, as if the man weighs nothing at all. That seems to break the spell on Mary, who spins to scamper toward the garden shed.

The moment she disappears from view, I open my mouth to tell him he doesn't have to help us, but he cuts me off with a look. "I'm sorry," I say instead. Apollo tilts his head in question, prompting me to further explain myself. "I shouldn't have gotten you mixed up in... this."

He snorts, an unhappy sound but not a scolding one. Apollo's bright eyes dart toward the shed for a moment before he turns to me again. Even with a corpse slung over one shoulder, Apollo moves with so much grace. He's standing in front of me before I know what's happening, one large hand tipping my chin up until our mouths are slotted together.

The kiss is over almost before it begins. He slips back to the base of the stairs right as Mary comes around the corner with two shovels in her hands. She stops several feet away from Apollo, holding one of the shovels out to me. Before I have a chance to reach forward, it's snatched out of the air between us. Apollo shakes his head at Mary, the shovel held tightly in the hand not holding the dead man over his shoulder.

"What?" Mary demands, her usual fire back now that she's reasonably sure Apollo isn't going to kill us.

He gestures with the shovel, first to Mary, then to himself, before finally pointing at the forest. Mary frowns, but she doesn't have much ground to stand on in this argument, and Apollo doesn't wait around to hear it anyway. He turns on his heel, strolling toward the forest without a care in the world. I watch from the steps as Mary follows him into the woods, panic slowly rising in my chest with each step.

Three people go in, but how many will come back out?

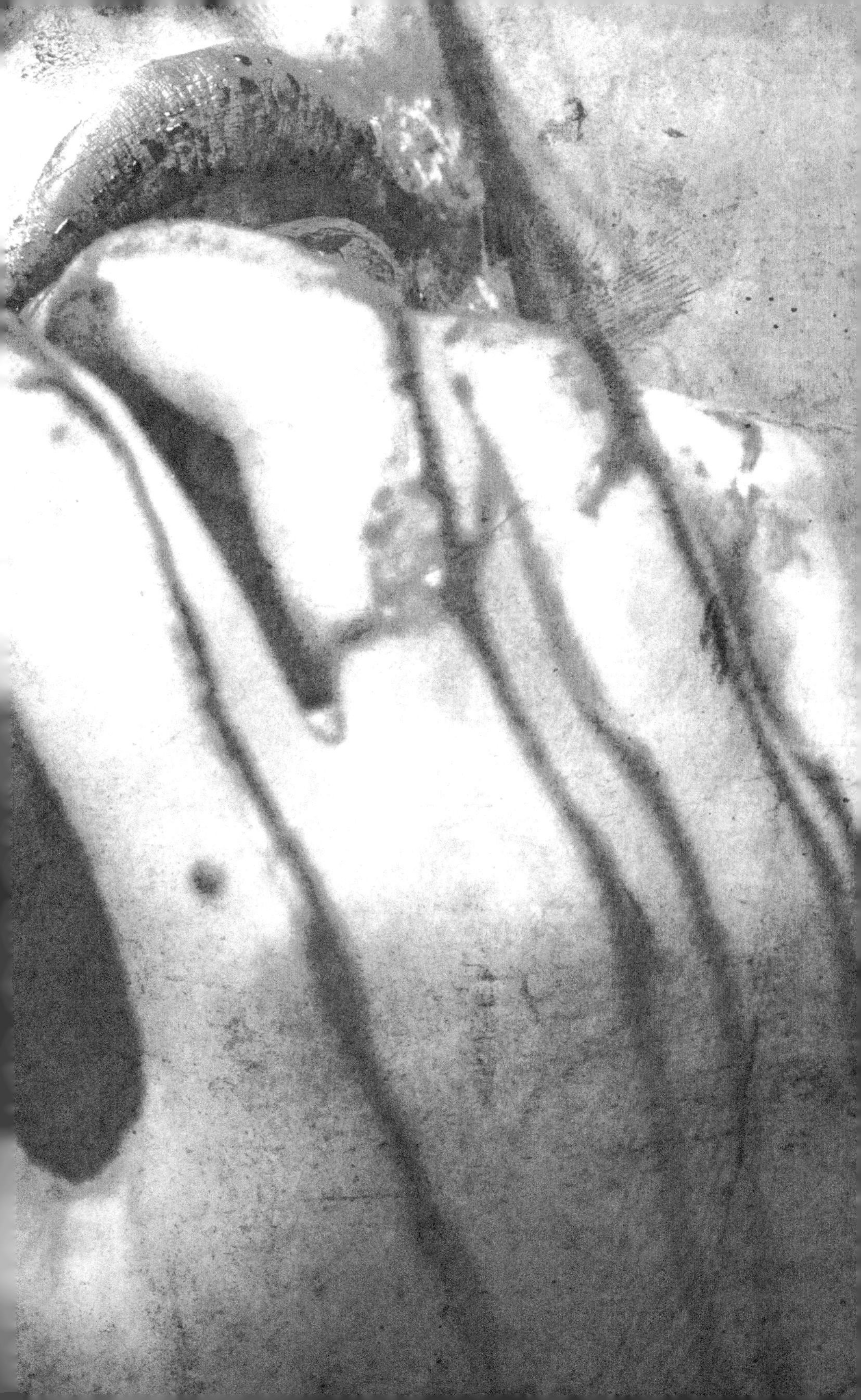

Chapter 6

Bloody Mary

You don't know the true meaning of silence until you're digging a hole in the middle of the night with only a corpse and a mute for company. Nothing is said as we dig the long, shallow grave. Nobody tries to dissuade me from cracking through ribs with my shovel and pulling out the silent heart within. No words of comfort are given for the rapist as I kick his body into the waiting cavity, and no one makes a sound as we shovel the dirt back over him.

When Legacy said I might like Apollo, I thought she was just trying to see the best in a bad situation, but now, I think she might have been onto something. A man who keeps his mouth shut is a man I can appreciate.

We've just broken through the woods into the moonlit front lawn when a large hand wraps around my bicep. Apollo is frowning, his blond brows almost invisible in the soft light, but the look isn't a harsh one. It's almost like a question, but I don't know what he could be asking me.

After several long moments of staring at one another, I finally ask, "What?"

Apollo's frown deepens, but he lets go of my arm to gesture toward the house, then to me. When I still don't get it, he sighs, drops the shovel, and brings both hands between us. He points first to his ring, then to the house.

"Legacy?"

He nods, pointing from the house to me.

"Me and Legacy?" There's no hiding the surprise in my tone, but my question is met with a swift nod of his head. I wasn't sure if he saw the kiss, but I assumed he hadn't, based on his total lack of reaction. My fingers tighten around the wet heart still clutched in my hand as I fight back the instinct to panic. "What about us?"

There's a long moment of silence, during which Apollo's face slips through a gambit of emotions. Finally, he settles on some kind of resolve, bringing his hands up again for me to see his wedding ring. He points to the simple gold band, then to the house, then to me, then back to the band again.

It takes several more pointing roundabouts before I understand what he's asking. "I am in love with Legacy," I agree, hoping that's truly the point he's getting at. Otherwise, I'm admitting to things that could harm a whole lot more than just my pride. "But she belongs to you. There is nothing that can be done about that. If you wish me to leave—"

Apollo cuts me off with a sigh, a dejected look on his face. He shakes his head before he bends to pick up his shovel. We walk to the tool shed in silence again, tossing the shovels into the darkness before turning back to the house.

I'm up the front steps and through the door, my mind focused solely on preserving the heart before getting in a hot bath and a warm bed. I'm fighting back the thoughts that it might be my last time experiencing those things outside of prison when a hand stops me before I pass the stairs. Apollo is watching me again, his eyes hidden in the shadows cast by the darkened house.

"What?" My hissed request echoes through the hall, making me jump. I hadn't meant to say it so loud, and the way Apollo's jaw tightens tells me he isn't overjoyed by my volume either. With a sharp tug, he pulls me toward the stairs, holding one finger in front of his mouth as a reminder to be quiet on the steps. I nearly huff out an annoyed breath but manage to bite it back in the spirit of staying alive.

I'm not sure where I expect him to lead me, but Legacy's bedroom is the last place on that imaginary list. I open my mouth to ask what we're doing, but he gives me a hard look over one shoulder before I can say anything.

The soft rap of knuckles on wood isn't any louder than my question would have been, but it sounds cacophonous in the silent hall. There's a moment when I think she might not answer, or that she isn't in the room at all, making me wonder whose room she might be hiding in. Then, the door swings open to reveal a beautiful, confused Legacy, all loose curls and soft curves beneath her dressing gown.

Dark eyes bounce from Apollo to me, then to the still-dripping heart in my hand before settling on Apollo again. She takes a step back, allowing us to pass into her bedchamber.

This room is larger than mine but just as plain. It's nothing more than a four poster bed, a fainting couch, and a small fireplace. There's a wardrobe tucked in the corner, an empty vase on the windowsill, but that's all she brought into the space. Legacy hasn't put anything of herself in this room, and I can't help but wonder what has kept her from making herself comfortable.

"Did everything go alright?"

Her hesitant question is directed at both of us, but it's easier for me to answer. "Yes."

"Then what are you doing here?"

That, I cannot answer. All eyes land on Apollo standing near the fire. He's not looking at us, however. His attention is focused solely on the notepad in his hands as he quickly writes something, scratches it out, flips the page, and begins again.

When he finally turns the paper around, I have to take a step closer to read what he wrote.

No one will bother you here.

"Apollo," Legacy whispers his name, taking a careful step toward the man. "What are you talking about?"

He gives her a look I think he intends to be soothing, but it comes across sad from where I'm standing.

You asked for a husband in law alone, and I am a man of my word.

Legacy seems to connect the dots faster than I do, her eyes bouncing between Apollo and me before settling on him again. "Why would you do that?"

I can't stay in the dark any longer. "Do what?"

Neither of them answer me as Apollo goes back to writing in his little book. When he turns it around, there are two things written on the same page, but with a great deal of empty space between them.

I want you to be happy here.

Tonight, I watched her rip a man's heart out and don't desire a similar fate for myself.

Legacy's laughter is soft, but there's a watery edge to the sound, as if she's trying to hold back tears. "I wouldn't let Mary kill you."

I want to tell her not to make promises she can't keep, but I stop when Apollo tears the bottom half of the paper out of the book and tosses it in the fire. He immediately begins writing something else, but I've stopped paying attention. My eyes are locked on the little piece of paper shriveling in the fire as I connect the dots on my own.

Apollo is offering Legacy and me a safe place to be together. The idea he would give her wholly to me is an appealing one, but looking at them now, I realize it's the wrong one. There's something between Legacy and Apollo that I don't understand, not unlike what exists between Legacy and myself that seems so confusing to Apollo.

Something else is said between them, a quick flash of Apollo's notebook I miss while lost in my thoughts. Whatever it is makes Legacy laugh again, a joyous sound brought down by an inescapable sadness.

The heart drips a thick splat of blood onto the carpet near my feet. None of us notice.

"He should stay."

Two sets of eyes turn toward me, equal in their confusion. There's no simple solution to this situation, but if Legacy wants him, I will be damned if I don't let her have him—just so long as he doesn't get all of her.

"He should stay," I repeat, taking a step toward Legacy. My empty hand slides around her waist, turning her until we're both facing Apollo. "He can sit in the corner," I murmur against her ear, my eyes still firmly locked on the man across from us. The barest hint he isn't interested, and I'll back away. When he meets my gaze with his own, an understanding passes between us. "Would you like for him to watch me take you apart, my love?"

Legacy sucks in a breath as I pull her against me, but she doesn't object to my suggestion. She seems to be waiting for Apollo to give his answer, and she doesn't have to wait long. Apollo takes two quick steps toward the fainting couch, spinning to drop onto the overstuffed seat. He folds both hands in his lap, waiting for us to make the next move.

I graze my teeth against Legacy's earlobe, reveling in the way her body shivers against mine as I bring the heart into her line of sight. The sticky, dead muscle brushes against her bottom lip, causing Legacy's mouth to open on a gasp as my eyes meet Apollo's again. "Let's give the man what he wants, shall we?"

Chapter 7

The Virgin Mary

Apollo's eyes shift from mine to Legacy's, the hunger unmistakable in the forest green depths of his gaze. He wants whatever comes next, whatever Legacy is willing to give him, and he's going to sit still and take it like a good boy.

"Bite."

My command is soft, but the sound carries through the room. There's a moment of hesitation—not from my beautiful Legacy, but from the man she so desires. He isn't sure how to feel about his bride eating a man's heart, and I can't say I blame him, but it's only because he hasn't seen it yet. He hasn't had the absolute pleasure of watching this gorgeous, strong woman turn to her baser instincts. Once he sees it, he'll understand.

Once he sees it, he'll never look back.

Legacy leans forward on instinct, her lips pulling back as her teeth sink into the heart still in my grasp. It isn't my best work, the muscle having been cleaved from his chest cavity almost as an afterthought. When I decided to take it, I had thought of it only as a trophy—as proof of another woman's safety. Now, I can't imagine a better fate for the dead man's heart than sustenance for the woman I love.

There's a moment of complete silence, the seconds passing without even the metronomic tick of the clock Legacy still hasn't moved into her room. My hand moves along her waist, dropping to press against her lower abdomen until her body is molded against mine. With a rush of air through her nose, Legacy moans around a mouthful of heart. Her pleasure rings so true, I hear myself mimicking the sound.

"That's my girl," I murmur against the side of her neck, pressing kisses into her skin as she chews. "Are you happy, love?"

"Yes," she sighs, eyes closed and head tipped back, as if thanking God above. "I've missed this."

I can't stop the snort of amusement that slips out. "The heart or me?"

"Both," she admits with a soft chuckle, but the sound dies when she remembers we're not alone. I wish I could see what Apollo is witnessing —Legacy's mouth dripping with blood as she smiles like a lovesick fool, the heat of my gaze as I brush my clean hand along the front of her skirts. It must be as erotic of an image as I'm picturing it to be, because he suddenly shifts in his seat, drawing all our attention to the line of his erection pressing against his trousers.

Legacy sucks in a breath, and I know what she's going to ask before she can even put words to it. "No, he cannot join us."

"Why not?" she whines, an honest-to-God whimper in her tone. "He'll be very good."

Apollo nods in time with Legacy's declaration but doesn't try to get up from his seat. Unfortunately for me, that's further proof he would, in fact, be very good. Apollo appears to be the only man in existence who is a natural born follower. He doesn't ask questions, not even with that little notepad in his hand, and he doesn't ignore direction. When push comes to shove, he will take control, but never with the intent to keep it. He let me choose where we buried the body, how deep we dug the grave, and he made no move to stop me from taking the heart. Legacy told me he signed all the contracts without reading them, didn't bat an eye when she surprised him with a house full of refugees.

That doesn't mean I'm ready to share her yet.

"I will consider letting him touch you if he can remain a very good boy while I'm fucking you." I pin him with a look, and Apollo nods once to show he agrees to my terms. Annoyingly, I have to admit, I really could get used to having a completely silent man around. "Get on the bed, love."

Legacy doesn't need to be told twice, slipping from my hold and scurrying to the four poster bed. I wait a moment, my gaze locked on Apollo, his dark eyes never leaving Legacy as she strips beside the bed. I see the moment he gets his first look at his bride in all her glory, and it nearly makes me laugh.

Poor bastard never stood a chance.

When I turn around, Legacy is fully naked, spread across the bed on her back. She has her knees bent, legs falling to either side, giving us an unobstructed view of her perfect pussy.

"You little devil," I chide, stripping off my shirt and unbuttoning my trousers. I don't turn to see if Apollo is looking at me when I drop the dark material to the floor. He isn't my concern at present, even if it's putting me a bit on edge knowing he's seeing all of me too. Crawling onto the bed, I settle next to Legacy and run a hand along the soft skin of her belly. "You really are desperate for him, aren't you?"

"Both of you," she corrects, meeting my eyes with her unflinching gaze. "I want you both."

When my eyes snap to the man in the corner, I see he's sitting on his hands, leaning so far forward, he's an inch from falling out of the seat, but he isn't moving. In fact, Apollo doesn't move a single muscle as he watches my hand dip between Legacy's spread legs, but I hear his sharp exhale at the sight.

She's so wet, I'm quickly distracted from the man in the corner. In all my years of having my hands on Legacy's pussy, I can't say I've ever felt her this ready at the first touch. Her body responds instantly to the glide of my fingers against her clit, her back bowing off the bed as she sucks in a gasp.

"You're already so close, love." My surprise is echoed by a harsh sound from the corner of the room. Apollo appears to be sucking air through clenched teeth as he tries to remain completely still on the fainting couch. I can't help but tease the two of them a bit, dragging my fingers on either side of Legacy's desperate clit, spreading her open that much further. "Do you think she's ready, Apollo?"

His eyes flick to mine for a brief moment before falling on Legacy again. I don't miss the sharp nod of his head or the way he quickly shifts his hips. Legacy unintentionally mimics his movement in an attempt to rub herself against my palm, and her low growl of annoyance when I pull my hand away makes me smile. I'm surprised to find I quite enjoy the power of having both of them desperate for release, but the truth is, I'm not in the mood to draw this out any further.

Shifting on the mattress, I drag Legacy around and position myself between her thighs until my mouth is inches from her clit. She sucks in a breath in perfect sync with Apollo, making me smile. "Time to put on a show, love."

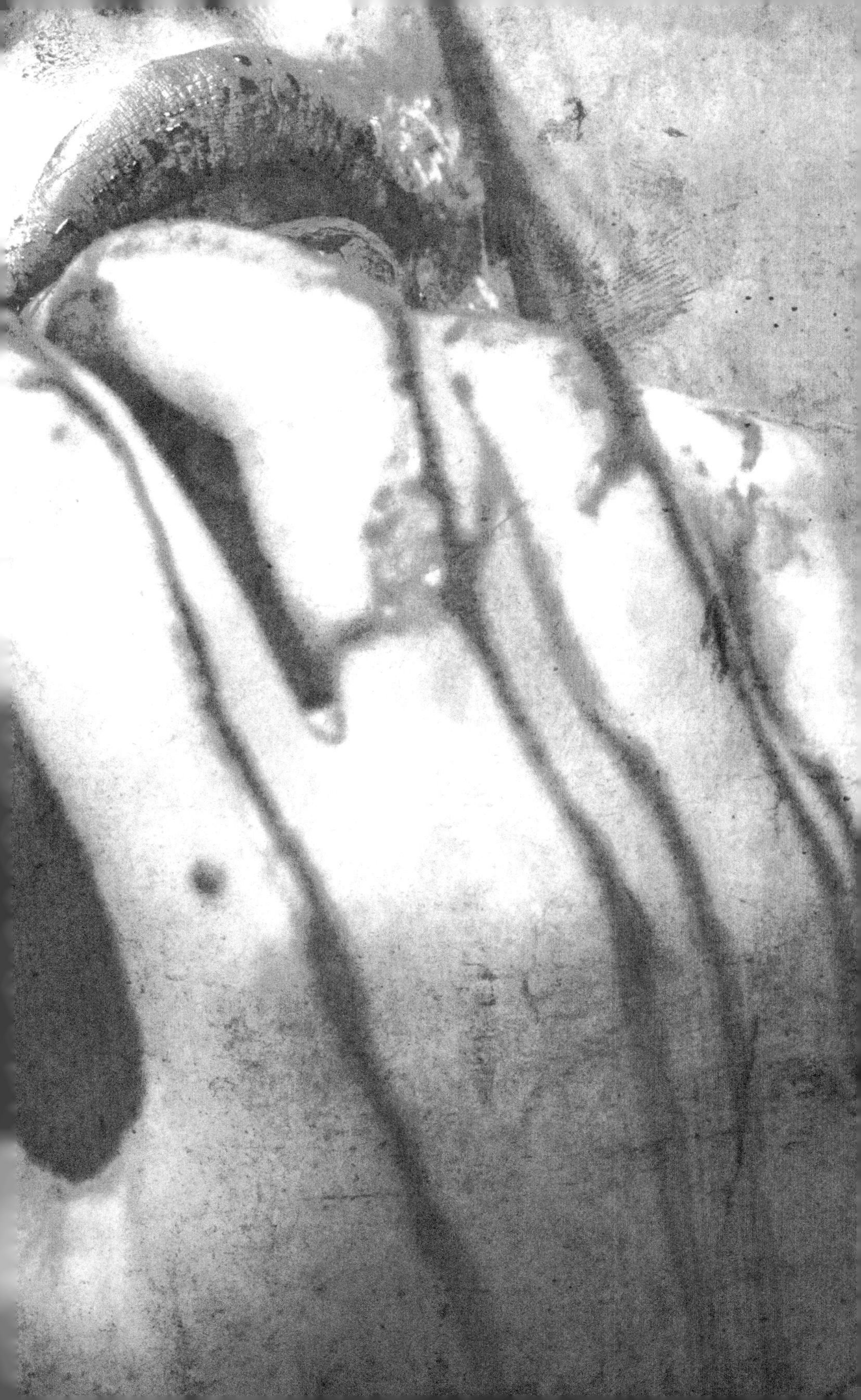

Chapter 8

Apollo's Plan

I'm not sure how many men Mary has killed, but I'm at least the second this evening. So far, I'm faring better than the first man, whose half-eaten heart is laying discarded on the nightstand, but not by much. I didn't think I would survive Legacy stripping out of her nightgown, but I managed it. Then, I was certain my heart had stopped when she laid herself across the bed, yet I held on. It wasn't until Mary ran those dainty fingers through Legacy's dripping cunt that I realized I was well and truly done for—beyond saving, six feet under, dead.

My cock has never been this hard, pressing insistently at the fabric caging it. I want to reach into my trousers and jerk myself in time with the rocking of Legacy's hips as Mary eats her out, but I somehow know that is against the rules. Breaking the rules is the opposite of being a good boy. I can't lose the opportunity to have Legacy in my arms, to taste and touch her however I want.

However she wants.

She begged Mary to let me join them, and even with the blood dripping down her chin, it was the single sweetest sight I've ever beheld: my Legacy begging for me, asking for me to touch her and wanting to touch me in return. I'll never forget it as long as I live.

Which is about twenty more seconds.

Legacy lets out a low moan as Mary's grip on her hip tightens. I can only see one of Mary's hands where it's wrapped around Legacy's thigh; the other has disappeared between their bodies. Legacy cries out again, her hips bucking as much as they're able with Mary holding her down, and it's only a moment before I see it—the sharp expansion of her ribs, the tensing of every muscle in her body, the way her jaw seems to unhinge to ease the way for her silent scream of pleasure.

Legacy is coming, and I want it to be the last thing I ever see.

Mary eases her through it, whispering soft encouragements I can't quite understand through the relentless pounding of my heart. Legacy says something that makes Mary look at me. There's the briefest moment when I think she might be about to invite me into the bed with them, but the way Mary's eyes dart away from mine make it clear she isn't ready for that yet.

For now, I sit in the corner.

For now, I wait in silence.

For now, I watch.

For now.

"Apollo!"

Mary hisses my name, admonishment clear even in her brevity. She's dressed in her trousers again, the dark fabric blending her into the shadows beneath the stairwell. Unfortunately for both of us, no amount of darkness can cover the way her voice carries through the dark.

"Who's there?" A booming voice follows the sharp snap of footsteps on the stairs. There's enough moonlight coming through the curtains in the front room for me to see the shape of a massive man thundering down the steps. Mary's safe from view, tucked away in the dark, but I'm left standing defenseless in the moonlit room. "Who the fuck are you?"

The demand seems to reverberate off the walls, shaking the entire house with the force of it. He doesn't slow once he reaches the bottom of the steps; if anything, he seems to gain speed in the open field of the hall.

I brace myself for impact as all two hundred and eighty pounds of him slam into my chest. It takes every ounce of my control not to fall on my ass, but it's a near thing. He gets a solid punch to my cheek and another to my temple that has the room spinning. I'm about to say fuck it to Mary's plan and attack the bastard when I see it—a glint of light in the darkness.

The needle slips into his neck, and he hits the ground before he even registers the sting. Mary stands triumphantly above him, a vicious grin on her face as she wiggles the spent syringe in his face. She's all but singing when she proclaims, "A taste of your own medicine, asshole."

Mary's eyes meet mine, the wild gleam of her excitement unmistakable, even in the dark. Apparently, I'm not hiding my emotions any better. "Oh, come on," she sighs, her slender shoulders slumping in defeat. "That was great."

I raise a brow in clear disagreement.

"We got him!"

Both arms cross over my chest as I tip my head to the side.

"I'm sorry he hit you."

I snort a derisive laugh at the obvious lie.

"Fine," Mary huffs, dropping the capped needle back into her pocket. "I'm not sorry he hit you, but only because Legacy always gets all maternal when you're hurt, and it's hot."

She gives me a look, as if daring me to disagree. I do nothing of the sort.

"Exactly," she laughs, bending over to pat the guy down. It wouldn't be the first time one of these asshats had a second weapon hidden on them. Since I don't fancy the idea of dealing with another situation like that, I move to help her flip the man over to search his back. "Nothing on him."

Mary nods once at the body, then a second time at me. In the year since I first met Mary, I've come to learn nodding means a lot more to her than a simple agreement. Taking it as the queue I know it to be, I bend to lift the man to his feet. He's more than a little unsteady in his heavily drugged state, and we nearly crash through the living room wall before I'm able to get us heading toward the front door.

This is so much easier than dragging dead bodies around. When I first started going on these little murder outings with Mary, she always seemed to kill the guys in the worst ways—blood everywhere, brains out, bones snapped. It was brutality at its finest. The only problem was, brutality doesn't make for the easiest cleanup, at the crime scene or in my basement.

Nowadays, we're a well-oiled, well planned operation.

"How much beef stew do you think we'll get out of this one?" Mary's question pulls me from my thoughts as I heave the drugged man through the doorway out to my waiting car. Legacy is there, sitting prim and proper in the passenger seat as she watches the street for any sign of trouble.

Mary makes a beeline for Legacy, leaving me to guide the massive man across the street and into the back seat. All the fight seems to bleed out of Mary as she settles into the seat behind Legacy, the very sight of the woman she loves seeming to calm her.

Come to think of it, that's exactly how I feel when I see Legacy. She's my everything, the eye of my storm, and I love her more than I ever thought possible. I love Mary too, though in a slightly less all-consuming kind of way.

Mary slides into the back seat, propping up our guest as I settle behind the wheel. There's a brief beat of silence, a moment of nothingness in the darkened cab, as the three of us breathe out the stress of the evening.

Then, Legacy turns to me and says something that nearly has me laughing out loud.

"We should start a cult."

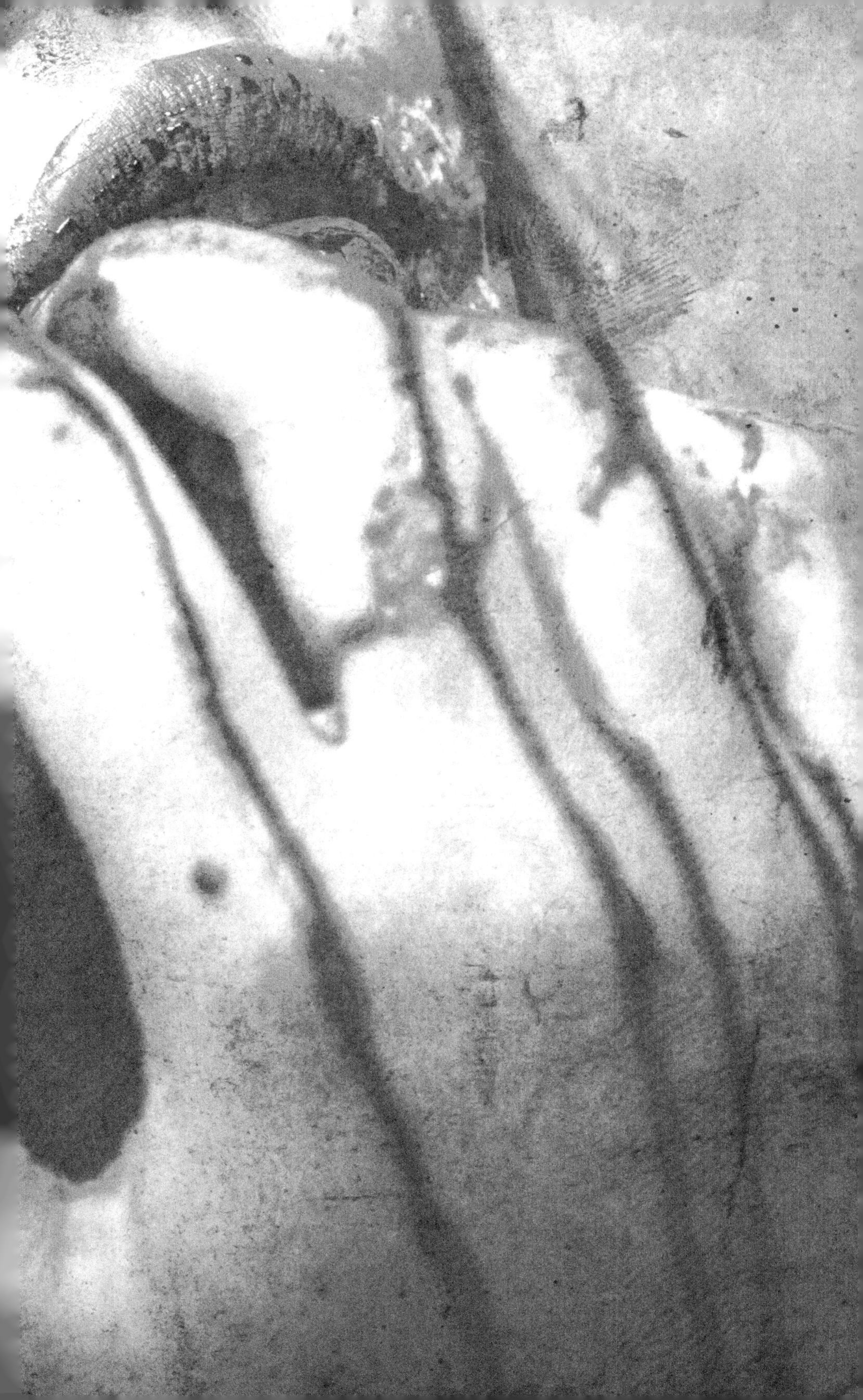

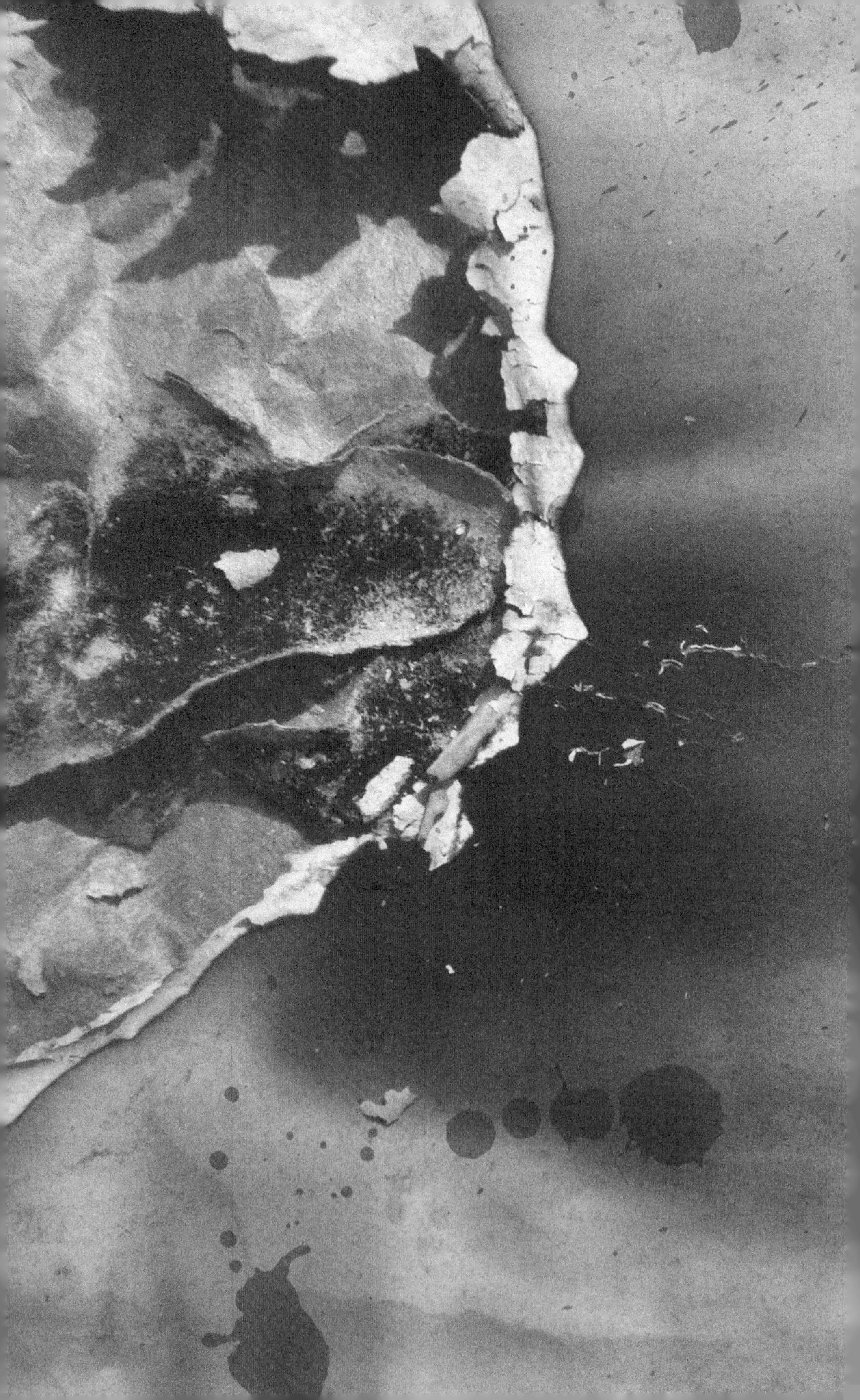

Naught Before One

Sasha Onyx

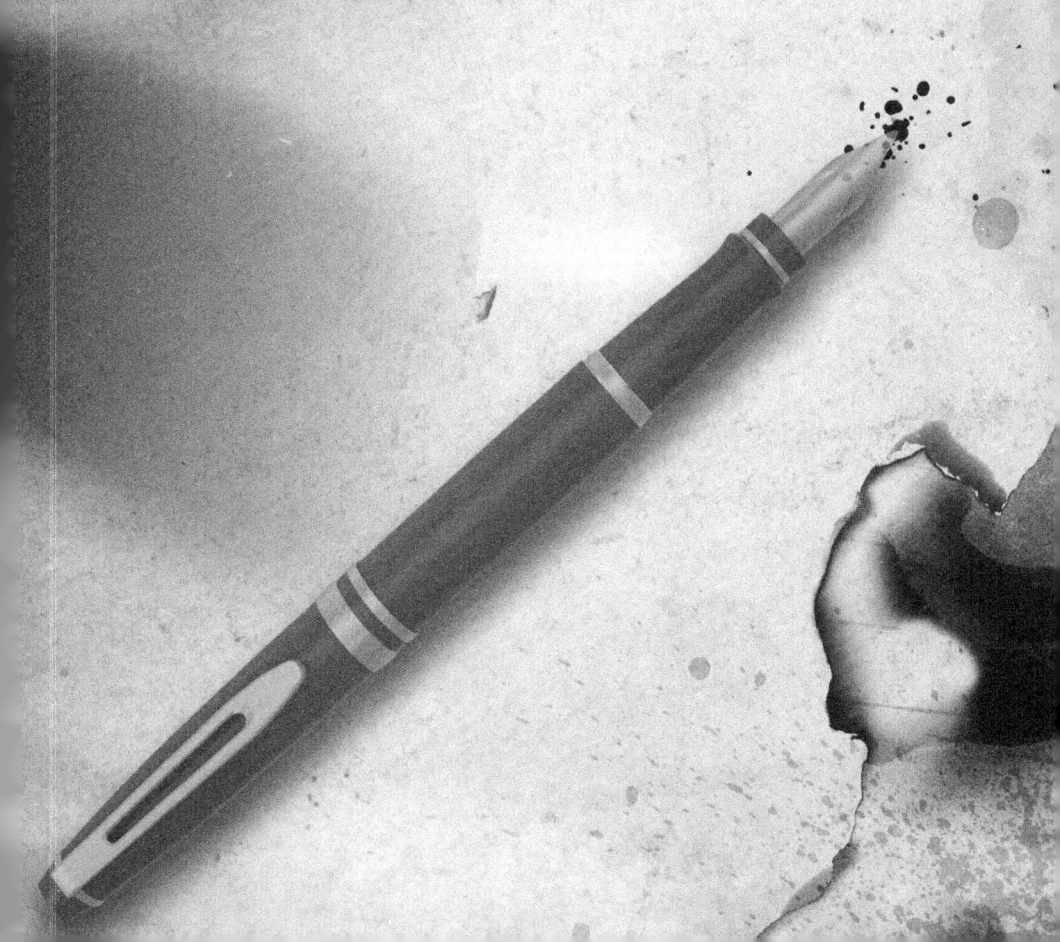

Chapter One

Nature and I had always perfectly blended, for I, disciple of the first gods, was born into it.

    Except on this night.

The stony path clearly resented every erratic step I took. Roots laced at my ankles while a continuous flow of dislodging rocks crushed my toes. My gait might have been stilted, barely gingered, hurried. I clung to my invaluable cargo with more tenacity than a wrym's coil.

Even as fear roosted in my mind, fluttering in and out, despite my efforts to expel it through tired, flared nostrils.

Even though there was no other hand to hold on to than the one of uncertainty.

Even... By all the damned blisters ruptured, and those about to bloom, the most important thing was that I walked.

An ordinary human would've said alone, but no one was ever alone in the Emerald woods—the viper between the leaves, the northern winds at my face, the creak of pines. Throughout it all, I was never unseen, never untethered. But I was silent, darkly draped, and made myself uninteresting.

A snap under my weight—loud enough to startle a stonebitten rabbit. It sprung out of its hidden burrow, and I stilled.

The point of my crescent ears twitched, and every bone in me fell silent. Ripples of grit, slate-against-slate diluted in the distance, betraying the rock-armored back of the flinching creature. A sound receding ever deeply north, ever closer to the Scrying coven, toward the cusp of a choice I had yet to make.

Any respectful witch would raise a brow at the frantic state of mind I found myself in—ridden with a sinister purpose, reluctant to follow the forest trail leading to the Scrying coven and, foremost, a tangent from everything eclipsing my kind.

You see, I'd found something.

It disturbed the order of nature, the coven, and my heritage. But who on earth could ignore what had triggered light into one's darkened bones?

Be damned the coven and its rules. I was keeping it.

My arms firmed around my possession, and my head dipped. For the first time, I spoke at *it* with words, fainter than a whisper. "You might not know, but your soul is lost and gone. I heard it ringing, mighty and sharp, and I, Raven, promise to return it to you."

Black feathers brushed against my cheek as Marvenous shrugged, claws curling in disapproval, tips digging into my shoulder without a care for the cloak she was needling into. *"Tis not yours to take. Not yours to keep."*

I sucked in a cheek, almost falling onto a boggy patch. "I just did, and I am keeping it." Of course, I was. *It* was there, under my clothes, in a warm place against my chest. It wasn't going anywhere.

"Your name doesn't even do you justice, Naught Before One. More like Naught Before Everyone!" Marvenous's wings ruffled once more, and a featherlet settled in the trench of my lips.

I ate it.

"You are more exasperating than famished hatchlings!"

I turned my head, only for intelligent black beads to stare right back at me. "Don't you have something else to do? A decaying measle you could dig your beak into?"

"My beak dug into your morbid cloak already; I've had my fill." Ravens possessed the cunning of witches, but Marvenous went far beyond the skill. *"'Tis not yours to take!"* she croaked before taking off, vanishing into the specter of mist, vanishing out of my well-deserving sight!

What my familiar thought didn't matter—only *we* did, and that alone prompted me to hug the small *nestling* in my arms.

Of course, I had no right to keep it. The idea itself went against

Chapter One

the third principle of the Scrying, a swamp of boundless spirited women and wasted dreams.

No gifted shall bear seed.

Quite the thorn in my side for a sworn sister like me. As much as I'd entered the coven—a young and filthy soul, denied of a mother's touch—those beginnings failed to define me. Yes, I'd been forged in the same fire. Yet, my edges were not as blunt as those of my sisters.

The second rule of the coven, however, had spoken to me by far and away.

A sister shall only find her power in a darkened path. For her purpose sleeps in its crevices where the glow worm hides.

A purpose found and tasted; its vessel cradled in my embrace.

And I wanted more. Could've been for pride, could've been for greed, seeking a power that awakens when purpose is found, and sacrifice endured. But I'd just undergone both, confirming the coven rules were based, not on what had once been tried and outlived, but on mold-eaten lies.

Yet, even as the fact was a moment of reckoning, no hate festered, not even frustration.

Because I'd done it for a whole different reason: the hole inside me, an abyss, that no spell, potion, or gold coin had filled until now.

Drat, if I was to follow my will, one issue needed exorcising: my integrity—a blood pact that had left a scar in the palm of my left hand—a blue jay-colored circle cut into thirds and edged with three moons, no less the symbol of the Scrying. The coven had taken me in as a newborn found drowning in the shite of a tar pit, and once you were in, there was no way out.

Nevertheless, I needed to part ways with my ethos if I went through with my decision. Hence, here I was, spearing against wicked punishment and desertion, my mind clanking with confusion.

The culprit—yesterday. The dawn had always hated me. Though, this time around, it had shown a certain kindness.

I should've known better.

Yesterday.

It was Ostara, which meant a one-week revelry, with our heads dusted with hawthorn berries and wreathed with wild vines and oak leaves, swaying bodies, drunk off wine and carnal desire, bursting to the tongue and the shaft.

I said *'meant,'* not *'was.'* Not this time. The Scrying coven was celebrating the end of a twentieth-year cycle, the Nosferus Beltane.

As the youngest members of the coven, Orakle and I were experiencing it for the first time. The ceremonies were unlike any Ostara festivals held before—overly pious and loathsomely ascetic. Somehow, prostrating to a goat-man, chanting vivid descriptions of our sufferings should we ever go against *his* holy teachings was far more elevating than honoring mother earth.

As it turned out, Beltane and his shadow, Nosferus, *apparently* wished for it. Anything for the illustrious god. Even sacrificing an antlered forest king who had outlived the hunt, parasitism and deadly winters, everything but the poisoned apple, for the trickster is victorious when dressed in innocence. *What cowardly route had we, witches, taken?* For truth's sake, I was as guilty. It could've been for my bogus prayers as I had inwardly cussed while dabbing my fingertips on the elk's bones—*though I did ensure to draw the phallus as small as possible*. It wasn't. I had brewed the poison, dipped the apple in the cauldron, and handed it to sister Madalet. She told me it was for the ghoul that stalked our nights…

Orakle was right. I had a brain the size of a bird.

The sun hadn't risen, but my sisters and I were already on our knees, faces bathed in a warm glow as we gathered around the skull of the flame-eaten elk, the jaw-grinding phalli etched over its ivory spears. Its sacrament had been agony. Each stroke a pox, and my fingers, coated with a coalescence of coal and tar, clingier than snail slime, would remain stained for weeks.

While Orakle and I huddled and took in the scene, I strove not to break a tooth at what my sisters were singing.

"The roots of attachment are twisted. Oh, to cling to them is to walk the line of ruin. A heart seeps from fleeting flesh and falls, falls into the fire of torment and sin."

"Praying to ashes and cocks," my voice croaked, nearly drowned out by those of my cheerful ravens—unneeded. The unkindness and I

Chapter One

differed quite a bit about Beltane. While they saw this eidolon as a protector, I viewed him as a tragic symbol of a pointless quest. Not to add the coven's growing obsession with *the male* bothered me, their worship silencing the three goddesses might, leaving my nerves choking in its grip.

Orakle nudged me with her elbow. "Concentrate on the earth under us, not the empty idol."

"I am. Grinding hard."

"I can see that," she whispered, her head tilting to the rift between our touching thighs. Below, my hand dug a hole that felt like a crater and our shoulders brushed lithely against one another, our stifled laughs torturing us. She thought no less.

"Nosferus, we summon you!" Across the bonfire, Dakanesh rose from her sitting position, arms open to the sky, her crown of bone, long twists of ivory, and dried ligaments dangling down her shoulders. She could've been a dead one, but alas, no. "Shadow of Beltane, Great Nosferus, come to your maidens, claim your brides!"

A pang in my chest, and I snarled, scanning the impassive expressions of the old crones around the fire, drinking hypocrisy emboldened in cunning promises like nectar. I couldn't fathom witches debasing themselves as merchandise for a shadow whose spirit's only ambition was to leave a veil of green in his wake.

But here we were...

While my teeth bared wider and my frown deepened, I tilted toward Orakle. "I wonder which stiff arsed hag taught her this?"

Orakle stayed silent, and I glared at her, captivated by a vision only she could perceive. Foresight across the Veil was her most envied, yet burdensome ability, and I knew she *saw* something when her fingers curled over mine, the nails sharp in my skin.

"What cold thoughts have your spine stiffening? Allow me to divine. Bride," I rasped.

"Nosferus." Green eyes shifted from the fire to me, widening, and the thought of them swallowing me crossed my mind. "The name comes with the skull of an unknown beast with the sharpest teeth."

I wrapped my hand over hers. Nosferus might have been new to us; I wasn't half as gullible as her. "Never as sharp as those of my unkindness' beaks. Worry not."

"A skull has nothing left to be stripped off." Anger stroked the hushed tone of her tongue, and I left the myst of this exchange for a noxious one where Dakanesh's dramatic rant thrived.

"Maidens of the first crop…" A laugh scrapped at my tight lips. "…for your endless power. One of life, one of eternal might." Dakanesh brandished a staff crowned with a purple stone—the Moon Path. At her sodden words, it glimmered, and I was confident I saw it flicker to an adder-gray. It was said that she carried the key to the Spirit World. Likely a fantasy, like anything that slipped out of her.

As Dakanesh droned on, the elk's charred skull bleated and quieted. An omen.

Then came in cries, those of a newborn, falling from the sky.

My sisters traded glares with each other, while others pointed their noses at the stars. As for me, my undisciplined glance went furiously inquisitive and had to land in the matron's milky one—Dakanesh's.

I bit my cheek at my childish reaction, but then I had an excuse. Dakanesh was the closest thing I had ever known to a mother—if such a mother had once thrown undercooked mice at me, had stumped teeth, nails, a double inward curl, and bats flying in and out of her grizzly rough mane.

One screeched out from behind her ear when she pointed her almost necrotic finger at me. "You, Raven," she said from across the flames, a face as smoked as her voice.

My chest filled. "Yes, matron?"

The snarl she wore might have seemed ominous had her mouth not been a wasteland of broken tombstones. "The wind calls, begs for our help. Seek what is causing its distress."

"The things that happen to you." Orakle's voice sounded like a scream tarried in her throat, the noxious fumes of the fire ever wafting toward us. I dared not look at her. Nothing ever tarried in me, starting with luck. Fortune's favor was as good as a hole in a web. "You provoked it, didn't you?"

I frowned, attempting a strained smile, uncertain if I should be amused, even though I knew her meaning. A handful of sisters, including Orakle, believed the wind's shiftings mirrored those of my mood—only a whiff—of utter nonsense. The wind was my mother, despite Dakanesh barely dressing as one. She fed me not with rot and varmint, but with scents and dreams, stirring in ways that seemed to seek my understanding. *She* was never a power to claim. Plus, how could I have? My purpose hadn't yet come to light, and with it, no power.

I played coy and she pinched my nose. "Don't you get it. The wind called, 'Naught'."

Despite her suffocating naïveté, a savage grin spread across my face. I had been freed from the choir.

The cry came from the newest of voices, thinner than a crystal shard. It sounded far, farther than where my coven had settled—at the farthest reaches of ordinary mortals. To find its source would take me at least a day or two, if not longer. A most wondrous conclusion. Any journey, unsuccessful or not, was always a better option than supplicating the goat-man.

So I stood, and as I did, my sisters, too. To consider it an act of respect would be a presumptuous assumption amidst the pursed lips and grumbling. Only Orakle grinned, one that held no kindness—and I liked that. It was cruel and genuine, utterly complicit. Because, at long last, a stroke of luck.

Marvenous perched on my shoulder. *"Near the village of Bokkerydim, dark one."* Her talons firmed. *"I do not like it. No, I really do not."*

My familiar had a keen instinct never to underestimate. I would, however, do so this time, my own instincts clawing at the deepest of my soul, and my unflinching would not be swayed by her croaks. Newly awakened breath wailed. A calling that echoed deep within my own. No force could hold me from seeking it, and I would listen only to those who ordered me onward. I stroked her, and whispered, "Let your worries be for your young."

In return, a croak, black eyes blinking furiously.

"What did she say?" Orakle nudged between our glares, gliding her fingers down her onyx sheen.

"A stretch of wings would do me good."

"Nought." A tired smile curved her lips, crinkling the corners of her eyes. "Be prudent."

Furious wood collided with stone and drew our attention to Dakanesh, her shaft's tail pounding the ground. "Raven, *my* Nought Before One. Press on."

Fingers furled over Marvenous' back, her beak swaying curiously at my clinging gesture. A presence in Dakanesh's eyes sparked new and offensive, wavering from mint to carnelian with every syllable she uttered. "The ceremony shall resume upon your return."

I kept aim at my food tosser's cruel eyes, feeling abused. The gratuitous nature of her words was excessive.

"Now go," she gritted, ravens swooping from the trees as she spoke.

I nodded and faced the wind. Frost-white feathers pushed out of my skin, along with talons of charcoal. From head to toe, I became an airborne creature and launched into the night.

My unkindness gathered close, mostly to cloak my disturbing size and shape, too extravagant for the common mortal.

When the scent of *non-gifted* slipped into my beak's slits, I plunged, barreling between the burly oaks and the slim pines, hooked on the trail of the newborn's echoes.

South.

Furthering away from my territory invigorated my senses. The tips of my wings teased the drooping chains of sprigs, needles raining in my wake. The crisp susurrus was a song of praise I could've croaked at but refrained; a dragonish screech was very much uncalled for.

With every hour I flew, every league I crossed, time bent, and I knew my freedom was but a silver breath on a cold night—short and fleeting. So I breathed it in with fervor, leaving no wisp unclaimed.

The cries…they ceased.

"Faster, ebon ones!" I shrieked.

My blood slammed against my veins as I dived. There was no faster term than speed, yet I pushed beyond it.

A throng of black tightened at my bristles, and my ravens faltered. On my right wing, powerful claws locked at the shoulder, forcing me to veer in that direction, and Marvenous' gruff caw snapped at the peace that had ebbed from our tails until now. *"Heed, dear one."*

I did. Half a league from where we circled, thatched roofs hung in tatters, with gaps wide enough for rain, snow, and critters to enter. Witches might have no coins to trade with, but still, we lived in the Weeping Cravta, a sacred willow tree hiding vast underground chambers brimming with fur pelts, an ever-burning fire, the chimney, a gaping wound at the summit of its hollow though beating core. Decency.

Ordinary mortals had none. Insufficiently graced to be animals, but damned enough to be their own downfall.

A clearing.
Plush of pink heather.

Chapter One

*There, a daughter's preacher lies.
A mourning, a farewell,
Beyond doubt, a raven's calling.
But beware the blue ax, for it hides a shaft.
And hard on the bone, it will hit.*

An omen, quite menacing, but my landing area no less. My claws brushed over the swaying reeds until they found a grounded, firm connection.

Wings broke, feathered blades sheathed back into me, cloak shimmied.

And my nose crinkled. *This smell—*

Blood.

Fresh.

Ravens waned at my feet, our attention scouring the glade when an intuition tugged at my senses, sight first. The sunset draped a thicket of shrubs, flanked by heather, in a rose-tinted halo, a faint incessant whirring threading around the scene. I frowned. Its aspect was magic.

Nonsense. I spat and kept walking toward a glow too brilliant for the chicory-root hue of flames. It came from a beam of dying sunlight spearing into the underbrush. As I plowed through the heathers, my smile stretched to find it igniting the hollowed core of an oak's broken base.

The zephyr picked, bleaching my vision with bothersome strands. I was the daughter of wind, and my mother—both a guide and a shield—had carried me to my destination, yet she was now pulling me away from the source of the call.

But I was Raven. I was curious.

My dark birds, no less. Hundreds of gleaming beads converged around the well of light, croaks cleaving the stone-cold silence. The ravens did so until the crunch of leaves under my feet quieted, and I clutched the sides of the stump.

My head dipped slowly as I stared into the dimness, stickiness crackling upon my parting lips. At the bottom, a toss of rag barely folding over the smallest body I had ever seen.

I then looked behind me.

Twice, perhaps three times; I couldn't remember. All I was in that instant was for *her*.

My hands plunged into the dim. I battled with the knot, nails, a proud inch from the skin, catching in red gauze. No matter how fast or carefully I untied the swath, the color remained.

It was me; those blood-stained hands belonged to me. But my focus was so jarred on what truly mattered that this detail sank into irrelevance. Pulling out my discovery, a spark of blue I knew only I could see flickered out of the baby. I caught it in one clamp and raised my fist to my eyes.

First, a rift, a small line, my clasp breaking in halves as I monitored my sprite—something I didn't want to lose. Then, an unfolding of fingers, slow and delicate.

Under the cover of my hand, a speck-like energy, a bulb lighter than air. A soul. These had a habit of evanescing at first sight, so I hastened to swallow it—it was invaluable, and I was instinct. What I would do with it, I didn't yet know. But with every passing second, the seed of a possibility sprouted, growing taller, sturdier.

And upon casting a glance at what lay dormant in my other arm, it turned into an imposing tree, its branches scraping at a dream. It was beautiful, far too precious to be wasted, so I tucked it beneath my cloak.

I now stood damned, waiting for thought as my scarlet fingers confronted me. This blood wasn't mine. Mine was dark red.

My eyes slit at what I saw between my digits, the jagged rim of the stump. Marvenous was perched on it. Beneath her claws a dripping crimson handprint, too small to be mine, hugging the side of the bole.

A croak, then an entire sung line of them came rolling at my back, and I pivoted. Just a few paces from me, feet, ten toes turned up to the sky, springing out from the tufts of heather.

A woman my age, a bet out of eight, with black hair, pulled skin hanging from her belly, a white dress, creases rippled with red.

Someone had butchered the work.

Perhaps a benevolent one.

No doubt unskilled. It was easy to guess what had happened. Someone took on the role of a midwife, her charge died, and in the bitter indifference of early spring, abandoned the newborn to its cruel fate.

Too afraid of us to seek help. Not enough of death, *their* so-called faith getting the worst out of them. The irony to call us the devil's

Chapter One

spawn, when the devil himself smiles back at them, their last breath fogging the death watch mirror they called upon themselves!

The tasteless forbidden arts of necromancy flashed in my mind. To revive the child, perhaps even the mother…find the culprit.

Kill it.

Ravaging envy gripped every limb of my being, all too ready to do so. *Squealings…a heart fighting for a beat as my nails press into it—*

A small cry shot out of me as my vicious hands instantly softened their grip on what was dormant in it. Unbidden malice threatened my composure, but I couldn't let it touch this little one. Not in any way.

Even my sigh felt brutal against it. How miserable must one feel to find solace in something so fragile, undone, and gone? Enough to cradle the tiny skull so silent in my folds, and I noticed my usually weak and bony fingers, now almost graceful, as if designed for that very purpose.

My shoulders drew inward, and the birds fell silent. *My purpose.* Like smoke, fingertips coiled about the temples with as much care as if it were an eggshell. By the earth's breath, how my heart pounded.

It betrayed a feat I did not need to contemplate. To be tied to a pole in the middle of a beautiful *ex-terra* bonfire, flames that scorched the soul, not the flesh, pleading forgiveness as my sisters danced and sang Beltane's words, *"The roots of attachment are twisted. Oh, to cling to them is to walk the line of ruin. A heart seeps from fleeting flesh and falls, falls into the fire of torment and sin."*

The thought rose within me like a poisonous brew, thick and foul, I quickened to purge out from my throat. "May the venom in my breath be your burden, Nosferus Beltane!"

Fizzing pricked my ears as I glanced at my feet. Lay hanging on a brown toadstool, my *spite*, seared, orange ringlets swelling throughout the cap. A spatter for *the goat's shadow*. I hope Nosferus tastes it. How lethal and bitter it is. *Bloody scriptures.*

There was never a time I never embraced my virginity, honored our beliefs, or avoided men. Even though the excruciating need to have a child of my own clashed with the coven's norms.

But days before the Nosferus Beltane rite began, Dakanesh introduced Orakle and me to its scriptures. It crushed every hope I had left of having a small heartbeat against mine…

"Nosferus, Beltane's Shadow, protects us from attachment, the cause of many wars and deaths, for if torn, it turns the mind mad.

Grief often walks hand in hand with wrath, and it is a most dangerous alliance for a witch," Dakanesh had said.

I glared at the ravens, heckling me to leave ever since the newborn found my arms. The breath I took was as though I were crafting air from the very ether, yet it was never enough—my ribs ached, caught between hesitation and the joy I barely dared to embrace. Marvenous skipped closer, her head twisting inquisitively.

I wet my lips. "What can I say? I need a moment?"

"*Too much thinking leads to misery.*" Marvenous was, once more, spot on.

All that, the Nosferus Beltane and everything that followed, had done was strip away the little trust I once had in my matron and her sacred parchments. The novelty of Nosferus Beltane puzzled me, even though it clarified why Dakanesh had treated me like an animal all those years. But if I had any ounce of respect for Beltane, no matter being male, it was because he was a god of nature—the embodiment of everything pulsating and alive. Why, then, would his shadow say otherwise? Why was adoption exemplified through me tolerated, but the love that should come with it denied? The answer I found was charred from cowardice—the fear of loss.

I had no reason to fear. The child had been met stilled. Grief required history, and I had none.

I eased the linen aside, folding it back to reveal the belly. She was perfect. The right amount of toes and fingers, lashes, wisps of silk furled skyward, as if she had always been desperate to look upon the yonder. She was just that, perfect. With a swift bite, I severed the umbilical cord, my teeth cutting through ties that were not meant to be.

The cord dropped.

Two ravens hopped close, and the fastest snatched it, before both took off, bickering.

'*A heart seeps from fleeting flesh and falls, falls...*' The sacred excerpt kept rolling in the back of my mind as I stared hollowed, at two black dots fighting in the sky. If I overstep Nosferus Beltane's words. I overstepped Dakanesh's...

A shiver won over me.

But one alone. Because then again, a cadaver had no longer *fleeting flesh* but was rather dead. And so, I felt safe knowing I respected this principle.

Overall, I had yielded to my matron. *"Seek what is causing its distress."*

And here was the cause, gentle against my chest.

I had lingered long enough for it to stir my soul. The idea of resisting something not meant for me was to lie to the very essence of my desire. It had taunted me, and I, hungry for it, took it in the end.

Chapter Two

My familiar's talons sank into my shoulder. *"Return to the Scrying. Drop this stupid idea of necromancy and bury the child."*

"You're rambling again, Marvenous," I said, stroking the rigid stalks.

From the clearing, the cornfield *had appeared* tranquil and easy to cross—a hint I neglected, for I should've known the humblest of things at first glance always proved to be a challenge once in hand.

Yet a challenge serving as my last rampart between me and civilization.

I had no specific fear of it, only hate.

My blood ran deep with it. *Thek!* I was born in an age where religion thrived and women died.

As a fief of Delos, Bokkerydim village perfectly exemplified its tenets—pervasive, toxic, sapping any strength of a free wanderer like me. Before I came into this world, women, once hopeful, had attempted to break into the tight hermetic circle of men and the beliefs they held dear. But defying the authorities had been a losing battle. Only humans bled, not convictions.

I wouldn't worry; this wasn't a crusade. I was engaging in a killing spree.

The thought made my blood race, and I wrenched apart two corn stalks, glass-like fibers biting into my skin.

But just as my heel lifted, a tickle crept up my ankle. Lilies of the valley.

To find them here saddened me. They usually flourished at the edges of woodlands and within them, and those little white bells were but fragments of a once-forested landscape.

Mother Earth gives. Men take. The hurdle of ivory florets eyed me, and I sneered. *And Mother Earth gives lilies which poison men.*

I gathered a handful into the smallest of several pouches hanging from my belt, inhaled long and hard, and stepped into the plantation.

Threading my way through stalks with only one hand and the weight of one's body was daunting—I barely had enough limbs to address the infant's safety. But I worked from a strength rarely called upon, fueled by grisly images of a dismembered man, pondering if I should collect the father's blood from the throat or his torn belly. Then, would it even matter? Necromancy was all about the parents' blood, anyway.

Marvenous flew close to my ear, clapping her beak. *"What you take, you must give back."*

Due to struggling lungs, I threw a questioning glance at her.

"Nothing can be left uneven."

"The newborn?"

"The lilies!"

I frowned, irritated enough from laboring through dense, inflexible deadlocks, her patronizing almost spilling my anger forth. "I am not a childling. I know!"

"A few steps on your right is a wider path."

I listened and wedged between two stems, my face creasing under leaf blades. "What foul luck is this?"

"You summoned it upon yourself!"

"Don't you know scheming is progress?" I said, sighing in relief when my foot settled on an aisle wide enough to walk, an endless stretch of tilled soil threatening its narrow end.

But so was I. I progressed fast, my panting and the sharp clink of shod horses crisping a testament to my effort. The corridor's dimness receded until it fully unveiled the twisted outline of human presence.

There, I made myself small. Toes and fingers dug into the earth as I neared my face at the village's threshold.

A silver mist drifted from my lungs, to which I tightened my cloak's collar, forestalling the giving-off of cold exhalations into the felt. I was to be a shadow, and shadows did not breathe.

Caw. Caw. Caw! Shadows did not croak, either, but my unkindness didn't care. Mother wind came, blows roaring against the croaks, where below, a hay wagon wheeled unhurriedly on a cobbled road—cleaved in its center, a dirty silver glaze of ice on the flatter sides.

My nostrils flared, an askance glare on the cleft pavement, no less burdened with the weight of accumulated shite—a waft even the dead could not emanate. *Pigs.*

I waited for the lone cart to pass, transfixing yet another pig and its conical hat. The corner of my lip twitched at it. It was a curious hat. Made of straw, it frayed in many parts, the tip twisting into a tight coil akin to a folding claw, and I liked that. Very much so, it was worth nagging for. My tongue curled, a song for my *mother*.

> *"Billow, billow, sudden, brusk*
> *A sharp hat begets interest.*
> *It is your daughter's desire.*
> *And what she wants, she gets."*

The peasant gasped as a rough current snatched the hat, swirling it ever high for the yonder to swallow. He pivoted his head, eyes astray, and these wandered toward me, toward unashamed raven croaks! I huddled closer to the ground, shrinking. My curiosity stayed within the bounds, for it always came back in kind, and attention differed from what I sought—silence. And the ravens were bursting fury at the beak.

Only when the wagon passed beyond the hillock did the wind fall. Grit gnawed at my feet while my hunched angered frame whirled. My teeth gnashed, eyes a curse to a moving veil darker than the night. "Would you wish your Naught to perish? By all means, increase your ruckus!"

None of the ravens had seconded my plan, regardless of why it hatched, and they made it clear. I grabbed a stem, plucked a cob, and threw it farther down the field, hoping the kernels would fill their talkative mouths and distract any passerby from me because I was to step into the village.

I pulled my hood over my head and cloaked my child.

There wasn't a soul now. Only straw from thatched roofs strewed over a patchwork of uneven stones, scurrying then halting at every wind drop.

My first step felt bare, a free fall without wings, holding on to little but my senses.

A most regrettable instinct.

The air hung heavy, stagnant, like sealed refuse. And now that the wind had faltered, it was far worse than unbreathable. It had become edible.

I skittered across the road, jumped over the festering rift, and flanked the housing walls. My throat tingled, eye-swelling piss corrupting every crevice of the inferno I admitted had called upon me. As much as morbidity beckoned me, human feces didn't. My nose twitched until I gagged, and all I wished was to stuff fresh moss into my nostrils.

"What business have you here, beggar?"

In the swirl of a cloak, I faced my first opponent, whose sticky and wilted voice had rung out many moons ago. There, a shadowed stick sat in a rocking chair under the cover of a darkened porch, and only the twinkling of starlit eyes and the hems of a withered shawl floating about the breeze gave way to an old woman's presence.

I crept up toward her. I needed direction, and she was the start of it. "Greetings, wise one. Simply wandering, without harm or arm. And like you, I am alone."

She chuckled, pointing to the right of the porch's steps. A small patch of what I thought was a garden, freshly turned earth, and three small monoliths for a tombstone. "Rid of my husband. How did you guess?"

The unevenness of her face sliced through the clarity of the night; a bumpy mound slanting down her cheek, as though it had been struck and broken time and again. Her left shoulder jutted unnaturally, slightly twisted. I held my frown at bay, even though a corner of my mouth ticked. She had survived him; the dignified response to her question was no other than herself. Her resolve commanded respect, and so I acknowledged it. "What once trampled is now trampled on; what once destroyed is now destroyed."

The elder's expression came to a sharp still, if not for her lips. "Speaking in patterns, are we?" The spark in her eyes reduced to a slit. "A witch's sickness, I was told. Spawns taught incantations before they can talk."

Chapter Two

I lowered my head, a corner of my eye always well settled on her. "Sounds contagious."

She mumbled under her voice while lifting her chin, and I scowled at what had caught her eye. "Them, too?" she asked.

While she alluded to a contagion, the ravens indeed multiplied on the lengthier ridge of her cross-shaped roof. My smile stretched onerously thin across my face. "I crossed the field. The ravens want the corn, not my lead," I lied between my teeth.

Her chair creaked, and a rushlight kindled and rose up to her face. Two feet stomped down the stairs leading to the road, and the croaks vanished.

"Not many pass this way without a reason. What's yours? Don't tell me you're lost. My beddings count for one."

"No one is ever lost without reason," I said.

"Make it die." The spear of my ear ticked at Marvenous' purr, my searching gaze falling upon the elder's roof, now pitch black from the weight of my unkindness. *"Make it die and return to the woods."*

I could.

I wouldn't, my attention straightening on this little person, whose angst began wafting as her eyes fell from the ravens to me. "Where do you come from, child?"

The needle of an unknown ache twisted into my eye, and I took it in with a tight smile. "From a tar pit." I chuckled barely, momentarily staring at my feet kissed from a wilderness these pigs called dirt.

There was a light tug on my head, and my focus drifted from the ground to the strand of my hair spitting out of my hood, firm in the elder's fist. "A bonny one like you…" she muttered, rolling it between her dried fingers. "Attracts the worst."

My lips twitched. "Sometimes, bony ones, too."

I then leaned in, locked eyes, and, with a voice threading into threat, whispered into her foul face, "I lied…" The glow of the rushlight jittered, mostly fear at the handle. I tried to find an understanding in the shallow depth of her eyes, cowering under a sag of skin, but I found nothing. "I am looking for someone. Would you be the one?" I wished her gone, even more so the stench of tallow.

"My old bones?" Her fingers stilled, ice against my strands, and my smile sharpened.

"Perhaps. Unless you can tell me where to find the preacher of this village." If the omen was right, the father of my child had to be one.

Her mouth twitched. "All men are preachers."

I had no time for the same tired, verified drivel. I seized the woman's unyielding hand near my face and pulled her close. "Tell me, brittling, where can I find him?"

"The Arden preacher is the one you want!" The spit of her words fell on my face as she shoved her fist away and leaped back.

My arm rose, one single finger lifting with a certain intent I did not hide. The old woman flinched, her clogs jolting as my touch skimmed over her. "I deserve no hexing!"

A glimmer of a smile tugged at the corner of my mouth as my supposedly hexing finger traced remnants of her saliva on my cheek. I took it to my lips and my eyes closed at the taste of her honesty. More lingered on her tongue; it was a certainty. "And where could this Arden preacher be dwelling at this very instant?"

Her ashen brows knit together, her gaze honing on the bulge beneath my cloak. "You're looking for trouble, and the man has many. He doesn't have food for the litters he breeds. Why would he…" her nose crinkled, "for the two of you? What is this smell?"

One swift leap and I cupped her face, my nails learning the soft curves of her lines, paper skin I could puncture if I firmed my clasp just so. "Tis not food I seek."

Though bright and round, her eyes now held a piercing gaze, softening her once-taut face. "If so, you say." And down the road, her finger pointed. "Where the three Arden brothers carved in stones stand, you'll find a chapel. His 'gathering' is behind, a refuge for the lost and ailing travelers. Be cautious; we live in a world where a woman's beauty is a savage curse, and men will do anything to control it, if not break it."

I left her cheeks alone and snorted. "I am well versed in curses."

"In that case, you'd better keep your friends close," she said, an earnest smile toward her roof.

To that, I bowed and veered my heels toward the gathering in question, a pointy straw hat falling from the sky onto my head.

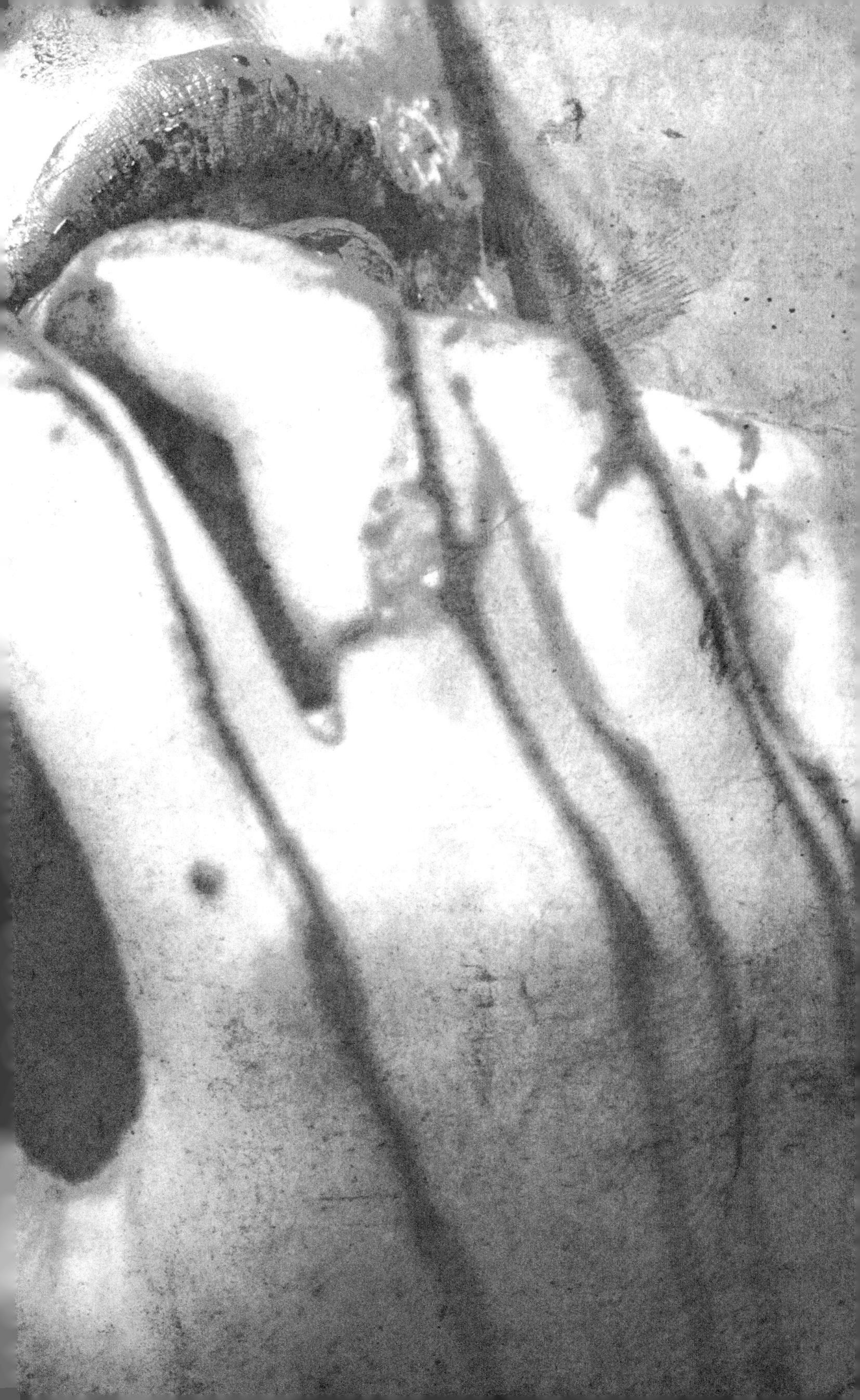

Chapter Three

My footsteps on the cobblestones were whispers. On the inside, though, chaos reared at my edges. My heart was pounding, thoughts spinning. To venture that deep into the ungifted world, to have spoken with one… I was a coalescence of both euphoria and anxiety.

I wanted more—

My brow arched as I glanced upward to what sounded like coins raining from the sky.

"Bats!"

I threw a hopeless stare at my hissing familiar, hovering defiantly beside my head, thrusting her beak toward the darkness rushing down.

It split at my sides, wings abrading my skin. A cut on my cheek, and I gasped.

"You've angered your familiar, its unkindness, and now Beltane."

"The bats came from their own."

"Of course. Bats are known to slip through the heart of a village."

"No Beltane talk!" I cried, crouching and shielding my face with my hands.

Marvenous and the unkindness squawked, drowned in the chatter of flying mice.

It wasn't until the cries broke and the night fell still that I unfurled around my knees and rose, eyes gazing skyward. *Mother* was already dipping into the far east.

A frown crossed over my face. I had to hasten, for my child and her rite urgently called. Necromancy was like a twister, the *Tenebros Libren* doors its eye. To summon it, conditions had to align: a name to call, bones of the lost one, the secret spell, and a personal sacrifice—preferably one's own life or a loved one. Quite tacky.

However, morality was not my concern, not anymore.

Her vessel was. No matter how I liked it—small, delicate, meant for her—it defied the usual prerequisites: skulls and bones. I was to perform a variation, overhauling its laws as taught by Dakanesh with a kit. She had gutted the animal for study, then she did the same with the mother and all the males, as we could not tell who the father was. *"Life of the mother, life of the father. Tenebros Libren Havad Heriomis. You took once, I give you twice. Take what you need but return the prize,"* she had said, wringing the dead creatures over the kit's body, their blood soaking it. The youngling came back to life. However, with that take, one crucial rule had to be respected: a point in the cycle of death not to trespass. The cadaver must not ooze brown.

I tugged at my child's cover and exhaled sharply. She was bloated. I had a few hours left, be it half.

And my lips curled, my heart hammered, the pulse of my blood begging to let out, for some had to spill. I'd already agreed some of it would, but simply out of pleasure. As for the rest, it had to come from the father of my child, and it had to pool at my feet. The night could run fast, bats come and go; nothing could tinker with my ambitions, not even Marvenous or… a god.

"Return to the Scrying, Naught!"

I raised a silencing hand. An omen was taking hold.

By six, they go
Behind idol and stone
One to kill,
And three to maw.

I straightened my hat and walked on, mulling over far more important things than angered gods. The omen.

It had been precipitous, unwarranted. *Two* were unaccounted for, and nothing of six went before or behind me. As hundreds of obsidian wings silently flew overhead, searching for three hand-sculpted abominations, my imagination ran wild. *What happened to the other two?* A tremor ran across my lips as my head swayed, blindly searching for two missing pieces I couldn't picture.

All I saw were the batten shutters slamming down upon my wake and the hasting of men and their swords unsheathing behind doors. Naturally, fright should have festered in my bones. But I had none. Instead, my lips quirked. I was *Nought Before One*, after all.

Despite never truly engaging with the *non-gifted*, I had never known defeat or the measure of it. I kept my stride casual, aware that without a decent horde of men huddling behind shields, none would be brave enough to step out alone.

Witches were feared, and fear was a weapon I welcomed. But however icy and sharp, a blade of ice is ultimately destined to melt.

I hurried onward, the wind billowing my cloak open to reveal the wonder inside. I brought my child to my lips, and, ignoring the scent of what had been, kissed the tip of her nose—a first kiss, a blessing. "Blood from your father, your mother, and the spark of yourself shall return to breathing flesh. You shall be alright." Her mother's blood mingled on her skin; as for her father, I just needed to drain it out of him. As the village thinned, its scent was already perceptible to me and grew raunchy when I neared a barren, circular area.

In its heart stood three sandstone statues: knights twice the height of our oldest cedars, swords dug into the earth, gathered around a well. Despite the clear moon, the dimness choked them, as if what they symbolized sucked up all the light. The Arden brothers.

I stooped from a stone bouncing off my head. Followed a hail of pebbles and twigs, the ravens scolding me for having wandered further than any witch of the Scrying. *"I warn you, child. Keep going, and we shall leave. I shall bear no witness to your charred bones. This is the edge of our patience. Return to the woods."* Marvenous was my familiar, but she was also the matron of her feathered coven. Blessed was I, for she had chosen me. Why, though, she would never tell.

But regardless of our bond, my anger still flared. "Marvenous, a mother of many hatchlings, let me be one," I said, the frame of my face sprigging with bristles.

"Tis not your child."

"It's all I have!"

"And you for us. Return to the woods!"

"When tested, your trust truly feels sharp!"

"Not as sharp as this." She perched on my hood, and I staggered as her beak viciously poked my head.

A grunt rose in my throat, my hand chasing her away as I careened back into a dignified gait. "Find shelter. It's not safe for you."

"No." Her claws ran into my shoulder as a croak ripped my ear apart. *"I want to be the first to feast on your dead eyes!"*

Her rant followed me as I walked past the monuments. Marvenous and I had our moments, and this was one.

I stopped, fingers clasped to the weathered stone of one of the Arden brothers. Before me, six thatched houses, different from those of the village. Spaced out, broader, the walls thick of waddle and timber, with curious gaping holes reminiscent of moth bites, only larger.

"And by six, they go," I muttered, skulking toward the closest house.

Creeping along its timbered walls, I inadvertently treaded past a strange aperture, a blur of two figures swirling behind it, voices muffled. *People!* A gasp nearly escaped me as I crouched from the sudden openness.

Sometimes, defying conventional wisdom led to discovery, or so that's what I told myself as my finger hovered near the brink of this odd portal, where the wind somehow could not go through—a *wind door* of some sort. Hollowed in shape, it was a gap carved into the wall and lit from within. A jolt ran through my arm as my skin met what felt like a sheet of pure frozen water without the expected melt or ice. What strangeness…yet adorned a lively home, bursting with greasy laughs.

"Please, Father. No." A plea, one of a youthful voice, big enough to tell me it was a girl.

I already knew my numbers. My nails flicked, hungered, back straightening as I stepped in front of the door, a last adjustment on my new headpiece. It was time to gut.

A flurry of wings flew into my face. *"Enough!"*

Once more, Marvenous and I found ourselves at odds with the subtle nuances of words. This one wasn't 'yours,' or 'return,' but 'enough.' I curved my hand into a tight ball, and with a sneer streaked over my jaw, tapped it defiantly against the door.

"Witch!" Marvenous darted away as a crack of light widened across my countenance.

With utter slowness, I drank in the silhouette, not leaving a drop unaccounted. First, boots with red blots on the tips, followed by forest green trousers, the coarse texture stirring an itch in my skin. A shirt ripped open, three red lines at the center of the man's hairless chest. I believe he spoke to me, but all I could think of was how the brightest colors and fullest tails were the surest marks of virility, and the man bore no trace of it. Only a thin, gray beard provided a glimmer of hope. Actually, even that fell short.

There was a snap, and my eyes widened, not at the insolence, but at how soot entrenched the crevasses of his fingers: ruined, bloodied skin framing the nail, the quick too short to be well kept if not by nervous teeth. To it, a glorious smirk etched over my cheeks that the man surely ignored. He had sown cruelty—for how long, I would never know—his soul, though, did, and it reaped its due with crippling anxiety.

The man's eyes set on my feet. "No beggars."

The non-gifted seemed inclined to judge a person based on their feet. If so, he should've found me grounded.

The heat of such offence pulsed, and I removed my hood, the hat falling between us.

Chapter Four

There was a fireplace behind the man. Thin, it panned through the door's cracks, curled about the hinges to loiter like a sea as anemic as the hair the man was ogling.

I knew time was unfurling faster than a striking snake. I had to hasten this splendid exchange. "Greetings, good sir. Would you be the preacher?"

As I stood there for what felt like the span of a throat clearing and three interspersed owl barks, he did not seem alive, save for the slick film over his eyes and the heaving of his chest.

Eventually, he nodded.

Wonderful.

"Who goes by?" Another voice, neither feminine nor masculine, muffled as though buried in a blanket in a distant room, likely the girl behind the wind door?

Orange haze flickered across the preacher's bumpy scalp. Like an egg, it tilted to one side, and at last, his mouth opened, though he turned his chin to his back. "Tis a woman."

I corrected him. "A wanderer, seeking information."

His attention snapped back to me. "I'd add a pliable lass, too. Ears like yours could've only been sharpened by hands."

No one had ever touched my ears. They were what they were, crescented and sharp at the tip. My chest puffed, the heart aggressive.

It ripped red when a fusty, meaty hand clamped my face and flicked it from left to right. "And still, ye wear that smile."

My perfect ears burned. Utter fury, if that was what it was, shook me in ways a blaze would, a searing whoosh consuming me in places so secluded, I boiled...but with a smile.

Hopefully, the emotion would last until I killed him.

"Would ye look at that..." The preacher's smile groaned as his eyes straggled down my body. I let him. Even lifted my chin for a proper assessment. Nothing fueled me more like raw, aggravating humiliation.

I wanted it all. It condensed in my firming clasp, nails hooking into my flesh, absorbing the faintest trace.

Until now, thoughts had been racing about what to do with the preacher. But as I breathed in his bond-repellent sweat, the answer came in pleasant—hang him, head down with a string of his guts. Immediately, my glance searched for the nearest beam.

"What yer grace doing here at such a late hour?"

"Well..." A grin slashed across my face as if flaunting wet blades. While ensuring he took in the sharpness, my *beggar's* foot slipped onward. *Eyeballs happen to be my favorite part of the body, and I come to eat yours.* "I have been told you take in the weak and the poor. May I enter? I promise I will ask for nothing more." I chewed my lips as my thoughts skid out in a murmur. "Granted, we all know there is always...more." *The eyes. I'll start with the eyes.*

The door yarned wide, and an arm stretched low, bowing to invite me in. The sudden shift in the preacher's mood was overly obsequious, off-cuts of a disastrous attempt to lure. "Make ya self at home."

My gaze hadn't begun sweeping the room, and it hooked onto the girl seated near the fireplace to my left. Although she had appeared warped, I was sure it was the girl I saw behind the *wind door*. Her age seemed to match mine, though it felt stretched by something worn. When I noticed a doll made of straw and string clutched in her hand, my jaws tensed; she was much younger than I wanted her to have been. The flames behind gently stroked her back, and I wondered if those were the only affections she had ever known, if not for ridiculous burly walls that seemed yearning to embrace her.

From the outside, the house sat generously, but inside, it was bloated, as if someone had carved one room from a massive log—thick, roughened walls enclosing the smallest of spaces. I suspected many more could've existed, had the house hadn't been burdened with superfluous wood. Speckled light filtered through, barely touching the penumbra. A blue curtain half-drawn partitioned this only room, swallowing what light there was. I noted two distinct breathings curdling behind it.

Then a realization struck me like bird shite. There were not two, but four people. My senses exploded. The embers crackled too brightly, the ceiling was too low, and the smell fornicated with liquor and something oddly animal. Though my composure showed nothing, I was clinging to the world's edge. Too many non-gifted around a witch often ended with a bonfire.

I inhaled and dipped my chin, centering.

"Ya alright, lass?"

I moved a step as the planks creaked behind me. "Settling, good sir. Settling." I never valued caution, however prudence now seemed necessary to avoid disaster. And method was caution's twin, proceeding as such, a fundamental requisite in brewing. Every ingredient, every potion, every word had its order. With that in mind, I gauged my options. *Watch. Identify the weakest. Kill.*

My gaze sharpened on the young girl. The thinnest gown, dirty gray linen, harsh and hole-eaten, hung on her like a shredded sheet, its hem stopping just below her calves as she quivered at the hearthstone's edge.

The quills at my neck tingled for a stomach I'd barely noticed, now appearing impossibly round. I locked eyes with the girl's ghostly gaze, striving not to dissociate. "What a lovely family. Your daughter?"

"My wife."

My gaze shot upward at the sound of an unknown voice. Skimming further along the fireplace wall, beyond a chairless table, beyond two axes leaning against the wall, stood a figure in a dark corner. His features were impermeable to even the most middling of fire glares. I would have been fine with the latter if his shady outline hadn't been so tall.

Not four, but five people. My smile, which held more ice than a winter's tarn, rifted, and I breathed in deeply and long.

His silhouette sharpened as his shoulders drew inward, and only a shard of firelight glinting off his hair revealed that he was red-headed. "Where are your manners, Izobel? Greet our guest!"

I nearly jolted. Even a fox's sick, foamy bark would've been less unsettling.

The young girl, Izobel, reached for the upper chimney's ledge. Her whole body trembled as she gripped it. She looked heavy, and every movement was a huff, a wince, a moan as she attempted to lift.

The scent of aged iron rose to my nose. I swept through the living space and seized the girl's searching arm. "Stay where you are, seated." I watched her stare widen at a part of my cloak. I followed her gaze. Pride swelled within me to see someone so intrigued by my *treasure*, and I murmured, "Tis mine. Do you like it?"

She nodded, a vague smile haunting her lips. The smile she bore prompted my own, but it faltered as I caught her frantically blinking. My eyes narrowed to her dried, pearly lips, then to the wrist I held in my grip. It was pale and clammy. I looked further down. Blood, left to dry, clung to her ankles, creeping up into the shadows between her thighs.

My voice faltered, then firmed. "Stay just as you are." She was with child, and threat clung to both of them. Priorities blurred. I shuddered, the cloak rustling as I caved inward toward my secret, my concealed hand closing over the littlest shoulder.

"Would you be a healer? If that's so, we got no coins," the husband said. "Ya can just leave her. I 'ave another wife in waiting."

A surge of unfamiliar emotion caused my skin to rise; Marvenous and the unkindness felt it, and a storm of caws broke out above the ceiling.

"Bloody crows. We ad 'em all night." Behind the curtain, the same blanketed voice from earlier, breath broken and languid, one I decided to pay no heed to. My present time was between the girl and me. I pinched her chin, raised her stare, and weighed her in. Hazel eyes, *grounded eyes*, a gap in the middle of her front teeth peeking from her parting mouth. *Good fortune.*

A cup clanked on a surface where the girl's spouse cowered. "Took a liking to Izobel, I see? Might I be of yer fancy, too? Come closer."

I slowly turned toward the dark corner where her husband was, fighting the urge to kill him. "The cold has numbed my bones. I shall have to decline, but ay, children are what freshwater is to the trout." The fish died on my tongue, my face heating before it fell. My glance never reached where Izobel's husband stood.

It puddled in dread at the curtained room fronting the fireplace. Peeking in and out, a rocking chair rocked with a woman in her fourth decade, dark hair cascading over her bare features, her thighs draped across a man's lap, his britches at his ankles, before vanishing behind the curtain again, only to reappear as briskly. Both were utterly unbothered by my presence, and I realized my plan was as sterile as their hearts. I'd thought of killing on sight, collecting blood, and leaving unashamed. But now, nervousness latched onto my limbs, and I fought trembles. This was far from a religious sanctuary; this was hell.

Two hands clamped down on my shoulders, fingers burrowing into the fabric of my cloak, pushing aside my discomfort for another. "You'll be fine here. We'll keep you warm," the preacher said. I'd forgotten him, though his presence never ceased to prey on my back.

I spun, rid of his filthy grasp, and met him with the same excruciating smile I battled to keep. "Would you not care about my name?"

He sent his foot back, and the door slammed shut behind him. "We have all the time in the world."

My brow lifted at the absurdity. I hadn't a moment to spare, so I edged closer, the preacher's smile flattening as his nose wrinkled. His head jerked at two buzzing flies, then a tiny swarm. He waved his hand, scattering them. "Why would grace like yours reek so foul?"

"It's your offspring. Look." Finally, my child would meet her father. With a quick tug, I pulled open my cloak.

His expression shifted into a snarl. "I'd remember if I'd fucked a white-haired head like yours."

"No, no. Not me, not my person." My cloak slid from the crook of my elbow, tilting my arm as I shifted the child toward the firelight, toward him. "I don't know what color her hair will be. It's too early to tell."

He leaned in, his nostrils flaring. I mirrored his expression, wondering why.

An agonizing breath barely made it to sound. "It's…" His eyes dragged from the babe to me, his face paling as his gaze met mine. "Dead."

A fierce desire to tear into the responsible who twisted my child's fate broadened my rabid grin, and my whisper shot out. "Ay."

"Has…" He stumbled toward the entrance, where his ax rested behind the door. "Has anyone seen Marideth and Helna?!" Finally, there was a hint of distress in the air.

"Maybe one's in a clearing, feeding the wolverines," I said. Then, I realized that what I thought had been a fantasy dream wasn't one. I never really glazed over this detail until now, but honesty demanded that I faced it. "And perhaps I ate the other, a girl I encountered soon after discovering your child. Quite justified. My meal had admitted abandoning the baby to die in the cold, though she did admit the father was a bastard."

The wooden clang of a cup, followed by a slosh of spilled liquid, clamored behind me, making me focus intensely on Izobel's shadow-husband. He took two quick steps, stopping just short of his dark corner, likely because the quills had reached my face.

"And I have come to kill one…but I might as well kill you all." I had pent-up those words for so long, their release felt cataclysmic.

"Her hair is feathering…" A meek voice from behind the curtain, and I glanced toward it. The rocking chair creaked as a black-haired man sprang to his feet, the woman gasping as she fell to the floor.

My neck twitched at him. "I will kill you last."

The lecher pulled his breeches up, his arms tangling in the straps. "Wha-what?"

"Weaklings die first, but the sick…" I watched him, watched them all frozen in their stance, my gaze narrowing as it returned to the man near the rocking chair. They circled me, but little did they know they made the pecking easy. "They endure. They suffer until the very end."

The black-haired threw a worried eye at the preacher, his voice ruinous and thin. "Witch?"

"Yes, but I like to think of myself as…" My third eyelid flickered upward, a subtle shift beneath the mask of my human face, prompting a gasp from Izobel's husband. "A little more than that."

A shadow hammered down at my side, and I revolved, dodging the preacher's arm. My spit shot forward, missing his boot by an inch. The wood sizzled, and for a moment, the preacher froze, his eyes wide as though he had been burned. His skin turned pale before rage overtook him, and his gaze lit as it met mine.

I stooped, my feet tracing a slow, tight arc, ears tuned to every shift in their movements. One was too silent. Izobel's husband, the coward.

"Denrius, ring the chapel's bell! Inform the village!" The preacher's voice boomed toward the black-haired clutched at the curtain, poised like someone torn between stepping back or forth from his rocking chair.

Denrius scrambled for the door, followed by the naked woman, fingers fumbling on the iron handle before disappearing into the night.

I sneered. The preacher seemed to think that would change anything, but I knew better. The bell would not alter his fate.

I hastened to place my child into Izobel's arms, who took it without even raising an eyebrow. A faint smirk tugged at my lips; her unflinching acceptance spoke volumes about her. She was on the right side of the three goddesses.

Wood grating against wood, followed by the sharp ring of honed metal in motion. "What ya fucking want, witch?" the preacher hollered.

My cloak and spine contracted in a single, fluid motion as I spun to find an ax in the preacher's grip. "I want to make you bleed. You see, you spoiled *her* fate before her first breath. Now, I have come to restore it." As I spoke, my shadow swallowed the light. I grew, towering over them, my head curving beneath the creaking beams, my tail spreading toward Izobel's husband. His feet jittered as they brushed against it. I sensed fright. It was well.

"What is this thing?!" Izobel's husband deserved an answer for having shown a mere figment of courage.

Feathers stilled against my back, sharp as blades. Ravishment stirred, my name, pulsing through my mind into a cavernous rasp. "I am Raven of the Scrying. The Nought Before One."

The preacher's gaze darkened. "Oracio!" Izobel's husband burrowed in the corner, I presumed. "Grab a kni—"

He stood, clutching his belly, holding on to the thread of life slipping from his fists, a fumble to the left, then one to the right, reduced to gurgles and shock. In my beak hung a rope of his gut, only to be pulled further out.

Amidst the tolling of nearby bells, blood poured from the preacher's jagged crevice. The flavor was nutty, ashy, dusty—as unpleasant as the girl I found in the woods. But I tugged harder as screams ricocheted in every direction. Drat, I was frustrated. I wanted to start with his eyes.

No matter, I swiftly gauged them before the preacher, dropping to his knees, plunged headfirst into the planks.

A sharp clank echoed from Izobel's side. "Bird lady."

I turned, the gelatinous texture rolling down my throat. There, standing before me, Izobel held my child to her chest, one hand gripping a rod.

She pressed it against me. I frowned as an unexplained instinct to grapple gushed through me. My transformation flashed, feathers drifting from my fingers as I reached for the rod.

But her hand trembled, and my eyes shot up to hers. Izobel's mouth tore apart. "Behind you!"

I saw black as a force slammed into the back of my skull, sending me stumbling two steps forward. I coughed up rust, the world spinning as I fought to stay on my feet.

Izobel and the fireplace pitched, and my vision bounced against the floor with the rod.

My gasp blew as I dragged my arm up the floor. I couldn't let my mind cloud. I had to persist.

The croaks turned desperate, and the brisk scratch of beaks and wings rapped against the door.

"At the end of the day, demon, you're just another woman, weak and wishful," Oracio said.

A heavy foot hammered down my traveling hand, and I gritted my teeth, my cry locked in my throat. The distant bleat of a beast cut through the air, but Oracio's rant never wavered. "Messing around with a dead child for what?"

"For a roof? To eat us? Damn us? Well, not today." A forceful shove flipped me onto my back, and Oracio straddled me. My arms felt heavy as I clawed at him, uselessly flailing. He caught them effortlessly, pinning them beneath his knees.

"She's in there! She's in there!"

"Hear that? They're coming for you. But I won't let them rob me of the pleasure of killing you. The man you killed? He was my brother." Oracio loomed over me, his hands closing around my throat with a ruthless grip. My mind convulsed, hopelessness blighting me as I fought to shift back into my raven form.

"Can't turn into a bird?" Oracio teased, pulling a pendant from beneath his shirt and dangling it before my eyes. The black- and yellow-striped stone swayed before me, its colors flashing as he ripped it from the chain. "Lepitor. A gift from a wizard." The name *Weesard* hardly registered as he shoved the stone into my mouth, a hand over it, two digits pinched on my nose. I fought to spit it out, but a reflex seized my throat, and I swallowed. "That is but the start."

Tears welled as he fumbled with my clothes. "Now, let's move to the main dish, witch."

I fought. I scratched. I broke inside. My restless mind spiraled with the weight of all the choices I had made until now. They crashed into me, sending the pieces that defined me to shatter. Yet, no matter how Oracio's grip tightened around my throat or how much he was about to rip from me, the shards struck back because I refused to regret the one thing that had made me feel alive. *Her.* That little non-gifted. I regretted nothing.

Yet, I ached. Born a female, revered for my gender in my culture, yet reduced to a vessel in theirs. It made no difference. Cruelty persisted on both sides. My arms fell limp.

A bleat rang out, its wail stretching into the distance as the door slammed open, the invading gush disheveling his brittle red straws. Oracio's gaze snapped to the doorway, and his grip loosened, easing a breath on me.

Beneath the elk's wail, the sparse, yet timely flutter of ravens into the house, and a brisk metallic rattle. My head shifted toward it, and Izobel's feet came into view. Dangling inches from her ankles, the rod's tip mottled in pale umber and soot.

Izobel shoved the rod into the side of his neck. She gasped upon meeting resistance, and I winced at the strength no mother in labor should have to summon. Splatters shot across my face as I watched Oracio's throat throb, red oozing down his shoulder. Izobel may not have skewered him entirely, but she had opened a window of opportunity. Oracio slapped a hand at his wound, wide eyes swaying to Izobel. Closing the gap, I replaced her grip and pushed. My grin broadened as his body slumped, relieving me of his burden.

A cackle erupted from the confines of my lungs as I shoved him aside. I was alive. And soon, my child.

"Witch! Come forth!"

But it faltered as fast, cut off by a shout that came from outside. I tilted my head back against the floor, eyes wide toward the door's threshold. A gasp escaped me, the raw truth of my first real fear crashing over me as the world blurred into a field of hay forks, torches, straw hats, and miserable faces.

"Marvenous," I called, a shudder in my voice. I needed her—only she could summon the unkindness, make it listen. "Where are you?!"

I scrambled to my feet, stumbling toward the preacher, panic deep-set as I realized I'd forgotten to collect his blood. Kneeling, I shuffled beneath my cloak and pulled a small empty vial from the string at my girdle.

A hand caught my wrist. "Please. Take me with you."

I paused, the bottle's rim hovering just above the preacher's shredded wound.

Izobel was a non-gifted—my kind had sworn never to help them again after the witch hunts became a decree. And yet, the child I took was non-gifted. To deny this woman now would betray the very thing I had already done.

"Can you run?" I couldn't bring myself to look at her. I felt wrong. My question felt wrong. Yet it rang right. Blood dripped slowly into the vial as I waited for an answer I thought would come in sharp.

Izobel's voice cracked, a burst she quickly fought to clamp down, and I turned to face her. Quick gasps escaped through her clenched teeth, tears streaking down her face, dark hair clinging to her damp cheeks, falling like a shroud over my child in her arms.

I sighed as a tortured, thin grunt escaped her. "Yes."

She could barely walk.

"Take nothing. I wander light," I said, pressing the bottle deeper into the wound.

I stood, almost immediately flinching as a torch swooped near my face, evading it by a hair's breadth. Men rushed through the door, their iron prongs angry, and a bird I thought had cruelly abandoned me zipped above their heads. I grabbed Izobel, my mouth opened, and the words spilled out. "Feast, but leave the girl."

One powerful caw, and a torrent of ravens flooded the house and yard. The screams of my harassers lasted only moments, the ravens leaving nothing but a sprawling of glistening, jumbled bones.

I meandered, eyes scanning every corner until I found my hat jutting out from behind the door.

"Where were you?" I asked, settling the strew piece atop my head.

"Gone to fetch help, you blighted dolt!" she snapped, nipping at my nape as she followed me toward Izobel. *"More are coming. The road ahead burns with torches."*

The girl's shallow breath rattled as I lifted her, my grip slick with urgency. "I beg you, it isn't the coven you've gone to seek," I muttered, the girl's weight in my arms stifling any hope of a swift escape.

"We have no time for idle chatter," she hissed. *"Hurry!"*

I sped us toward the exit. "I need an escort. Now."

Her wings came beating my face as she hovered before me. *"You need nothing! Fly on your own!"*

Chapter Four

"Not for me. For a young..." the word stung my tongue, "girl with child."

Marvenous did not make us wait. A black maelstrom erupted at the heart of the room, instantly shrouding Izobel and my child. Within moments, all that remained was a mass of shadow, dragging them into the open night.

I skittered to the door, the last remnants of ravens' feathers swirling in my wake. My blood surged as I halted at the threshold. A line of flickering flames snaked around the statues of the Arden brothers. Another mob.

I ran, bare feet skidding on the rotten planks of the stairs. I lost my footing once, then twice, before my soles slapped against the wet earth.

The mob drew nearer. Cries. Slurs. Threats.

I ran, fought to shift, to become a raven.

Nothing.

Not a darn feather. The stone Oracio had forced upon me... That could only be it. The weight of it held me, bound me to those abject grounds.

I contoured a block of houses to my right, avoiding the route I'd taken earlier, now threatening with fire and murder. My pulse shook, a flash of relief breaking through as I spotted the cornfield ahead, its towering stalks once intimidating, now inviting cover.

"Other there!"

"The field. She's escaping!"

I plunged into the stalks, their bite no longer an issue. I stumbled and tripped with every step, the menacing yells behind me drying my throat.

At last, the clearing. I dashed for it.

My cloak caught in the wild grass. I stumbled, my arms betrayed me, and I collapsed wholly.

"She's ours—"

"Get her—"

A frustrated moan rushed out of me to a river of fire pouring from the cornfield, spilling thick.

Waves of horizontal thunderbolts, and my body shook, sheer chaos scalding my moves. The sound fused with the ground, hissing close to my ear as stones thrust into the surrounding earth. My body cramped, every sense screaming as magic collided with this unusual, vicious weapon.

I dared not rise. The noise felt too deadly, and my survival mattered. But then, a sudden tremor quivered through the earth beneath, and I thought the end of me.

My gaze searched upward for the origin, ears tugging at a pattering. The more it grew into heavy thuds, the less proud my breathing felt, and I finally held it back when the thrums escalated into a relentless pounding.

A colossal bull elk emerged from the forest's edge, its head a polished bone, eyes flashing red, flames flickering out of the orbits as they frayed in the gusts. Its body was a tangle of moss, bone, and vine, limbs woven with roots.

The instinct to cover my head never hit me. Instead, I watched it leap over me.

A piece of moss dislodged from its chest, a balm falling softly before me. But as tender and soothing as the moss looked, fierceness was what shone in the owner's eyes.

Hooves struck, antlers thrust forward, igniting in flames.

I watched as power surged down the field, a trail of white blossoms blooming in its path.

With incendiary force, the elk charged into the frenzied village folk, claiming what had once tried to claim me.

I blinked a few times, flies in my belly as a forbidden thought stirred. *What would it be like to be his…his do*e. A longing coiled within me, evaporating as quickly as I fixed my eyes on the paling sky.

The moon had vanished, swallowed whole by the horizon, leaving the sky to bleed into a violent purple.

And the heart in me wilted. The sun was rising. The wind dropped.

Not a sound pulsed from the trees.

Everything lifeless.

It was too late. My child would never be.

My knees buckled before my cry could break free, necromancy slipping through my fingers like swamp muck. Though I fell apart, the earth never touched me.

Feathers whispered about, enveloped my limbs, an embrace of infinite wings lifting me into the sky. Out of all the ravens, one nestled into the crook of my neck—the one I needed.

Shame washed over me as I surrendered, the breeze, motherly, stroking me in waves, pushing my tears forth when all I wished was to hold them back.

Chapter Four

Marvenous buried herself deeper. *"Stupid child. Why cling to the vessel when you possess its soul?"*

"Why cling to a day's warmth when you have night's cold?"

"The night holds many secrets. The day spits them out bare. Doubts poison a witch's heart."

"As does clinging to fleeting flesh…"

"Speaking of which, the un-gifted's health is fading. You must tend to the girl. And please, make her life last."

"I need tending as well. I swallowed a stone and cannot shift."

"The horned god… Have you—Kraa—his call? He—Kraa—you his maiden. He will help you."

I should've worried about the bizarre caws interspersed in her words.

Instead, my face warmed. "His?"

Chapter Five

The scent of belonging instantly poured into my nostrils, and I closed my eyes. Feathers left my skin, wild grass swished, and solid ground pressed against my back.

I lay like stone, wanting to be ingested by the forest meadow. A blade snapped between two of my fingers, which then strangled its brokenness. My throat gasped, waves of shuddering breaths I no longer cared to control.

My eyes ripped open to a sky smothered by pines, bloating gray and green, and bursts of water.

I was the water. A torrent of cries. Tears scrawled down my face like salted landslides. Spirits rose in a contagion of chuckles, eerie coos feeding more tears. More children's laughter, more dread.

I was the rain.

I dripped, watering down. Boldness, determination, curiosity—empty shells in a tarried ditch.

Giggles left me no respite. They bounced about the barks, emptying me.

And once everything drained, I noticed the blatant symbol of failure was missing.

I had lost myself.

My breath clawed at the air, spasms possessing me, and I would have done anything to reverse time and the winds, never to let the wails of a newborn reach my ears.

To push back sorrow demands a strong command of oneself. I only commanded tragedy. Yet, I hung onto the knowledge there was a little soul in me, and my tears ceased.

An unknown cry burst through, and a hidden flock of birds scattered two feet away. I jolted as an anarchy of cream-colored featherlets drifted over me, the ferns coughing and flattening with each bird's brief flap and hop—pheasants. *Sheck!* I was still at the fringe between wood and grassland.

Gathering my legs under me, I charged out an exhale, as though trying to slice through agony. Then wiped my face with the sleeve of my arm, blood and salt clinging to my lips, thinking I must have been a sight to behold.

Izobel. I scoured the woods for where the cry came from.

"Kaa-Kraaa."

Dressed in molten black pearl, Marvenous stood perched over the sag of a pine branch a few feet up and away. A rainbow blue glint flickered across her feathers from the first rays.

"Marvenous, why are we so close to the plains' border?" I gathered myself, each movement a painful cramp, swaying but never toppling. May the hit I took at the head be undeceitful, for my skull felt hewn in two, and the ground shifted more than it should've.

"Kaa-Kraaa."

I blew the world's misery in one breath. "Save me from your silent treatment. Where is the baby? I must bury the body, allow it to reach the Summerlands." I couldn't refer to the newborn as *her* anymore. The word had silenced itself without my will. I attempted to rise, but my mind throbbed, a fist punching at the insides of my skull. "Then I shall return to the Scrying."

The way of the Scrying. Maidens of the first crop. I spat, blood mingled, a thin thread of smoke wafting from the grass, and I dipped my chin. I grew faint, my backbone falling into a drowse.

A flower tinged with the color of midnight sky bloomed, its stem rising to support me, coaxing my posture upright. If it was him, Beltane stirred something inside me I hadn't known existed. His shyness threaded through, and something else, a certain tenderness tugging at parts I disapproved of. Not entirely.

Chapter Five

"Kaa-Kraaa."

As I leaned on petals' silk, Marvenous's cold barks struck what she failed to offer: to be comforted, to be touched, cradled, lodged in someone's arms—and I craved it all too much. Drat. Was that so?

A silent groan sounded in my throat.

I pushed myself off the giant flower and braced myself, nails scraping an itch at the sides of my shoulders. Emotions like these—such putridness, stains of greed and selfishness. Marvenous's stone-cold demeanor toward me was as justified as the consequences of my intense affliction, for I was sure an ailment had closed its grip on me.

I chased prying vines, scratching them from my face and shoulders until they folded back as if retreating from searing heat. I needed no one—no child, no Beltane, nothing.

"Kraa-Kraaa."

"A witch needs a moment, as sparse as a familiar can allow it. Allow it," I said, my voice choked, as I gathered my legs to my chest, then buried my head in the only burrow at my disposal.

Vines returned, slithering slowly out of the earth, curling over me, pausing at each of my movements as if startled at my every chest heave. But they kept going, tendrils wound around my limbs, earth-laden wisps brushing every fragment of who I was.

"Kaa-Kraaa."

I tilted my head up. "Marvenous?"

Such a black bow, Marvenous descended from the trees, her tips arcing stiffly as she swooped toward me, talons grazing the high blades before landing beside me. "Kaa-Kraaa."

My yell fell apart. "Speak!"

A coil of roots tightened around my chin, forcing it upward, and my gaze stretched beyond what my left side would allow. The pressure on my neck made me twist to see what lay behind me.

Izobel sat leaning against a trunk, her breath hollowed and ruined, like mine. My chil—the small body lay beside her, as still and lifeless as any other ordinary bindle, and nausea swamped over me.

"Kaa-Kraaa." I took full cognizance of the urgency as a spread of ravens anchored on the small prairie. These spattered at me, while a frenzied Marvenous hopped back and forth from me to Izabel.

She kept screeching at me, and…my hair stood on end. I could no longer understand her.

To realize that loneliness doesn't arise from physical proximity, but from the fear of being lost with no one to understand, I was suddenly the loneliest creature in the Emeralds.

My voice sank. "Marvenous. Something is not quite right, isn't it?"

My familiar sprang into my lap, her head twisting between the dirt-gray strands that draped over my bowed face. "Kaa-Kraaa." She pecked at the region of my dress covering my stomach, over and over, then clamped her beak on my fingers, guiding them toward my mouth.

"I am not hungry enough to eat my own fingers."

In a flash, she took off, only to return almost instantly, dropping a stone in my lap.

"One stone is enough. I dread what it will do to my digestion."

Again, she returned with a stone. Five times, she repeated the cycle, each stone growing larger until she began dropping them on my head. Despite it all, I was strangely relieved to see we hadn't lost the balance of our healthy relationship.

Trading stones for my head, she perched on it, her upside-down gaze lowering over my eyes. With a violent snap of her beak, the most ear-splitting croak rang out, drying my eyes. Then, as if to punctuate her fury, her feral little head bopped down, pecking fiercely at my lips.

Marvenous left, but I braced myself as she returned, her wings splashing against my face as she flitted on the spot. Her beak cut through my lips, and the harsh taste of slate coated my tongue, along with a pebble.

I spat it out and shooed her away, my breath frazzled. "What is it? I don't understand you!" The gush picked, but it felt strange. Strands moored about my eyelashes. Dark ash. My hair had always been whiter than bone.

I suddenly understood. It was the stone I had swallowed. Like poison, it ate away at my seventh sense, the fulcrum of my soul, and how it spoke through enchantment. My powers, still in their infancy, were like teeth, an extension of me that couldn't be removed. Yet this stone, like a clamp, was pulling at every holy fang.

A hand on the grass, my face to the ground, I stuck my finger down my throat, hoping to dislodge the stone. Dramatic thoughts swirled about purging the stone, unsure if it still loitered in the food pouch of my belly or had moved elsewhere.

I crouched, gagging, saliva dripping from the sides of my chin. My throat burned, expelling acid mixed with the undigested flesh and gut.

No sign of a stone.

Chapter Five

I pressed my finger deeper, my nails scraping.

A lump shot out, falling mute and slimy in a bed of red and white. I rose it to the sun, wondering how such a small stone could outsmart a witch. The word 'weesard' flashed through my mind. *What is a weesard? A demon?* Would the non-gifted tame a power I was unaware of? Harness something beyond the grasp of witches?

I tilted toward my familiar and opened my palm. "Marvenous, keep this safe somewhere but far from me. Drop it in an abandoned nest and remember the location."

She croaked, and before I could react, another raven swooped down and snatched the stone.

I smiled when she perched on my shoulder. *"Never have I seen a witch slower than you."* She preened my hair, and I petted her back, resisting the urge to squeeze her.

"Marvenous, forgive me for thinking I could outrun fate."

"You still can. Bokkerdym men are sifting through the woods, searching for you. You must hurry. The young girl needs your skilled hands!"

My eyes warred with Izobel, a broken stare, void of anger, yet as shattered as mine.

Hesitation—my rage entwined with the mother wind, gusts slammed against my back, driving my hands into the slick ground, which slid toward the non-gifted girl. I was still ridden with grief, but nature remained deaf to it. I bitterly accepted the necessity of such, for if it conceded, it could no longer prove itself cruel. Yet, I wondered if it wasn't my reaction altogether that was proving heartless.

I crawled. "Izobel."

Nothing of her moved aside from her blinking and her chapped lips. Placing my hands over her belly, I waited for movement. My eyebrows furrowed at how hard it was. I shoved closer, my ear against it.

To truth as ordained as seasons come and go, I leaned back with neither pinched lips nor gaping ones. Izobel breathed fear, so I could show none. Her heartbeat needed to steady, and quickly. My hand searched for the contact of her skin, then froze mid-air—a habit. "It will hurt. It always does. But pain strengthens. Do not fear."

Izobel nodded. I assumed she must have gone through a living hell to have placed her trust so quickly in a witch she knew nothing about. Pain and suffering were no strangers to her; she had been schooled in it.

Without lifting my gaze from what had to be removed, I asked the ravens, "The thinnest needle. The warmest blanket. The freshest water. Find a woman's gown and cloak." I needed an element that would cleanse, heat, and heal. "Wait. Bring me dried sticks, moss, two flint rocks, and the strongest thread—make it thin."

Izobel winced. "What are you going to do to me?"

"I shall remove what makes you ache."

Izobel released a freeing breath I partly understood, then fully grasped as I shoved my grief aside. She must have hurt all her life, for she never held control over her body—only the men did.

Twigs dropped beside me; two pieces of flint, moss. Once hastily gathered into a heap just inches away, I hit the stones together under Izobel's strained moans. The friction sparked, and the fire breathed to life. I trusted the ravens would finish their tasks on time. And so the fabric of her dress tore beneath my forcing grip, serving as gauze for what was about to flow out the ragged tear.

The ground rumbled beneath my thighs, the earth caving in a few inches from me as if something had pierced it from below.

Water welled up and gleamed the color of the purest void.

Beltane was more than curious; he wanted to play his part.

I touched the grass with a fragile smile and whispered, "Thank you."

My motion stiffened, buttercups thriving between my fingers. An unfamiliar heat rose within, and surely, it couldn't come from me, so I turned toward my brittle fire, barely strong enough to withstand a sigh.

The croaks came, welcomed, pulling me from the maze of confusion Beltane had planted. Above, black blotches coalesced until talons anchored near my feet: amongst a few black feathers, a measle's dried intestines, and a bone fragment—all new additions to my stockpile.

It was time.

I stroked the flames with a fragmented finger bone, its provenance irrelevant, then helped Izobel settle onto her back. As delicately as bark wraps a birch, I pressed her feet to the ground, ensuring her thighs splayed just enough. I needed to check that the baby hadn't moved down. I exhaled in relief when I found it hadn't. Had it been, I would've lost both.

Stygma slid out quietly from my thigh strap, the metallic hiss wanted muffled as I kept the dagger out of Izobel's sight. With a soft grip on the handle, I inched between her legs and firmed a hand on her chest. "Simply breathe."

She nodded as roots bound her wrists and ankles to the ground. She did not protest; instead, she remained calm as though she, too, were a witch. None of what she saw seemed to faze her, and I believed she had enough presence of mind to get through this. "Izobel. All shall be well."

Chapter Six

Two corpses lay beneath a pine three trees away, the ravens perched, watchful eyes prying on the daring scavenger. Be it my mind or my body, one had been too weary to dig graves. I would do so tomorrow. Tomorrow made sense. Tomorrow would bring a new day, a new beginning.

All was well.

I pulled my cloak over Izobel's shoulder, trading my own for one silent, sleeping blanket made of birds.

All was well.

My chest wrung from a fist of guilt, the child's death tearing through me once more. I winced. The attempt to save it haunted me still, no matter how hard I fought the memory.

Izobel's hips had been unfit for labor, a detail that had never been one. The child had suffered from the moment of its conception, fragments of its skull missing. Its heartbeat had ceased when I sectioned the umbilical cord. There was nothing to be done.

By the Crone, one ought to believe me; I had proceeded with care, my stitching as thin as a stone fissure. The lilies of the valley, more curative than deadly, had steadied Izobel's erratic heartbeats. I had done everything I could.

But as I curled around the non-gifted, whom I felt safe calling a friend, doubt crept in, with it, my intrusion into the village, tossing guilt in all corners of my mind. I miscalculated; I should have let the ravens handle these men, but I thought myself righteous and carnage justified.

The finality of it left me bereft of even a speck of motivation. My lips gave up a sigh as I turned onto my side, faint beak clicks protesting as I moved, Izobel's sporadic breath frightening my skin. But she breathed, and that was all that mattered.

Marvenous took shelter in the crook of my neck. *"When are we leaving? We must go up north. We will die here."* Her purr betrayed her. Marvenous was as depleted as I, and in ordinary times, a croak would signal her pressing. But I had learned that both beasts and men speak not what they must, but what they desire. She was a liar. And I swallowed her words, only to spew them back, for I wasn't like her. Not entirely. The overall of what made our relationship beautifully antagonistic. I appreciated that. It was raw.

"No one is coming, Marvenous. And if that were true, let us die. I am worn."

"Brainless aphid! They might not be moving in our direction, but they're still siphoning every trail."

Fatigue overwhelmed, the ache of my bruises dulling, thoughts collapsing—one chance to bloom, only to be torn asunder.

Sleep swept in and smothered me, and, blessed be the limits of my body, I relinquished.

Senseless dreams pulled me in and out. I kept waking, my anxiety unwilling to sober. But never strong enough to spare with my physical exertion.

Vegetal hisses.
Slithering.
"Wind—"
A growl. Dragging, denser than the one of a wolf.
"Skin."

I sprang up to my waist, my blanket of croaks and chaos darting moonward.

"Beltane!" Marvenous shrieked before her wings shot open, a giant fist of pine needles burling over us.

Her wings beat, her beak snapped. She fought to stay, but the brown swarm divided into five fingers, a veritable hand, parting at her attacks to then thrust onward. Marvenous squawked as her eyes met mine, both of us understanding she had no choice but to leave.

Croaks turned distant, and needles dropped lifelessly. I twisted and turned, as beneath me the ground shuddered. Behind my tense toes, a mass of thorns spun, arching over my head into a frustrating, tangled green yet immense cage; a thousand fireflies, giving off a warm glow.

Now the only light.

My fingers caught in the thicket of trampled grass as I crawled backward. The ravens hadn't even picked up the sorcery until too late. Someone had torn me from Izobel. Someone had dragged me. Somewhere.

"I...found." The thrumming etched into an articulate tone. It was neither beast nor man, but *other*. "You."

A dream? I drew Stygma for a bite of blade over my palm and cursed at myself, for blood and pain grimed my reality with acute precision.

"Wind-skin."

Again, the tortured whisper, and I gasped, my eyes wide as I saw them—*the newborns*—two small outlines, mistaken for somber burrows.

Shock struck as roots crept over their swaddles of fortune, harassing every ragged inch of Izobel's reused and torn dress.

I scrambled forth, my hands reaching, scratching, tearing apart the woods that had turned on me. I could not—*would not!*—lose them. Hysteria carried me as every vine weeded out, three more slithered to take its place.

"No!" I had laid sight upon the rare. The ancient comet a scar upon the sky. The mountain, weeping scorching blood, the great auroras of the northern wastelands. A sister's last whisper, gaze, breath. And in my arms, I had held a newborn, blessed be me, two.

But I had laid eyes upon the rare, now threatened to be swallowed into the earth's belly. I had brooded over what I could offer: a proper burial, to honor them, thank them for the knowledge they imparted through the preacher and Oracio—the truth about witches, not as demons to be burned, but as women, used as vessels for their filthy seed.

Or perhaps, I had laid sight upon the rare, and I valued it as much as the Mother with her infant night threatened by an eclipse, her blood moon taking in the burns for as long as she can. In my case, holding the newborns.

One last time.

A wisp of rose bush lashed at my hand in reprimand. I caught it, the prick of thorns cutting into my skin, and wrenched it free.

More sprigs, sharp tendrils scraping across my arms, while white sap dripped down my face from the roots I had bent. My feet kicked air as they lifted me, winding around my ankles, entwining at my waist, wrists, neck.

Desperation shot out of me. "I am not ready!"

"Trea-sures must be bur-ied." Those molten words, an inexplicable furnace for me. Tears threatened. An envy to be embraced, outrageous, tolling my bones. The discrepancy between my sentiments clashed like two opposite waves. I disgusted myself.

I shoved down the feeling, coaxed by wreaths weaving over the small heads, buttercups blooming, turning, curling like drops falling upward.

My breath held. Crowns—*two little moonlings of the woods*—and a chill ran through me. I needed time. Time to bid my farewells. Time to call upon the three goddesses to take them—carry them, to safer shores, to the Summerlands where the shadows turned to light and cast upon the Veil. An imperative.

"Beltane. God of the First. Enlight a dark creature. It seeks your motives and their values." My voice pushed sorry. The nightmare unfolding had already turned me to dust.

The voice shifted. Guttural. "Wha-t one takes. One must give ba-ck. As all things must re-turn to the earth."

My chin quivered. "Is it because of the lilies of the valley?! I have a stone I am certain will be of your liking. Don't take them, not now." I grew desperate, even more so to Marvenous' muted croaks emanating from behind the thorny tangles.

I wrestled as fronds spun around the corpses. "Stop! *Stop it!*"

But Beltane did not listen.

He was cruel. With slow diligence, he maintained my suffering, the two childlings disappearing, swallowed into the belly of earth.

Forever sealed.

My head hung low. I thought about dying altogether, and I would beg him to kill me if I had the boldness.

The forest grumbled, quakes vibrating through my soul, and I watched aghast, two saplings shooting up from the ground, fanning proudly. Leaves unfurled like those of nascent butterflies. Buds prospered, studding the length of every branch with golden fruits. Apples. *Symbol of immortality. Symbol of youth.*

Chapter Six

I could not move, wouldn't. The respect Beltane displayed baffled me, a burial no witch could never hope for.

The trees, stouter, grew and breached Beltane's cage, which parted for their tops, then closed around them to let nothing else pass...

When their trunks merged into one, the world hushed. My lips pressed, and so did my eyes. Beltane had done what, deep down, I knew I could never. I would have carried their rot until my death, unable to let go.

But he had also robbed me of the moment to hold them one last time. *Had I known...* I would've coiled around them, constricted every muscle, not let the night see them, not even air pass. I would have kissed them, dug my nails into their little bones, held onto them like a fever, as a good mother would have done. As a mother should have done.

No tears fell. I forbade it, undeserving of any outlet. My wretchedness could drown its vessel.

The whole of me fell limp, my nape bowing, secretly wishing for a raptor to nip it. I just wanted to hold them. Look at them. At *her*. Just one last time.

The whisper thickened; a warning before the pounce, but I gave no heed. "Nought Be-fore One."

A firming shoot forced my head up, and the night opened its eyes, two savage almonds, iris-flames dancing in the dark.

"Rav-en."

A languid moan of despair rushed out of me, but a vinelet coiled over my cheek, barely grazing, and I wondered if Beltane feared breaking me.

The voice crisped. Singular. "Wind-skin..."

Twin fires blazed before blinking, their glow magnifying a coil of horns that framed a figure's head surfacing from the black of the bushes. I thought of him bragging with his stellar apparition, while still pondering his obsession with me.

"Moon–drop." Now the sound came from the throat of a man. "Fea–ther–light."

I watched a fox-masked creature hatching from the wall of vegetation, as if born from it. Dishonest would I have been to say I did not hold my breath. But at the same time, I wasn't surprised. Every witch knew the god was shy.

Yet somehow, Beltane drew closer, flowers unfurling at the edges of every dragged hoof. He carried himself not as a conqueror, but as a mourner. His defeatist head slant had his gaze invariably meeting the tangent of his brows—strips of lichen spread over the fox fur like outstretched wings.

He looked beaten.

A fragility that gave life to my hope.

I scuffled with my bonds. Groaned, lambasted by the tightening of the vines.

Spent, my harsh breath sent my strands flying from my face, and I saw what swayed in the breeze: long charcoal-blue hair, the color of night itself, trussed by a more vivid shade. If only those silken strands could've concealed what hung beneath his hips.

My eyes rounded.

Perhaps in shock, to an accidental glimpse at what an experienced person would indeed have found satisfying from a suitor. But I was not experienced. I yanked my gaze to one side. Unbidden tingles spread throughout me, Beltane's aura perverting my shivers. I expected fear, but even that coiled warm inside me.

The grass quieted as he halted a few feet from me. I had many questions, but the scorching ash in his gaze consumed them all. He tilted his head, red fox ears sharp against the dark green, and reached for my face. His hand moved unhurriedly into my vision, its skin betraying the ichor of which Beltane was made—an amalgam of flesh giving way to bone, wood, then stone, ending in nails of rock-solid amber. These stretched out and stopped a thread from my eyes. I kept them open.

Beltane held me captive in ways too many to count, and my chances of escaping him amounted to none.

Even divine intervention would not save me, for no mortal could behold the bodily appearance of a deity without death following. Beltane was a god, and I had seen him. It didn't matter whether my mind blurred between fascination and anguish; the truth remained—I was staring death in the face.

His form solidified as he leaned in, his hand hovering just above my skin without contact, our lips a mere flutter from each other, and I suspected I was but a touch from my demise.

A possibility I accepted. My *death* was exquisite. The Scrying would have surely guffawed, reeled, or gasped at my resilience. But worse than surrendering, *sheck, damn poorer,* was the warmth creeping up my thighs.

This uncalled reaction froze me, apprehension paired with a longing I knew not if it was for death or something else.

"Not a bird can en-ter this place. Do you like it?"

I would have berated the god, but the innocence in his voice confused me—I even softened at it. "Birds never liked cages."

A slab of pliable wood and leather pressed against my body, and my lungs burned from the taste of his breath. Slate, petrichor, and something sweet, intoxicatingly too close to my lips. They quivered. Beltane was obviously blind to intimacy, as was I, a stranger.

"But they'll fly away if I o-pen the…cage." His last word came out dry.

I straightened my head, locking my gaze on him. "By all the wild you embody, I know you hate cages! Why do you harass me?"

The said cage of green groaned.

"Sor-row. Pain. Hope-less-ness." Behind the kind silks of his lips, wolf's fangs adorned his gums, and I bit my tongue. Ravens and wolves were like snow and rain; I could not measure up to him.

"De-votion's affli-ction."

"What would a heartless god know about it when he steals a witch's offspring?!" I waited for punishment, my gaze fixed on the fox's mask, most of all keeping watch on the flames dancing in his irises.

Beltane swayed his head to one side, casting a contemplating glance over a moss-laden shoulder, before his eyes returned, snarked and flared. "A wit-ch's?"

Dissecting speech. I didn't need or want to. "Tell me!"

The flames in his eyes weakened at his almost imperceptible whisper. "At ev-ery dis-ease gripp-ing the moose… The brare-bull's snare… And the ooz-ing from its se-vered horn… The blood… of the bear-er."

My face tilted askance. "The blood of the bearer?"

"Through-out *her* life, *she* will have spilled more blood than the sum of what a hunt-ing party carries with-in their veins. And I suffer for the tro-phy always matt-ers. Never the sa-cri-fice."

"You suffer? Cowering behind those pitiful leaves, spying on young witches?" My chest locked with what rushed out of me. I expected a swift neck break from the vine rippling up my nape, but I felt cradled instead.

"The three godd-esses' servant, the fruit tender, the war-den… I am but the Emer-ald's gard-ener, cursed. Each time, an in-sufferable struggle to see all the flowers bloom be-cause I know I'll have to watch them die."

A frown of reluctant empathy crossed my face as the mask's snout slanted down. Boned, teeth jutting out, the fox's pelt might have snugged his face, but it failed to conceal the lower part. Beneath the fangs' shadow, a straight nose, broad nostrils flaring as if he forbade himself the unforgivable. I maddened, the envy spilling at the edge of whatever power he wielded on me.

"But late-ly…" As suddenly as the wind, Beltane shifted his expression altogether, switching unstable apathy for something entirely different. He locked his hysterical eyes with mine, flashing parching blue. "Only quel-ling when I am close to you. And I know you as mine and I as yours will re-vive me."

My stomach sank from a sudden reckoning. Beltane was too *man*.

Too near.

Too promising.

Too treacherous.

Of all the things I had knowledge of, *I* was the least of things. Because when Beltane's nails grazed at my lips and an odious mewl rushed out of me, only then did I learn how unprepared I was to *succumb*. "God of Old, I am not your follower. I am not your maiden. I am not one to be *claimed*." My lips trembled, dignity decayed. "I will hex you!"

Beltane's torso swelled, pectoral strings apparent, and I inwardly braced for his retribution.

Instead, a tide of green whisked me into his arms.

"Wind-skin." The horned fox loomed over me, its human smile breaking knowingly, as ten claws secured my thighs and shoulders. "You al-ready have."

Flushed wasn't enough of a notion for the firestorm he set in me. And my reason, a stranded snail on a rock, cooked.

So I breathed; enough to keep a semblance of body function.

This time, I didn't fight my way out because I reckoned gods don't fight mortals; they play games with them, and the entire woods knew who had lost. I didn't mind. I was far too curious about the loser's fate. I. Was. Raven.

The dome of lush green did not recede to let in the night sky. Instead, the grass, vines, and roots distorted and spun, evolving into a living corridor that expanded with each step Beltane took. As he held me in his arms, heartbeats, two distinct ones—my buried one, and another, glistening crimson and wreathed, interlaced with vines and tiny white buds, pulsing behind a wooden ribcage. They struck together in perfect time, and I couldn't tell them apart. I had more exhaustion in me than a dying river, barely clinging to its thin trickle.

My eyes searched for the unnoticed and my ears tuned to the void left between two sounds, begging for an omen. But the forest remained stubbornly silent.

I could do nothing but let grief upend me into the creature I had always been.

And the witch strengthened.

The hooves led. The unknown unraveled.

But whether a god claimed, that was still up to me.

Chapter Seven

Twilight's dew edged squamous across my eyebrows and arms. It pearled about the hair, smaller than grain, before settling coolly upon my skin as oblivion chased me from its kingdom.

Pieces of what I last remembered assembled wrongly: Beltane. His inexorable march. The trees, my eyes fighting to stay open as a forest god cradled me, and a hoard of words...

"Surely, there must be other reasons than just finding sorrow within another?" I had asked Beltane, prepared to be ignored. Gods never spoke second to mortals.

A pause stretched longer than ten strides. By then, I believed our unborn conversation had ended until a husky voice broke the silence. *"Trees grow with wa-ter, but a for-est thrives with the win-d."*

"Why did you choose me? Gods and mortals do not belong."

By then, my eyelids had already closed, his last words following me in the dark. *"We were nev-er chosen. We were al-ways meant."*

My ear twitched first. The jarring sigh of a cascade trickled listlessly; it mirrored my disheartened soul, so terribly acceptable for a witch of the Scrying that a dissenting grunt seethed my throat. *I am not like them.* But I couldn't avoid thinking that the Bokkerdym village had been the pivot of Dakanesh's teachings combined with Nosferus' words, a lesson I presently deemed of unimaginable worth, one I would ensure fills the emptiness where my heart once was. Adding to this, a vow: forever renounce motherhood. My nostrils expanded at the conclusion, and crystalline air and leaf decay rushed in. That encompassed the totality of my environmental awareness. And it suited me well. I didn't want to wake up. The darkness was safer than facing yet another disappointing *unknown* lingering beyond my closed lids. I was through with it.

I had to go home.

If Beltane wished it so.

Some of me dreaded the Scrying, a liberating realization akin to a bird escaping its cage. I had flown perhaps too high, but I had flown far…

A wave of sickly floral sweetness rose from the depths as though the earth sensed my unease. It bound my turmoil in such an intoxicating embrace that my eyes snapped open.

Green glows speckled the scene, clinging to the rocks, roots, and trees—bitter oysters surrounded a brook flowing seamlessly into a chasm of stars. I lay on a bed of surprisingly soft, dry moss, with comforting warmth at my back. I dared not move as two hooves jutted above my line of sight, antlers following long. An elk was curled around me.

From the rhythmic push of its chest and the fragile chuff of its barely groaning nostrils, it was asleep. I sat, legs folded, a smile unseaming my lips. *A snoring elk.*

Beltane's neck, mahogany, taut even at rest. A primal detail witches chanted. Hooves heavy with gold robbed the stars' light… I closed my eyes at what I dared chew over. Only to open them to antlers, strips of frail mineral, silver, and bronze entrenched in length. Their fragments struck me, as bright as the water splashing behind me, and I felt it more. The heat. The hunger. A thirst so palpable it seemed to burn. *Theck…* I needed water.

Then to fly. It would be easy, so very easy. The roots may cling, but they cannot follow. Again, fear wasn't there, and my priorities unfolded with outstanding clarity. *What is terror when the god sleeps, and the wings stir? Naught.* A cackle hissed, mute, from the treacherous within. But it quieted just as quickly. I still needed water, and I still mulled over my puzzling countenance toward Beltane.

Gingerly, I rose, a straggling sensation clutching at me as I glanced downward, the lower hem of my dress ensnared by the weight of the

Chapter Seven

beast. I considered *forcing* myself to stay, but a feral *no* slammed into my mind.

I tugged, freeing it, and walked toward the brook.

Toes dipped, ripples spreading in crisp circles. I unbuckled my girdle, and my waist swelled; freed skin tingled, as charged as the storm gathering in my chest. *Never again*. I hurled the belt into the ferns, which hissed in complaint, then yanked my garment up.

My blood gasped—a cognitive enlightenment, tempted to say rare lately. The dress sank back, edges sodden, as my feet jostled with the wet shingles. The fact was, I had company. No matter creatures roving in the woods, the elk over there wasn't one entirely.

I crouched and spun on my heels, grass weeping beneath me. *What if he catches me naked?* The idea of it felt like a half-formed claw around a fawning throat, as uncomfortable as the word *half* appeared in my mind. Poised like a skulking badger, puzzling excitement and unease sent my chest as I shed my stained, tattered dress. My eyes never left him—his resting lithe ears, antlers tangled and balanced toward me, while I lifted one foot after the other from my emptied rag, more unhurried than growing moss.

I would admit it. I was the lurker, and the elk wasn't even dead.

Dehydration, that was what it was. My mind was clouded.

I waddled until the waterline licked at my collarbones, cupped my hand and scooped up some river to my mouth. Soothing and fresh, the liquid trickled down my throat, and as I mused over the glowing bitter oysters, a genuine breath escaped my lips. This place *wasn't* a green cage, but a sanctuary.

I could fly. I should take off right now before the god awakens—a rational thought, after Beltane had forced me into this place. But as I neared the unguarded edge, the night air greeting the fang beneath my smirk, he would now have to wrestle me from it. A cascade tumbled from the plateau above, and the brook I was in spilled over a steep slope of trees and slate. I edged the night; the currents were kind yet pulling, and I held onto a rock.

But what charged in my eyes was gouging. My breath hitched, and I clutched the stone.

Men had ravaged the forest for land, destroying it. My face creased, a legion of goosebumps spreading throughout as the expected green dissolved into turned earth and farms. I had assumed Bokkerdym to be the only threat of the Emeralds, but as my gaze widened at what warned in the far-off horizon, I realized how gravely mistaken I was. Trust in my soul, the distance between me and vile was close. Two hundred leagues from the dying edge of the forest stood a castle. Though I had not seen it, I knew it was the citadel of Delos. Its spires, broken fangs of onyx, tore the night as if thrust from hell's jaws.

I needed grounding, to lean my face into the breeze, to seek reassurance. Strands of white pulled toward Delos, and for a heartbeat, I felt like I was being *drafted*. But it then shifted, hair flurried, and I stilled to *nought, to who I was*. I chinned down. In the water, the ghostly quarter of the moon marking where I stood in time—marking where I stood with myself.

The Mother was gone, and with her, a piece of me. For a witch's sake, I fought to let go, but somehow refused to.

And I prayed, broken whispers I hoped the wind would carry up to the Three Goddesses.

> ***"Life, stale, everything is and remains as.***
> ***A wasteland I taste, feel, see, for men tamed it without mercy.***
> ***I am but breath and feather where nothing must grow.***
> ***Goddesses have pity.***
> ***If I could just become in the eyes of mine.***
> ***Hold purpose and kiss its newborn skin.***
> ***Let a child bless my fate.***
> ***It's all I ask.***
> ***Without witches,***
> ***Without chains.***
> ***Without men.***
> ***Take my bones, my soul, and magic***
> ***For the price of a child.***
> ***It's all I ask."***

"I will ful-fil your wish."

Water barely shook as I steeled, horrified at what someone *had caught* from my flimsy whining. A mass of black dripping hair breached the pale reflection of the moon—Beltane, horns aglint, the fox's mask wrapped around his eyes, incredibly alive. "Bir-d…" The mist swelled, tiny bolts forking around his horns, wrapping around him like a possessive demon. "God-dess."

I stumbled backward as vines rose, dripping tendrils snaking closer. My voice was not proud. "What I wish is out of reach. From you. Undeniably from me."

The roots trailed over my shoulders and locked behind the small of my back. "Noth-ing is ever out of my reach, Wind-skin." His gaze deepened, the fire in them curdling deep red, almost dark, yet the slight slant of his eyes removed any trace of wrong intentions. It mirrored an aching hunger, a wistful kind, as if he too held by a thin thread of hope. I'd scarcely ever been so understood in my whole life. Blessed be Orakle and Marvenous, no matter how they tried.

A brusque spray of droplets slathered my eyes.

One blink, and he was before me; the next, I was in his arms, his *ambergrised* breath fanning over my face as he observed me with the diligence of a scrutinizing snake. In return, I concentrated on the wildfires in his gaze, so intense that mist erupted between us.

"I have wai-ted." My skin bastardized, rogue featherlets shedding at the birth of my temples at his voice, trailing grit similar to what layered his bones, a most appealing trait for a scavenger like me. "A thous-and moons for you." A fissure split my mind. No one had ever spoken to me this way. With Beltane, I was collecting *firsts*, more than I ever had in my life.

I should've been writhing in his embrace, spitting my acid ire at him, extinguishing his eyes, making him stagger in blindness. But I lacked the time, barely *pity*. He'd apparently lost his mind, consumed by grief I couldn't help but think reflected my own. But I wouldn't *waste* the time on this, either. I wanted him to grant me my wish.

Though odd, if alternatives had been available, I would have still chosen his, and his alone, as incomprehensible as it was, as raw and intense as I felt when I looked at him, and as wholesomely unnerving when his eyes searched for me.

Yes, pitiful.

"I'll share my knowledge, one you held, for we were once each other's pu-pils. "

I had no memory of whatever he was implying. And as if a mere glance or the touch of skin against mine had erased all traces of sorrow, I saw his true nature emerge: brash, impulsive, the smirk, evil and depraved, the god, taunting. He was a changeling in every aspect of his being, his mood no exception.

A row of sizzling cracks like small thunder strikes echoed around his shoulders, and his arms firmed against me. My throat dried. Any woman would scream at the storm building behind him; any witch would present a dead rabbit as an offering, bowing before him.

I did nothing.

My mind blanked, and only reflexes moved my body. Beltane's growl rippled through, and I held onto the raw muscle strings and bone of his neck, my head pressing into his chest as he pushed against me with terrifying speed.

My ankles hit the bank, and I fell backward, a controlled fall from Beltane as he followed me down.

Drops streamed down taut muscles, seeping into the moss of a pectoral, pooling at the sharp bone of an exposed rib. They fell, heavy and cold, down slabs of stone, a curtain of hair spilling over my chest like nightfall.

I dared not move a toe. Beltane's arms and thighs caged me. His head dipped, lips halting an inch from mine. "A con-tract. A seal. A pro-mise to give you what you desire."

My cheeks heated. *That is too close*, I thought, but my hands remained locked around his neck, a reckoning too late to gasp at, so I left them.

"What are the terms?" There was no need to ponder on that. But I did.

"Your heart in return for *life in you*."

"It is yours."

The mention of my heart, and he wanted it. A spark, a blossom, a fragment of moon in the hands of fate; I became everything at once.

A vine teased the edge of my mouth, which I opened with trust. A strange pressure left me as it curled beyond my throat, twisting inward as it removed a pound of myself I could no longer carry.

The wisp retracted, heat grazing my front teeth. In its coil, the orb I'd ingested. It beamed, an almost blinding glow of blue as it hovered toward Beltane.

Realization struck: the god hadn't scolded me the first time; he had been wanting to retrieve the soul I had stolen. Why he changed his mind mid-course? I would not know.

But I would not ask, either.

The vine slackened, the speck floating out into Beltane's palm. "I mis-took you for stea-ling it, but I'm con-vinced now it has always be-longed to you."

Chapter Seven

His hand closed over the orb, and his other reached out, fingers elongating into gnarly roots. They crawled up my temples, and I felt myself veined into him.

My pulse, a flash flood, swept everything down my core, building up at a pace I utterly judged dangerous. I knew next to nothing; fear scythed into my limbs, but my heart and the heat building beyond said otherwise.

Beltane dived against the crook of my neck, and the sweetest of deaths unfurled within. Up and down my ear, each tender racking of his lips pulling me deeper toward my end. My inexperience had hidden such forbidden desires; I shattered a little more, each piece of me fragmenting into Beltane's mystic abyss.

"Wind-skin..." His groan stretched, rising as his teeth rasped over my flesh. My bones could've splintered at it. "When the men you call un-gifted settled in the west and the south. When the tim-ber fell, and the trees bled, a white ra-ven was struck with an arrow."

I held my breath as his mouth chased my jawline. His wording, a birdsong for the witch, grimmed my cantering heart, which only picked up faster, and I listened close.

"How I experienced ev-ery creature's death when you dropped from the sky."

I could not stir away from his gaze, beyond the flames, irises the color of embers, normal ones a man bears.

"Daught-er of wind and the last breath. Pa-tron of crows, mai-dens and young-lings."

The pith of my voice emerged from the vocal string of a dying corpse. "Am I?"

He smiled against my flesh. Then a kiss. A deliberate one.

I tumbled as if falling from a cliff. *My first kiss.*

"You shall realize who you are. But first, let us bond..." Murmurs of a god pressed on other kisses. I gave a shuddering sound to each of them, and he caught it with his lips every time. "As se-cond time has gran-ted me."

His unfounded certainty fed my wish. There was no reason for battles. Nothing pulling me away from him. Everything to lie about. I was there, complete, with no apparent purpose except to return to *Orakle*. Nothing was urgent.

Except the tension. The pull. The need.

Tendrils erupted from the thickets, winding slowly around my legs.

Their thorns scraped deep, drawing blood in thin, burning lines. But these did not force my thighs to spread. I widened them myself.

Beltane's face darkened, the very shadows of the forest seeping into his skin. "Do not run now."

"I won't," I said, my breath catching as his came ever increasingly slower. I sensed it building over my stare, fixed on the filaments of lightning crackling at the edge of his lips.

With furious slowness, his body slid down, fur and stone meeting my curves.

A frail cry shot out of me, Beltane bursting into thousands of glow flies before reassembling again. His only response to this was a chuckling huff. His reputation fell short on him. He wasn't shy. He was restive.

I instinctively secured his horns in my grips. It wasn't an act of control—no, it was the only thing stopping me from unraveling completely. And maybe I didn't want him to *swarm* off after all.

Truth surged forward. "Let it be known, I am a virgin." I could have simply said no and protected my virtue, but none made it to my narrative, instead a vomit of words. "I am a witch. From the Scrying. Not *Wind-skin*. A witch as unseasoned as the first spring."

At that instant, Beltane tucked his head and shook it once, and another kind of fright invaded me as he shifted even slightly.

I tugged on his coiled bones. "Remember your promise."

My small, telling movement drew his untamed features forward, the snout of the fox a near rasp over my nose. "I give myself to you," I whispered, fearing now that he would leave after what I said. Even gathered another shame laden breath. "Stay."

His growl contained a hint of laughter. "I am but with you. And you are but with me. Where we both be-long."

He then brought his hand forward, glowing blue as the soul levitated in his palm, and gave me a cocky inclination of his head. "Nothing hurts more than hindered de-sire, and my pain is excru-ciating, Wind-skin." I did not know yet how he would take my heart, but I couldn't fathom someone as infatuated as I—he was that he would be capable of ripping it from my chest.

He raised the soul to his mouth, and my jaw clenched.

He. Ingested. It.

The glowing soul descended, its spark spearing along the strips of

Chapter Seven

his root-entwined neck down to his torso. Behind his rib cage, a green veil, just as vibrant, flowed across the sprite. Bleakness washed over me.

His face dipped inches from mine as he caught my horrified gaze. "Some of me is re-quired."

Very well.

Beltane's mouth found the dip of my collarbone, a languid trail between my breasts. I bit down a gasp upon the capture of my nipple, enduring the heat, the irresistible, the rogue tongue as dark magic swiveled around my tip. I couldn't imagine needing any other tool from him at that moment.

The lack of air left me turning red until he stopped, but even as I exhaled again, I found little comfort. His lips brushed past my navel, fleeting kisses leaving a stream of black petals in their wake. Skin rose, fingers staining as I chased them down the turbulent waves of my belly. Beltane was plowing down a path I didn't want but needed. *So much.*

My heart pounded like tumbling boulders upon a petal brushing over my clit. The last one, as ephemeral as his departing mouth.

A conclusion I hadn't expected.

I heaved, tucking my elbows at my sides. The god had halted his gaze on my core, which I knew was slick. The flames in his eyes starkly flared and rose toward me, his lips curling as he licked them. I flinched, unable to process.

Then, a voice I barely recognized was mine. "I wish to know what you are about to do."

The outline of his head, now black against the moon, swayed enervated, his claws digging around my calves. "Giv-ing what I pro-mised." He then growled, his forceful breath sending a tingle across my wetness.

I had to measure up to the heart bestowed upon me, brave, for it would be the last time I would own it. The ground be witness—grass and shoots curled, kissed, and grappled at my skin while Beltane disappeared beneath me.

Tipping my head back, I moored my gaze at the stars peeking through the gray, and quivered at wisps growing at the ends of his fingertips. These conquered, invading my inner thighs, and I shut the whole of my face in a tight, hermetic wince when these parted at my seams and joined over the velvet of my pelvic bone.

My fingers dug into the moss, and my breathing shattered at the thirty-seventh kiss celebrated on the inside of my thigh. A burning tide swept through every vein, and a moan escaped before I could stop it.

Other kisses, more heat than I thought I could sustain, and I stopped counting the score of his lips. The moss in my grip was a mess of frazzled filaments and earth.

Then, a touch, a finger running over my center. I shut my mouth, taming the violence beneath my ribcage. But Beltane paced up and down. Twirls and swirls began, and the rubbing of a thumb sent me into deep agony. My hips charged at him, nails folded into my fists at the unbearable need to be stroked over and over.

Beltane praised me with a low growl, and I rewarded him by bringing my leg over his shoulder, then the other.

Moss powdered under my clench when he slipped a finger inside. "Oh, God."

A second one. My heels pressed against Beltane's back, for I needed him to preserve his posture exactly as it was.

"I've sought the pur-est springs, tast-ed the sweet-est honey…but none could match your ess-ence," he said, his touch leaving me entirely.

The god seemed inclined to torture his *untouched* witch, dragging his movement, pausing as the flames licked at the last of my decency.

I raised my head, confronted.

What I saw only quickened the pulse between my legs. My wetness tinged Beltane's fingers, which he plunged into his mouth. "I have missed the taste of your desire, Wind-skin." He threw his head backward and released a shrilling sound as blossoms thrived at his shoulders, more on his back, disappearing under a veritable coat of starflowers.

I hadn't had time to ponder this before his arms circled my hips and his palms pressed into the curve of my spine.

Not comprehending the situation, I found myself face down on the ground.

Gripped by the waist, my knees grated against the earth as he pulled me toward him, and another growl shredded what air had dared lingered between him and me.

I barely stood on my hands that Beltane chuffed at my rear. "Heated creature." He was a filthy, wicked animal, and I bit my lip, an evil grin more akin to a snarl than a smile.

Transfixing the still of pine trees had never been so intense as his hands swept down my waist, sliding into the crease of my legs and hooked there. The ridges of his horns pressed at my thighs, and I shivered upon his mouth, taking me whole.

I moaned before he groaned against me. Moaned again when a tongue thrust into me. And moaned as I fell onto my forearms.

Moans. I was but that. *More, more.* It shortened at every swift turn of his tongue, lingered over every pressure exerted. Every dragging swipe.

I whimpered at a nip. Nibbles. Whimpered more, my hands turning feathery as quills pushed over my skin.

Beltane snickered, sultry air pulsing against throbbing ache, and my moan staggered.

I'd call upon all the dark forces to keep him there, imprison him into an eternal loop until he collapsed from exhaustion. I'd reached the point where I would stay by his side so the god could feast on me for as long as he cruelly desired. And I would return the gesture—give him my kidneys, my guts, and whatever parts of me he wished to have.

I tried crawling away; it was too much. Searing. A hand drove down my spine, pushing into my feathers, and clasped my nape.

"I must give now, and you must take." His voice was but a broken heap of trembles, exciting every drop of blood in me.

Two solid arms dropped like columns beside my holding ones, heat as never behind my back.

A grip, neither rough nor soft, pulled at my scalp, and my eyes dilated at what had just entered. Beltane was like birth and death. I lifted from a fistful of my hair, my hands wading as one powerful stroke swelled within. Light pulsed teal, a glow blinding the brook. I saw it beneath me, reflecting across the pines. The entire woods flared as a star bloomed in the shelter of our joint bodies.

My cry merged with a thousand rutting bleats, a clap of thunder throughout the Emeralds.

Yet, as my uproar subsided and I shut my eyes, it felt as though I'd only just opened them. Beltane stood before me in a void of white, golden ram horns, shone with a purity as if recently forged, the fox mask gone.

He was beautiful.

Ebon hair of the wildest length flowing into mist, pupils, veritable ember stones, holding no fire, fear, or hate, but raw nature, the blood of trees, gleaming gold in their oval pattern. He smiled, a broad one, teeth of men. His hand moved toward me, and a smile touched my lips.

Until a sharp pain pierced the moment.

When I looked down at what caused it, there was only a gaping, bleeding hole in my breast.

I glanced up, unable to think straight.

In his trickling fist, my part of the bargain.

My heart.

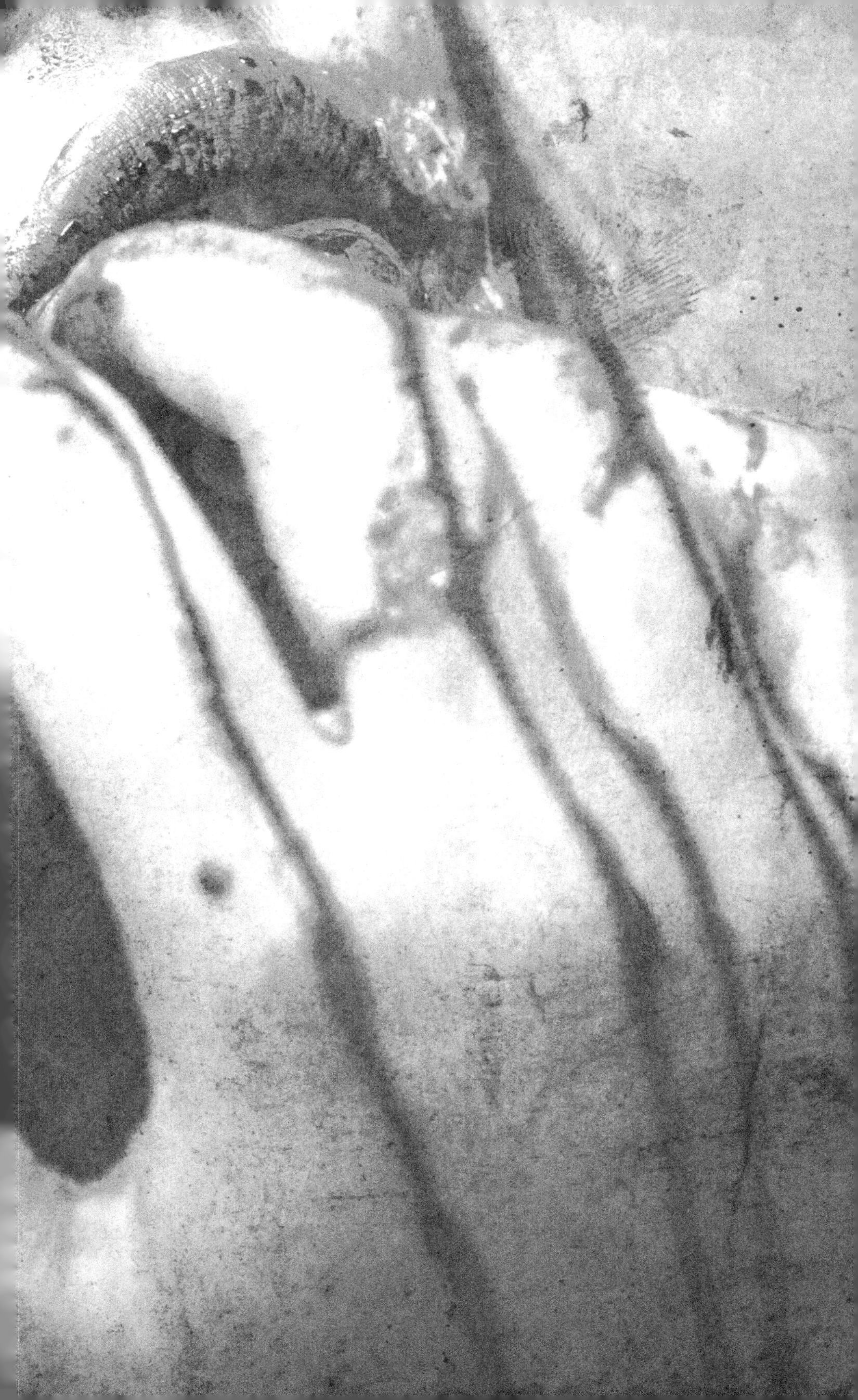

Chapter Eight

My throat cluttered, and I coughed blood.

Beltane's expression iced. "What one takes, one must give back." The fur in his voice had left for unbending metal.

My knees buckled, and I swayed, only to be caught by him. Speaking was impossible, even if my lips moved.

I had been perfectly aware that Beltane's involvement would lead to my death, but I did absolutely nothing. Then I figured out I was an omen, and I didn't listen.

Witnessing Beltane thrust his hand into his chest, shattering his ribs to retrieve his own dripping heart did nothing to ease my numbness. "You gave my pur-pose back. In ex-change, I will give you what keeps me a-live."

Beltane placed my heart in the cavity of his chest and plunged his hand and his heart into the cleft of my own.

Scenes from my life—childhood memories, swirling forests, hags, and scattered bones, erupted around me. All crumbled away, revealing what I had never seen but remembered with startling clarity. Snow-capped mountains, the Emeralds stretching endlessly into a vast expanse of green where the plains should have been. Only the wild remained, the shadow of Beltane stretching before me, his hand warm in mine.

A row of blinks passed in quick succession until drowsiness faded into confusion. I was beneath the same stars as earlier. The fog had lifted, and from the solid fawned colored knees in my vision, my head rested on Beltane's lap. A blanket of powdered gray silk covered me, a hem splayed across my hand, just an inch from my face. It fluttered.

A voice, soft, drifted across my face. "Windskin."

Beltane's heart held memory, and I remembered everything.

Fingers toyed with the pike of my ear, a flicker here, a rub there. "Tell me you won't return to the coven that raised you."

I pushed myself up, as if emerging from a nightmare, the blanket vanishing into moths.

There was a crinkling sound as I gathered myself. My gaze followed the sound and settled on my skin, golden-leafed from my feet to my neck, right up to my jawline to my raised puzzled hands. Beyond them, Beltane.

His stare, unbreakable, had already ensnared me.

"Shyhorned."

Fox ears melted against his skull while I stilled upon my voice, a finger over my mouth. *Shyhorned*, a moniker I once called him, had naturally etched on my tongue, as foreign as it was familiar. A remnant of a past life.

Our gazes remained anchored, as if afraid a stray glance would pull us apart. Two strands of lichen arched over Beltane's eyes as the embers in them swayed in brutal disarray.

Had I not known him, I would have recognized him the same; an intensity bled with the lava flowing beneath the earth's skin. A starving gleam in the eye. My husband's.

Joy fluttered up my belly like sunrise, and my chin wavered. I rushed at his neck, his arms scooping me up. "There exists no greater torment than beholding you and yet failing to recognize my own reflection." His murmur shuddered, and I quickened to press my lips on it.

"But you persevered, as intoxicatingly elusive as you are, drawing me to you with every fleeting root." My feathers rose, pressing over the gold of leaves as I teased him. Unnatural at first, yet the words felt right.

I had recollection, but I felt out of place, as if all the richness of experience had been emptied, except for the ones I had in this life.

The moment was relief but also shock.

Acid climbed in my throat, and the world swayed as I adjusted to a

Chapter Eight

new reality. Mushrooms of increasing size pushed toward me, and I tumbled onto puffballs, dusting me with spores. "I had forgotten your antics, always so full of chivalry."

"I'm going to drive you mad, Windskin. I have endless moons to catch up."

I snagged at a mushroom cap, ready to throw it at him until a wince crossed his face and he clutched his chest.

I dropped the pulp where I had bruised the mushroom. "Forgive me. I didn't mean to harm you."

A burl of forest litter washed over me in retribution. My cry was joy as I braced an arm over my head.

"Cruel bird. Will you ever cease to make my heart ache?" I couldn't see him, but I detected a smile in his voice, flaunting. Showing off heated and it wrapped around me like a sweltering mantle. My vision blurred, not from the shower of crust, but from him. I had never had enough of him. Somewhere deep within, I thanked the three goddesses who ruled over our ancient selves. To be parted from him…only death had made it sweet. Never a moment had I not craved him. An impulse as raw as sinking teeth into a beloved's flesh.

In a fluid motion, he sat, sliding beside me, making me sway on the mushroom cap. We were like children. "Had enough, moondrop?"

My cheeks tingled despite my old soul. I pressed my hand on his face, which he bit a finger, and I fussed lightly, a brusk jolt. Something shifted atop my head, which I grasped and brought down—a headpiece of black feathers, fashioned in the manner of raven wings. One quill brushed against a soreness. My chest.

When I glanced up, Beltane watched me with a shy smile, and I detected a ripple of anxiety in him.

"You took my mortal heart for yours." I braced a strand behind his ear, silk slipping between my fingers. "Why so?"

He straightened, a warning burgeoning at his cheekbones, spikes. "To ensure that whatever may come to us, neither will endure the agony of loss. I could no longer wait for your memories to wake."

The suffering. I understood the holy teachings about fleeting flesh. Beltane had been but mourning, and mortals took it for word. When the gods roamed the world, we were told by sprites that two-legged creatures, resembling us in a few ways, lived in small, secluded tribes like the witches with their covens. But when the world turned blank for me, my eyes never beheld them. And the holiness upon which the gods would later depend had remained unknown to me until this life.

A breeze pulled his hair back. I wanted to see him, entirely. "We are not bound by decaying flesh but by souls."

As instinct is to breathe, I cradled my belly. "Soon, we will be bound by another."

"Later than sooner."

I shot him a glare. "Later?"

His chest heaved, flowers at his strands closing, leaves purling in the coil of his horns. "Patience."

A gust of wind shook the trees. One broke in half, a torturous creaking as it wrecked off its neighbors' boughs. To this, Beltane evanesced into the night.

I stood and roved along the brook, blood simmering. "Beltane."

"I would have expected you to be content with your awakening," echoed against the rocks.

My eyes narrowed into thin slits as I sifted through the trunks. "Show yourself."

Leaves rustled gently against my back. Night turned powdery at my waist until solidifying into encircling arms, a soft kiss grazing my neck. "You shall bloom in time. I simply need to find *this time*."

I turned and faced him. "Time?"

Despite towering over me a good few heads, he seemed small. "Once I am made whole again."

"Once you are made whole," I repeated.

The wind whistled, and Beltane's gaze shifted to it before pressing swiftly against me. Little tempests brewed around his horns as his chest rose and fell in heavy breaths. "Do not return to the coven that raised you. Stay—"

"Silence, if you would." I stared at my moon-fed shadow stretching over the pines, my lips rifting slack at what had always outgrown mine, now missing. "Where is your shadow, dear husband?"

"You speak as you always have." He leaned into me and pressed his irresistible lips to mine. The taste of honey lingered, addictive, but I pulled away. "You are a raven of the utmost kind."

"Yes," I replied dryly. "I am curious. Where is your shadow?"

A faint, tortured sound escaped him as a dry leaf drifted between us.

I frowned. "Your shadow."

Chapter Eight

With casual nonchalance, he pricked a leaf from behind his horn, seemingly fascinated as he made it twirl between his fingers. "Fall is coming. How I despise it."

"Your shadow." I spat, searing a mushroom cap.

Beltane exploded into bats, blankets of shrieks and wings flashing between the trunks. An eerie voice curled around my ear. "Nosferus is what *they* call it now. Do not ask me more."

I walked at the stream's edge, Beltane emerging beside me. Dakanesh's wisdom. She knew everything about Nosferus. More than its *owner*, as it appeared. "I must go."

"Where?" A growl etched at his last word, a possessive grip on my arm.

I raised my gaze to him. "The Scrying coven."

"You are not safe. You bleed like them. You are weak like them. They will hurt you." Vines latched at my ankles, little bonds I ignored.

My attention swapped him for the moon, unsure of what I truly grasped. "Who will hurt me?"

"The witches."

I stood, struggling to put the pieces of the previous events in order, and Izobel once again struck me. "I thank you for helping me with the girl. Is she out of harm's way?"

"She is. And is resting where you left her. Safe for now."

"I must go."

"Don't!"

I shifted before he could reach me, shivering from a freedom I had never known until now. "You are everywhere I fly." My talons gathered, the tips of my wings beating down, grazing the river, vines chasing me as I leaped into the night.

Leaving Beltane had been easy; the wind thrust at my back, yet the *tearing tore*, and would persist until I landed at his side again. The aching parting stretched into the very length of my wings. Irrepressible. Life was like that, and Beltane, mine.

In my flight path, an unkindness, not easily forgotten, joined, forming a perfect arrow in the sky. I soared at its point, and a cunning presence appeared in my left peripheral.

"*Little pest. Do you know how many feathers I've molted since you left my sight?*"

"Glad to see you, too, Marvenous."

"*Where were you?*"

I turned my beak toward her. "With my husband."

"Nought…"

"I might think you know me as Windskin."

As I uttered my name, Marvenous croaked, a call for her flock. *"Memories have been unbound. And so have yours."*

The memory of who I was settled in them, feathers of black drifted down, and I released a shriek call. Countless weightless daggers drifted into the opacity of night, my protégés freeing themselves from the Tenebrae of my mind that had kept us all dormant.

And we had now all risen. For beneath the shedding, a plumage emerged, honoring the three goddesses: nacreous.

"I could not reveal something you had to find out for yourself, Windskin."

"I am still Nought."

"That I know!"

I smiled inside. I was still Nought Before One, Raven of the Scrying.

"Where to now?"

"We're going to retrieve a god's shadow."

And Orakle. I stirred for the north, and the arrow veered.

A windstorm howled at our backs, the elks bleated in the distance, and the ravens cawed. And with the inert force in my belly, I couldn't wait to *take back what once was given.*

To be continued - abridged excerpt from the novel 'The Heart of the Untamed'

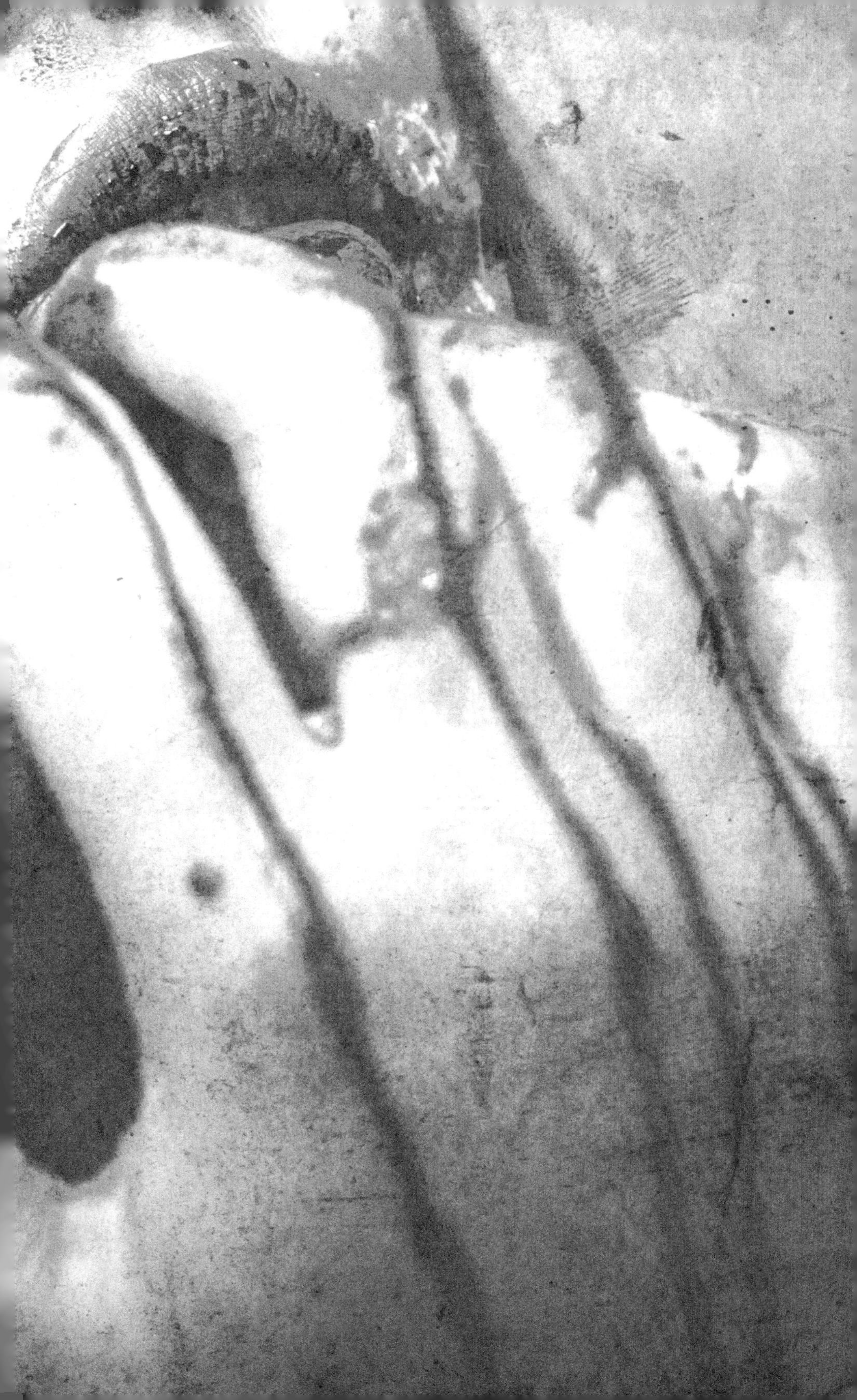

Content Warnings

Please check the content warning for the story you're about to dive into. The last thing any of us want is for our content to be triggering. Protect your mental health at all costs!

Ava Jay
   Graphic depictions of rape within flashbacks and present, Menstrual blood & products, Alcohol abuse, Substance abuse, Flashbacks of driving while intoxicated, Inappropriate therapist and patient relationship, Panic attacks, Denied abortion care, Intentionally induced miscarriage, Purposeful car crash, Attempted suicide, Medical, abortion / D&C, Murder, House fire, Arsen

CJ Riggs
   Murder, Gore, Drugging, Torture, Pear Of Anguish, Bleach, Salt, Revenge, Burning Alive, Castration, Disemboweling, Lingchi

DK
   Murder, Genitalia Mutilation, Mentions of rape, Drugging

Kamila Garza
   Author's Note
   Due to their work out in the field, the ladies of Silhouettes of Sin

use code names during a mission. However, some of these nicknames are used outside of work, so I will be adding each of their nicknames called by each girl and for whom. Lastly, this book does contain graphic violence, gruesome details of attacks, preempted SA (stops before anything happens), murder of men, bloody details, explicit on-page sexual content, FF relations, group sex scenes, fire play, edging, and past sex work. Please do not proceed if any of this is a trigger for you. Your mental health is more important.

KM ROGNESS

Even though this is a short story—very short—it's dark, bloody, and filled with extreme feminine rage. This isn't made for everyone to read, but with all the hate and corruption going on in the world, this story needed to be told.

This isn't meant to be a dark romance, or any romance at all. This is an **erotic horror** that ends unexpectedly with a temporary HEA. It'll be short, violent, and smutty.

Check out the triggers and tropes below. Your mental health matters, so if this is too dark and triggering, please don't read it. If you like what you see below, dive right the fuck in.

Extreme femme rage, SA in the military, recorded GR, corruption, military/marines, noncon, dark and disturbing flashbacks, revenge, blood and gore, mutilation, unaliving, false captivity, blackmail, violence that causes loss of pregnancy, threats, age gap, dark secrets, dubious consent, graphic violence, explicit language and sexual content, unhinged, pitch black, morally black MMCs, Scorned FMC, taboo/forbidden, twin stepbrothers

Lamia Lovett

Mention of rape, mentions of abuse, mentions of forced pregnancies, mentions of infant deaths, mentions of still births, On page murder, kidnapping, forced medical procedures, Anxiety/Panic attacks.

Nicole Banks

Talks of sexual assault, talks of suicide. There's an on-page sexual assault (it's a simulation but can be triggering for some) and murder. Please protect your mental health and if anything is too much, please put this story down.

S. Manship

Cannibalism, Mute Character, Mutilation of Corpses, Corpses - in General, Various forms of Murder (Including but not limited to: head wounds and forced overdose)

Sasha Onyx

Violence and gore, Child abuse, Emergency C-section procedure, Cannibalism, Death of a child, Explicit depictions of body parts.

E.L. Emkey

Graphic sexual content, which includes consensual sex and sexual assault, alcohol use, murder, drowning, torture, mutilation, and mental abuse.

Made in the USA
Las Vegas, NV
06 May 2025